The First Compact

Books by
Marc Alan Edelheit

Chronicles of a Legionary Officer:

Book One: Stiger's Tigers
Book Two: The Tiger
Book Three: The Tiger's Fate
Book Four: The Tiger's Time
Book Five: The Tiger's Wrath
Book Six: The Tiger's Imperium (Coming 2020)

Tales of the Seventh:

Part One: Stiger
Part Two: Fort Covenant
Part Three: A Dark Foretoken
Part Four: **Thresh (Coming 2021)**

The Karus Saga:

Book One: Lost Legio IX
Book Two: Fortress of Radiance
Book Three: The First Compact
Book Four: (Coming 2021)

Nonfiction
Every Writer's Dream

Way of the Legend:
With Quincy J. Allen
Book One: Reclaiming Honor
Book Two: **Forging Destiny**(Coming)

The First Compact

The Karus Saga: Book 3

By
Marc Alan Edelheit

This book is a work of fiction. Names, characters, places, and incidents are either the product of the author's imagination or are used fictitiously. Any resemblance to actual persons, living or dead, or to actual events or locales is entirely coincidental.

The First Compact: The Karus Saga, Book Three
First Edition

I wish to thank my agent, Andrea Hurst, for her invaluable support and assistance. I would also like to thank my beta readers, who suffered through several early drafts. My betas: Paul Klebaur,Melinda Vallem, William Schnippert, David Vernon Houston, David Cheever, Bruce Heaven, Erin Penny, Tim Adams, Sheldon Levy, Walker Graham, Bill Schnippert, Jonathan Parkin, Jimmy McAfee, Marshall Clowers, Phillip Broom, Joel Rainey, James H. Bjorum, Franklin Johnson, Sally Tingley-Walker, Tom Trudeau, James Doak. I would also like to take a moment to thank my loving wife, who sacrificed many an evening and weekend to allow me to work on my writing.
Editing Assistance by Hannah Streetman, Brandon Purcell, Audrey Mackaman
Cover Art by Piero Mng (Gianpiero Mangialardi)
Cover Formatting by Telemachus Press
Agented by Andrea Hurst & Associates
http://maenovels.com/

Author's note:

Writing *The First Compact* has been a labor of love and a joy. I am so excited to share this next action-packed and exciting chapter in Karus and Amarra's adventures. It is my sincere hope that you love it as I do.

I also want to take a moment to thank you for reading and keeping me employed as a full-time writer. For those of you who reach out to me on Facebook, Twitter, or by email, I simply cannot express how humbling it is, as an author, to have my work so appreciated and loved. From the bottom of my heart… *thank you.*

You can reach out and connect with me on:

Facebook: Marc Edelheit Author

Facebook: MAE Fantasy & SciFi Lounge

Twitter: @MarcEdelheit

You may wish to sign up to my newsletter by visiting my website.

http://maenovels.com/

Or

You can follow me on **Amazon** through my Author Page. Smash that follow button under my picture and you will be notified by Amazon whenever I have a new release.

Reviews keep me motivated and also help to drive sales. I make a point to read each and every one, so please continue to post them.

Again, I hope you enjoy *The First Compact* and would like to offer a sincere thank you for your purchase and support

Best regards,

Marc Alan Edelheit, your author and tour guide to the worlds of Tanis and Istros.

Table of Contents

Chapter One

It was raining, a miserable downpour, and had been for the last hour. As the two dragons descended toward the ground, the wind whipped past and buffeted around Karus. The raindrops, like tiny bees, stung his face.

Even with his cloak wrapped tightly about himself, Karus was thoroughly soaked through and chilled to the bone. The sky above was filled with dark, angry clouds. The land below seemed shrouded in an early dusk, one that Karus thought quite depressing.

Karus leaned forward and braced himself, gripping the nearest of the dragon's spikes tightly as the ground rushed up to greet them. His stomach did a backflip as Cyln'Phax extended her wings, flaring them outward as she slowed, then landed with a hard jolt.

She flapped her wings mightily as she worked to arrest her momentum. The red dragon took several awkward steps forward before bringing herself to a complete halt. A moment later, she folded her wings back and settled down onto the ground so her riders could dismount.

Cold and miserable could easily describe the last three days in the air. Shortly after leaving the Fortress of Radiance, poor weather had moved in on them. Throughout the three-day journey to find Dennig's warband, it had routinely rained, making even the nights difficult for those riding upon Cyln'Phax and Kordem's backs.

Karus began hastily untying the straps that held him in place. Around him on Cyln'Phax's back, the elves, along with Dennig, were doing the same.

Karus found he was having trouble undoing the knots that held him securely in place, for his fingers were numb and shaking slightly from the cold. After some effort, Karus managed to untie the first knot. He began working on the next one. Soaked through, the leather had constricted and tightened, making the job harder. He had to use his nails to pry each knot free.

For a moment, he considered cutting the remaining straps with his dagger but disregarded that idea. He would need to reuse the ties for the journey back to Carthum. So, he continued to work at it, picking each one free.

Then, finally, the last knot gave way. Stiffly, Karus pulled himself to his feet and began climbing off the dragon's back. He used the spaces between the massive scales as handholds and carefully worked his way down the creature's side, jumping the last two feet.

His sandaled feet smacked down upon bald stone. Karus took a moment to glance around. The two dragons had landed them along the crest of a wide ridge, much of which was weathered stone. A few hardy plants grew here and there, along with isolated strands of grass. Beyond that, there was nothing remarkable about the ridge, other than its height, which nearly made it into a small mountain.

Lightning slashed at the sky, illuminating the clouds in a flickering flash. Thunder followed a few heartbeats later, rumbling dully off in the distance. Karus stretched out his sore and aching back, then moved forward to a sheer drop-off of several hundred feet. He gazed outward, down the steep slope of the treeless ridge.

Less than a mile away was a town surrounded by a tall stone wall that seemed quite hardy. Despite the downpour of rain, smoke from burning buildings drifted up into the sky. He could smell the smoke hanging heavily on the air, along with another smell... the sickly stench of death. Rain always seemed to make both worse.

The town was situated in a small valley hemmed in by rocky ridges. A muddy river meandered down the valley and through the town. Cultivated fields, ready for harvest, spread outward, like spokes from the town.

Once, the valley must have been a peaceful place. Now... death and destruction had found their way here. The town was besieged by a small army and, from what the dragons had told him in the rush before landing, it was an army of orcs.

The Horde had beat them here.

Karus surveyed the scene before him. A sour feeling settled in the pit of his stomach. The enemy certainly seemed highly organized. He knew he should not be surprised by this, but he was just the same.

The orcs had built a fortified encampment four hundred yards back and away from the town. The tents inside the encampment had been arranged in neat, ordered rows, as if planned out in advance. There was twenty yards of space between the encampment's defensive walls and the nearest tents. A trench surrounded the entire camp. Roman encampments used a similar practice. If the encampment came under attack, the closest tents would be out of light missile range.

The enemy even had a wagon and animal park located safely within their encampment. The organization told him the enemy besieging the town were highly disciplined, which made them even more dangerous in Karus's estimation. A disciplined enemy was one that would stand and fight.

His eyes shifted from the encampment back to the town, which had been completely ringed by a siege trench and earthen wall to keep the defenders from breaking out. This told him the siege had been going on for more than a handful of days.

The enemy was actively in the process of assaulting the town. From this distance, the figures of both the defenders and attackers looked tiny, almost toy-like. Thick with orcs, dozens of scaling ladders had been raised against the stone walls. Even more ladders were being carried forward. Then there were the reserves. Thick, block-like formations of orc warriors stood just out of missile range, clearly waiting for their turn to try at forcing the walls.

Even at this distance, the fighting for dominance of the town's wall looked hard, brutal, and determined. From the numbers of bodies lying in heaps near the scaling ladders, this wasn't the first assault either. But from the looks of it, this one might be the last.

The defenders appeared to be making a desperate effort to keep the enemy from securing a foothold over one of the walls. But there seemed precious few defenders compared to the number of orcs pushing forward or waiting in reserve.

The town's gate was also being assaulted. The enemy had brought up a battering ram and were hammering away. From the ridge, Karus could hear the steady, deep *thump* from the repeated hammer blows. All the while, the defenders above the gate shot arrows down at those doing the battering or dropped rocks on their heads.

"We're too late," Dennig said, having come up next to Karus. "Oh, Great and Mighty Thulla... were it not so. I have failed."

Karus glanced over at the dwarf. Dennig loosely held the magnificent axe he'd found in the Fortress of Radiance in one hand. The dwarf's shoulders slumped. He looked defeated, broken, and more wretched than when Karus had first seen him as a half-starved prisoner of the elves. Along with the rain, there were tears of frustration running down Dennig's cheeks and into his neatly braided beard.

Behind them, Kol'Cara snapped an order. Karus glanced back. Arrows and bows held ready, the elves of the Anagradoom spread out across the ridge and around the two dragons. They took up defensive positions, gazes fixed outward, watchful.

What with the dragons, Karus did not know why they even bothered. Were there any enemy within easy reach, they would be foolish, perhaps even suicidal, to venture forth against them. But still, security was security and the elves knew what they were doing.

Si'Cara and Tal'Thor had climbed down off Kordem's back. They made their way over to the cliff face to look out at the town. They stood a few feet away, silent, staring, inscrutable.

Karus turned his gaze back to the town that was being assaulted. Despite the downpour and the distance, he could plainly hear the clash of weapons, screams, shouts, and the general din of battle. It was an all too familiar sound, the chaos of a fight, and a hard one at that.

A catapult, one of three set behind the enemy's defensive berm, launched a large stone. The shot arced up into the air. It sailed easily over the wall, before crashing into the roof of a building inside the town. The building shuddered violently under the impact before collapsing a heartbeat later in a heap.

Smoke shot up into the air, and despite the rain, flames could be seen rapidly spreading over the ruins. Several buildings in the town were already burning sullenly under the downpour.

Amarra stepped up on his right. He tore his gaze from the town and glanced briefly at her. She wore a forest green cloak over her white dress. One of the elves had given it to her. The hood was pulled up to shield her from the rain.

In her right hand, Amarra held the High Father's crystal staff. It glowed faintly with an internal light that occasionally throbbed. She studied the view for a long moment, then turned her gaze to him, giving Karus a determined look he had come to know only too well.

"Karus." Amarra spoke in the common tongue. "We must do something. You must."

Rubbing his hands together for warmth, Karus felt himself scowl slightly. He turned his gaze back to the town, wondering what he could do, if there was anything that could be done.

His hand reached down to the magic sword, Rarokan. The familiar tingle, which he had come to expect, raced from his palm up his arm and into his body. As the High Father, Jupiter, had commanded, he'd successfully retrieved the weapon from the Fortress of Radiance.

He sucked in a breath. With the sword's power, the day seemed to imperceptibly brighten, and the chill in his bones, particularly the numb ache in his hands, lessened.

"What is there to do?" Dennig said, anguish making his voice tremble. "My warband is trapped, surrounded by the enemy. We've arrived too late. From the looks of things, my boys will soon be overrun. It is only a matter of time now. I should never have left them to seek help from the elves."

Karus turned his gaze back to the town. He estimated the enemy army numbered somewhere around ten to fifteen thousand. There was no telling how many dwarves were trapped, but it couldn't be many, for the town wasn't that large. Even if the defenders managed to throw the assault back, the enemy would only reorganize and come again. Dennig was right. They were watching the destruction of his warband.

Amarra caught his gaze and raised an expectant eyebrow. Karus felt his scowl grow. The defenders needed a miracle and he did not have one handy. He wanted to tell her there was nothing to be done but knew she would not accept that. Instead, he turned to Dennig.

"How many are in your warband?" Karus asked. "When you left them, what was your effective strength?"

Dennig was silent for several heartbeats.

"We had no more than forty-five hundred, with almost a third of that number walking wounded. Now"—the dwarf gave a shrug of his shoulders—"who knows? I have been away for weeks. There may only be a few hundred fit to fight or march."

Karus looked back at Cyln'Phax and Kordem, rubbing his stubbled jaw as he considered the two dragons. He sucked in a deep breath and slowly let it out. "On the way here, how far back would you say that enemy army we flew over was?"

Karus well remembered the long column snaking its way along the road. The line of march had stretched out for as far as the eye could see. He had found it a sobering sight.

At least fifty of your miles, human, Cyln'Phax responded in Karus's head. *Two or three days of marching… depending upon how fast they move.*

With luck, Kordem added, *they will think we were two of their own. We really don't need the enemy sending wyrms after us. It would complicate our return to Carthum.*

Karus could not help but agree. He'd seen enough of the enemy and their dragons. He had no desire to tangle with more, even with Cyln'Phax and Kordem present.

"And you're sure?" Karus asked. "They're marching here? Do I have that right?"

The road they are using leads here. In truth, we can't say if they are marching to this very spot, Cyln'Phax said, *but they are moving in this direction… and as we've told you, this same road that leads to this town also takes one to Carthum.*

If I had to guess, Kordem said, *Carthum would be their ultimate objective. That and the destruction of your legion. The elimination of the dwarven warband was likely a bonus, or an opportunity too good to pass up.*

Karus gazed up. With the low-lying clouds, it was hard to tell, but he figured that they had around three hours of light left, maybe four at best. His gaze returned to the town. The entire situation was maddening.

The enemy army they'd flown by numbered around fifty, perhaps even sixty, thousand. He knew the legion could not stand up to such a force. And though they had not seen any wyrms with them, he understood without a doubt the enemy had them.

If the legion stood a chance of survival, he needed allies, and badly. Below, though surely weakened in number, were those potential allies. No matter what Dennig said about dwarves refusing to fight alongside humans, Karus had a feeling they would. That was, if he could extricate them from this mess, show them the value of having allies. And yet, he did not see how he could save them or, for that matter, help. The enemy besieging the town was just too numerous.

"Do you think you can get me inside the town?" Dennig asked the dragons. "Let me die with my boys?"

That would be unwise, Kordem said. *There is no love lost between our peoples. Were we to attempt to land inside the town, it is quite possible your warriors might think we were of the enemy and attack. It would be very hazardous for us.*

We could fly up high, Cyln'Phax suggested, *where there is no risk and simply drop you into the town.*

Dennig turned a hard look upon the dragon. His hand tightened on the shaft of his beautiful axe, and for a moment Karus thought the dwarf might attack the dragon. "I'd be dead."

You wish to die a useless death, Cyln'Phax said. *Why does it matter how you achieve that end?*

"That's not helpful," Karus said, before Dennig could respond. "We don't need to be fighting amongst ourselves."

Dennig shifted his gaze back to the fight. Karus could only imagine what was going through his friend's mind. If it was his men down there, Karus knew he would feel the same, would want to be with them in their final hours.

But what could they do? Even if the dragons took him back to Carthum, it would be days before he could return with sufficient reinforcement to help break the siege. Dennig's warband would not last that long, and if it could manage the impossible, the larger enemy army would soon arrive. There seemed nothing to be done. The dwarven defenders were surely doomed.

Or were they?

He scanned the enemy army, then the encampment, and finally the fields around the town, looking carefully.

Karus turned slowly back to the dragons. "Is there anything you can do to help?"

Us? Kordem asked, sounding surprised. The dragon cocked his head at Karus, like a dog might. *What are you thinking?*

"I don't see any wyrms. Could you scatter that army down there?" Karus asked, gesturing toward the town. "Give the defenders a chance to break out?"

You want us to save them? Cyln'Phax asked, clearly incredulous. Karus could sense the dragon's disbelief in his mind. *You want us to save dwarves? You know there is bad blood between our peoples.*

"Aye," Karus said. "I know there is not much love there. But still… the Horde is coming for us all. Whether we like it or not, we are on the same side. If we don't begin working to help each other, I can see no end other than the Horde crushing us all, one after another."

Dennig turned around, his eyes suddenly hopeful. The heat had left his gaze. He looked between the two dragons and his mouth worked as if he was having difficulty speaking. The dwarf took a deep breath and then swallowed. "I would be in your debt were you to help us."

Kordem's eyes narrowed as he studied the dwarf for several long heartbeats. Then both dragons turned and swung their heads around to face one another. Karus suspected they were in silent communication, discussing the matter.

"They surely spotted us landing," Karus added. "With all this rain, I am thinking they believe you both to be wyrms, their allies. It would come as a rude shock to find out otherwise. Don't you agree?"

Kordem swung his large head to look out at the fight raging less than a mile away. The dragon was silent for some time. Karus noticed that Cyln'Phax had become agitated, claws digging into the stone of the hillcrest.

Kordem flicked his tail hard, smacking it against the stone of the hilltop several times, and turned his gaze back to his mate. Karus felt the impact of the repeated blows through his sandals like tremors from an earthquake. It almost seemed as if the hill itself shook.

Cyln'Phax issued a low, almost dog-like growl.

"They will help," Amarra said.

We have not even come to an agreement yet on whether or not we will help, Cyln'Phax said, turning his head to her. *We are still talking the matter through.*

"Yes," Amarra said, tone becoming firm, "you will . . . You must. It is as Karus said. You don't need to like it, but we are in this together."

She tapped the butt of her staff on the stone. The crystal flashed briefly with light and there was an audible snap as the rock underneath cracked and splintered.

Are you certain? Kordem asked. *This is not without risk for my mate and me. Though there are no wyrms in sight, they may have priests with* will *or perhaps even a wizard.*

Karus turned his gaze to the town and then back to the dragons. "I see no other way we can help. Do you?"

Cyln'Phax let out a small gout of flame from her nose. Kordem stood and unfurled his massive wings, shaking the rain off.

We will help, Kordem said, sounding resigned, head swinging to look at his mate. *Perhaps it is time we begin putting our differences aside.*

"Thank you," Dennig said.

We do this not for you, Cyln'Phax said, standing as well, *but for Amarra, our mistress. We do not want your thanks, dwarf.*

"Regardless," Dennig said, "you have it."

Remain here, Kordem said. *When we are finished, we will come back for you. If there are wyrms nearby… we may need to leave in a hurry. Be ready.*

With that, the green dragon leapt into the air and gave a mighty flap of his wings. Karus was forced to brace himself against the sudden gust of wind the dragon generated. Kordem gave another great flap and the wind was almost enough to push Karus over the cliff. He reached out a hand to Amarra, helping to steady her.

Karus, Cyln'Phax said as she too leapt into the air, *you are becoming overly fond of these dwarves and… elves. One day it may cost you more than you know… as it has us.*

Wings beating at the air, both dragons began climbing, circling higher and higher, until they disappeared into the clouds.

Karus heard the scuff of a boot on the stone behind him. He turned to find Kol'Cara had joined them. The elf had the hood of his cloak thrown back. His hair had been tied into a single braid that ran down his back.

"Why did they leave?" the elf asked, glancing skyward. "Where are they going?"

"To try and save my warband," Dennig said. "I pray to Thulla they are able to do it."

The elf turned his gaze to the town and the assault that had continued unabated. He seemed about to say something, but a shattering cry rent the air. It was primal, bestial, the sound of it battering the ears painfully.

A powerful stab of fear struck Karus through the heart. He'd never felt anything like it and it unmanned him. All he wanted to do was find someplace to hide, but he seemed frozen in place, rooted like a tree. The others seemed similarly affected. Even Kol'Cara, who, with a stricken expression, stumbled and almost fell.

Karus's hand brushed against the hilt of his sword and instantly the fear retreated. He gripped the hilt like a drowning man might latch onto a floating log. The fear was still there, but not as bad as it had been. He could move again, breathe even.

There was another roar from above. Then Kordem emerged from the clouds, wings tucked close to his sides. Like a bird of prey, the dragon dove down on the town. Cyln'Phax followed close on her mate's tail. Both dragons were moving at incredible speed, hurtling precariously toward the earth. The sight transfixed Karus in its fearsome beauty.

There was another shattering cry as one of the two dragons roared. It seemed as if the fighting in the town instantly ceased. Karus could well imagine every single eye, attackers and defenders alike, looking skyward in sudden fear and terror as the two dragons bore down upon them with frightening speed.

Kordem's wings flared out as he leveled out, skimming over the tops of the buildings with what looked like just inches to spare until he was over the enemy. Cyln'Phax banked in the opposite direction, to the right, following the wall around the other side of town.

Both dragons spewed a rain of fire down upon the enemy. The fire was brilliantly orange, an incredible contrast against the drabness of the day. Then they were beyond the town and the enemy. Both creatures were beating at the air again, gaining altitude and curving away, leaving utter destruction where they had struck.

Even under the downpour of rain, the dragon fire continued to burn brilliantly. It seemed as if the rain had little effect upon it and perhaps even made it worse, spreading the flames outward. The fire burned everything it touched.

The terrible, agonized screams of the dying and injured could be plainly heard. Then came a hearty cheer from the town's defenders. It sounded as if they were cheering themselves hoarse at their sudden deliverance.

"Great gods," Dennig breathed. "Great bloody gods."

The dragons continued to climb up into the sky, almost to the clouds, before banking back around and diving once more toward the ground. As they did, the terrible fear returned. Karus placed his hand upon Rarokan's hilt, and once again, the fear retreated.

The dragons swept over the enemy, raining fire and burning great swaths through the ranks of the enemy's reserve formations.

Karus was utterly shocked by the violence of the attack. He could not see how any army could stand in the face of such power. It was an awesome and frightening display. He was grateful the dragons were on his side.

Of the enemy formations that had not yet been attacked by the dragons, a handful broke ranks and fled out into the trampled farm fields. They sought to escape the wrath of the two massive beasts as the dragons climbed once again, preparing to make another run.

Almost touching the clouds, both dragons swung back around, seeming to hang motionless in the air. The fear returned, even more powerful than before. Karus felt it pulse strongly against the sword's power. He wondered on the magic the dragons were using, for that must be what it was. Then, there seemed to come a mass groan from the enemy army as a whole.

Like a dark tide flowing back out to sea, the enemy began to draw back from the walls. All organization had disintegrated in a flash, the terrible fear overcoming their discipline. Throwing away their weapons and shields, orcs were running in all directions, fleeing for their lives, just as fast as their legs could carry them.

Cyln'Phax extended her talons and landed amongst a group of fleeing orcs, slamming violently into them. Roaring with a terrible rage, she blasted fire all around her, in a near circle, burning hundreds. Those trapped inside the ring of fire faced the dragon herself. They stood not a chance. Claws lashed out, ripping and tearing, as did her massive tail, which swung about, smashing and tossing orcs bodily into the air. Karus stood there taking in the scene with wide, stunned eyes. He was no stranger to the bloodshed of battle, yet even he had never seen anything that could rival the carnage being wreaked upon the enemy before him.

Above her mate, Kordem continued to circle, shooting balls of fire downward onto the fleeing enemy, harrying them onward and away from the town. Each fireball exploded upon impact with the ground, not only burning the enemy but knocking those nearest off their feet.

"See?" Amarra said, pointing at the town and looking over at Karus first and then the dwarf. "We have helped. We stand stronger together than apart. You must see that now, Dennig. We must all work together if there is to be a chance."

Dennig, for his part, seemed unable to tear his gaze from the destruction the two dragons continued to wantonly wreak upon the enemy. He just stood there and shook his head.

"Well," Karus said, glancing over at the dwarf, "I think it's safe to say you're in their debt now."

Dennig slowly turned his gaze to look over on Karus. Eyes wide, he could only nod.

Chapter Two

Karus stopped twenty yards before the main gate of the town. The roadbed was raised and paved with stones. On either side were drainage ditches that ran with streams of muddy water.

Amarra stopped too. Dennig had halted a couple of steps before them and was looking around at the devastation while stroking the braids of his beard somewhat thoughtfully.

Karus glanced up at the rapidly darkening sky. It was still raining, though not as heavily as before. They were all miserably wet and would likely be for some time to come.

The elves of the Anagradoom spread out, creating a protective bubble about them. They moved with bows and arrows held at the ready. Si'Cara and Tal'Thor had remained close at hand. Both elves seemed tense, ready.

Ahead, the town's defenders had opened the gate. The wood had been blackened by fire. It had also been badly pitted and holed from the repeated hammer blows of the ram. It was a wonder the gate still stood. Karus wanted to meet the builder and congratulate him, only he was likely long gone, like everyone else in this land who had fled westward, away from the Horde.

The battering ram lay discarded in the drainage ditch on the left side of the roadbed. It had likely rolled partially into the ditch after the attackers had dropped it and run. The ram was no more than the trunk of a sturdy tree that had been crudely shorn of its branches. The water in the channel rushed over and around it.

There were bodies nearly everywhere the eye traveled, lying in the mud or grass where they had fallen. Most were orcs, but mixed amongst them was the occasional dwarf who had somehow died outside the confines of the walls. Karus supposed they had died before the siege had even begun. But there was no way to be certain.

Along the walls of the town, wherever the scaling ladders had gone up, were piles of bodies. Corpses spread outward from walls, back to and over the enemy's siege works. Thousands had died during the fighting, and even more when the dragons had struck.

Spears and spent shot from slings littered the ground and roadbed. Arrows by the thousands peppered the muddy ground to either side of the road. Discarded weapons and various types of equipment and shields lay amongst the bodies.

More than a few of the enemy lived. Karus even supposed some were playing dead, waiting for nightfall. Most were wounded. Several orcs were attempting to crawl or drag themselves over the siege wall and away. An orc carrying a bow picked himself up and, holding his injured side with his free hand, began staggering toward the wall.

Without hesitation, Kol'Cara raised his bow, calmly nocked an arrow, and loosed. The missile punched through the orc's back armor with a solid-sounding *crack*. The orc was driven forward by the strike and went down hard. He did not rise again.

Another elf moved to a badly injured orc who was dragging himself toward a sword just off the roadway. An arrow protruded from the orc's left knee and another from his side.

The elf drew a curved, elegant dagger that was more short sword than anything else. He grabbed the orc by the hair, pulling his head back, and then quite casually slit the creature's throat. The orc kicked violently and then fell still, green blood flowing out onto the ground in a gush.

Karus glanced back at the dragons, who were waiting out in a wheat field. The dragons had landed them two hundred yards from the walls, well outside missile range. Both were looking his way, watching warily.

He turned his gaze back to the aftermath of the battle that surrounded them. Karus was sickened by the sight of so many dead and wounded, even if the majority were the enemy. The stench of charred and burned flesh was overpowering. He found it almost an effort not to gag.

"Holy High Father," Amarra breathed, her hand to her mouth. "So much slaughter … so much suffering …"

"Such is the way with war," Karus said. "It is never a pretty thing. War's best face is always an ugly one."

"No matter how ugly and awful," Dennig said, with a pleased air, "this is victory and I will take it. We got here in time to save my warband. That is all that matters, isn't it?"

"True," Karus said.

"Had we been delayed or arrived in a few hours," Dennig said, "we would have been too late. The gods were surely on our side."

"Don't forget the dragons," Karus said.

"Aye," Dennig said.

Karus's eyes swept the walls of the town. Hundreds of dwarves lined them. They gazed down silently at their warchief, the humans, and the elves. The dwarves who had manhandled open the damaged gate stood and, like those on the wall, simply stared at them.

"I think they are waiting for you to do something," Karus said.

"I believe they are," Dennig said.

The dwarf took two confident steps forward and raised the magnificent axe he had taken from the Fortress of Radiance. He shouted a few words in his language. He finished by pumping the magnificent axe in the air above his head.

The dwarves along the walls gave a hearty cheer in reply. It quickly morphed into a chant.

"Shoega . . . Shoega . . . Shoega."

The dwarves were quite enthusiastic and Karus thought they should be. Their leader had not only returned, but he'd come with dragons and had rescued them from certain death and destruction. Only they didn't know that rescue had been grudging on the dragon's part.

The cheering died off as two dwarven officers walked through the gateway and out of the town. Both stopped, turning to speak to one another. Then, they moved forward. Their armor was spattered with orc blood. They were fairly covered with it, a testament to how involved in the fighting they'd been. Their expressions seemed as hard as granite.

"Martuke, my second in command," Dennig said sourly as both approached, "and his aide, Thaldus. I give you fair warning, they are not the most pleasant of my people."

Karus glanced over at Dennig and saw him once again run his hand though the braids of his beard. Karus's friend was annoyed, perhaps even troubled.

Martuke and Thaldus stopped before their warchief and saluted, a touch to the right side of their helmet. Dennig hesitated a long moment, then returned their salute. The three dwarves spoke in their own language, which sounded harsh and guttural to Karus's ears. Or perhaps the harshness arose simply from mutual dislike?

Martuke's eyes went to Karus, then flicked to Amarra. He eyed the crystal staff, then turned his attention to the elves, before finally moving to the dragons out in the field. Martuke's expression was a schooled mask as he said something to Dennig, who stiffened, clearly not liking what he'd heard.

"What did he just say?" Karus asked in Common.

"I said, *human*"—Martuke made the word sound vile as he spoke in fluent Common—"that it is good to see our warchief alive and well. However, after such a long absence, I did not expect him to return." Martuke glanced over at Thaldus. "We all thought him dead and feasting in the halls of our ancestors."

"You should know by now I am not so easy to kill," Dennig said, his eyes squarely on his second in command, "even in an adjudication circle."

It was Martuke's turn to stiffen as he turned his gaze back to Dennig. Karus wondered what an adjudication circle was. But he was more than certain there was no love lost between Dennig and Martuke.

"Gods be praised," Thaldus said hastily, though Karus thought he detected some sarcasm in the aide's tone.

"Martuke," Dennig said, and half turned, "I have the honor of introducing Camp Prefect Karus, commanding the Ninth Roman Legion, and Amarra"—the dwarf hesitated a heartbeat—"High Priestess to the High Father."

Martuke scowled slightly as his gaze traveled back to Amarra and hardened ever so slightly. "It seems you willingly consort with humans now."

"I do," Dennig said. "Do you have a problem with that?"

"Don't forget us elves," Si'Cara said. "You've been consorting with us too."

Martuke did not immediately reply, but his gaze flicked to Si'Cara with a look of utter distaste. Karus had difficulty concealing a smile, but Dennig showed no restraint. He grinned broadly at Martuke.

"And elves and dragons too," Dennig said, then sobered. "Karus I have even named a friend."

"Friend?" Martuke seemed truly shocked. His face twisted with loathing. "Is it not enough that you disgrace yourself? Would you now dishonor our ancestors? Would you ignore their sacrifices, their suffering?"

Dennig's tone hardened. "I dishonor no one, and I ignore nothing. I owe him my life and he has more than earned my friendship. Were it not for Karus, I wouldn't be here." Dennig jerked a thumb behind them. "And… neither would those dragons who broke the siege. In a way, Martuke, you now owe Karus your life, for the dragons are his and Amarra's allies, as are the elves. Were it not for them, trust me, orcs would be feasting on your flesh this night. The warband would be destroyed. Instead, you and I, along with the warband, will live to fight another day."

Martuke and Thaldus said nothing to this, but shared a glance. If possible, Martuke looked more disgusted than ever.

"Where is my son?" Dennig asked, clearly having tired of the game. He frowned slightly, looking beyond the two officers. "Where is Kelgan? I would have expected him to be with you to greet me."

The disgust left Martuke's face and suddenly he appeared uncomfortable. He hesitated before answering. "He was injured in the fighting."

"Badly?" Dennig asked sharply.

Thaldus gave a nod.

"The surgeons do not expect him to survive the night," Martuke said.

It was as if Dennig had been gut-punched. He took a half-stumbling step backward, a profound look of grief overcoming him. He looked around, bewildered. A heartbeat later, he recovered himself and straightened. When he spoke next, his voice was harsh. "What happened?"

"This morning, the enemy gained a foothold on the wall," Thaldus said. "He was the nearest officer and threw himself into the breach. Kelgan held them off long enough for reinforcements to arrive. Before he fell, your son fought bravely, earning himself and your family great Legend."

Dennig turned his gaze to the cobblestone ground and remained silent for a long moment, the grip upon his axe tightening.

"My friend." Karus rested a hand on Dennig's shoulder. "I am sorry for your loss."

Dennig gave a curt nod, sucked in a deep breath, and looked over at Amarra.

"My lady, perhaps you might help?" Dennig asked. "Like you did with Tal'Thor?"

"I will need to see him," Amarra said. "However, you must understand, it is up to the High Father to grant such a blessing. It is not up to me. I can only ask for a healing. I cannot promise one."

"You would let this witch, this human, this false cleric, near your dying son?" Martuke asked. "Where has your legend gone? Tell me, for surely it is beyond salvage."

"Hold your tongue," Dennig snapped, "or by my Legend, I will see that you lose it."

Martuke's jaw flexed. And with that, Dennig began striding forward. Karus went to follow, but Martuke shook his head in the negative and held out his palm.

"Not you," Martuke said. "You and your elves will remain here."

Dennig stopped, turning back. He stepped close to Martuke.

"Never forget, I am warchief," Dennig said in a low tone. "You may have been appointed by the Thane as my second in command... my watchdog... his spy... but never forget I command here. I trust these people with my life. They are not to be harmed, hindered, or molested in any way. Do you understand me?"

The look in Martuke's gaze spoke of intense dislike and a base hatred for Dennig. After a moment, the dwarven officer gave a reluctant nod and took a step back.

"As you say, *sir*," Martuke said, making the word sound grudging. "You are in command and answerable to the Thane."

Dennig spared Martuke a long look, then motioned for Karus and the others to come. The elves closed in around Karus and Amarra as they started forward.

"Elves guarding humans," Martuke said, with a slight shake of his head. "I never thought to see such a thing. What is going on here?"

"There is a lot you do not know." Dennig let out a weary breath. "Now, we've wasted enough time talking. I am wet, cold, and tired. I would see my son. Take me to him."

"Yes, sir," Martuke said, and led them into the shattered town. Thaldus followed them to the gate and then remained behind.

Passing through the gatehouse, they found the town a thorough mess. It was almost unrecognizable as once having been a settlement. The buildings nearest to the walls had either been reduced to complete ruin by the enemy's artillery or had outright burned to the ground. Rubble and debris were everywhere, clogging the narrow streets. Paths had been cleared to allow passage, but for the most part they were very narrow.

Battered and weary dwarves watched them pass. Karus saw no looks of hatred or dislike directed at Dennig from his warriors. In fact, he saw what he took to be a deep respect and trust, perhaps even relief that their warchief had returned.

"How many effectives do we have?" Dennig asked Martuke.

"There hasn't been time to make a proper count, yet," Martuke said, "but if I had to guess, maybe a little less than a thousand. We should have a better idea within an hour or two."

Dennig stopped and swung around. "That's all? That's all that's left?"

"Since you left us for the elves, it has been difficult going and we've seen some heavy fighting," Martuke said. "It has not been easy, sir."

"No, I imagine not," Dennig said, glancing around at the destruction of the town. "How many injured would you say?"

"That I do not know either," Martuke said. "After this day's assaults against the walls, the number is surely quite high."

With a hand, Dennig motioned to Martuke in the direction they had been going. Martuke took the hint and led them deeper into the town, past a building that burned fiercely.

A team of dwarves had formed a bucket brigade. Drawing from a well, they were passing buckets filled with water forward to be tossed upon the inferno. Even with the rain to assist, as far as Karus could see, they were having little effect upon the blaze. Karus thought the heat from the fire was welcome enough, for he was still very cold and wet. He was so chilled, he was almost at the point of shivering.

Martuke led them to what appeared to be a central square. Karus felt it was almost like a Roman forum. But . . . the square had an alien feel to it that reminded him he was far from home. Karus was struck with an acute pang of loss. He and the rest of the legion would never be going back. They would have to find a new home.

Dennig stopped cold, surveying the scene that spread out before them. The entire square was filled with the injured, either lying upon the cobbled stone or leaning against the walls of the buildings that had remained standing.

There were hundreds of them and each had taken a serious wound, for Karus had seen plenty of walking wounded already. These before him were no longer capable of defending the town.

Even more wounded could be seen along some of the side streets that led out of the square. Some were silent; others cried out in agony or moaned their misery to the world. The cobblestones at their feet were slick from the rain and blood of the injured.

A pathway had been made between the injured. It led toward what Karus thought was a tavern on the far side of the square. A wooden sign with a faded mug hung out before the door, which had been propped open. Yellowed light from inside spilled out.

Two stretcher-bearers, wearing bloodstained tunics, emerged carrying the body of a dwarf between them. Both dwarves looked exhausted, as if they had been pushed almost beyond reasonable limits.

They unceremoniously dumped the body onto a pile of corpses that rose chest-high to the right of the door. Then, bringing the stretcher with them, they went back inside the building.

Karus had seen such things before. Though Dennig's people were not human, he found it still tore at his heart to see good soldiers suffering so. The dwarves seemed to be a proud and brave people. He could respect that and them. Surely many, if not most, here would perish, succumbing to their wounds and to the elements. Not for the first time did Karus think it a harsh world.

"Can you help them, my lady?" Dennig asked, having stopped. He gestured around the square with his axe. "Can you heal them?"

Amarra had been gazing around at the wounded. She looked blankly at Dennig for a long moment then blinked before focusing on him.

"I… I don't know. Let me see."

She closed her eyes, breathing in. Her staff flashed with muted light. She gasped sharply as she opened her eyes, her chest heaving… as if she'd run a great distance.

Amarra turned to Dennig and seemed suddenly hesitant. A tear ran down her cheek as she shook her head. "There is nothing I can do for so many. I cannot heal your people."

"Why?" Dennig asked. "You were able to heal Tal'Thor. Why not them?"

"I do not know," Amarra said, sounding thoroughly wretched. "When I searched within, the sense I got was that the High Father would not permit such healing." She paused. "There will be no healing this day. Dennig, I am truly sorry."

Dennig had become perfectly still, his gaze upon Amarra intense. The implications of what she'd said had sunk home. Karus could not believe what he was hearing either.

Amarra cleared her throat. "It is possible that since your people follow Thulla, he will not grant his favor."

"Thulla," Dennig whispered. "I don't understand. Our god sits with the High Father. Why won't he help?"

"I don't understand either," Amarra said. "But, as I said, there will be no healing this day. That much was made clear to me."

"My son …"

"I am so sorry," Amarra said.

Dennig gave a grim nod and looked around once more. "This is the price of victory, the cost of saving the warband. Perhaps, if we'd had more faith to begin with, things might be different."

Martuke shot Amarra a deeply unhappy scowl, then gestured toward the tavern. "Your son waits. I will show you the way."

Dennig followed after Martuke. Amarra caught Karus's arm and drew him close.

"I reached within," Amarra said to Karus, lowering her voice. "I am not permitted to save them, to squander the staff's power. The High Father made that very plain, almost painfully so."

"Well," Karus said, "the High Father must have his reasons."

"He must," she nodded. "We just do not know what they are."

Karus started after Dennig and Martuke, working his way through the square to the tavern. Those wounded that were conscious and aware of their surroundings watched them pass with deadened gazes.

Karus found the small common room a charnel house. There was blood seemingly everywhere. Amputated body parts lay in a small pile. The blood had coated and stained the floorboards red. Blood was even on the walls. The stench of it was powerful. So too was the smell of loose bowels. Karus had come to associate that smell with death.

A fire burned in the hearth, along the back wall. With the door open, it did little to warm the room. A table had been moved to the center of the common room. Directly overhead hung a lantern. Working under the dim light, two surgeons were bent over a patient who had been placed on the table.

The patient grunted loudly as the surgeons worked on his left arm, which bled profusely. In a waterfall of red, blood ran from the table to pool onto the floorboards. It was clear an artery had been cut and the surgeons were working on repairing the damage.

Off to the side, there were three dwarves lying on makeshift stretchers, clearly waiting their turn before the surgeon's knives. All three had been severely wounded. An assistant was kneeling next to one of the injured, holding a flask to the patient's mouth. The wounded dwarf moaned in agony, but he wouldn't drink. Another, in a weak voice, repeated something over and over again in his own language.

One of the surgeons looked up and froze in his work. The other turned his head to also stare in astonishment at the humans and elves, along with their warchief, as they filed into the small room.

"As you were," Dennig said, and with that, the spell was broken. The two surgeons returned to their work. Dennig turned to Martuke. "Well, where is my son?"

"This way." Martuke led them to the stairs at the back of the tavern, next to the fireplace and up to the second floor, where there was a small corridor that led to the boarding rooms. Martuke brought them to the first door, which he opened, and then stepped aside for his warchief to enter. Dennig hesitated in the doorway. Karus stepped up behind him, gazing in.

On a bed lay a wounded dwarf, who appeared to be sleeping on top of soiled and dirty sheets. His face was bruised, and his stomach had been wrapped tightly with a bandage. His left leg had also been bandaged.

The dwarf opened his eyes at the intrusion and slowly turned his head toward the door. He blinked several times, focusing as he took in his father. Realization dawned, followed by disbelief. He tried to sit up, but groaned and gave up.

Dennig had gone ashen. He stepped into the room and carefully leaned the axe against the wall, before kneeling by his son's side. Karus stopped at the door, resting a hand upon the frame. The boy appeared no more than a youth in his teens. His beard only reached down to his upper chest. His hand shook slightly as Dennig took it in his own.

Dennig said something in the dwarven tongue, tone soft, filled with feeling, grief. Kelgan gave a nod and replied. Karus glanced back toward the stairs. Kol'Cara and Si'Cara had been the only elves to follow them up. The others had remained below. With Martuke, the small corridor suddenly felt crowded.

"Wait downstairs," Karus said to them. "I have no need of a guard here."

Kol'Cara gave a nod. Si'Cara appeared reluctant, but she too followed her brother back down the stairs.

When they had gone, Martuke rounded on Amarra.

"Like so many others before you," Martuke said in a tone barely above a whisper, "despite that pretty staff, you are no more than a false prophet preying upon the hopes of others. A true priestess would heal our wounded, thus proving the truth of her words, the very proof her position is representative of the divine."

"Just because one makes demands," Amarra said, "does not mean the gods will answer. Belief is a personal thing. Martuke, you either have it or you do not. If you have belief, you must be willing to sacrifice to be rewarded…"

"Sacrifice," Martuke huffed. "What would you know of sacrifice, girl?"

"More than you can possibly imagine," Amarra said and tapped him on his chest armor. "I have given up everything that I was for my faith. I have sacrificed much." She glanced over at Karus. "Sacrifice comes in many forms, and even then, the reward might not be what you believe you want or need."

"My lady," Dennig said, interrupting them. He was struggling to contain his grief as he looked back on them. "I fear there is not much time. If you cannot heal my son, would you be kind enough to give him your blessing? Though my people have largely lost our faith, I would send him onto the feasting halls of our ancestors with the comfort of at least the High Father's blessing."

Martuke looked as if he wanted to object but said nothing.

"Of course." Amarra moved past Karus, her dress whispering across the floorboards as she entered the room.

She knelt next to Dennig. Kelgan eyed her warily.

"This is Kelgan," Dennig said in a gentle tone, "my firstborn, a great warrior and… a loved son."

"It is an honor to meet you, Kelgan," Amarra said.

Kelgan spoke in heavily accented Common. It came out as a mere whisper. "My father tells me you are a true priestess of the High Father. That he has seen you perform miracles. Is that so?"

"I am blessed," Amarra said, "to be the High Father's instrument upon this world. It is as he says."

"Do you"—Kelgan sucked in a weak breath—"think if I pray... to Thulla with you"—his voice cracked and he spent a moment clearing his throat—"our god, Thulla, might listen?"

"In truth, I do not know," Amarra said. "I am willing to try. That is, if you are. I have a suspicion he will listen to both of us."

Kelgan seemed to gain strength from that. His voice became stronger, deeper. "Like most of our people, I have turned from Thulla. I would ask forgiveness before I cross over. Do you believe he might forgive me?"

"I have recently found my faith," Dennig said, laying a hand on his son's shoulder. He looked over at Amarra. "It is fitting you should find it as well."

"I understand Thulla, like the High Father, is a forgiving god," Amarra said.

"Then I will pray with you," Kelgan said.

Amarra gave a nod, then looked back on Karus and Martuke meaningfully.

"Leave us," Amarra said, "if you would."

Martuke gave a disgusted grunt, leaned forward, and closed the door.

Chapter Three

Karus had spent an uncomfortable night. He and the elves had camped out in the field with the dragons. Kordem and Cyln'Phax had harried the scattered enemy onward, driving them miles away. He doubted the remnants of the enemy army would be able to easily reform or would willingly linger nearby.

That they had to spend the night in the field bothered Karus little. There had simply been no shelter available for them inside the town. The dwarven injured had needed it more.

With Kordem's assistance, they had been able to get a good fire going. That had helped a great deal and made things a little more bearable. Karus had even managed some sleep, though when he'd woken, he'd found himself stiff and sore.

The first of the two suns had just come up and the sky was clear, almost incredibly blue. The rain had finally left them, and for that little blessing, Karus was immensely grateful. The warmth had even returned, and for the first time in days, Karus felt dry.

He glanced back toward the town. Amarra was still in there with Dennig. Si'Cara had come to tell Karus that Kelgan still clung to life and had yet to pass on. Karus felt terrible for Dennig. He couldn't imagine what it was like to lose a son. How much worse was it to watch it happen, and slowly at that? He hoped and prayed he never had to experience what his friend was now going through.

Karus turned his attention back to the enemy's camp and the open gate that loomed just before them. Since there was nothing else to do but wait, he had made the snap decision to explore the encampment before the dwarves got into it. He wanted to study his enemy and get to know them better. This was the perfect opportunity to do that.

The defensive wall that surrounded the enemy's encampment had been built of earth. The wall rose to a height of ten feet and traveled outward from the gate in either direction. A wooden barricade topped the wall and a six-foot defensive trench surrounded the entire encampment.

The gatehouse was constructed completely out of wood, with thick support beams that had been emplaced into the earth of the wall. A shielded platform over the gate allowed the defenders to rain death down on anyone who attempted to batter down the gate.

Karus stepped through the open gate and looked around. Five of the Anagradoom had accompanied him as an escort. Karus thought the elves looked menacing in their black armor. They moved with a predatorial grace that was almost unnerving. Kol'Cara remained at his side, while the others moved forward a few paces.

Arranged in orderly rows, hundreds of communal tents, separated by wide streets, spread outward before them. The camp was unnaturally silent, eerie, ghostlike even. The canvas of the nearest tents rustled as a light breeze blew by and around them. Other than that, nothing stirred or moved, at least nothing they could see.

"We should be cautious," Kol'Cara said, breaking the silence. "The dwarves have yet to make certain the camp is empty of the enemy, and we have not checked it either."

"Do you think there is danger?" Karus asked, his eyes scanning the tent line. He personally doubted any enemy remained. With the dragons and the army scattered, they would have been foolish to do so.

"Danger?" Kol'Cara asked, glancing over. "There is always danger. Sometimes it's not as apparent as one would expect."

Karus shot the elf a slight scowl, wondering if he was being toyed with.

Kol'Cara gave a sort of half sigh. "I don't think any of the enemy remain. They've surely fled."

Karus said nothing. He suspected the elf had more to say, so he waited.

"Still," Kol'Cara said, sounding almost wistful as his gaze drifted back to the tents. "There are things that could be dangerous in this camp."

"Like what?"

"Items that are best left undisturbed," Kol'Cara said, "religious relics, artifacts, and the like. You may not realize it, but the soul can be easily contaminated by such evil talismans."

"You're not jesting," Karus said, "are you?"

"I am deadly serious," Kol'Cara said.

"Well," Karus said, "if you see anything I shouldn't be touching, you let me know."

Kol'Cara gave a nod. "Agreed."

Karus was about to start forward, but then stopped, looking back over at Si'Cara's brother.

"Why do the Anagradoom wear black?" Karus gestured at the black armor. "The other elves do not."

"It was our choice," Kol'Cara said.

"That doesn't exactly answer my question," Karus said. "I am thinking with you elves, there is a reason for everything you do."

"You are becoming more insightful by the day," Kol'Cara said, with an ironic tinge to his tone.

"Uh huh," Karus said.

Kol'Cara sucked in a deep breath and let it out. As he did, he briefly gazed up at the blue sky, then turned his gaze back over to Karus. "Because we are the Anagradoom, the exiled, the cursed."

"The cursed?"

"Yes," Kol'Cara said. "We are the cursed. The High Master saw to that. We stand apart from our people. By our actions, our willing choice to protect the sword and guard its bearer… you, we cast ourselves out of elven society, forever turning our backs on the light of the people"—he tapped his black leather chest plate—"so we thought black appropriate under the circumstances."

"One day," Karus said, "perhaps, when this is all over, you can go back."

"I fear this will never be over," Kol'Cara said. "The gods are eternal and so too seems the war. It raged before my birth and will likely continue long after my death."

"I'd like to think, one day, this madness will end," Karus said.

"One day, for us, it will end. For others it will continue—or begin a madness they can hardly imagine."

"Are you trying to cheer me up?" Karus asked. "Because if you are, you're terrible at it."

A hint of a smile formed on Kol'Cara's face. "Shall we go in? Or do you wish to stand here all day? I give you fair warning, elves are known for their patience."

Karus gave an amused snort and started forward. He was coming to like Si'Cara's brother. Kol'Cara snapped out an order in Elven and two of the elves jogged ahead of them, over the open ground between the wall and the tent line. They began checking the nearest tents. The other two spread out, bows held at the ready, watchful.

The camp was just as organized as Karus had thought when he'd seen it from afar the previous afternoon. He looked inside the first three communal tents he passed. Each tent slept nine and was clean, the bedrolls laid out neatly, as if the soldiers expected an inspection at any moment. The personal possessions of the soldiers who had occupied each tent were in medium packs set against the canvas walls.

Stepping over a guy rope, Karus moved to the next tent, pulled back the flap, and ducked inside. Kol'Cara followed. Curious, Karus opened one of the packs. He pulled out a haversack filled with what looked like salted pork, bread, and what appeared to be some sort of fat in a cork-stopped jar. He did not taste it, for there was no telling what it actually was.

Karus set the food aside and explored the contents of the pack further. He found a cloth bag that held a flask of oil, along with a small clay lamp and a number of uncut wicks. The lamp was shaped in the image of a fish. The detail was excellent.

Also inside the bag was a needle and roll of coarse thread. He set that to the side and pulled out a spare tunic, a whetstone, a stained cloth for cleaning, and another flask. Karus opened it and smelled the contents, then gave a grunt.

"What's in it?" Kol'Cara asked curiously.

"Vinegar." Karus set the flask aside too. There was a mess kit and a handful of personal possessions at the bottom of the pack, which included a pair of dice and a plain dagger, likely used for eating. There was no purse. Just like legionaries, the enemy soldiers most probably carried their wealth on their person, rather than leave it behind in camp. He also found a waterskin. Unstopping the skin, Karus took a sniff and smelled the sour vinegar-like stench of poor-quality wine.

Karus rubbed his jaw as he considered what he'd just learned. The pack was not all that different from what you might find in a legionary's pack and kit. There were, of course, serious differences, but it was similar enough that he found it troubling. He gazed around the tent once more, impressed by the cleanliness and order. The fetid, lingering smell of unwashed bodies was absent. That meant the orcs bathed regularly and kept good hygiene.

"It would seem they are not complete savages," Karus said, looking over at Kol'Cara as he straightened up.

"No, they're not," Kol'Cara said. "Do not let their bestial appearance fool you into thinking they are mindless animals. Orcs are quite intelligent, perhaps one might even call them sophisticated. I have never seen it myself... but before the Last War, I understand they were known for their culture and great works. At least that is what my grandfather told me."

"Great works, huh? I would think this camp counts as one." Karus moved by the elf. Lifting the flap aside, he stepped back outside into the sunshine. Pausing, he glanced over at the nearest tent, before turning his attention to the defensive wall that surrounded the camp. Kol'Cara emerged behind him.

Everything Karus was seeing seemed to indicate order, organization, discipline, tradition even, something the legion was well-known for. He had the suspicion the camp was laid out the exact same way every time the small army rebuilt it. The defensive wall was too well-made to be a one-time construction. His gaze settled on one of the enemy's large stone throwers. It was a sophisticated piece of engineering too.

The enemy had engineers. That was plain enough. He found that thought alone disturbing, for the Horde had to have some sort of formal education or training program. That meant not only did they study and learn how to build things like this camp, but, like the Romans, they also studied war.

He already knew the Horde was a determined enemy…but now…he understood they were truly dangerous, unlike any he—or perhaps even Rome—had ever faced.

Troubled, Karus began walking, moving deeper into the encampment, absorbing all he saw. He passed cook tents, portable forges, armories, and animal pens filled with strange-looking cattle, domesticated pigs, and lots of other interesting things.

There were seemingly endless picket lines, with teska tethered to stout poles that had been sunk into the ground. The animals' waste smelled terrible, so strong it made Karus's eyes water. He passed supply dumps, stacked high with crates, jars, and bales of animal feed.

Then, there were the heavy wagons and carts, several hundred of them, and well-maintained, too. He looked them over longingly, for the legion badly needed the transport.

They passed a sick tent. The sides of the tent had been rolled up. Karus was startled to see several dozen patients lying on pallets. He still was not accustomed to the sight of the enemy, orcs. With their green skin and tusks jutting from their mouths, they looked so alien. And yet, at the same time... so familiar... very close to being human, uncomfortably so.

Those that had been able had clearly fled. The rest had been left behind, but not before their throats had been slit. Someone had seen to it that none had been left alive for the enemy.

Karus wandered the camp for more than an hour, until he came to three large iron cages. There was a group of live humans in one, six in total, all sitting upon the dirt floor. They looked dirty, ragged, half-starved, and had clearly been abused to some degree. Several of them sported bruises about the face.

In the other two cages were small, almost tiny creatures, wearing gray tunics. There were ten of them, five in each cage. They were half the size of a dwarf and skinny as could be, with a grayish pall to their skin. Their hair was short and black. They stared at him silently, with small, beady, unblinking, black eyes. Fascinated, Karus stepped closer to the nearest cage. The creatures had no pupils.

They were filthy and stank badly, as if they'd been in the cages for a long time. The small creatures fidgeted continually, almost like they had too much energy and could not stand still for long.

"I would be careful, were I you," Kol'Cara said. "Those are gnomes. They are allies of the Horde and are very unpredictable, not to mention dangerous."

"These?" Karus was surprised by that. "They're no bigger than a child. I doubt they could stop a stiff wind if they tried."

"And yet," Kol'Cara said, gesturing at the cage, "the orcs saw fit to confine them. It is my understanding the orcs fear their kind."

"Their allies?" Karus asked. "They fear their own allies."

"That is my understanding."

"Well," Karus said, "I guess, in a way, that makes sense. Rome's own allies fear her strength."

Kol'Cara did not reply.

"Are you certain they are allies of the Horde? Penned up, they look like slaves," Karus said, "or prisoners, condemned for some crime."

"We no slaves," one of the gnomes said in Common, with clear indignation. His voice was squeaky and high-pitched. "And we do no crime. We free people."

Karus was surprised the gnome spoke Common. "If you are free, then why are you locked up in a cage?"

"Orcs no trust us," the gnome said. "As elf say... they fear us, and they should too."

"Why fight with them?" Karus asked. "Why fight with someone who does not trust you?"

"We no want to, no like them." The gnome gave a shrug of his tiny shoulders. "They are allies, so we fight. Is hard to tell why."

"Try," Karus said.

Another gnome spoke. "It just is how it is and has always been. We rather kill orcs. We like hunt orcs. They no like so much... don't see the fun."

Several of the gnomes in the same cage snickered at that.

"The dwarves will just kill them when they come to see what they can salvage from the camp," Kol'Cara said. "Gnomes are the enemy. They are nothing but trouble and will lie to you. Do not waste your time speaking with them."

Sparing one more look at the little creatures, Karus moved over to the cage with the humans. They were squatting or sitting on the ground. As he approached, they stood. There was no fear in their eyes, no trepidation. They stared at him, almost defiantly. Each had a thin steel collar secured about their necks, which marked them as slaves. Karus found it interesting that slaves would dare meet his gaze in such a challenging way. This world was so different from the one he'd known.

"Who are you?" Karus asked in Common.

They stared at him in confusion. It was apparent they did not speak Common. It was either that, or they were very good actors. Karus glanced over at Kol'Cara with a raised eyebrow. The elf said something to them in another language. Again, there was no comprehension in their eyes. The elf tried again ... Nothing.

"Those are all the human languages I know," Kol'Cara said. "It is possible the dwarves may be able to communicate with them."

"Do you think the dwarves will kill them too?" Karus asked. "Like they would the gnomes?"

"They may just take them as slaves for labor," Kol'Cara said.

Karus did not like that. The idea of humans serving as slaves for the dwarves was somehow repugnant, wrong. He studied the men in the cages a moment more. It appeared as if they had been though a tough time of it.

"Do you think they are a threat," Karus asked, "if we free them, that is?"

"To the Anagradoom," Kol'Cara said, "these humans are no threat."

"Look at the ears," one of the human slaves said. "He looks like a man but is not."

Karus's head snapped around. It was a strange accent, but he understood the words.

"Pointed," another said. "He is no man."

"You speak Greek?" Karus said, switching to their language. "How?"

There were stunned looks inside the cage.

One of the slaves stepped forward. "We do. How is it you speak our tongue?"

"Years ago, I learned it from a slave who hailed from Athens," Karus said. He doubted they knew where Athens was, but as these were the first of a new people they had not met, he decided to be open. "I wanted to read some of the masters' works in their original Greek."

The slave ran his eyes over Karus's armor. "I do not recognize your armor. Where are you from?"

"I am of Rome," Karus said.

"I have heard of your city and of your people," the slave said, then turned to the others in the cage. "He is from our world."

"Truly?" another breathed. "We thought we were the only ones."

Karus felt rocked to his core. He was having difficulty believing he had heard correctly. Was it true? Had others been brought to this world, just like his legion had? Then, something occurred to him. The Greek had called Rome a city. The empire had conquered Greece and absorbed it. Surely they should know that. What was going on here?

"What is your name?" Karus asked, struggling to contain and conceal his excitement.

"Adrastus," the slave said, "spear brother to King Leonidas."

"Leonidas?" Karus almost took a step back. It could not be the same Leonidas? Could it? He had read about King

Leonidas. Most Romans knew his tale, honored his bravery. Was this a link to home? Perhaps they were not so alone on this world. "Thermopylae?"

"You have heard of that blasted place?" another Greek in the cage asked, stepping up to the metal bars and gripping them. "You know of Thermopylae?"

Karus gave a slow nod. A great battle had been fought at Thermopylae. The Greeks had withstood the might of the Persians, at least for a time. That had happened hundreds of years ago. Leonidas had been a king of one of the Greek city-states, a great warrior and leader of men. He had died, sacrificing himself and his warriors to buy time for his people and Greece.

"We died there," Adrastus said.

"You died?" Karus was confused. "What do you mean you died?"

"We died in battle," Adrastus said, "and woke up on this strange world, at least some of us did. Soon after, I was visited by Zeus. It was he who told us we were saved for a reason, a purpose."

"Zeus?" Karus said.

"On this world," Adrastus said, "we have learned, he is called the High Father."

Karus's mind raced. The High Father was also Zeus. He should have realized that. "My legion was brought here too."

"What is a legion?" Adrastus asked.

"A small army," Karus said. "Are there more of you?"

Adrastus gave a nod.

"How many?"

"That," Adrastus said, "I will not tell you."

"What are you saying?" Kol'Cara asked.

In his excitement, Karus had forgotten the elf did not speak Greek.

"They are from my world," Karus said, switching back to Common. "They are a people called the Greeks and they're warriors. Very good warriors too, if they are who I think they are."

"Are they friendly?" Kol'Cara asked.

"Friendly?" Karus asked himself. "Seeing that they are in the same boat as me and my boys are, they should be. But… that is yet to be determined. Oh, they also follow the High Father."

"Better than Castor," Kol'Cara said. "There are more of them, then?"

Karus gave a nod. "I do not know how many. He will not tell me. He clearly does not trust us."

"I would not trust us," Kol'Cara said.

Karus glanced at the cage, then switched back to Greek. "How did you come to be here, in this camp? Prisoners?"

"About a week ago we were taken, four days' march from here," Adrastus said. "This land is cursed. It has been stripped bare of food and people. We were out foraging, when those green creatures fell upon us. In the beginning, we thought them demons sent by the gods, but now… after watching them from this cage, we think they are just a strange people, much like any other… an alien people."

Karus fell silent for a long moment as he considered what he'd just been told.

"We have plenty of food," Karus said, "in a city named Carthum several days' march from here."

"There is food here in this camp," Adrastus said. "Free us and I will bring our people. It will sustain them."

"When the dwarves get here," Karus said, "they will likely take it all. There will be nothing left for your people."

"Dwarves? Who are they?"

"The warriors defending that town," Karus said. "They are another people, not like you and I. Different than the orcs."

"Orcs?"

"The green creatures that captured you."

"So," Adrastus said, "orcs ... and dwarves"—he pointed to one of the cages with the gnomes—"and those? What are they?"

"Gnomes," Karus said.

"We had heard the fighting and seen the dragons," Adrastus said. "The ... orcs ... all left after that, in a hurry, too." The Greek paused. "These dwarves hold the field?"

"In a manner of speaking," Karus said, "yes."

"And they will not let our people have anything?"

"I think that unlikely," Karus said. "But we have plenty of food and will share, if you will come. Well, that really depends upon how many mouths you have to feed and if you will work with us."

"You would share your food with us?" Adrastus asked. "But you want us as allies?"

"My legion thought we were alone in this land. Together, we will be stronger. We should work together." Karus paused as he considered his next words. "The High Father visited me as well. He gave me a job to do and I mean to do it."

"Greeks and Romans working together," Adrastus said, as if considering.

If Adrastus had indeed come from Leonidas's time, that meant he had lived hundreds of years in the past, many hundreds of years before Karus had been born. Just the thought of it was incredible. The ways of the gods were truly mysterious indeed.

Karus did not tell him that, in his time, the Greeks now lived under Roman rule. Since there were Greeks amongst the camp followers, if Adrastus agreed to join them, then it was a certainty he would learn soon enough. When the truth came out, he might take it very badly. Karus knew he would have to be proactive and, when the time came, handle breaking the news carefully, for he had enough enemies as it was and did not need any more, especially a Spartan.

The flap of great wings drew their attention skyward. Cyln'Phax landed a few yards away, flattening a number of tents. The ground shook with the impact of her landing. Eyes incredibly wide, the Greeks in the cage drew back and the gnomes became quite agitated, jabbering amongst themselves.

Ah, Karus, Cyln'Phax said, *I see you've found the others from your world.*

"You knew there were others and said nothing?" Karus asked, jerking a thumb at the Greeks in the cage. "This is getting tiresome. Why withhold that information?"

There are five hundred of them, Cyln'Phax said, ignoring the question. *The last we saw of their little band, they were a day or so's flight from here, hiding out in the mountains.*

Karus just shook his head in utter consternation.

"Are there others like them?" Karus asked. "From my world?"

That I do not know, Cyln'Phax said, *but as you and they are already on Tannis, it is a possibility.*

"The beast speaks in my head," Adrastus said, disbelief in his tone. "It talks."

I am no beast, Cyln'Phax said, leaning her head toward the cage. She opened her jaws, exposing long rows of serrated teeth. *If you continue to insult me, I shall eat you, puny human.*

Adrastus snapped his jaw shut.

"Cyln'Phax is an ally," Karus said and pointed at the dragon before gesturing at the elf, "and so too is Kol'Cara and his elves. As I said, the High Father gave us a holy mission. We are to gather allies and flee this world to a safe haven. If you want, you may come and fight with us."

"You already have powerful allies," Adrastus said. "Why do you need us?"

"You have seen the enemy," Karus said. "There are a lot more coming."

Adrastus tore his gaze from the dragon. "Zeus told me the same."

"Then let's work together," Karus said. "It was clearly his intention."

"How do I know I can trust you? You might be lying."

Trust him, Cyln'Phax said, *trust him not. It matters little to me, but honestly… I think you would be a fool not to. Your people are starving and Karus offers to fill your bellies. Besides, the two of you are from the same world…*

Adrastus's eyes went to the dragon and then back to Karus. He was silent a long moment. "I will have to discuss such an offer with my people. Since we came here, things are different. We are from many states and have no king. None of our leaders came with us."

"You're from Sparta," Karus said. "Do I have that right?"

"I am of Sparta and those with me are too," Adrastus said. "There are Tegeans, Corinthians, and Myceneans in the mountains at our camp. As the dragons said, we number a little over five hundred."

Karus had not heard of the Tegeans, but he had heard of the others. They were city-states of old Greece.

"Can you open the cage?" Karus asked Kol'Cara.

"Are you certain you want to do that?" The elf looked skeptical.

"They are potential allies," Karus said, then turned to Cyln'Phax. "Can you tell them how to get to Carthum?"

I suppose I can, Cyln'Phax said with a huff.

"We will free you," Karus said, turning back to Adrastus. "You can take all the food you can carry and a couple of teska… Are you familiar with them? They are the six-legged, shaggy things, the local beast of burden to these parts."

"We know of them," Adrastus said. Then his eyes narrowed. "Won't these dwarves you spoke of object to us taking food?"

"I will see that they allow you and your men to take what you can and permit you to go. The dragon will tell you how to reach the city of Carthum."

Adrastus's gaze went to the dragon again and then returned to Karus. "Free us if you will, but upon my honor, I promise nothing other than we will discuss your offer. We may not even come."

Karus thought about telling Adrastus more or making a stronger argument. But after some thought, disregarded that idea. He had made his case, and now he would see them freed. The Greeks would either come or not. It was that simple.

"I find that fair," Karus said. "And before you go, you should know… there is another army of orcs out there. They are marching this way and for Carthum. We won't be staying long… so don't take too long in deciding."

"Another army?" Adrastus asked.

"Far larger," Karus said. "The orcs are of the Horde. They are the real enemy in this land and they have dragons of their own."

Adrastus's eyes once again flicked to the dragons.

Karus, Cyln'Phax said, *try not to compare us to wyrms. I find it insulting.*

"Free them," Karus said to Kol'Cara, switching to Common and ignoring the dragon, "if you would."

"Are you certain?"

"I told them they can join with us," Karus said, "and leave this world and the Horde behind when we go. They are going to discuss the matter with their people."

"You leave world?" the gnome he had spoken with asked in Common from the other cage. "How? How you go? You tell."

Karus turned back to the gnome as Kol'Cara drew a dagger and began to work on the lock to the Greeks' cage. He moved back over to the gnomes' cage.

"What concern of that is yours on where we go?"

The gnome did not immediately reply but seemed to eye him shrewdly. Karus turned away to watch Kol'Cara work.

"Two World Gates are in hands of Horde," the gnome said, drawing Karus's attention once again. "But third is locked, sealed, lost. Its location is not known to Horde. They search, on orders of the Krix, but not know where is."

Karus felt his heart almost skip a beat. There was a third World Gate? And the enemy did not know where it was? How was that possible? He also wondered what a Krix was.

Do not listen to him, Cyln'Phax said. *Gnomes cannot be trusted. Were there another World Gate, I think we would know.*

"I not lie," the gnome said emphatically. "I not lie. There is third World Gate."

He lies, Cyln'Phax asserted forcefully.

"Noctalum know truth," the gnome said. "You ask them."

Not likely. Cyln'Phax sounded disgusted. *And I very much doubt one would speak to the likes of you, gnome.*

"We no talk to them," the gnome said. "We watch them. We watch everyone. They no know."

Cyln'Phax raised her head at that, eyeing the gnome intensely. The little creature did not flinch under the scrutiny.

"And why would I believe you?" Karus said. "You are allied with the Horde. Gnomes, like the orcs, are our enemy."

"Yes, yes, I know," the gnome said, as if it were not such a big deal. "We part of Horde. But if you take us with you … my people not be. We be free. We leave Horde behind. No war on you once we go to Istros. On that I promise, give word."

"You cannot trust them," Kol'Cara said over his shoulder as he worked on the lock. "They are gnomes."

Istros is a world I have heard of, Cyln'Phax said. *It is a world that is said to be free of the Last War… the War of the Gods. If there is a third Gate… it could lead there.*

"So, you believe there is a third Gate," Karus said, "and it goes to this world, Istros?"

"It go Istros," the gnome said, nodding his little head emphatically.

Gnomes do watch, Cyln'Phax said. *They are like vermin and sometimes it is impossible to rid your lair of them, even when you burn it out. In the deep dark of the world, they are nearly everywhere on Tannis.*

Karus found that last part both troublesome and worrying.

"What is your name?" Karus asked, thinking escape from this world could not be that easy.

"Klegg, leader to my people, the Malshar," the gnome said. "Long has Istros Gate been lost to all but few. Key that opens it has been lost." The gnome pointed at him with a tiny index finger. "I think you have Key, yes?"

"Why would you think that?"

"Because High Father involved," Klegg said. "Oracle said he hide. Take and hide Key. I think he gives it to you."

The oracle again, Karus thought. When time permitted, he really needed to visit this oracle.

"You know where this Gate is?" Karus asked, deciding not to answer the gnome's question.

"No," Klegg said.

"Then you are of no use to me." Karus started to turn away again. He should have known it would not be so easy. Nothing ever was.

"I know how to find it."

"Tell me then."

"No," Klegg said. "You think I stupid? I not. Free us. I bring people to Carthum. Then…we help each other. I helpful you. You helpful us. We find Gate together. We go."

Karus considered the gnome for several silent moments. He knew there was no way he could trust this creature. But, at the same time, he realized he might have to.

"We not friends," Klegg said. "We not allies. But we work together for time. Escape Tannis to Istros, then go separate ways. We no trouble you."

Karus hesitated a moment, then gave a mental nod. He'd made his decision and, for better or worse, would live with it.

"Free them too," Karus said to Kol'Cara.

"Karus," Kol'Cara said, straightening from his task of picking the lock to the Greeks' cage, "this is a mistake." He pointed at the gnomes with the dagger. "If I let them go, they will pass on word of us to the Horde."

I cannot believe this, Cyln'Phax said, *but I am inclined to agree with the elf. This is an uncommonly bad idea.*

"The enemy already knows we are in Carthum," Karus said. "I think we have to take the risk. If a third Gate exists…we need to find it. It could be what we need to escape this world."

Kol'Cara gave a disbelieving grunt and turned back to the cage. A moment later, the lock came free and he swung the cage door wide.

"Thank you," Adrastus said as he stepped through the door and up to Karus. He held out his arm, which Karus clasped. Adrastus's grip was firm. "The dragon has already told me how to reach Carthum. As I promised, I will speak to my people. If there is agreement amongst us, we will see you there."

"Good." Karus gestured back the way he'd come. "The food and supplies you will need are that way. The teska are picketed right behind the supply dumps. There are also packs with precooked rations in the tents. You may want to grab a few of those too. With that other army marching here, there is no time to waste. Understand?"

Adrastus gave a nod.

"Good," Karus said, "best get moving."

"Thank you again for freeing us." Adrastus paused, as if he would speak more, then motioned for his men to follow. A few heartbeats later and they were gone.

There was a heavy chink, and with it, the lock to the gnomes' cage came free. Kol'Cara stepped back as the gnomes filed out. He moved over to the other cage and opened that lock too. The elves had moved closer to Karus. He noted they held their bows at the ready, arrows nocked. Were the little creatures that dangerous? They were the size of small children.

"We go now," Klegg said.

"Betray me," Karus said, "and I will kill you, Klegg."

The gnome flashed him an evil smile. "You no first to try."

Chapter Four

Karus was absorbed in the maps scattered across the table. He heard Kol'Cara say something from the other side of the tent and looked up to see the elf set a wax tablet he'd been idly studying back down on the camp table.

For the last hour of their explorations, the elf had seemed bored, almost to the point of distraction. They had found the enemy's command tent or, more appropriately, what the orcs likely considered their headquarters.

Karus had been impressed with all he'd seen so far, and the enemy's headquarters was no exception. The tent was open, as all four sides had been rolled up. It was large, with a thick central support pole and four outer supports. The canvas of the tent was good quality and had been well waterproofed. A large banner with a red skull emblazoned on it flew from the top.

There were four long tables for the clerks. Each table held a clay lamp. Tablets, stacks of parchment, styluses, and ink bottles lay on the tabletops, right where the clerks had left them when they'd fled. So hasty was their flight that one of the tables and a couple stools had been overturned. There was even a half-eaten meal of what looked like pork and some beans on one table.

Karus thought it interesting that there were no bugs. Had they been back in Britannia, flies would have been buzzing around it. Strange…

Trunks full of neatly organized tablets and parchment had been set around the main support pole. Karus supposed that they were reports, the kind of mind-numbing work the military bureaucracy seemed to eagerly require—well, at least the legion did. Over the years, Karus had frequently wondered if anyone had ever read the vast multitude of reports he had been required to submit to headquarters.

"What did you ask?" Karus said.

"I asked if you found anything interesting." Kol'Cara moved over to him. The elf gazed down at the map before Karus. There were other maps scattered about on the table.

"Yes, I believe so. I think these maps are very interesting," Karus said. "This one in particular is of the local region and the surrounding lands. The X mark here is the town, the one the dwarves were holding."

"I see." Kol'Cara leaned forward to get a better look. "That does appear to be the river running through the valley, and these are the ridges surrounding the town." The elf glanced over at Karus. "It seems you can read a map. I am so pleased for you. I might even admit to being slightly impressed."

Karus flashed the elf an amused grin. "Yes, I can read a map. A soldier who can't is doomed to die an early death or wander forever… lost to his own incompetence as many junior officers learn to their own chagrin." Karus grew serious and tapped the town with his index finger. "What I find particularly interesting are these other marks on the map. The lines under these X's here, likely also towns and villages, could indicate enemy garrisons. If so, it marks the farthest advance of the Horde westward, which would be where we are now."

"Or they could simply be marking the towns and villages they've sacked, looted, scouted, or whatever. Have you considered that?"

Karus scowled as he touched the map again with a finger. The elf had a point. Under one of the X's was a strange, blocky script that had been penciled in. "Can you read this writing?"

"I don't read orc."

"Well," Karus said, "that makes two of us. Still, I believe I'm right. See this circle under Carthum?"

"I do," Kol'Cara said. "Are you certain that is Carthum? Before we went into stasis, that city did not exist. It might have been a simple farming village. Human lives are so short and fleeting compared to ours."

"How old are you?" Karus asked, looking over at the elf, for Carthum was an old, even ancient city. He understood elves lived many lifetimes… but he had no idea how long.

"Old enough to know better than to answer that," Kol'Cara said. "Back to my question… Are you certain that is Carthum?"

"Yes. I am sure. I recognize the positioning of the forest here, along with these other towns and cities. We found a map in the city that matches this one exactly."

"I'll take your word for it," Kol'Cara said. "All right, let's say I am convinced."

"This circle, I believe… means the city is not occupied." Karus touched two other X's with circles under them. "This one here is clearly Caradoon. My men scouted the city before I left for the Fortress of Radiance. It was abandoned and, like most other towns and villages, stripped of food. Still, the Horde had not gotten there yet… hence the circle."

"You may be on to something." Kol'Cara leaned forward again. All traces of boredom gone, he began studying the map more intently, then slid his finger back to the town the dwarves had been defending. "So, this town is indeed their farthest advance."

"It would seem so," Karus said. "That tells us the threat is coming almost directly from the east. It appears we don't have to worry about something coming out of the north and south. Though I believe the dwarven armies are somewhere to the west, and from my encounter with one of their generals back in Carthum, a dwarf named Torga, they don't exactly seem too friendly."

"Dwarves by nature are not. Dennig seems the exception." Kol'Cara gave a nod and then touched the map. "If you are correct, it means the orcs have a very long supply line. The nearest occupied town would be this one, way over here." Kol'Cara trailed his finger almost halfway across the map. "That's a long way, several hundred miles at best. It could explain why this advance force brought so much supply with them. I wonder how much the main body is hauling with them or if they are relying upon a system of replenishment trains."

Karus was silent for a long moment as he considered the elf's words. It was a good question, one that was worth exploring.

"You think the army that was here…was like a reconnaissance in force?" Karus asked. "Is that what you are saying?"

"It is certainly possible. They might have been pushed forward to see if there were any hidden threats and then stumbled upon the dwarves and decided to act."

"The enemy's line of advance seems like they're making a beeline right for Carthum," Karus said. "You may be right. The dwarves might have been too good an opportunity to ignore." Karus fell silent again, then gazed back down at the map, his thoughts on the army they'd seen from the air. "Their line of advance is too much of a coincidence for me. Their objective is surely Carthum."

"Agreed," Kol'Cara said. "This land is empty of its people. Barring Dennig's dwarves, your legion is the only organized force about. They're aiming to eliminate you, then move whenever they are ready and at their leisure to seize the rest of the region."

Karus gave an absent nod, suddenly feeling ill at the thought. As if he did not already have enough problems, the enemy was coming for him.

"If that is the case, when we pull out of Carthum, they'll likely follow us," Karus said.

"Again, I agree. If the destruction of your legion is their objective, they will follow. A pursuit may already be a foregone conclusion." The elf paused and glanced back down at the maps. "Do any of the maps detail the west, beyond Carthum?"

"This one here." Karus pulled a small map from under the one they had been studying. It had clearly been hastily sketched and seemed to be as basic as they came.

Kol'Cara examined the map for several long heartbeats. "This map is far from complete. It's missing two mountain ranges that I know of and an extremely large lake with an island at the center." Kol'Cara paused. "It was likely drawn by a team of scouts who did not do a thorough job of exploration or lacked the time to do so."

"Their picture of the west is incomplete," Karus said. "We might be able to use that in some way to our advantage. That is, if we can find detailed maps ourselves."

"I know the terrain beyond Carthum quite well," Kol'Cara said. "Land does not change that quickly over a few hundred years."

"A few hundred years?" Karus asked. "Is that all?"

Kol'Cara pointedly ignored the comment. "Cities, towns, and villages, that's another story. When we get to

Carthum, I can sit down with one of your scribes and help build a map of the west all the way to the Barrier Ocean."

"An ocean?" Karus asked. "How far westward from Carthum?"

"It's a long way," Kol'Cara said. "Maybe a thousand of your miles."

There was so much of this land Karus did not know. It was incredibly frustrating. And it put him at a serious disadvantage. He needed to correct that deficiency, and as rapidly as possible.

"This map tells us there is a good chance their advance scouts have penetrated a little beyond Carthum," Kol'Cara said, "but not much farther."

"As we move west, my cavalry will have to be on the lookout for additional scouting attempts," Karus said. "If we can keep them off the line of march, we might even be able to slip away at some point."

"Cavalry?" Kol'Cara said, looking up, his gaze intensely focused on Karus. "You have horses?"

"We do," Karus said.

"This world is without them," Kol'Cara said. "Do you have many such mounts?"

"Yes," Karus said, "and I intend to use that to my advantage."

"The orcs of this world may not be prepared to counter them or comprehend how dangerous cavalry can be," Kol'Cara said.

"Based upon an encounter with an advance force we caught foraging, they're ignorant of how to handle or face cavalry."

"My Anagradoom might be able to help you uncover enemy scouts," Kol'Cara said. "That is, if you will allow me to send out a couple of my best with your cavalry."

"Are they good?"

"Good?" Kol'Cara asked. "They are the best."

Karus gave a grunt at that. He'd seen the elves in action. If they were as good scouts as they were fighters, he did not see a downside.

"We might even be able to teach your scouts how to do their job better," Kol'Cara said.

Karus eyed the elf for a long moment. "Very well. If you believe you can help, I have no problem with letting you try. Can your boys ride a horse?"

"If they can't," Kol'Cara said, "they will figure it out easily enough."

Karus turned his gaze back to the map as something occurred to him. "From the air, we only saw part of their army, but I bet the main body's line of advance is quite long, stretched out over many miles, perhaps a hundred or more."

"Most likely," Kol'Cara agreed.

"It's an opportunity for the cavalry," Karus said.

"How so?"

"Well," Karus said, "we could strike at their supply train. Or, if they're relying upon a replenishing system, as you suggested, ambush their resupply trains. An army can't march very far if it can't eat."

"Interesting," Kol'Cara said. "Deprived of sufficient food, they would then seek to forage what they can from the countryside. That also presents an opportunity."

"As we move westward, we will need to destroy any food stores we happen across and cannot take with us," Karus said. "We can also ambush their foraging expeditions."

"I would recommend burning everything," Kol'Cara said. "Leave nothing for the enemy, including shelter. Make life as difficult as possible."

Karus glanced back down at the maps again and was silent for a long moment. "I want to take all of these maps with us to study them further when we're back at Carthum."

"Tek'Deeth," Kol'Cara said to an elf who was standing a few feet away, just outside the tent. There were no other elves in view, but Karus knew they were near. "Gather up the maps. See that they go back to the dragons and are safely secured."

Slinging his bow over his shoulders, Tek'Deeth replied in Elven and stepped into the tent. He began rolling up one map after another. There was string on the table, which he used to bind the rolls of maps, or if they weren't meant to be rolled up, he folded them.

Karus turned his attention to the rest of the command tent. It reminded him very much of his legion's mobile headquarters. He scanned the worktables, not for the first time wondering how his legion was doing. He'd been away for almost three weeks now, a near eternity and much longer than he had initially anticipated. Worse, when he'd left, disease had been burning its way through the ranks. He wondered how bad it had gotten. What would he find when he returned?

Rapping the table lightly with his knuckles, Karus eyed something strange on the next table. He stepped over and picked it up. It was a long wooden tube, about two feet in length, and larger on one end. The wood was etched and carved in flowing geometric patterns that were so intricate, they were almost mesmerizing. A closer examination revealed a piece of shaped glass affixed inside the tube on either end.

"What is this?" Karus said to himself, turning it over in his hand.

"I have not seen one of those in a very long time," Kol'Cara said. He took the tube from Karus and looked through the smaller of the two ends, then handed it back. "If I am not mistaken, it is gnome-made and very rare."

"Is it dangerous?" Karus asked, still wondering on the device's purpose.

"Dangerous? No," Kol'Cara said. "Well, not to its user anyway. A spyglass is what I believe it's called. You use them to see far distances up close."

"Really?" Karus was intrigued.

He put the device to his eye, just as the elf had, and pointed it out the side of the tent. He blinked in surprise and took a stumbling step back. The next tent over appeared incredibly close, almost on top of him. He pulled the spyglass away and saw the tent at its proper distance, then brought the telescope back to his eye.

"Magic … wonderful magic," Karus said, looking over at the elf.

Kol'Cara seemed amused by his reaction.

"No, just a clever invention is all," Kol'Cara said. "It has to do with the shape of the glass, a trick of the eye is all, I think. We do not have much use for such things. Though, before the Last War, there were elves who made devices like this one to gaze up at the sky, particularly at night."

Karus studied the device a moment more, fascinated. "This may come in handy. It is small enough that perhaps Valens might find a use for it when he scouts or raids the enemy's supply train."

"Valens?"

"He's the commander of my cavalry, one of the best horse soldiers and mounted commanders I have ever known. I think I will bring it with us and give it to him."

"If you wish," Kol'Cara said.

Using a thin leather strap that had been lying on the table, Karus tied the device onto his sword harness while Tek'Deeth worked behind him. Once it was secure, Karus gazed around, searching for other interesting items.

His eye was next drawn to an elegant dagger that had been left lying on the same table, half concealed by a tablet. It was beautifully made, clearly a master's work. The hilt was bejeweled and must have cost a fortune. He moved over and reached for it. Kol'Cara's hand snapped out, grabbing his wrist in a vice-like grip.

"I would not touch that," Kol'Cara said. "That dagger is a priest's holy symbol. It may be dangerous."

Karus found the elf's grip so hard, it was almost painful. Kol'Cara released him after a moment.

"Is this one of the corrupting things you mentioned?" Karus asked.

"It is called an athame." Kol'Cara gazed at the weapon as if it were something vile, like a venomous snake. "Castor's priests use them for ritual sacrifices. And yes, the dagger might be... dangerous... very dangerous. I think it better to be safe than not, don't you agree?"

"Right." Karus blew out a breath as he gazed about the command tent once more. His mood had soured and he felt the itch to go, to return to his legion. Things had been so much simpler before they had been transported to this world. "I've seen enough. Shall we go?"

"I thought you would never ask," Kol'Cara said.

They stepped out of the tent and back into the sunlight, which seemed intensely bright. Both suns were now up, having climbed high in the sky. The day was beginning to grow warm, hot even. To their left, down the street that led toward the gate they had entered, came a harsh shout. It sounded like an order.

Karus saw Dennig approach with an escort of two warriors. Behind them, farther down the street, was a formation of dwarves, several dozen strong, that had been marching in a column. They'd come to an orderly halt and were dressing their ranks. The officer in command moved to the side of the column and shouted another order. The warriors in the formation faced left, toward the officer.

The dwarves had clearly come to salvage what they could from the enemy's camp before they moved on. Karus's gaze shifted back to Dennig. He studied his friend as he stopped before them. Dennig's face was grim, hard, and his eyes bloodshot. He appeared much older and worn than when Karus had last seen him the night before. It was apparent he'd not gotten any sleep.

"Karus," Dennig greeted, the exhaustion plain in his voice. "Kol'Cara."

"Dennig," Karus said, "I want to express how very…"

Dennig grimaced and held up a hand, forestalling what Karus had been about to say.

"I do not wish to talk about it, Karus," Dennig said. "The hurt is too fresh and there is much that needs doing before the warband can march. Perhaps, at some point in the future, we can talk about… my son, but not this morning, please. Give me that, if you will."

"I understand," Karus said.

"Thank you," Dennig said, gazing briefly over at the command tent and Tek'Deeth securing the maps. He scowled slightly, then turned back to his guards. "Give us some space to talk."

Both guards stepped back several paces.

"Where is Amarra?" Karus asked.

"She and Si'Cara are back with the dragons," Dennig said. "They are waiting for you. Kordem said you had gone into the camp. I told them I'd find you." Dennig paused. "I take it you will be flying back to Carthum?"

"That was my intention," Karus said.

"And you plan on leaving Carthum, just as soon as you can?"

"We have your supplies there," Karus said, "but transport is a problem. We're short on wagons and carts. When I left, my boys were building them as quickly they could. That said, with the enemy army on the march, we're out of time. We will, unfortunately, be leaving a lot behind."

"Well, there's transport here," Dennig said. "We'll be taking every wagon and teska the orcs brought to carry our wounded and as much food as we can. We're out of time here too. Much of the enemy's stores will be left behind. I estimate that more than half of the wagons will be empty when we go."

"What are you proposing?" Karus asked, cautiously hopeful.

"That you wait for my warband," Dennig said, "and together we move westward. With what's coming, I am thinking strength in numbers will be more important than anything else, at least for the foreseeable future."

"Are you suggesting an alliance?" Karus asked. "What will Martuke think?"

"Martuke?" Dennig said, with a heavy breath that was filled with exhaustion. "He will hate it and so will my people. It might even cost me my head were I to enter into such an arrangement." Dennig paused and blew his breath out through his teeth. "No, there can be no alliance. I am simply proposing we travel west together. You have my supply in Carthum and I have the transport you need. Think of it only as a brief marriage of convenience, nothing more. We collaborate as long as it suits both our interests."

Karus thought for a moment, considering the proposal. It wasn't exactly what he wanted, or the alliance he badly needed… but perhaps it was a start. By working together, they would begin marching down the right path.

"Dennig," Karus said, deciding to press a little further, "you know what we face. It makes sense to ally."

"That is not my decision to make," Dennig said firmly, then softened his tone, lowering his voice. He glanced at his escort, which waited a few paces away. "After this fiasco, I will be lucky to keep my warband, that is, if I can make it back to the army. I have no idea how the Thane will react to our losses. Karus, I have barely five hundred warriors capable of fighting and another thousand that are either walking wounded or thoroughly incapacitated. We left Carthum over four thousand strong and I have a fraction of that remaining. I should never have left my post there. The price… even to save our own, has been too high."

Silence settled between them. Karus decided to break it and ease Dennig's troubles a little.

"I accept your offer," Karus said. "We will be waiting in Carthum for you. We can move west together, and if it comes to a fight, I will be there at your side."

"Thank you," Dennig said, sounding immensely relieved.

"No need to thank me, my friend. An alliance"—Karus paused and glanced over at Kol'Cara—"or really a coalition of races, will, I fear, become only too apparent in the months ahead. Your Thane will surely see that."

Dennig gazed at the elf for several heartbeats as he ran a hand through his beard and then turned his gaze back to Karus. "I pray it is so, for my eyes have been opened."

"When will you march?" Karus asked. "After all they've endured, I bet your boys are pretty spent."

"Spent or not," Dennig said, "we must go. I can't afford to have the enemy catch up with us and complete the destruction of the warband. As soon as we hitch the teska teams to the wagons and load our supplies, along with what we can easily grab from this camp and our wounded, we will march. I want to be on the road before evening or just after dusk. And I intend to march straight through the night. If I have any say about it, I will be in Carthum in four days' time."

"Right," Karus said. "We will be waiting for you. You have my word on that."

Dennig glanced behind him at the dwarven formation up the road. It was clear he wanted to get to work. Karus followed his gaze. The officer was speaking to his warriors, undoubtedly giving instruction.

"I freed some human prisoners," Karus said. "They are people from my world. I told them they could take a couple of teska and some supply back to their band. With any luck, they will join us in Carthum."

"More people from your world?" There was a flicker of surprise in Dennig's tired and weary gaze. "I had not considered that possibility."

"Neither had I, and if what they tell me is true, they are skilled warriors. I would appreciate if yours do not hinder them."

"I will see that they are allowed to go unbothered," Dennig said. "Now, if you will excuse me, the next few hours will be very busy. I have a lot to see to. Until we meet again … my friend."

"Until then," Karus said. "Stay safe."

"You too, Karus." The dwarf turned on his heel and started back the way he'd come, toward the dwarven formation, which had fallen out. Dennig's escort followed after him.

"You did not tell him about the gnomes," Kol'Cara said, once Dennig was out of earshot.

"No, I did not," Karus said.

"Why?"

"I didn't think it the appropriate time. He needs us and we need him. There is no need to complicate things until they need to be complicated."

"I like that," Kol'Cara said, suddenly amused. "'There is no need to complicate things until they need to be complicated.' That's almost elven in nature. Quite witty, actually."

Karus suppressed a scowl. "Well, there's nothing keeping us here now. I've been gone from Carthum long enough. Let's get back to the dragons and be off."

Chapter Five

Karus, wake up.

In his mind, Cyln'Phax's voice was loud, insistent, impossible to ignore. He opened his eyes and looked around, blinking away the sleep. They were still flying; the wind was rushing against him, whistling through his helmet. The suns were out and the air warm, though the wind made it slightly chilly. Wrapped up comfortably in his cloak, he had dozed off.

"What is it?" he called into the wind.

We're landing, Cyln'Phax said and banked sharply to the left. Karus's stomach did an uncomfortable flip as the dragon dropped downward. Caught by surprise, he braced himself, hanging onto the dragon's nearest spike. Ahead of them and below, Kordem was already in a wide lazy spiral, dumping altitude as the dragon descended rapidly toward the ground.

"Why?" Karus shouted.

Amarra asked him to land, Cyln'Phax said, sounding none too happy. *Really... she insisted, said it was important we land near the hill below, the one with the ruins.*

Karus glanced downward. They were flying over what looked like a series of small rolling hills, really grasslands, with a scattering of isolated wooded areas.

He could see no cultivated fields or buildings, except what appeared to be a ruined stone castle sitting on a lone hilltop a few hundred feet below. It wasn't a large castle, but he was sure at one time it had been an imposing edifice and had likely commanded the land for miles around. Karus wondered what had happened to the people who had once lived in this land. As he looked around, farther out, he saw the occasional ruin, but no towns, villages, or cities.

Cyln'Phax continued to swing around as she followed Kordem in a downward spiral that brought the ground closer by the moment. The castle was abruptly lost from view. Karus glanced over at the others on the dragon's back.

Just as he was, they were holding on tightly to the nearest spike. The elves seemed to be enjoying the experience, with several grinning and one outright laughing. Karus, on the other hand, had had enough flying to last him a lifetime. He was a soldier and was convinced his feet belonged planted firmly on the ground.

A heartbeat later, Cyln'Phax flared out her wings and the dragon landed, almost smoothly, with hardly a bump. She folded her wings back and settled down to the ground.

Glancing around, Karus saw that they had landed at the base of the hill. A small wooded area was to their left about twenty yards distant. It was more a stand of trees than anything else. The hill with the ruined castle was not that tall, perhaps only three hundred feet in height and rounded, with an easy sloping grade up to the summit.

The elves were already feverishly working at the knots to the straps that held them in place. Unfastening his cloak from about him, Karus began to undo his own ties. The knots came away quickly. By the time he was free, the elves were already climbing down the dragon's sides to the ground. He followed after them and, using the armored scales for handholds, Karus began working his way down.

Kordem had landed about forty yards away. Amarra was climbing off the dragon's back. Tal'Thor and Si'Cara were already moving away from the dragon, as were the four other elves from Kol'Cara's bunch that had ridden with them. Karus noted they had their bows up, with arrows held at the ready, their heads swiveling as they scanned the area for potential threats. Below, Kol'Cara and the other elves were doing the same.

"Safeed ta," Kol'Cara snapped and pointed at the wooded area. Two elves began jogging away toward it.

"Is there some danger about?" Karus asked as his sandals touched the ground. His hand strayed to the sword, coming to rest on the pommel. The tingle of energy from the sword ran through him, in an almost comforting manner. Any aches and pains or stiffness he'd had from hours of flying vanished in a heartbeat.

Not that I can tell, Cyln'Phax said, bringing her head around to look. *The elves seem a little paranoid.*

"Being paranoid," Kol'Cara said to the dragon, "keeps one alive. Until we know otherwise, we shall assume there are enemies about."

That is quite delicious advice, Cyln'Phax said, snaking her head toward the elf and snapping her jaws loudly. C*an I eat him now, Karus? Please? It's been days since I've had a snack.*

"I think you'd choke on me, dragon," Kol'Cara said with a grin.

You might be right, elf, Cyln'Phax said sullenly. *I might just choke on your bony frame.*

The wind took that moment to blow. It wasn't a strong gust, but it pushed the heat back a little. It brought with it a smell Karus knew only too well. He gazed toward the ruined castle, for the gust had come from that direction, blowing down the hill.

"Death," Karus breathed. "Death has followed us here."

Kol'Cara had smelled it as well. The elf's eyes were on the ruins above, scanning what little could be seen. Her nostrils flaring, Cyln'Phax lifted her head toward the ruins and let loose what could only be described as a low growl.

"Am I the only one," Karus said, looking between them, "who thinks this reminds me of the Fortress of Radiance?"

Kol'Cara shot him a hard look. Karus gave the elf a shrug and decided to find out why they had stopped. He started over for Amarra. Behind him, Kol'Cara snapped a series of orders in Elven to the five other elves. Each went in a different direction. Karus recognized that Kol'Cara was establishing a perimeter around the two dragons. With death on the wind, he did not see cause to question it.

Moving through the knee-high grass, Amarra had started over toward him. Si'Cara and Tal'Thor walked with her. They met halfway between the two dragons. Amarra had discarded her cloak and carried only her crystal staff, the bottom of which she rested in the grass as she stopped before him. In the daylight, the staff was glowing almost brilliantly, something it did not do very often. That in and of itself was an ominous sign.

"Karus," Amarra breathed. She looked excited and pointed up at the castle. "We must go up there."

Karus was silent for a long moment, his gaze traveling up the hill to the ruins at the top. For the most part, the top of the hill looked overgrown, wild even.

"I was afraid you were going to say that," Karus said. "Why must we go up there?"

"I don't know," Amarra admitted.

"What do you mean, you don't know?" Karus asked, a feeling of deep unease settling over him. It was not a good answer, at least not the one he was looking for. "Something recently died up that hill. You can smell it on the wind and I very much doubt it was an animal."

Amarra switched her staff from her right hand to her left and touched her chest. "The pull is very strong. The High Father is telling me to go up there. Even now, it is almost a torment to stand here speaking with you, delaying. There is something very important up there and all I want to do is start climbing that hill. It is almost like he is telling me to hurry… before it is too late."

Karus suddenly felt intensely frustrated. Too late for what? According to the dragons, they were only a few hours of flying time from Carthum. He wanted to get back to his legion and yet here they were. The High Father, it seemed, had different plans for them.

"We must go," Amarra insisted.

Kol'Cara joined them. Karus scratched at an itch on the side of his neck and turned to the elf. "You sent two of your boys into the wood over there to check it out, right?"

"I did," Kol'Cara said. "They should report back shortly."

"As soon as they return," Karus said, turning back to Amarra, "we will go up to the ruins."

"Thank you," Amarra said, with evident relief.

"Why?" Kol'Cara asked. "What is up there?"

"We don't know," Karus said, "but Amarra feels it is important we find out."

"Perhaps it makes sense to scout the hill first," Tal'Thor suggested.

"We could go and look around, mistress," Si'Cara said, "make sure it is safe before you and Karus make the climb."

"I agree," Kol'Cara said.

"No," Amarra said, firmly. "Karus and I must go. And we must not delay. That much I know."

"Alone?" Karus asked, suppressing a frown. "I don't think that is a very good idea."

Amarra closed her eyes, clearly searching within, where Karus understood she found her direct connection to the High Father. She opened them after a few heartbeats and sucked in a deep breath. "It is important that you and I go together. Why, I do not know… but it just feels right. I sense nothing about the others coming or not coming. There is no direction there."

"Then we all go," Karus said, "just as soon as the scouts return."

"If the High Father wills it so," Kol'Cara said, "then that is how it shall be done."

Karus drew Amarra away a short distance.

"I do not like this," Karus said to her, lowering his voice, "not one bit. We're to go up there and we don't know what we are walking into."

"Neither do I," Amarra admitted, "but it is as he wills it. We must have faith."

"Faith," Karus breathed. "I have faith, especially after we both were visited by the High Father back in Carthum. I just want to be back to my legion. I've been away far too long as it is."

"Yes," Amarra said, "but we will be back soon, tonight even. This is important. We must believe it will all work out."

"Faith again," Karus said and glanced once more toward the hill. "This all comes back to faith, doesn't it?"

She leaned forward and planted a kiss upon his cheek. "I love you."

"I know," Karus said. "It was a very lucky day when my men pulled you out of that dungeon."

"Yes," Amarra said, "you are a very lucky man."

Karus saw both scouts emerge from the wooded area and come jogging back. He had a stab of intense resentment at their appearance, for it had ruined the moment with Amarra. Reluctantly, he broke apart from her and they moved back over to Kol'Cara, where the scouts had begun to report.

"In Common please," Karus said, "so that Amarra and I may follow."

"My apologies, sword-bearer," the elf said. He was shorter than the other elves by about a foot but was just as fair and youthful-looking as the rest. His hair was black and had been tied into a short braid.

"Call me Karus, and I would know your name." It was past time he got to know Kol'Cara's boys.

"Aven'Terol," the elf said and then grinned, as if amused. "As you request, I shall call you Karus, sword-bearer."

"And you?" Karus said to the other scout.

"Havren'Fen, at your service, sword-bearer." Havren'Fen had sandy blond hair that had been pulled back into a ponytail. He had a thin, horizontal scar almost dead center on his chin, maiming his features slightly.

"Now," Kol'Cara said, "report."

"The wood is clear," Aven'Terol said, "however, we found goblin tracks."

Amarra sucked in a startled breath.

"Goblins?" Karus asked. "What are they?"

"They're pests," Amarra said, "that live in the underground spaces. Once an infestation is discovered, goblins must be eradicated, for they breed rapidly."

"Pests, like bugs?" Karus asked.

"What are," Amarra asked, struggling over the unfamiliar word, "bugs?"

"Small winged pests," Karus said. "Others crawl on the ground and are small, tiny even, usually with many legs."

Amarra still seemed to be confused.

Kol'Cara, however, clearly understood what Karus meant. He shook his head. "I like that word better than the Common version. There are no bugs, as you call them, on Aragavorn."

It was Karus's turn to be confused. "Aragavorn?"

"This continent." Kol'Cara pointed to the ground at their feet. "The lands around us. Across the Barrier Ocean is another continent, named Solestra. There are bugs there, but not here."

"Ever since we arrived on this world, I've been wondering on that," Karus said. "Why there and not here?"

"Long ago, before we elves came to this world, there was a wizard who detested bugs," Kol'Cara said. "At least that's what I've been told. He cast a web across this land, and for the most part, smaller bugs and other minor pests disappeared. Even though the wizard has long since died, they never came back."

"Well, isn't that handy," Karus said, marveling at such power and wondering if the story was true. "There were times when I wished I could banish pests as easily, and rats too." Karus paused as a thought occurred to him. "You said smaller bugs?"

"I did," Kol'Cara said. "The larger ones were never affected. Some of them are quite dangerous, lethal even, and they have many legs."

Karus recalled the thick webs he'd seen in the Fortress of Radiance and suppressed a shudder. He hoped he never met what had spun them.

"Back to the goblins," Karus said, returning to the matter at hand and shooting a glance up at the ruins. "Tell me about them. I take it they are dangerous?"

"They are thinking beings that are quite dangerous," Kol'Cara said, "but not overly bright. They are tribal in nature and live primarily underground, usually only coming to the surface at night."

"They're pests," Amarra said, with clear disgust, "stealing food and occasionally killing or raiding."

"They have also been known to fight with the Horde," Kol'Cara said, "usually grudgingly."

"Great," Karus said and turned his attention to the hill, gesturing at the ruins. "And they're likely up there, right?"

"The tracks lead up the hill," Havren'Fen said.

Karus glanced up at the sky. It was nearly midday, with one of the suns almost directly overhead. "You said these things only come out at night?"

"Not quite. They prefer the darkness," Kol'Cara said, "but they have been known to venture out during daylight hours."

"That's what I thought," Karus said and, feeling sour, turned his gaze back to the ruined castle. What was waiting for them? At times, it seemed to him this world was filled only with horror after horror and death.

"Goblins, like orcs, see better at night and in near darkness," Si'Cara added. "Their vision is not so good during the day, especially when the sun is bright."

"We must hurry," Amarra said. "I feel the pull to do so. The High Father wants us up that hill."

"Well, then," Karus said, "I see no reason to delay. Are there any objections?"

There were none.

"Right then." Karus clapped his hands together. "Let's go see what's up there."

With Amarra by his side, Karus started up the hill. Si'Cara moved slightly ahead with Tal'Thor. Kol'Cara snapped an order and the elves of the Anagradoom fanned out to either side, though three remained behind with the dragons.

The climb did not take all that long. The slope was an easy one and the hill not terribly high. Before Karus knew it, they were at the remains of the outer wall of the castle. The smell of death was much stronger and had grown more powerful with every step up the hill.

The ruined castle was clearly ancient, for the stone, which in places was covered in carpets of moss or overgrown by brush, was well-weathered. The wall was no more than a jumble of collapsed stone blocks. The mortar that had held the blocks in place had long since crumbled to dust.

Si'Cara stopped before the wall, crouched down, and pointed, looking back on Karus and Amarra. "See here? Goblin tracks. No more than three days old."

The tracks were unlike any footprint Karus had ever seen. They reminded him of large bear prints.

"These three points," Si'Cara said, "are foreclaws. These marks here are the toes, and this is the heel. The goblin was going that way." She pointed to their left, along a path that followed the wall around the hill. "Goblin feet are webbed, which is why the print is so wide. Don't let that fool you. They are generally on the smaller side. A full-grown one will come up to your chest, Karus. Because of their webbed feet, they can swim quite well."

"If you see one that is unarmed," Tal'Thor added, "don't assume it is helpless. They prefer to use their claws over weapons. The claws are razor-sharp."

"I already don't like them," Karus said as Si'Cara stood and began climbing up, over the wall. Tal'Thor followed after his wife.

"When I was a child," Amarra said to him, "there was a bad infestation that went undetected for months in the catacombs under Carthum. Many people died before the city guard was able to clear the catacombs and eradicate them."

Karus glanced at the wall, feeling apprehensive about going forward. Only, he knew he had to. The High Father demanded it. So, he stepped up to the wall and began climbing the pile of stone. It took some scrambling and he had to push aside brush, which had grown up amongst the stones. He almost slipped when a loose bit of stone shifted under his foot, but he was able to get himself up and onto the top of the wall. Climbing in armor was not the easiest of things to do. It took effort.

He stopped and turned back, holding out a hand to Amarra. Scrambling the first few feet, she gripped his hand tightly and he pulled her up to him. She shot him a wink and then made her way deftly over the other side, following after Si'Cara and Tal'Thor. Both elves had already made their way over the wall and had begun moving cautiously out into the courtyard.

Karus remained where he was on the wall, studying the interior of the castle and the remains of what looked like a vicious fight.

Where buildings had once stood was now only a tangle of overgrown, mismatched piles of stone. What had been the central keep was a ruin too. The top of the keep had fallen in on itself. An entrance, where a door had once stood, had been recently cleared and dug out. The hole was overly small, about four feet in height and three in width.

He could not see inside and felt a sense of unease wash over him. It was as if the hole led to an ominous pit of darkness.

Karus shifted his gaze away from the hole and whistled softly, for one heck of a fight had taken place here. There were bodies lying all around the entrance. The bodies were small, the skin greenish. Birds of all kinds hopped around the dead, worrying at the flesh. Disturbed, they squawked loudly as the two elves moved amongst them.

"Goblins," Amarra breathed in disgust below him.

"Yes," Si'Cara said, looking back. "There may be some live ones about. We must be cautious. If you would, mistress, for your own safety... please stay close to me."

Karus ran his eyes over the bodies. There were dozens and each had seen a violent end. He wondered what had killed them, then spotted a larger body, about the size of an orc, only he knew it wasn't. The shape was wrong. The body lay in the shadow of one of the ruined buildings and it was hard to make out, for there was a bush growing in the way. Carefully, he climbed down the other side of the wall as Kol'Cara's elves moved into the courtyard, spreading out, disturbing the hungry birds even more. One elf went to the entrance hole, peered into it for a long moment, drew a sword, and then disappeared inside.

Kol'Cara knelt next to a body. He looked over at Karus. "They've been dead no more than three days."

The smell of death was overpowering now. Karus glanced down at the body of the goblin, feeling an instinctual distaste and loathing. The goblin, though bloated in death, had been a twisted and ugly thing. Strange tattoos ran over the exposed skin.

He moved on, past Kol'Cara, stepping around and over the bodies. Squawking loudly in protest, the birds scattered out of the way. Each goblin had taken a gruesome wound, likely from a sword or some other edged weapon. One had been nearly chopped in half at the waist.

Karus continued slowly through the field of bodies, working his way toward the body he'd spotted lying in the shadow beyond the bush. He stepped around the bush and stopped. Karus stared in amazement at the creature that lay dead at his feet. It was most definitely not a goblin and the birds had completely avoided disturbing it.

"A Vass," Kol'Cara said at his side.

Karus almost jumped, for he had not heard the elf come up.

"A what?" He glanced over. "What did you call it?"

"That is a Vass," Kol'Cara said, in a tone filled with awe, and a healthy mixture of what Karus took to be horror. The elf shook his head slightly. "I had not realized there were any on this world. This is most definitely not good, for where there is one, there are many more."

Karus turned his attention back to the creature. It was clearly male and had long since died. The creature had sat down and leaned back against a pile of fallen stone before it expired.

For lack of a better description, the dead Vass looked like a cross between a tiger and a man. The face was fearsome, animalistic, and covered in orange and black patterned fur. The jaw was slack, mouth open, revealing a set of yellow canine teeth.

A beautifully crafted longsword lay at its side. The weapon was almost too large to be practical, and yet Karus could easily imagine the creature wielding it with ease.

By the size of the Vass, it had stood over eight feet tall and had clearly been strong. Its arms and legs were thick and muscular. The Vass had not died easily. There were dozens of slashing wounds all over its body, some superficial and others quite deep.

Even its black chest armor was badly scratched and clawed. A deep gash along the left side of its neck had likely finished the creature. The fur was matted with dried blood, which had run down its side to the ground where it had pooled and then dried.

Half a dozen goblins lay a few feet away. The Vass had clearly taken them all down before succumbing to his own wounds.

"Death from a thousand cuts," Karus breathed, trying to imagine the terrific fight that had gone down in the courtyard around them. As imposing and large as the Vass was, he had difficulty believing it had single-handedly killed all of the goblins he'd passed.

"Indeed," Kol'Cara said. "The Vass are fearsome warriors. It is said amongst my people, the only good Vass is a dead Vass."

"They are with the enemy, then?" Karus asked, looking over. "Part of the Horde?"

"No," Kol'Cara said, "the Vass are not of the Horde. They are everyone's enemy and walk their own path, for reasons known only to themselves. I have never heard of them allying or working with another race. Karus, the Vass are feared and respected by all sides. That they are here, and so close to Carthum, should be of great concern. In the days ahead, we must watch out for them."

Karus turned around, gazing over the ruins of the castle courtyard and the numerous bodies that lay scattered about. The keep's entrance, only feet away, looked like a forbidding black hole, a portal that opened to another world, one of eternal darkness.

The thought of going into such darkness fed his unease, for who knew what horrors waited within, perhaps even those larger insects that Kol'Cara had mentioned. He wondered if more Vass were in there.

"Do you think this was where they lived?" Karus asked. "The Vass?"

Kol'Cara shook his head. "No. There is clearly a goblin den under this hill. The Vass are more civilized, a sophisticated people, like yours and mine. They build villages, towns, and cities on the surface. They educate and love their children. They do not live like animals in the dirt."

Karus thought about that, his gaze returning to the tiger-like man. It looked like an animal, but then again, so too did the orcs. He had to adjust his thinking, for neither were animals, but people like himself, capable of reasoning.

"Do you think he stumbled upon this place," Karus asked, "and was surprised by the goblins, ambushed?"

"No," Kol'Cara said. "Such a thing is very unlikely."

"Then why was this Vass here?" Karus asked.

"That is a very good question." Kol'Cara glanced around. "This ruin is remote. He must have had a good reason to come here. Perhaps he was searching for something."

"Karus, Kol'Cara," Tal'Thor called from across the courtyard. The elf was waving at them. "I have found a live one, a Vass."

Karus and Kol'Cara shared a quick look. They moved over and found Tal'Thor standing a few feet from the Vass, staying out of the creature's reach. The Vass lay on its back, looking up at them, badly injured and clearly in a weakened state. That Tal'Thor was standing just out of reach gave Karus pause.

Its thigh had been ripped open, exposing the bone within the leg. There were dozens of slashes and cuts across its arms, legs, and face. The creature had lost a lot of blood, which had stained the ground around it. The black leather chest armor was also scratched, pitted, and dented from battle with the goblins. The creature had removed its helmet, which lay discarded a few feet away, as if it had been tossed there. So too had an empty waterskin, which had a deflated look to it.

There were drag marks through the dirt and vegetation, as well as a trail of dried blood, where the Vass had clearly pulled itself out of the direct sunlight and into the shade.

Amarra, along with Si'Cara, joined them. She sucked in her breath at the sight of the creature and became very still. Her staff glowed brighter and then faded back to its normal sullen throbbing.

"There is the body of another one on the other side of the keep," Si'Cara said. "He clearly put up a fight." She glanced around at a dozen or so goblin bodies that lay within fifteen feet of one another. "And it seems this one did as well."

The Vass bared its teeth at them, whether in pain or defiance Karus did not know.

"I suggest we kill it," Kol'Cara said to Karus.

The Vass's yellow eyes went to Kol'Cara. The two furry ears atop its head seemed to shift in his direction as well. Karus could see the intelligence in the creature's gaze. It was weaponless and at their mercy. Its longsword, which was covered in crusted green blood, lay a few feet away in the dirt and out of arm's reach.

The Vass opened its mouth to speak and struggled, working its jaws, but no words came out other than a weak gasp. The creature swallowed. It seemed to make a great deal of effort and then tried once again to speak.

"I would ask that you do it quickly, elf," the Vass rasped in Common, barely above a whisper and clearly a struggle. "I have suffered enough. I would die and see my maker."

"Very well." Kol'Cara handed his bow and arrows to Tal'Thor before drawing his dagger, an elegantly curved weapon. "I will do you that honor, though you have done nothing to earn it."

"No," Amarra said, in a firm tone. "There will be no killing this day. He is why we are here."

"Me?" the Vass rasped, his eyes narrowing as he studied Amarra.

"Are you certain?" Karus asked. He did not know who was more surprised, he or the Vass. "We're here for him?"

"Yes," Amarra said, her gaze focused intently upon the Vass. "Yes, we are."

"How—?" The Vass coughed, a weak sound. "How could you know we would be here? Who … told you? Who betrayed us? I … must … know."

Ignoring the Vass's question, Karus glanced over at the keep and felt a sudden wash of relief. The elf emerged at that moment and started over to them.

Karus turned to Amarra. "We don't need to go in there, do we?"

"No, we do not," Amarra said. "We have found what we came for."

"I did not want to go into that hole either," Kol'Cara said to Karus. "I too am feeling great relief. You may not know this, but we elves prefer the outdoors. I was not looking forward to exploring a goblin den, a difficult and dangerous task during the best of times."

Karus wondered what Kol'Cara meant by the best of times. He could not imagine there ever being a good time to explore a goblin den.

The elf who had emerged from the keep stepped up to them. He gazed briefly down at the Vass before turning to Kol'Cara. "I did not go far," he reported. "There are more bodies inside, all goblin. I saw nothing living."

Kol'Cara gave a nod and then turned his attention back to the Vass.

"What is your name?" Amarra asked before Kol'Cara could speak.

The Vass had not taken his eyes from Amarra. He had been studying her critically. His eyes lingered on the crystal staff. "You are a priestess, human woman, are you not? You are directly blessed by a god."

"I am Amarra, High Priestess to the High Father."

"High Priestess... we honor your god." The Vass paused, his eyes closing, as if he'd gone to sleep. They opened after several heartbeats. "But... we do not worship him. Does that bother you?"

"No," Amarra said. "Each must follow their own heart when it comes to faith."

"Truer words were never said..." The Vass coughed, bloody spittle flecking the fur around his mouth. "You will not heal me?"

"I cannot," Amarra said. "I am not permitted to do so. I think you know that."

The Vass gave a nod of agreement and turned his eyes back to Kol'Cara, whose knife was still drawn. "Do the honorable thing and kill me, for I will not be held captive."

"Permit us to help you." Amarra took a step nearer. "You will not be our captive."

"Amarra," Karus said sharply and grabbed her arm to keep her from getting closer and within reach of the creature.

"Vass are not to be trusted," Kol'Cara said. "It would be best to put him out of his misery, as he has asked us to do. To take him with us would be dangerous. Besides, his wounds are grave. He may not even survive the trip."

"What would you know of trust, elf?" the Vass hissed through clenched teeth. "Your kind has betrayed many over the long years."

Shooting Karus a hard look, Amarra pulled her arm from his grip. "What is your name?"

"Ugincalt. You can call me Ugin. I like it better than my full name, always have." Ugin coughed and then grimaced, his hand going to his leg, gripping it above the wound. Karus noticed a tourniquet had been tied there, which was likely why Ugin still lived.

"We will help you," Amarra said, "if you will allow us."

"And then I will be your caged pet?" Ugin said, face twisting with what Karus took to be derision. "Will you lock me up in a cage for your people to gaze upon? Will you make me into an object of curiosity? Is that it? Thank you, but no. Death is preferable."

"As I told you," Amarra said, "you will be no one's captive. When you are able, you may leave of your own free will."

Ugin eyed her for a long moment before responding. It was as if he was weighing her words, thinking them through, deciding whether or not she spoke truth. A spasm of pain overcame him. He grimaced, baring his canines. It passed in a moment and left him panting. When he recovered, he spoke again. "And will they agree to the same terms?"

"They will," Amarra said, "unless you seek to harm us or our people in some way or manner."

"I would hear them agree to the terms," Ugin said, "before I do."

"It is as she says," Karus said.

"And you, elf?" Ugin asked Kol'Cara. "You seem to be the leader of your people. Will you give me your word of honor?"

Kol'Cara gave a slow nod. "I do not like it, nor do I trust you, Vass, but I will abide by such a deal."

"Bargain fairly struck, then," Ugin said to Amarra. "You have my word of honor, and to my people, nothing is more important than honor. I will not harm you or yours"—Ugin coughed lightly—"as long as you live up to the terms of our agreement, priestess." The Vass seemed to relax a little. He loudly cleared his throat before speaking again. "Do you have any water?"

Karus unhooked his canteen from his harness, unstopped it, and stepped forward, cautiously handing it to Ugin. The Vass drank deeply before handing it back.

He closed his eyes for a long moment, as if in bliss, and then opened them. When he spoke, his voice was stronger. "Thank you. I ran out of water the night before last."

"Why are you here?" Karus asked.

"I will not speak on it."

"Why not?" Karus asked.

"That was not part of our bargain," the Vass said, "and besides, it is none of your business what Vass do."

"Right." Karus glanced over at Amarra, wondering what she had just tied him to. He looked to the entrance to the goblin den. "Can we go now?"

She gave a nod.

"We need to tend to his wounds," Si'Cara said, "before we move him. And even then, he might not live to see Carthum."

"Will you allow us to help you?" Tal'Thor asked, pulling bandages from a small pack he carried, along with a stopped jar of what Karus took to be vinegar. "We will clean and bind your wounds."

The Vass gave a nod and the two elves approached and set to work, first examining the leg wound. Ugin kept his eyes upon them as they worked. They set about first cleaning and then bandaging the leg, tying the bandage tight. Ugin said nothing, made no noise, and gave no indication that their ministrations were causing him pain, other than the occasional grimace.

"Do you think there are any goblins left?" Karus asked, looking over at Kol'Cara.

"If there were," Kol'Cara said, "I think they would have finished him. The fight here seemed to the last."

"There are none left alive," Ugin said. "I dispatched the last goblin with my bare hands, choking the life out of him. Their womenfolk and children fled into the deep. You need not fear them, as they are not aggressive."

Kol'Cara regarded the Vass for a long moment.

"Make a litter," Kol'Cara said to Havren'Fen. "When they are done, we will need to move him back down the hill."

"My sword," Ugin said. "I would not leave it. The weapon has been in my family for generations."

"I will bring it," Havren'Fen said, "and make sure it travels with us."

"I also have a pack," Ugin said. "We left our packs at the base of the south side of the hill. Mine is brown leather. There is a small clay jar with a potion that will kill the pain. I would ask you bring the pack too."

"Demanding, aren't you?" Kol'Cara asked.

"I am only asking for some relief from the pain," Ugin said. "Surely you would not begrudge me that?"

Havren'Fen looked to Kol'Cara, who, after a long moment, gave a reluctant nod of assent.

"Thank you, elf," Ugin said, "for your generosity."

Karus thought Ugin's tone lacked sincerity. There was clearly no love lost between Vass and elvenkind.

"Ugin," Kol'Cara said, turning back to the Vass. The elf's lips twitched with sudden amusement. "How do you feel about dragons?"

The Vass eyed Kol'Cara in question. "Dragons?"

"Surely you saw us arrive?" Kol'Cara said.

"I awoke to find this one standing over me." Ugin nodded toward Tal'Thor. Then his eyes narrowed. "You have dragons?"

"Oh yes," Kol'Cara said, "and they are not part of the bargain you struck with us."

Chapter Six

Karus sat down on a small tree that had fallen down some years before. Tall grass had grown up all around the trunk and it made for a natural seat. It felt good to sit down and take a load off.

Amarra was over by Kordem, digging through her pack, likely for food, for they had not stopped for lunch, nor brought food up the hill with them. Karus did not feel like eating. He wasn't hungry. He was tired, bone weary. The only problem was that he knew when they returned to Carthum there would be no rest, just lots more to do, for an enemy army was marching against them.

It had taken over an hour for the elves to fashion a litter and move Ugin down the hill. Because of the serious nature of his injuries, the going had been a slow, careful process. They had just now reached the dragons and set the Vass down, a few yards away from where Karus had sat.

Both suns had moved across the sky. With their movement, the heat of the day had increased. It was more than warm, and Karus, from his exertions, was perspiring heavily. He untied the straps on his helmet and removed the heavy thing, setting it down next to him. Karus ran a hand through his sweaty and matted hair and then cracked his stiff neck.

He turned his gaze to watch as Si'Cara checked over Ugin's bandages, making certain none had come loose on the journey down the hill. With an inscrutable expression, Tal'Thor stood by and watched, as did two of the Anagradoom who had helped take turns with the litter.

During the trek down the hill, Ugin had repeatedly slipped in and out of consciousness. Now, however, he was fully awake. His eyes were on Cyln'Phax, the nearest of the two dragons. Karus wondered what was going through the Vass's mind.

Cyln'Phax was simply staring back at Ugin, studying him. She'd said nothing since they'd arrived, which had surprised Karus. He'd expected some type of protest or caustic comment. Instead, neither dragon had uttered a word. Karus got the impression both were concerned, perhaps even worried, by the presence of a Vass. Karus knew the elves were troubled too.

Compared to the Horde and their immediate threat, the Vass seemed like a secondary concern. Still, Karus was too weary to worry much about it. He would cross that bridge when he came to it.

He supposed he was worn down from all that had happened since they had set out from Carthum. Even now, Karus was having trouble wrapping his mind around it. He was more than ready to return to his legion, craved it even. He wanted some semblance of order in his life, and the legion represented a return to that. At least it always had. Stranded and cast adrift on this strange world, Karus wondered if normalcy would ever return.

"In his weakened and injured state, he will still need to be watched, both night and day."

Karus nearly jumped out of his skin and turned.

"You need to stop doing that," Karus said, looking to his right at Kol'Cara. "You scared me half to death."

"Perhaps I should have made more noise as I came up." Kol'Cara looked amused. "I had forgotten you are only human and not accustomed to such things."

"Uh huh," Karus said. "And you're a terrible liar. You intentionally snuck up on me."

"If I had, I would never admit it. Besides, a deaf elf would have heard me approach." Kol'Cara chuckled. "You need to be more situationally aware. It might just save your life one day."

"Right," Karus said, "I'll try to keep that in mind."

Kol'Cara took a seat next to Karus, his gaze shifting to Ugin. The elf let out a barely perceptible sigh, as if he too were relieved to be finally sitting. They sat in silence for a time before Kol'Cara broke it. "We found and retrieved his pack, along with those of the other two Vass."

"Find anything interesting?" Karus asked, recalling the orc pack he'd studied in the enemy's camp. There had not really been anything surprising, only what one would expect to find in a soldier's pack.

"There was nothing in it to warrant concern," Kol'Cara said. "We will bring his pack with us and leave the others behind."

"The painkilling potion was there?" Karus asked.

"Yes." Kol'Cara held up a small clay jar he'd been holding and shook it slightly. The jar was so small it fit in his palm. The elf regarded the jar for several heartbeats. "If that is what this truly is. With the Vass, there is no trusting what they say. They are known to speak honestly but twist the truth to their own advantage, what we might consider bordering on a lie or outright deception. I am told they have a twisted sense of honor. You must measure every word." The elf glanced down at the clay jar. "So, I am hoping this is for dulling the pain."

"What else could it be?" Karus asked.

"Poison, perhaps," Kol'Cara said, studying the small jar. "Honestly, I really don't know. Whatever it is, he wants it and that concerns me."

"Have you looked inside?" Karus asked. "Poured some of the contents out? Given it a smell, maybe?"

"No," Kol'Cara said, looking suddenly horrified. "Whatever is in here, I might spoil it, waste it, or worse, if it's poison, become contaminated with it. I am unwilling to take that risk, for some poisons can kill from smell alone."

"Does it really matter?" Karus asked, feeling impatient to be off and on their way to Carthum. "He says it's for killing the pain. Perhaps it is; maybe it's not. I imagine, with the severity of his wounds, he's been suffering terribly."

"I suppose you are correct," Kol'Cara said. "It does not really matter. Still, I find I worry. Perhaps I am just overly concerned because we are dealing with a Vass."

They fell silent for several moments as he considered the elf's words. Karus's thoughts drifted back to the ruins on the hill. Three Vass had killed at least thirty to forty goblins and there was no telling how many they'd killed inside the den itself. That alone gave him pause, for he knew three humans would be hard-pressed to do as well.

"His people are really that big of a threat to us?" Karus looked over at Kol'Cara.

"We can only hope they are few in number."

"And if they're not?" Karus asked.

Kol'Cara did not reply, which was an answer in and of itself. Karus decided to change the subject.

"You were not born of this world," Karus said, "were you?"

"How can you tell?" Kol'Cara said with genuine interest.

"You knew what bugs were," Karus said.

"I could have just traveled to Solestra," Kol'Cara said.

"I doubt that," Karus said. "Elves seem to like their forests too much, kind of like a grumpy neighbor who is completely happy on his own property. Trespass and he will come after you. Leave him alone and he's no bother at all. Besides, your people are long-lived and came to this world from another. I'd bet you were not born on this world."

Kol'Cara laughed. "It seems you are getting to know my people well."

"I figured," Karus said, "there was a good chance you came here like us."

"Like you?" Kol'Cara shook his head. "My people came through the World Gate. Yours came another way, through an ancient portal that should not have been opened."

Karus thought on that. He did not really understand the difference between a portal and a World Gate.

"I was born on Longtow," Kol'Cara said. "It is a world that has since fallen to the Horde. My people came here when it became clear resistance to the enemy was a hopeless endeavor. The Horde eventually followed."

"What was it like?" Karus asked.

"Longtow?" Kol'Cara asked. "Or the uprooting of my people?"

"Longtow," Karus said. He imagined such a move of an entire people would have been a painful experience, and decided it was best not to probe too far.

"A world very different than this one, actually," Kol'Cara said, getting a faraway look in his eyes. "Longtow has vast and seemingly endless oceans. There are no large land masses, like here on Tannis, just many… many islands. Truth be told, it was a wondrous and beautiful place to spend time as a youth… exploring the marvels it had to share, sailing the waves. I miss that time." Kol'Cara fell silent for several heartbeats. "That was long before the Horde arrived."

"I never much liked the sea," Karus admitted. "I spent a summer serving with the navy. That well cured me of a fondness for ships and the water."

Kol'Cara shot him a slight understanding smile.

Thoughts of what Kol'Cara had lost stirred unhappy feelings of his own. Rome and all she offered, his extended family, retired life in Sicily... it was all lost to him.

His gaze slipped back to Amarra. She was chatting with Kordem while munching on a hunk of bread. He had lost, he reflected, but... he'd also gained much. It was something to be grateful for. That was for certain.

"Are there elves on Solestra?" Karus asked.

Kol'Cara gave a nod. "There are even elves sailing the Barrier Ocean, living much as we once did. Leaving Longtow saw a rift emerge amongst us. My people, once unified, fractured and split upon coming to this world."

Kol'Cara fell silent for a few heartbeats.

"Longtow was one of the reasons I chose the path I now walk," Kol'Cara said. "We as a people elected to flee instead of fighting for what we had. Upon reflection... I think we gave up too much, were too willing to leave, when we might have stayed. We surrendered who we were. The price for a temporary refuge was just too high."

Karus looked over at the elf, who met his eyes with steel.

"I swore," Kol'Cara said, his voice trembling with emotion, "I'd not run again. When the opportunity came, I took it, and so too did the rest of the Anagradoom. There are some elves who, just like you and your people, would stand against the dark tide sweeping across this world. That is why we are here. That is why we turned our backs upon our people. That is why we gave up everything we cared about. As I am sure you know, there are some things worth fighting for."

Karus decided it was time they got something out in the open between them. Kol'Cara needed to understand Karus's priorities, so that later there would be no confusion.

"The High Father gave me a mandate to find a way off this world," Karus said. "He promised an empire without end. I intend to find a new home for my people and rebuild, to begin that empire. You must understand, we're not standing and fighting for this world."

"I know." Kol'Cara sounded regretful. "This world is lost. The peoples that reside on this planet wasted their opportunity, squandered what time they had. No ... we do not fight for this world either. It is the next one I am fighting for. Karus, I will stand with you, so that those who settle there, those I love ... can finally have a permanent home, like your empire ... one without end. A home without fear of the Horde. That is the path I have chosen ... the one we will walk together."

As he stared into the elf's gaze, Karus found the bone-tired weariness had gone. He gave a nod. "You made the right choice, for some things are definitely worth fighting and dying for."

"I know." Kol'Cara's gaze shifted to his sister. In the elf's eyes, Karus saw a deep love and fondness. He turned back to Karus. "I am pleased we understand one another."

They fell silent once again. Si'Cara had finished her examination and handed the Vass a waterskin, from which Ugin drank deeply. Some excess water ran out of the corners of his mouth, wetting the orange and black patterned fur. As he considered the Vass, Karus placed his palm upon the bark of the fallen tree and felt its rough surface. Ugin was an unknown quantity, and a dangerous one at that.

"Do you think he will survive his injuries?" Karus asked.

"Truthfully, I don't know much about the Vass," Kol'Cara said. "What I do know has been passed down from others. I have only ever encountered their kind once before and that was simply in passing. We exchanged only pleasantries and went our separate ways without violence. The elders know them better and I learned from them what I know of Ugin's people. I understand the Vass are reputed to be a hardy race. Where there is a will to get something done, it is said, they usually find a way."

Si'Cara retrieved her waterskin and straightened before turning away. She made her way over to them, leaving Tal'Thor and the other two elves to watch over the Vass.

"We're almost ready to load him onto one of the dragons," she said. "Is that the potion he wanted?"

Kol'Cara nodded, but he did not hand it over.

"You're unhappy about this arrangement, brother," Si'Cara said, "aren't you?"

"You know I am," Kol'Cara said. "We're taking a potential enemy back with us and will ultimately release him to his own devices. Even if this is the High Father's will, I do not see the logic or the reason."

Karus saw where Kol'Cara was going. A cold feeling stole over him. "When he leaves, he can take back information on our strength."

"That is how I see it," Kol'Cara said.

"I am not so sure, brother," Si'Cara said. "There is a purpose here. We do not know the intent, but it is there nonetheless."

"Well, there's no helping it now," Karus said. "We're committed and we've given our word. We don't have to like it, but the High Father brought us here to save him. Give him the pain potion and let's be on our way."

Expectantly, Si'Cara held out her hand, palm up, to her brother. Kol'Cara hesitated a heartbeat, then passed the small jar over. Without another word, Si'Cara returned to Ugin, unstopped the jar, and handed it over to the Vass.

Ugin took it and gulped the contents down greedily, almost as if he were afraid she'd stop him. He closed his eyes and, with an audible sigh, dropped the jar into the grass. A moment later, he went completely limp, seeming to go to sleep. Then his body began to shimmer with a dull blue glow. Sl'Cara took a stumbling step backwards, as did Tal'Thor and the two Anagradoom.

The glow lasted no more than a heartbeat. It left Karus wondering if he'd imagined it. But for the elves' reaction, he'd have thought so. Something magical had just occurred. He was sure of it. Magic, Karus had learned, could be frightfully dangerous.

To his side, Kol'Cara stiffened and then slowly stood.

"What is it?" Karus asked and looked over. "What just happened?"

"That was no pain potion," Kol'Cara said, very quietly. "I fear Ugin had something infinitely more valuable in his possession, something so rare I find it difficult to believe such things from the Age of Miracles still exist."

"What did he have?" Karus asked.

"A healing potion," Kol'Cara said, his gaze fixed upon the Vass. "The art of making them has long been lost to the mists of time."

"A healing potion," Karus said. "Like how Amarra healed Tal'Thor?"

"That was a god's direct power," Kol'Cara said, his gaze still fixed upon the Vass. "Amarra was a conduit for the energy that provided the healing." Kol'Cara gestured toward Ugin. "This was something altogether different and, if I understand correctly, inherently dangerous."

"I don't understand," Karus said. "Dangerous? How?"

Kol'Cara shook himself slightly and turned to Karus.

"He should sleep for more than a day," Kol'Cara said. "He will heal as good as new within the week. I had thought we might get away with simply watching him while he convalesces, as his injured leg would have kept him immobile. Now, he will have to be watched closely... very closely. He cannot be let out of sight or allowed to wander."

"Fortuna seems to love complicating my life." Karus blew out a long, unhappy breath and stood. "Well, there's no helping it now."

"No," Kol'Cara said, "there isn't."

"I guess," Karus said, gaze on the sleeping Vass, "in a way, he didn't lie to us."

"You are right," Kol'Cara said. "The healing potion would take away his pain. I had not expected him to have something... so rare. One thing is for certain..." The elf's gaze returned to Ugin and he took a step nearer, voice trailing off, as if he'd just realized something.

"What is that?" Karus asked.

"We have to assume that amongst his people, Ugin is no simple Vass," Kol'Cara said, "for only someone of great import would have had so valuable an artifact in his possession."

Karus's eyes fell on the Vass, seeing Ugin with new eyes. When he woke, they would have a serious talk. If Karus did not like the Vass's answers, agreement or no... Ugin would be locked up, at least until the legion left Carthum. Karus would see to it Ugin learned little about the legion's strength and capability or where they were going. He sucked in a breath and let it out. Decision made, he turned to Kol'Cara.

"Let's get him loaded onto Cyln'Phax and be off," Karus said. "It's past time I returned to my legion."

Chapter Seven

The smell of smoke hung on the air as Karus climbed down off the dragon's back. Most of the elves were already on the ground and spreading out into the shrouded darkness of the empty palace gardens. Havren'Fen had remained on Cyln'Phax's back and was busy untying the packs. The Vass was also secured, but he was still out and had not woken since he'd taken the potion.

Karus could see the faint orange glow of fire from down in the city reflected on the low-hanging clouds overhead. As they had come in for a landing, it had rapidly become apparent a small section of Carthum was burning.

Several buildings near the north wall were fully engulfed. If the fire got out of hand, the entire city could easily burn. Should that happen, the palace district, though separated by a wall, would likely burn as well. Karus could not have that, for it would mean the destruction of the legion's supplies and difficult days to come. Still, he saw no reason to panic. The legion was likely battling the blaze, working to contain it from growing. They certainly had enough manpower to do so. He was sure he would get a report on the fire soon enough.

Feeling stiff, Karus stretched out his back and let out a groan of relief. After so many hours sitting, it felt good to be back on the ground and once again standing on his own two feet. Their journey was finally at an end. And yet, oddly, no one had come to greet them.

Cyln'Phax dragged her long tail around the side of her body, moving it out of the way of the elves. In the process, she demolished several of the remaining garden beds, uprooting the overgrown plants and weeds with appalling ease.

Clutching her glowing staff in one hand, Amarra climbed down from her perch on Kordem's back. She said something to Tal'Thor, who alone had remained on Kordem and was working on removing the packs. The elf looked down at her, replied, and then returned to his work.

Karus was looking forward to spending some time alone with Amarra. It had been more than three weeks since they'd had any semblance of privacy. A good night's sleep, under a roof and in a real bed, was what he needed. It had been an exceptionally long trip, and even the dragons seemed weary of travel. It was good to finally be back, where he belonged.

From the palace, there came a sudden shout and then the pounding of feet, mixed with the jingle and chink of armor. Karus's head snapped around. Ten legionaries had emerged out of the main entrance, shields and javelins held at the ready.

There was an officer with them. In the darkness, Karus couldn't see who it was. The legionaries rapidly made their way down the wide marble steps to the garden and then formed a line, with the officer to their side.

Whether it was an honor guard or not, Karus was unsure. They locked shields and that decided it. They were no honor guard. Cyln'Phax swung her head around and growled at the legionaries. It came out as a deep, menacing sound that set the small hairs on Karus's neck standing on edge. The legionary line uniformly took a startled step back as they suddenly made out the dragon in the darkness.

"Easy," Karus shouted in Common to the elves, who had brought their bows up. Arrows had been nocked and they were aiming at the legionaries. Though the elves were deadly, after he'd seen what they were capable of doing, he was more concerned about the dragons, particularly Cyln'Phax. "Do not attack. They're friends." He hastily switched to Latin and in his best parade-ground voice shouted at the legionaries, "Stand down, men. Stand down."

"Karus, is that you?"

"Flaccus?" Karus asked, recognizing the voice.

"Thank the gods," Flaccus said, then turned to his men. "You heard the camp prefect. Stand easy, boys, javelins down."

The legionaries relaxed, lowering their shields and setting the butts of their javelins on the ground. In response, the elves lowered their bows. Cyln'Phax issued another, almost grudging growl, before laying her neck and head on the ground with a heavy *thud*, accompanied by a tremor that ran through the garden.

Flaccus stepped forward toward Karus and without hesitation offered a crisp salute. Karus returned it.

"It's good to see you, sir," Flaccus said, relief plain in his tone. The cantankerous centurion seemed genuinely sincere in his greeting. "Very good to see you. I'm not afraid to admit, I thought you dead. I am pleased I was wrong."

"That sentiment seems to be going around," Karus said, thinking of the response Dennig had gotten when he'd returned to his warband. He glanced back at the dragons. "That wasn't very bright. Those two dragons could easily have burned you down and the men too."

"Sorry, sir . . . I did not know it was you," Flaccus said, with a nervous glance toward the dragons, who were little more than large shadows in the darkness. With the cloud cover, there was no moon and very little light. "I was told there were intruders in the gardens. I expected trouble, so I rounded up those I had on hand and we rushed out." He gestured back toward the entrance to the palace. "Going from the light to the darkness, we couldn't see the dragons until we got down the steps and formed a line. By then . . . well, it was too late. We were committed."

"You expected trouble?" What with the fire down in the city, Karus was becoming seriously concerned. "Flaccus, what's going on here?"

"Where to begin?" Flaccus glanced behind them at his men, as if he did not wish to speak in front of them. It was clear to Karus something bad had happened, and his worry reached new levels.

"I don't care where you begin"—Karus lowered his voice a tad, softening his tone—"just that you do, understand? I need to know what is going on."

Amarra joined him. In the darkness, her glowing crystal staff seemed brighter than usual. It shed a pool of dim blue light around them. Karus almost frowned as the light fell upon the centurion's face. Flaccus appeared as if he'd missed several nights of sleep. There were serious bags under his eyes and his craggy face seemed more lined than usual. In the three weeks since Karus had last seen him, Flaccus had seemed to age.

Flaccus's expression became guarded, wary even, as his eyes flicked to Amarra. There was no warmth there for her, only coldness. Karus wondered if Flaccus thought Amarra a witch, like many of the men. They believed Karus had fallen under her spell. It was concerning, for he'd thought Flaccus above that.

"What's wrong, Flaccus?" Karus asked.

At that moment, Kol'Cara stepped up next to Karus. The centurion's gaze shifted to the elf. Karus could see the shock as Flaccus realized Kol'Cara was not altogether human. The hardened centurion took a half step back before his self-control halted him.

"What is he?" Flaccus asked in a half gasp. "He looks like a man ... but is not."

"Flaccus," Karus said firmly, putting steel into his tone. It worked, drawing the other's attention back to him. Introductions could wait a bit. "I need to know what is going on. I want a report and I want it now. Understand me?"

"Ah, right, yes, sir," Flaccus said, with another glance thrown to Kol'Cara. The centurion took a deep breath and turned his full attention on Karus. "The sickness has gotten much worse. At least eighty percent of the legion and auxiliary cohorts are down sick. Those numbers are consistent with the camp followers too. Since you left, over five hundred have died from the illness. The clerks will have an accurate tally at headquarters. That band of refugees we accepted ... well, they've gone and revolted against us. They've taken a portion of the city into their keeping."

"Eighty percent? Five hundred dead? The refugees revolted?" Karus wasn't quite sure he had heard correctly. His heart sank like a heavy rock tossed into a pond at hearing of not only the sickness destroying his legion, but also the setback to his plans on building a coalition. It was a double hammer blow. What possibly could have happened? What madness had overcome them? Revolt?

"Yes, sir," Flaccus said, tone grim, hard. "There's been fighting. I've managed to pull the entire legion and auxiliaries into the palace district, including those who have fallen ill. It's a bit cramped, but we're all here and every man has a roof over his head. Right now, we're in a sort of general standoff with the refugees. For the moment, we have the strength to man the palace district walls. They don't have the numbers or determination to get in. It's that simple, sir."

"Eighty percent?" Karus asked again, reeling at how badly his men were suffering. He could scarcely believe it. "Five hundred gone to the sickness, along with eighty percent of our strength ineffective?"

"We lost about another hundred in the fighting." Flaccus paused again, seeming discomforted. "That's not the worst of it, sir. I know you were close, so I am just gonna come out and say it. Dio's dead."

"Dio." Amarra's hand went to her mouth. "Oh, no."

"What is happening?" Kol'Cara asked, looking between them and Flaccus.

Ignoring the elf, Karus closed his eyes at the unexpected news. The pain he felt struck to his core, threatening to overwhelm his normal iron-clad control. He had lost comrades before, but never like this. Dio was one of his oldest and most trusted friends. They had cut their teeth together as common legionaries. It was almost unimaginable ... inconceivable that he was gone. "How? Was it the sickness?"

Amarra turned to Kol'Cara and in a low tone explained in the common tongue what had just transpired. As Flaccus continued, she began translating for the elf.

"No, sir," Flaccus said, anger coloring his voice. "He was murdered by that bastard Logex."

Logex was one of the leaders of the refugee band they had taken in. Karus had offered them shelter in return for protection. He had given their ragged band a chance to survive. Karus felt his anger heat to the boiling point. This was how they repaid his generosity? Murder?

"Why?" Karus asked. "Why did they do it?"

"While you were gone, we took in another band of refugees Valens had found wandering about, around two thousand hungry mouths. With their added numbers, we formed another auxiliary cohort. As more of our people fell ill, even though none of their own got sick ... both groups became frightened. About a week ago, the training cohorts stopped taking orders. Though he could barely speak their language, Dio went to talk to their leaders, to reason with them, plead even." Flaccus sounded disgusted with that last bit. The disgust turned to bitter anger.

"Instead of listening, Logex seized Dio and his escort. They held them hostage, demanding we turn over our food and transport in exchange for the hostages. When Felix refused, they murdered him." Flaccus balled his fists. "Sir, they slit Dio's throat in front of me. There were no further demands or discussion. The bastards just killed Dio and his escort, as if they were making some point." Flaccus paused to take a heated breath. "After that, well ... Felix led two cohorts to punish them. The fighting was hard. You know how brutal house-to-house can get. That was when Felix was injured."

"Not Felix too," Karus breathed. The earlier blow now felt like a gut punch.

"He took a spear to the thigh," Flaccus said. "It went clean through the muscle and thankfully missed the artery. If the wound doesn't turn bad, he'll live. At worst, it should keep him off his feet for a few weeks. Ampelius says he may have a permanent limp."

Feeling relieved beyond measure, Karus gave a nod. He would have to check in on Felix later, but needed to hear the rest.

"What happened after that?"

"The bastards sealed themselves into a portion of the city and blocked the streets," Flaccus said. "We've been unable to dig them out. With Felix down, and the other senior centurions ill, command fell to me, sir. As more of our men fell sick, I didn't have the strength to continue the effort against the refugees. I deemed it best to move everyone into the palace district, at least until we could recover sufficient numbers to sortie out again. We have the food stores and good walls for defense." Flaccus paused to take a breath. "Some of the boys are getting better, sir. Those who don't die seem to recover without any problems or lingering effects. Fifty were able to return to duty just today alone and thirty the day before that. I am hopeful that in a few days a good portion of the legion will recover."

Karus was silent as he considered Flaccus's words. That men were recovering was a good sign. And yet, he knew the Horde was unlikely to give him the time he needed for the rest of the legion to recover. Karus shook his head slightly, feeling intense frustration. He now found himself in an impossible maze with seemingly no way out. He hadn't expected things to fall apart so badly.

"Command fell to me," Flaccus repeated. "I believe I made the best decision I could, sir, by pulling the legion back, that is."

It was apparent Flaccus was concerned that Karus might question his decision-making. Heck, Karus realized, Flaccus had likely been second-guessing himself for the past few days. It was clear the weight of ultimate responsibility had taken a toll on him. Physically, he looked terribly run-down. The man needed some positive reinforcement, for Karus could not fault his actions.

"You did right," Karus said. "Moving everyone to the palace district was good thinking. Above all else, the safety of the legion comes first. You looked after the boys. I could not have asked for more."

"I only did what I thought best, sir," Flaccus said. "I don't like the idea of leaving those traitorous bastards out there without paying them back in kind." Flaccus paused and then lowered his voice so the men could not hear. "I never wanted to be in charge, sir. I am a cohort commander, plain and simple. That is all I ever wanted. Now that you've returned, command rightly falls to you … Karus, I wish I was the bearer of better news … but, just the same … welcome back. The legion is yours."

Karus gave another nod and glanced over at the men behind Flaccus. They appeared tense, stressed … Having led men for much of his adult life, he could sense it in their being, their manner. He understood it was a microcosm of the pressure the entire legion was surely under … what with having been uprooted and transported to a strange world, the current sickness … all of it … He understood the strain on the men must be immense.

What he saw told him his legion was hanging on by a mere thread. All it would take was another major shock or setback for the thread to snap and then all would be lost. Discipline could only take one so far. If the thread snapped, there would be no more legion, just a mass of frightened men looking out only for themselves.

"Karus," Kol'Cara said, drawing his attention after Amarra had finished translating. "I have heard of other humans new to this world … those having come through the World Gate … becoming sick, just days after their arrival. It is possible your people suffer from the same sickness."

That, Karus thought, did not sound good. "Is there a cure? Or a treatment?"

"Not that I am aware of," Kol'Cara said. "The strong survive, but it seems to be something of this world that affects you humans in particular. Elves do not suffer from this disease. It must be some type of a sickness, perhaps for which your bodies have no defense until you survive it?"

Karus found it incredibly maddening. This disease had become as much his enemy as the Horde. Worse, he could not see or fight the enemy that was burning its way through the legion. Fortuna was playing a cruel game with him and it was costing him his men. It may even ultimately cost him the legion. On top of that, Dio had been murdered and Felix wounded.

He turned back to Flaccus and started to speak, then stopped. Karus felt a wave of intense guilt threaten to overcome him, a near tidal wave of emotion. Just as the High Father had asked, he had retrieved the sword, but... at what price? It had been his decision to leave, to effectively abandon the legion. What had followed in his absence was surely his fault.

Why had he left?

He should have listened to his gut and stayed. He should have heeded Dio's counsel. He had instead disregarded his friend. Karus knew now, without a doubt, he should have remained in Carthum. His place was with the legion. The sword could have waited. If he had stayed, perhaps things would have worked out differently.

"I'm sorry," Amarra said. She reached out a hand and gripped his, squeezing slightly. "I am so sorry, Karus."

For a long moment, Karus gazed back at her blankly. He felt the sting in his eyes of frustration and loss. He blinked away the tears before they could fully form.

"I'm sorry, Karus," Amarra said again with much feeling, "for Dio and all that's happened."

Karus sucked in a ragged breath. He cleared his throat before attempting speech.

"I'm sorry, too." Karus's voice was gruff, and with those words, his heart hardened, becoming iron-like. His anger mounted. He pulled his hand free from her grip. It came to rest on the sword. The tingle that ran up his arm and into his being had become a familiar and welcomed friend. The darkness lightened ever so slightly and so too did his grief. A sullen, burning anger filled the void.

He glanced once more at the men. The anger retreated, and as it did, cold calculation stole over him. He could not afford to wallow in self-pity or, worse, self-recrimination. Despite the sickness, the legion was still in danger. An enemy army was marching on Carthum, and Dennig was counting on him.

The dwarves badly needed his help and they would be at the city's gate in just three days… three bloody days! Grief would have to wait. But his revenge over Dio's death would not. Logex would pay for what he'd done. They would all pay. He would see that they did.

"Flaccus," Karus said, burying his rage, shoving it deep. The cold calculation shifted into hard, professional resolve. "I'd like to introduce you to Kol'Cara. His people are elves. They're here to help us."

"Elves?" Flaccus asked.

"Kol'Cara," Karus said in Common, "this is Centurion Flaccus, one of my senior cohort commanders and a trusted man."

Kol'Cara inclined his head respectfully to Flaccus, who gave him a nod of his own in return.

"He does not speak Latin," Karus said to Flaccus, "but he does speak Common."

"I've not learned it yet, sir," Flaccus said, scowling, his eyes shifting from Kol'Cara to the other elves. "I only know a word or two. There's been no time."

"I have made additional allies who are even now on their way, marching to us. They also speak Common," Karus said and paused as he considered Flaccus. "Just as I have, you're going to have to learn this new language quickly. You and the other officers will need to communicate with our allies."

"Yes, sir," Flaccus said. "I will learn the language. The allies you mentioned ... are they more of these elves?"

"Dwarves," Karus said, raising his voice a little so the men could hear him clearly. They needed good news, some hope to rally around. "We're no longer alone in this land. We have allies marching to us."

"The short disagreeable bastards?" Flaccus asked.

"Yes, them," Karus said and then decided to return to the matter at hand. The fire in the city concerned him greatly. "But right now, I need to know if there is an immediate threat to our position in the palace district."

"No, sir," Flaccus said. "We're secure."

"Why is part of the city on fire?" Karus asked.

"We don't rightly know, sir," Flaccus said. "It wasn't our doing, that's for certain. Someone from amongst the refugees must have been careless with a flame, or it could be something else. There's just no telling. I did spirit two men over the wall and into the city to find out what's going on. I don't expect them to report back for a few more hours."

"Right, then," Karus said, with another glance at the legionaries. "We need to get to work. Let's move this conversation to my headquarters and begin planning, for there is a lot we need to do, including deal with the refugees… sooner, I think, rather than later."

"Yes, sir," Flaccus said.

Karus turned to Kol'Cara and switched to Common before Amarra could translate. "We're going to my headquarters to plan and I want you with me." He paused and glanced over at the other elves, who had been watching. "I would appreciate your boys waiting here in the garden. With all that's happened, my men are on edge. They've never known of your people until today. It will take time for them to become accustomed to you… to see you as friends."

"You do not wish… any… shall we say, misunderstandings to happen between your people and mine," Kol'Cara said. "Do I have that right?"

"I've enough on my plate at the moment," Karus said. "I most certainly don't need any more headaches."

"I understand," Kol'Cara said and turned to his elves, speaking in Elven, clearly passing along instruction. He looked back at Karus when he was done. "My Anagradoom will keep the dragons company while we plan."

We don't need company, Cyln'Phax said. *But your elves may remain under our protection.*

"That is very kind of you, oh magnificent and ancient lady," Kol'Cara said to the dragon, while offering her a slight bow.

A gout of flame was snorted out of Kordem's nose, briefly lighting up the palace gardens. The dragon huffed in what was clearly amusement. Unsure of what was going on, Flaccus and the legionaries shifted uncomfortably.

Cyln'Phax lifted her head up off the ground and turned her baleful gaze upon her mate. She did not reply.

That was a good one, elf. Kordem made the huffing sound again. *I will have to remember that one… oh great and ancient lady.*

"It spoke," Flaccus said, in utter amazement. "I heard it in my head."

"That's right, they're not mindless beasts," Karus said. "They speak through your mind."

Mindless beasts… I think perhaps my mate might be one, Cyln'Phax groused.

Kordem huffed again.

"I'm coming, too," Amarra said to Karus.

"I wouldn't have it any other way," Karus said and truly, he wouldn't.

"Mistress," Si'Cara said, "I will accompany you. I am your guardian, your protector."

Amarra turned and looked to Karus in question, raising a delicate eyebrow.

"I have no objection," Karus said and started for the stairs. The legionaries drew aside, parting their line. Their eyes were on him as he passed between them. Karus could sense the hope in their gazes, the hope that he would make things right, fix it all.

Only, Karus did not know if he could. Regardless, he'd be damned if he let them see any self-doubt. They needed leadership and strength right now. He would give them both. In the coming storm, he would be their anchor. He would keep the legion together, unified, and see her through… ultimately guiding them all to a safe harbor.

As he made his way up the steps, the hobnails of his sandals cracked against the marble. At the last step, Karus hesitated and glanced back, first at the two dragons, then at the elves of the Anagradoom. It seemed they were all watching him, even the legionaries.

He suddenly felt the burden of responsibility weighing heavily upon his shoulders. Karus took a deep breath and let it out, resolved to let nothing stop him. No one would stand in his way. He had a job to do and the legion to preserve … to save. He owed his men that.

He also owed Dio.

The anger surged again. The refugees would most certainly pay the price for his friend's death. He would personally see to that. Logex, especially, would be called to account. The man would regret the day he crossed the might of Rome. With that last thought, Karus turned away and continued on toward the palace entrance, from which yellowed lantern light beckoned.

Chapter Eight

Karus had taken no more than four steps into the palace before he almost stumbled to a halt. Just behind him, Flaccus too came to a stop. There was a prolonged moment where neither said a word, then Flaccus spoke.

"As I told you, sir, every one of our boys has a roof over their heads. The palace district is large, but it's not that big. I've had to cram and stick them anywhere I could, and that includes the palace itself. Each man that's sick is out of the elements. Only those that are healthy are in tents and I've tried to isolate them to keep them from falling sick too."

The corridor was one of the main arteries of the palace. As such, it was wide, with marble floors and delicately arched ceilings. From the garden entrance, the corridor stretched out to his left and right. It was filled, packed even, with those who had fallen ill. Along the walls of the corridor, the sick lay on their camp blankets, with only a narrow path between them for passage.

A handful of the oil lamps that hung from the ceiling had been lit. Karus wondered if this was because it was night or Flaccus had been conserving the available supply of oil.

The intermittent lamps cast a dim, flickering light down on the suffering. It gave the setting an almost surreal look, as if he were in some strange nightmare. Though Karus well knew this was no dream. It was all too real.

The reek of loose bowels was plain awful and so powerful it stung the eyes. Buckets had been placed every few feet to act as mobile latrines. The nearest wooden bucket was full to the point of overflowing. To his left, at the far end of the corridor, a man in a stained tunic was changing the buckets out, emptying the contents into a wheeled cart.

Still, despite the nearness of the buckets, it appeared as if many of the men had not been able to make it to them, simply expelling their bowels on the floor or, worse, soiling themselves where they lay.

The human excrement, much of it liquid, ran freely across the once polished marble flooring, making it slick. In other places, the waste had long since dried, creating a dirty crust.

Karus found it stomach-turning. Worse, though, was the sound of hundreds of men coughing and hacking away. It grated at the ears, as those sickened seemed to be coughing up their very lungs.

So severe was the coughing that one of those nearest him had bloody froth running down his chin and onto his tunic. The crusted blood had dyed the tunic he wore from a pale gray to deep burgundy and given it a hardened look, as if paint had been applied to the wool.

It took Karus more than a moment to recognize the man as Optio Mettis from Second Cohort. The man's lips had a blue tint to them, never a good sign. Karus had last seen the optio a little over three weeks past. On several occasions, when he'd gone out and about in Carthum, Mettis had commanded his personal escort. The man had been fit and strong before Karus had departed for the sword. Now… he was but a shadow of himself and had lost much of his bodyweight. Karus could not believe how painfully thin Mettis had become.

Horrified by all that he saw, especially by Mettis, Karus found he suddenly could not move. It was as if he were rooted in place, like those skeletons they had found before the ruined walls of the Fortress of Radiance.

He stood there, frozen, just staring at Mettis. The resolve he had felt moments before in the gardens was gone. It was as if it had vanished into thin air, fled at what the diseased in this corridor represented.

The palace was a massive structure. In this corridor alone, hundreds of men lay, suffering, riding out the torments of the plague that was ravaging the legion. Being told most of the legion was sick was one thing. Seeing it with his own eyes was altogether a whole different experience. Karus's heart nearly broke, for before him... the legion he loved was dying a slow and agonized death.

"They don't deserve this," Flaccus said, in a near whisper.

"No," Karus said woodenly, "they most certainly do not."

Behind him, he heard a horrified gasp. Amarra had just entered, along with Kol'Cara and Si'Cara. The legionaries Flaccus had brought with him were lined up, just behind the two elves at the entrance. The horror Karus had felt was reflected plainly in Amarra's expression.

She stepped forward several paces, eyes incredibly wide. Amarra moved a few feet in the direction of the legion's headquarters and away from Karus and Flaccus. She gazed down the hall, saying nothing, but clearly taking it all in.

"Sir."

It was a weak and pathetic call... barely audible. Karus looked around for its source and saw Mettis had turned his head and was looking at him. The optio's eyes were bloodshot and watery. A solitary tear ran down the side of his face as he stared unblinking at Karus. And the optio wasn't the only one. Several others had stirred, propping themselves up on their elbows, and were looking his way.

"Sir…" Mettis tried again and then made to stand.

Karus found he still could not move as the thin man climbed to his feet. It was like watching a recently deceased corpse rise from his funeral bier. Mettis stood, wavering for a moment, and then with a groan collapsed to his knees. It broke the spell. Karus moved, caught the man in his arms, and helped to ease him back down to his blanket, which had been soiled and fouled.

Mettis's skin was clammy and cold to the touch. Sweat beaded his brow and, as Karus laid him down, he panted like a dog after a long run. Mettis was clearly exhausted by the effort to stand. Karus could hear the sucking fluid in the man's lungs as he struggled to simply breathe.

Kneeling at the optio's side, Karus spotted a full waterskin lying next to him. He unstopped it and held it up to Mettis's lips.

"I don't want to drink, sir," Mettis gasped. "It makes me go, and I've gone enough for a… lifetime."

"Nonsense," Karus said. He'd known men to die from an extreme loosening of the bowls, all because they stopped drinking. "You need to drink and keep drinking. Doing so will help you get better. That's an order, soldier. Understand?"

"Yes, sir."

Karus held the waterskin back up to Mettis's lips. The man drank, at first a little, the excess water running down the sides of his mouth, and then greedily, as if he'd been stranded in a desert and was dying of thirst. When Karus judged Mettis had drunk enough, he pulled the waterskin back, stopped it, and set it aside.

"Feel better?" Karus asked.

"I do." Mettis's voice was stronger. He coughed lightly. "I do, sir. Thank you."

Mettis coughed again, deeper, almost convulsing his entire body.

"We all thought..." Mettis gasped between coughs, "you'd gone, left us... to our fate... even though the centurions said otherwise."

"Never," Karus said forcefully. "I went to find something important to the legion's survival."

Mettis closed his eyes for a long moment, before opening them and coughing into his hand. It was a terrible cough and made Karus cringe on the inside. Mettis rolled onto his side, almost curling into a ball, hacking even harder. Blood spattered the optio's hand, which he held before his mouth. Karus rested a comforting hand on the man's arm and simply waited.

When he recovered, Mettis rolled back onto his blanket and lay there, exhausted, panting.

"Did you find what you were looking for?" Mettis asked, his voice hoarse from his latest coughing fit.

"I did," Karus said, "and I've come back with allies."

"That's good to hear, sir." Mettis coughed again. This time, the fit was prolonged and seemed harder on the optio. When he was done, Mettis sucked in a deep, gasping breath, then returned his attention to Karus. He lifted his head a little off the dirty, rolled-up tunic he used for a pillow. "Sorry I'm not fit to serve, sir."

"You'll be well, soon enough." Karus patted Mettis's arm and then gave a light squeeze. "It's time for you to focus on your health, son. Just rest. That's your job now. I need every man, understand? And you're one of the good ones, with a bright future ahead of you."

"Yes, sir." Mettis seemed to relax slightly, laying his head back onto the rolled-up tunic. "I will rest."

Mettis reached up a thin, bony hand to Karus, who took it. The hand was ice-cold to the touch and it shook.

"Sir," Mettis said, an intense look in his gaze. "Can you do something for me? Please."

"If it is within my power, it will be done."

"Check in on my men," Mettis said, "if you wouldn't mind, sir."

Karus regarded the optio for a long moment. His heart was tearing itself apart at Mettis's suffering, and this was just one man amongst thousands. "I will. You have my word."

"I have a wife"—Mettis coughed—"and daughter."

"I didn't know that," Karus said.

"Vita. She's a fine woman. She's always been good to me, even when I've not been nice to her. It's unofficial-like, sir."

"I understand," Karus said. Mettis had never received permission to marry. The policy was designed to limit the number of camp followers. Though, in Karus's experience, such procedures and rules did nothing to ease the legion's burden when it came to the camp followers.

Mettis and Vita had likely pledged their devotion to one another in a private ceremony. And so, like thousands of others, his wife had simply followed the legion whenever and wherever it moved.

"When you're better," Karus said, "you will have my personal permission to marry her, right and proper. You can make it official."

Clearly pleased by the news, Mettis smiled at him with blood-flecked lips.

"Thank you, sir." Mettis's expression turned sad. "But I don't think I am going to make it." He coughed lightly and then worked to clear his throat. It took several moments until he was able to speak again. "I hear the ferryman's call, sir. He's beckoning me to cross."

"What kind of talk is that?" Karus said. "Of course you're going to recover. You're a legionary, one of the toughest of the tough. We don't give up without a fight. What of your daughter? Would you have her grow up without a father?"

Mettis got a distant look, as if he were reliving an old memory. The smile returned, a tad wider. "Tiayus...she's the cutest little thing you've ever seen, sir."

"How old?"

"Five." Mettis coughed again, this time harder, wracking his entire body. When he recovered, the smile was still there. "She has long brown hair that's nearly as long as she is. Skinny little thing...There are times I think she's all hair." He gave a weak cough that might have been a laugh. "It bounces when she runs and, boy, does she love to run. My Tiayus is a fast little thing..."

"I'd like to meet her and your wife," Karus said. "After you've recovered, you will bring them to see me."

"Thank you, sir." Mettis closed his eyes. "Vita would like that. She's always had nice things to say about you, sir. The men know you look after them and so too do the followers. They appreciate that."

Squeezing his eyes shut, Mettis coughed again, long and hard.

"Gods it hurts..." It came out as a gasp. "Can you make the pain stop, sir? Please..."

Karus knew there was nothing he could do to ease the man's suffering, and that made it all the worse.

"Just you rest," Karus said, patting the man's arm again. "Rest and drink plenty of water. That's an order."

"Yes, sir," Mettis said. "Resting sounds good."

The optio sucked in a breath, gave a heavy sigh, and then appeared to fall asleep. His hand went slack in Karus's grip. Karus leaned forward and checked the man's pulse. Nothing.

Mettis was gone.

Karus gently set the optio's hand down and bowed his head, at first in what felt like defeat. He let out a long breath. Mettis deserved some words said over his body. It was the least Karus could do in return for the man's service to the empire.

"Jupiter…High Father," Karus said, "look after this man. He was a good soldier, husband, and father. See that he crosses over the great river peacefully. He deserves some well-earned rest."

Karus rubbed at his eyes. His thoughts turned to Jupiter, his god. A lot had been asked of him and the legion. He could not see how he would be able to accomplish it all without some divine help. The least Jupiter could do was lend assistance, and so, he decided, it could not hurt to ask.

"Jupiter," Karus said to himself, "oh great one, please help my legion. Save my boys before they waste away to this terrible plague."

Karus lifted his head, feeling a terrible frustration. The prayer had not helped his mood improve. He regarded Mettis and thought of the man's family. Life as a camp follower was not an easy one, especially for a widow. Mettis's wife and daughter were now alone in this strange world. That would make it more difficult on them, at least until Vita found a new husband. That was, if she could find one. After the disease finished ravaging the legion, there might not be enough men to go around.

"His wife and daughter died last week," Flaccus said, breaking in on Karus's thoughts. "Dio told me, just before he went to meet with the refugees. I didn't have the heart to tell Mettis."

Karus stood, his gaze traveling down the hallway. It was a veritable sea of misery and suffering. The world in which they lived was a cruel and hard one ... brutal even.

Karus rounded on Flaccus.

"This is a disgrace," Karus hissed, anger taking hold. He took a step nearer the centurion. Karus pointed down at Mettis. "You were in command. These conditions are a bloody disgrace." Karus tapped Flaccus on the chest armor with his index finger. "I expected better of you, Flaccus."

The centurion's lips drew together into a thin line and his jaw flexed.

"Well," Karus demanded, "what do you have to say for yourself?"

Flaccus stepped closer to Karus, their noses almost touching. The centurion's gaze bored into Karus's and he lowered his voice in an almost menacing manner. "The legion doesn't have the strength to man the walls and properly care for the sick. There are simply too many down. I barely have the manpower to make sure the men get fresh water and food. We're just hanging on here, sir. I don't know how much clearer I can make that. Now that you've returned, I am sure you can do better."

Karus wanted to argue and continue to rage at Flaccus ... but he knew the centurion was right. Flaccus was exhausted and, like the legion, at the end of his rope. In truth, Karus could not fault him, for he very much doubted he'd have been able to do better himself.

"Of course, you're right," Karus said, softening his tone. "That was unkind of me. Forgive me."

Flaccus said nothing but took a step back. The heated look faded from the centurion's demeanor and the exhaustion returned. "We may not be friends, but we go back a long way together. There's nothing to forgive, sir. You're just frustrated, as am I." Flaccus gestured down the hall. "Mettis and the rest of them do not deserve to suffer like this … to just waste away. That's not how a soldier should end his days."

Karus could only nod.

"We are few," Kol'Cara said, joining them. "Where we can, we will help, delivering food, water … making sure they drink, cleaning up even. If you will let us, that is."

"What did he say?" Flaccus asked.

"He said they're willing to help care for our people," Karus translated.

Flaccus gave a weary nod of thanks to the elf. "We need all the help we can get."

"Thank you," Karus said, to Kol'Cara. "We both thank you for that kindness."

"Bloody witch." A man at the far end of the corridor had dragged himself to his feet and was pointing behind Karus, at Amarra. "She's the cause of this sickness. She's to blame."

"As you were," Karus shouted back at the man, taking two steps forward and staring daggers. He put thunder in his voice. "You will stand down, soldier. That's an order."

The man hesitated. He suddenly looked uncertain, glancing to his left and right for support.

"She has the camp prefect under a spell," another shouted as he got to his feet next to the man. "We can't have that, boys. Can we?"

"No," someone shouted. This was followed up by a smattering of agreement.

"He'll see the light," the first man shouted, emboldened. "She needs to die. We kill her and we kill the sickness. It's that simple."

"I said, stand down." About to storm down the hall and shake sense into the man, Karus found himself restrained by Flaccus. The centurion had gripped his shoulder.

Incensed, he looked back on Flaccus. Before Karus could say anything, there were more shouts. The call was taken up by others. Within just mere heartbeats it seemed the entire corridor had erupted in shouting, drowning out those still coughing up their lungs. Dozens of men, in better shape than Mettis, had gotten to their feet. Screaming their rage and spewing bile, they started shuffling forward.

"Oh shit," Flaccus said, glancing around them, for enraged men were closing in from both sides.

Several had even drawn weapons, a mix of daggers and short swords. Karus's heart plummeted, for he knew, without a doubt, the thin tenuous thread holding the legion together had finally snapped.

"On me," Flaccus shouted to the men he'd brought to the palace gardens. "Protect the camp prefect!"

Chapter Nine

Flaccus pulled, half-dragging Karus backward toward the exit to the palace gardens. Karus resisted. Barely registering the centurion's efforts, Karus put his entire focus on scanning the crowded hall for Amarra. Incredibly, she was ignoring everything that was happening. It was as if she were in her own little world and nothing whatsoever had gone wrong.

Farther down the hall, she was crouched by the side of a gravely ill legionary. Like many of the other men stricken low, he had been terribly ravaged by the disease. He was filthy and painfully thin. He appeared, like Mettis had, to be just wasting away, barely clinging to the last threads of life.

The breath caught in his throat as Karus abruptly realized it wasn't just any legionary, but Junior Tribune Delvaris. The youth was the last surviving tribune, the only remaining aide to the legion's late legate. Karus had adopted Delvaris as his own aide. The boy had shown promise. Now, he'd most likely die a difficult and pointless death.

Amarra was holding Delvaris's hand in her own. She was speaking with him. Si'Cara was by her side. The elf looked grim and worried. She reached down to pull Amarra back to her feet. Amarra shook the elf off. Si'Cara tried again, more insistently this time. Amarra said something emphatic that, over the shouting and noise, Karus could not hear. Whatever had been said did not seem to please Si'Cara. However, for her part, she gave a reluctant nod of understanding and straightened.

Only feet away, a handful of enraged men had begun closing in on Amarra. The rest of those shouting had not yet worked up the courage to take action.

"Amarra!" Karus yelled, desperate to warn her as Flaccus continued to pull him toward the exit. His voice was drowned out. Karus watched in horror as one of the men with a dagger in hand and wild eyes reached for her. Her back was turned and she did not see the attack coming.

Thankfully, Si'Cara had seen them. She moved like lightning. While bending at the waist, the elf spun and kicked out. Her foot connected squarely with the side of the man's jaw, snapping the attacker almost completely around. He teetered for a moment unsteadily, then went down like a felled tree.

Without missing a beat, Si'Cara recovered and punched the next man in the face. She followed that up with a knee driven into his gut. He doubled over. She knocked him bodily aside, then drew her sword. Kol'Cara joined her and the two of them moved to shield Amarra from the growing attentions of the mob of men.

Having seen more than enough, Karus separated himself from Flaccus and started for Amarra. The centurion cursed and followed after him. Before Karus could reach her, two additional men, both with swords drawn, came forward. Si'Cara deftly traded a series of sword strikes with one, while Kol'Cara engaged the other. Almost simultaneously, two men rushed Si'Cara from the side and tackled her as she was trading sword strikes. She hadn't seen the attack coming and was caught completely off guard. All three went down in a tangle of arms and legs.

A heartbeat later, Karus was there and amongst them. He punched the man holding the sword, hammering him hard in the face. He felt the man's nose crunch as it broke. Crying out, the man dropped his sword and fell back, holding his face as blood fountained and flowed from between his fingers. At Karus's feet, Si'Cara was struggling with the two who had brought her down. One was straddling her and had his hands around her throat. He was a large man and seemed hardly affected by the sickness.

Si'Cara's face remained calm as she tried to protect her neck by digging her chin down into her chest as hard as she could. At the same time, she was trying to pry his hands, which were the size of meat cleavers, from her neck one finger at a time. Already, one of her attacker's fingers was bent at a sickening angle from her efforts. But the enraged legionary barely registered the pain, so intent was he on ending her life. The elf began to gasp for breath and was clearly beginning to lose the fight.

Karus kicked him hard in the side. The big man gave a deep grunt and immediately released his hold on Si'Cara's neck. Karus reached down and grabbed him by the hair, hauling him to his feet.

"Bastard!" Karus shouted and slammed the man into the wall. The man's head made a sickening thud as it impacted with the wall and the breath whuffed out of his lungs. He slid down to the floor, spasming.

Si'Cara elbowed the other man in the throat. He gagged and rolled to the side. Flinging her body up from the ground, she launched herself at his prone form, viciously punching him in the side of the head. He collapsed onto his stomach, out cold.

"Take my hand."

Karus held out his hand and pulled Si'Cara to her feet. She was bleeding from a gash along her arm and her neck was red where she'd been choked. Her ponytail had also come undone. Beyond that, she seemed all right, though winded.

Behind him, Karus could hear Flaccus and Kol'Cara fighting. Steel rang on steel. He glanced over and saw them facing off against three men weakened by sickness. A fourth man was already on the ground, mortally wounded and bleeding out from a bad stomach wound. Kol'Cara's sword was bloodied. He'd also received a cut on the thigh.

Karus knew it was time to go. In moments, the rest of those in the corridor would surely attack. He turned to Amarra, prepared to physically drag her away and back into the palace gardens if needed. But something checked him and he hesitated.

"Jupiter's grace ..." Delvaris said. "I see it. I really do."

Karus realized Delvaris was close to death. That thought saddened him greatly, for he genuinely liked the boy. He had personally saved the tribune's life back in Britannia. Amarra was clearly offering him some comfort. But that still wasn't what had stopped Karus. Something strange was on the air. He could almost feel it. There was something important going on here. He was sure of it.

The noise in the corridor seemed to increase in volume. It seemed like everyone who could muster the strength was screaming their hate and bile at Amarra. So far, only a handful had been bold enough to take action. Karus knew that would soon change. Mobs were like that. Eventually, everyone would join in and that was when it would really get ugly. Karus sensed that moment fast approaching.

"You see true," Amarra said, her focus wholly on the tribune. Over the din of the shouting and screaming, Karus could barely hear her. "And so too is your faith."

"Where are those men?" Karus shouted over his shoulder at Flaccus, who had just knocked a man down by slamming his sword hilt into his opponent's face. Flaccus did not answer, for he was immediately engaged by yet another enraged man and was hard-pressed. Karus turned his gaze to the armed legionaries Flaccus had led into the garden. They had not moved from where they stood by the exit.

Oh, no, Karus thought. Bloody gods…

Instead of coming to their assistance, one, with a determined look, lowered his javelin and started forward toward Amarra. There was murderous intent in his gaze. The others, clearly suffering from indecision, continued to hold their ground.

Between him and the legionary, sword back in her hands, Si'Cara turned to face this new threat.

"You," Karus shouted, pointing at the man and pushing past Si'Cara. "Stand down."

The man stopped, looking uncertain in the face of his enraged camp prefect. He raised his spear and stepped back, mumbling something Karus could not make out. However, two of his comrades who had not moved earlier advanced, leveling their javelins directly at Karus.

Something hard hammered into Karus's cheek, snapping his head to the side and staggering him. For a moment, he was disoriented and saw nothing but stars. Karus tasted the sweet copper tang of blood. He shook his head. There was a large chunk of plaster at his feet. Someone had thrown it.

Karus turned back to the two legionaries who were still advancing with the javelins. Hot wetness ran down his neck. He ignored it.

"All right, you treacherous bastards, come on." Enraged and hurting, Karus drew his sword. The magical tingle was a flood, a torrent of energy rushing into him. Time seemed to slow, perhaps even stop altogether. The shouting ceased and so too did the pain. Karus saw another chunk of plaster suspended in midair and marveled at it.

Kill them all, the sword hissed malevolently in his mind. *Give them some steel. Feed me their souls and together we shall grow in power.*

Abruptly, time began to move again.

Shocked, Karus glanced down at the sword, which had burst into blue flame.

Kill my own men? Never. Even as enraged as he was, he could not bring himself to do such a thing. The two men with the javelins were mere feet away. Karus took a step back, realizing he may not have a choice in the matter.

A small clay lamp someone had thrown shattered at his feet. The oil caught fire and startled Karus. He had to hastily jump to avoid being burned. Immediately, the anger and outrage slipped away. The blue flames licking the blade went out too.

The lamp seemed to break the dam. Screaming and shouting even louder, the mob now pushed forward as a group, almost fighting one another to be the first to get at Amarra. Karus lost sight of the two with the javelins as the press of men moved in. He violently shoved back a man who had gotten too close for comfort. Karus smashed another in the face with a fist, knocking him on his ass and tipping over a latrine bucket in the process. The foul liquid sloshed across the floor and over Karus's feet.

A hand grabbed at Karus's arm, pulling him. It was Flaccus again.

"It's now or never. We have to go, sir."

"No," Karus shouted back and looked for Amarra. "I'm staying."

"You stay," Flaccus shouted, "you die. The legion needs you, sir."

"No," Karus shouted again. "Not without Amarra."

The ground shook violently. The shouting almost immediately died off as the building around them groaned like an old man rising from bed in the morning.

As the building shook again, plaster, stone, and masonry crashed down from the ceiling. The floor trembled and then the entire building rocked on its foundation. Flaccus, along with many others, lost his footing and fell.

A large stone block crashed to the floor, killing a man two feet from Flaccus. The poor bastard had not even had time to scream.

Dust and debris raining down, the building shook yet again. Karus wondered if it was an earthquake. He glanced up as a large crack formed in the ceiling and saw a massive claw break through. Masonry was ripped and torn away. One of the dragons was tearing the palace apart to get to them. Again and again the claws tore at the masonry, pulling away whole blocks, making the opening wider. Then he could see the darkness beyond as a portion of the ceiling overhead was fully ripped away.

There was a massive roar of exultation that seemed to shake the palace even more. Karus felt fear descend upon him. It was like what he'd felt when the dragons had attacked the orc army. Though, once again, the feeling was muted. For everyone else, the fear was clearly overpowering.

Men fell back, collapsed to the ground, cried out in panic, and attempted to flee. Though for the latter, they were almost too petrified to move. Even the elves were not immune. Kol'Cara, sword in his hand, was shrinking back.

Flaccus had dropped his weapon and held his hands over his head. The centurion was cowering against the wall.

Nearly alone on his feet, and bracing himself with a hand against the wall, Karus watched as the dragon continued to tear at the building, ripping away the floor above, working frantically to make the opening wider.

Foolish humans, Cyln'Phax roared in rage. *Stupid, short-sighted men....so typical of your species. In your ignorance and fear you would destroy the direct instrument of your god. You would harm the High Priestess, your only path to salvation. Fools, the lot of you. You disgust me.*

A large chunk of the ceiling came away and the building stopped shaking. The dragon's head could be seen above, jaws parting slightly. She leaned forward, sticking her head through the gap in the ceiling. Flame began to build in her maw as her gaze bore into the cowering men.

And now you will pay for your lack of vision, Cyln'Phax said. *I will burn you all to ash.*

"Cyln'Phax," Amarra said in a calm voice that rang with inner strength. Until that moment, Karus had not realized how quiet it had become. "That will be enough, thank you."

With a loud clap, Cyln'Phax snapped her jaw shut.

They dared to attack you, mistress, Cyln'Phax protested. *They would have harmed you. They deserve this... and have earned death.*

Karus turned his gaze toward Amarra. She was still crouched by Delvaris's side. In one hand she held the tribune's hand and in the other her crystal staff, which had begun throbbing with increasing intensity.

"I assure you," Amarra said, without looking up, "I am and was quite safe. There will be no killing. That is the end of the matter."

The dragon hissed in reply.

Amarra bowed her head. A heartbeat later, there was a brilliant flash of light from the staff, nearly blinding. Karus was forced to avert his gaze. Then, abruptly, the light faded and the dimness in the corridor returned.

Amarra was glowing. There was no other way to describe it. White light seemed to encase her in a sort of bubble, rippling over her skin. It was the purest light Karus had ever seen and it made him feel good, soothed his worries and concerns. The feeling was akin to being comfortably wrapped in a warm blanket on a cold night.

"You have shown your faith to be true." Amarra spoke in fluent Latin to Delvaris, as if she'd been born to the language. "For your faith, you have been greatly honored. The High Father...Jupiter...grants you his blessing."

The staff flared into brilliance once more. A humming sound filled the air. Dust from the damaged ceiling cascaded downward in a shower. A beam of light shot out from the crystal staff, striking Delvaris's chest. He convulsed, as if in terrible agony, arching his back almost to the point of breaking. Then he fell still. The beam ceased, and returning to its normal sullen throbbing, the brilliance faded from the staff.

Everything had become deathly quiet. It was only then that Karus realized the fear had gone, vanished. In its place, an incredible sense of deep peace had descended upon him. All in the corridor had stopped cowering and seemed similarly affected. They had dragged themselves back to their feet. Those too sick to rise from their blankets, if they could, were simply watching. It was so quiet, a hairpin could have been heard dropping.

Delvaris opened his eyes and he blinked, looking around. He took a deep breath and exhaled mightily, seeming to savor the experience of breathing without difficulty.

The junior tribune sat up in apparent amazement. He was no longer a wasted mockery of a young man. Delvaris had been completely and fully restored to health. Barring his soiled tunic, he looked perfectly fine.

"You've healed me," he gasped, his gaze turning back to Amarra. It was as if he could not believe what had just happened. "You have healed me."

"No," Amarra said. "The High Father, whom you know as Jupiter, granted you his blessing. Your faith has been rewarded."

"Thank you," Delvaris said, "thank you."

"You would be better served," Amarra said, standing, "thanking him."

"I... I will," he said, "with all my heart and for the remainder of my days. I shall honor the High Father. I promise."

"A miracle," Flaccus breathed in awe. There were several other similar exclamations from those nearest.

Amarra stood, turned, and smiled so radiantly at Karus that it warmed his heart. The white light still surrounded her. She stepped up to him and put a hand on his wrist. Karus felt the sense of peacefulness intensify with her touch. It was pure and utter bliss.

"You will not need that," Amarra said.

Karus looked down at the sword in his hand. He knew she was right. He glanced around at the men. They were no longer gazing on Amarra with fear and hate, but what he could only describe as wonder mixed with shock. He sheathed his sword, and as he did, she removed her hand from his wrist.

The contact was broken and with it the sense of profound peacefulness was lost. It was almost painful, as if something dear to him had been ripped away. He recognized it as the High Father's touch.

"Their eyes have been opened," Amarra said. "As our god commanded, it is time to feed their souls."

Amarra turned away and started down the corridor, her dress whispering across the stone. The nearest men drew back, almost as if fearful.

"The High Father," Amarra said loudly, "who you know as Jupiter, welcomes *all.* Return to your roots ... honor him, love him as he loves you ... worship your god, fill your hearts with faith and you shall know salvation. I call upon you, Romans ... return to your god."

No one moved. It was almost as if they were afraid to. The silence stretched. It was broken as a legionary coughed, hacking so hard it bent him over double as he lay on his blanket. He recovered and climbed slowly to his feet, before moving through the crowd toward Amarra.

The sickness had taken a terrible toll upon him. His cheeks were gaunt and he was painfully thin. His tunic hung awkwardly on his bony frame. He appeared so ill, it was a wonder he could walk at all. There was a funny look in his eyes, as if he saw something in her ... that others did not.

He slowly stepped forward and reached a tentative hand out toward her white dress and the light that encased her. Amarra did nothing to stop him. He hesitated, abruptly becoming unsure. She smiled reassuringly and gave an encouraging nod for him to continue.

As he touched the fabric, the staff flared back to brilliance and a beam of light shot squarely into his chest. He stumbled backward. The beam faded from existence.

Gone was the emaciated, wasted man.

Eyes wide, he sucked in a breath and let it out. He looked at his hands and arms, gazing at them in utter astonishment. "I am healed."

"Your faith has been rewarded."

Amarra set the butt of her staff down hard on the floor. As it cracked the marble, the air rang with the sound of a bell tolling. "Hear me, Romans, the High Father is willing to bless you, to forgive your transgressions, those in the distant past and those committed this night. All he asks in return is faith, love, and devotion. I pose you this question … as he gives unto you, will you willingly give in return?"

There was a moment of hesitation, then almost en mass, the men pressed forward, each reaching out to touch her dress or the staff itself. The staff's light once again grew in brilliance. The air seemed to hum, and with every touch, a jet of light shot forth. The light intensified and more of the healing beams shot forth, each fully restoring a man.

Karus watched it all in amazement as Amarra healed every single man in the corridor who still drew breath. The white light around her had grown intense, to the point where it was almost painful to keep his gaze upon her. But Karus did not look away, not once. He was watching a rare event, a miracle, unfold before his eyes. It was simply awe-inspiring … incredible to witness. He found himself greatly moved.

Karus and Flaccus just stood side by side and watched. So too did Kol'Cara and, above them, Cyln'Phax. Eventually, Amarra walked back down the hallway to them. Si'Cara, following after her, looked a little disheveled and worse for wear. But despite that, there was a slight smile of satisfaction plastered upon her face.

Every eye was on Amarra as she passed. She stopped before Karus and Flaccus. She was still encased in a bubble of white light. It was then Karus noticed that Amarra's hair had turned perfectly white. Gone was the black hair.

Amarra fixed the centurion with her gaze. "Do you wish to receive the High Father's blessing also?"

Flaccus hesitated a moment, then slowly knelt before her and bowed his head. "I do. Though, I feel compelled to admit, I do not feel worthy."

"The High Father is a loving god," Amarra said.

"Still," Flaccus said. "I have sinned."

"The High Father is a forgiving god. He will weigh and judge whether you are worthy."

"I understand." Flaccus reached forth a hesitant hand to touch the hem her dress. A beam of light shot forth, striking the centurion's head. The beam ceased. He gasped, eyes going wide. Flaccus reached down toward his stomach.

"The pain is gone." Amarra was gazing down upon him. "You know of what I speak. It has been slowly eating away at you. Month after month, day after day, it has been getting worse."

"My stomach," Flaccus said. "My stomach has been healed?"

"You have been judged worthy," Amarra said.

"It was killing me," Flaccus said, looking over at Karus. "Ampelius said so... a cancer of the belly."

Karus had not known. Neither the centurion nor the legion's surgeon had said anything. Flaccus had likely sworn the man to silence, possibly under threat. And in truth, Karus could understand. He'd rather die doing something useful, working out his service, than being discharged. To die alone and without one's comrades close at hand was something Karus wished on no one.

"The cancer is gone," Amarra said.

"I will thank the High Father," Flaccus said.

"You will return his favor," Amarra said, "with your service."

Flaccus gave a solemn nod. "I will. I swear it to be so."

"Now, if you would show me to those others still afflicted, I will offer them the High Father's blessing."

Flaccus stood and glanced over to Karus. "With your permission, sir?"

"Do it," Karus said.

"This way." Flaccus led her back down the corridor.

Men freshly healed lined the sides of the corridor. As she passed, with Si'Cara following two steps behind, first one, then all the men took a knee and bowed their heads. Karus had never seen anything like it. Romans bowed to no one, not even the emperor... only the gods.

A few moments before and they would have willingly torn her limb from limb. Now they showed Amarra great honor, respect, and perhaps even love. The thread Karus had thought severed had been mended. It had taken a miracle, but it had been done. The legion would march on.

"You have an amazing woman there," Kol'Cara said, having come up to his side.

"I do," Karus said and started after Amarra. "That I do."

Chapter Ten

It took more than four hours for Amarra to work her way through the entirety of the palace district. With the High Father's power, she healed every man, woman, and child from the legion, the auxiliaries, and the camp followers. Throughout all of it, Si'Cara had remained close by her side. Karus and Flaccus trailed behind them, going from building to building until they found themselves out on the parade ground before the main entrance of the palace.

Here, tents had been raised for those who were healthy. Flaccus had told him it was hoped the fresh air would keep further men from falling ill. The legion's surgeon, Ampelius, had recommended it, and Flaccus had thought it a good idea.

Ampelius was a master at his craft and had saved many a man from death. He, with his small corps of doctors and medics, had always been an integral part of the legion. Now, with Amarra's miraculous ability to heal the sick and injured with the High Father's power, Karus wondered if it made them redundant and possibly unneeded.

Karus glanced skyward. Though still overcast, the darkness had finally given way to some color. The temperature had even begun to grow warm, which seemed to indicate a hot day was in the making. Despite having not slept, Karus found he wasn't at all tired. In fact, he was energized, as if he'd gotten a full night's sleep. Flaccus seemed to be in a similar state.

Just several yards away, surrounded by a crowd of legionaries, Amarra worked, spreading the good word and healing those yet to be afflicted with symptoms. According to her, all had been infected. She had chosen to visit last with those who had yet to fall sick, offering them the High Father's blessing. So far, none had refused her.

Most legionaries honored the gods to one degree or another, with many simply paying lip service. In their unique profession, soldiers could not ignore the gods and risk incurring divine disfavor. To do so was unwise, for the gods were known to be vindictive, especially if they were not regularly appeased.

Karus himself had always been religious. Dutifully, he had regularly offered devotions and sacrifices to Rome's pantheon of gods, all twelve of them. During the high holidays, he had even attended a service or two. But, for the most part, Karus had kept his beliefs to himself, as he felt it was a deeply personal thing. Forcing religion on someone typically did not work. The northern Celtic tribes were proof of that. Such attempts usually led to hard feelings and trouble.

He glanced over at Flaccus. Prior to coming to this world, there had always been a zeal of faithful fire residing within Flaccus's breast. The man's intense and open belief in the divine set him apart from most others who served. He frequently attended religious services and pressured his men to do so as well.

And now, in Flaccus's gaze, Karus saw the deep burning belief had been reinforced. After what had occurred this night, he understood that many of the men would undergo a revival of faith, and an intense one at that. He wondered, not with a little trepidation, what future challenges that would bring. Zealots, driven by fanaticism, could be trouble.

"Excuse me, sir."

Both men turned to find two legionaries standing at attention. They wore their service tunics and were armed with short swords. Their faces had been intentionally blackened by ash, which had run and been smeared by sweat. They offered Karus a salute.

"Optio Divius"—Flaccus pointed to the man on the left by way of introduction and then the man on the right—"and Legionary Lanza. Both are from my cohort."

"I know them," Karus said to Flaccus. Between the legion, auxiliaries, and the camp followers, it was impossible for Karus to personally know everyone by sight. It was more important that everyone else knew him rather than the other way around. But... he did know these two knuckleheads and almost smiled, for he was fond of them both.

Divius was a hard service veteran who was on track to make centurion. The man had rugged good looks and was known to be popular with the ladies. He also had a good head on his shoulders and was a respected man. In battle, Divius set the example for others to follow. Even when everything went to shit, he'd shown great courage and a coolness of attitude.

But, with all that going for him, he'd initially not qualified for promotion. Until the previous year, Divius had been mostly illiterate. To correct that deficiency, he'd diligently saved his pay and purchased an educated slave to teach him what he needed to know. Only those who could read, write, and do their numbers were eligible for promotion. In the end, Divius had learned what he needed and made it, receiving a promotion to optio, much to Flaccus's pleasure.

The next step for him after he gained more experience was the centurionate, and Karus had no doubt Divius would make it.

Lanza was another good man and a veteran of more than ten years of service. He'd distinguished himself in combat the previous summer against the Celts in a nasty ambush that had nearly seen an entire century wiped out. Lanza had been awarded a phalera for bravery and was another who showed promise.

Both men were fast friends and almost inseparable. They were known for finding trouble, and not the little kind either. Karus, along with many of the other senior officers, considered both to be blessed by Fortuna, perhaps even the High Father. On more than one occasion, by all rights, both men should have died … and yet somehow, despite the odds, they'd managed to survive.

Karus scowled slightly and wondered why their faces had been blackened. Then he snapped his fingers with sudden understanding and silently cursed himself.

"The fires," Karus said.

With all that had happened, he'd forgotten about them. In a city that could easily burn, with the legion inside it, he found that was an almost unforgivable sin. Karus became irritated with himself at the lapse.

"That's right, sir," Flaccus said. "These are the men I sent into the city to investigate the fires."

"What did you learn?" Karus asked, forcing the irritation away.

"The refugees have been fighting amongst themselves, sir," Divius reported. "We think they found a small warehouse with some food and … well, fought over the contents. It must have been something we overlooked, sir. Leading up to the building, there were bodies all over the place in the street. It appears after the fighting, they got around to extinguishing the fires."

"Are you certain the fires are out?" Karus asked, feeling instant relief at the news.

"We couldn't get that close, sir," Lanza said, "but we were able to climb a building that was tall and had a good view. Though it was still dark, all we saw was some smoke... not as much as before, but no visible flame. It certainly seemed like it was out."

"Do you agree?" Flaccus asked Divius. "That the fires are out?"

"I do, sir," the optio said. "I think they were extinguished when the fighting ended." Divius paused a moment. "It's just a guess, but it seemed like the Sersay and Taka'noon ganged up on the Adile."

Karus thought back to what he remembered of the band of refugees he had accepted into the city. Amongst them had been the remains of three entire peoples. They, like many others, were fleeing the Horde.

Xresex had been the headman of the Adile. Logex had represented the Sersay—Ord the Taka'noon. He'd thought he could deal with them, but he now understood how wrong he'd been. It wouldn't be the last time he would be wrong either. Karus knew at some point in the future he was bound to screw up again. Life in the legions taught you that you couldn't always have things go your way. No one was infallible.

Still, all that had followed was solely his fault. For the remainder of his days, he would feel responsible for Dio's death. He was in charge and it was his job to make the important decisions. That was the rub of it all. Command frequently came with a price. Make the wrong decision and it cost lives, and sometimes not just a few, either.

"How can you be certain they turned on the Adile?" Karus asked.

"In the short time they were amongst us, I got to know the refugees, sir," Divius said. "I even picked up some of their common tongue. Well, sir, I saw more bodies in the street from the Adile than I did of the other two. We also eyeballed men of the Taka'noon helping the Sersay haul carts loaded with food back to their camp in the city. We followed them, sir, and saw no Adile about."

"There weren't none in their camp either, sir," Lanza added. "It was like the Adile upped and moved. There's no telling where they are in the city, or if any are left. The Sersay and Taka'noon are not exactly the nicest bunch of barbarians we've met."

There was a strong chance the Adile had been the ones to find the warehouse. Once they had been admitted to the city, the refugees had turned over their food to the legion, which had been moved to the palace district. It was part of the arrangement Karus had made with their leaders.

If Karus had been a betting man, he'd have willingly wagered good money that the Adile had not told the Sersay or Taka'noon what they'd discovered. Hence the discord amongst them. It also told him they were hungry and becoming desperate.

"How do you know the Adile so well?" Karus asked, suddenly curious.

"Divius was transferred to the First Light Carthum Cohort," Flaccus answered for the man. "He took over after Ipax fell ill, while you were away, sir."

Karus gave an absent nod as he thought over what both men had told him. That there was a division amongst the refugees, and that they'd been killing each other, was welcome news. It ultimately meant the job of dealing with them would be slightly easier.

The legion would still need to dig the bastards out of the city, and something like that was never a simple enterprise. He just hoped that when they were dislodged, Logex was captured. Karus wanted him alive. The High Father might be in a forgiving mood this night, but Karus most certainly was not. The man would pay for his actions and what he'd done to Dio.

"Anything else you can tell us?" Karus asked.

"Not much, sir," Divius said. "Centurion Flaccus ordered us to be cautious and avoid detection. We couldn't get too close or we'd have run the risk of being discovered."

"You did good," Karus assured the man. "You have my thanks… both of you."

Karus saw both men's eyes widen as they looked beyond him. Karus and Flaccus turned. The mass of men had parted and Amarra, with Si'Cara still at her side, was approaching, walking confidently across the parade ground toward them. She was encased in the same bubble of white light. In the early morning gloom, she stood out brilliantly, a veritable pool of moving light. Karus had to admit, she looked quite the stunning sight. Behind her, after a slight hesitation, the men silently began to follow.

She stopped before them, her attention fixed on Divius and Lanza. With her nearness, Karus keenly felt the sense of peace… the High Father's power… almost pulsating outward in waves. The men who had followed gathered about them in a large circle, crowding around to see what would happen next, eager even.

"The High Father is willing to bless you," Amarra said to Divius and Lanza, "if in return you both are willing to honor, love, and give him your faith."

Divius looked uncertain, his eyes going to Flaccus. The optio's mouth opened, but no words came out. Like the rest of them, it was clear he felt the power radiating forth from Amarra.

"I would take what is offered," Flaccus told the two men. "This night the High Father healed the entire legion of the sickness… the camp followers too. Amarra is the god's High Priestess."

"Jupiter, sir?" Divius asked, looking to Karus. "The High Father is Jupiter… is that true, sir? Some of the centurions were saying it was…"

"I told you it was," Flaccus said, testily.

"It is, son," Karus said. "He's known as the High Father on this world. Jupiter sent her to be a light in the darkness for us." He glanced over at Amarra. That the legion had been saved from the disease was an incredible relief. The feeling of closeness to his god seemed to deepen, as did his feelings for her. Without Amarra, none of this would have been possible.

"Though it has not yet taken hold," Amarra said, drawing their attention again, "the sickness is in you both. Should you forego the High Father's blessing, in the days to come, you will both fall ill. Whether or not the sickness takes you… I do not know. The High Father gives us all free will of heart. As such, the choice is yours."

Lanza licked his lips and then swallowed. The legionary knelt almost reverently before Amarra.

"My mum taught me to honor the gods. You won't see me turn aside a blessing," Lanza said as Divius took a knee before her also.

"I would ask to be blessed," Divius said. "The High Father… Jupiter… has my faith… He always has."

Amarra held the staff toward the two men. It was glowing just as brilliantly as the bubble of light around Amarra. Both men looked at her, unsure, hesitant.

"Reach out," she told them and gave an encouraging nod.

Lanza did as instructed. When his fingers touched the staff, a beam of light shot out and into him. He gasped, eyes growing wider, if that was possible. Amarra moved the staff toward Divius. The man hesitated a moment, then grasped it, with the same result.

"That was incredible." Divius's breath came fast, as if he'd run a long distance. After a moment, he reluctantly released the staff and shared a look with Lanza. There were tears in his eyes. "Just incredible. I felt him. I felt the High Father's love."

"I did too..." Lanza whispered, almost as if to himself. "The love... I've never known anything like it."

"The sickness is gone. You have both been judged worthy," Amarra said, with a knowing smile. "The High Father loves us all, even if at times we forget. You may both rise."

"Thank you," Divius said.

"There is no need to thank me," Amarra said. "Trust me, your faith is enough."

Both men stood and then stepped back several paces as Amarra turned to Karus and moved closer.

"And now we come to you, my love," Amarra said. "Though you have already been blessed greatly by the High Father, the sickness is within and it's growing." She closed her eyes and held forth her hand toward his chest, palm held outward. "I can now feel the disease, an evil and vile thing... spawned by a dark god." She grimaced, as if she'd bitten into a sour apple. "It is spreading rapidly." She opened her eyes, lowered her hand, and focused on him intently.

"The sickness needs to come out, before it has a chance to become worse."

Karus had suspected he'd been infected. But the dark god stuff was new. That worried him, for he recalled the twisted creatures of evil in the city. He eyed the men circled around them. Their gazes were fixed on him and Amarra. Beyond just being healed, Karus suddenly realized this was an incredibly important moment for the men and, in a manner of speaking, himself too.

Though she'd already healed everyone else, he was keenly aware he would be setting the example for all to follow from here on out. The healing had begun the process, but Karus needed to strengthen Amarra's position as the spiritual leader of their people... harden the cement foundation. He would not see it questioned again, at least by the Romans.

He returned his gaze to Amarra and found her searching his face. Karus knew he must show not only his devotion to the High Father, but also his faith. He needed to give a demonstration of his belief, something he'd been loath to do in the past.

"So be it," Karus said softly to himself. He slowly and quite deliberately got down onto one knee, before bowing his head before her. Romans only ever knelt before the gods. They did not even bend a knee to the emperor.

"I thank the High Father," Karus said, loudly enough for the nearest men to hear.

He knew what he said here this morning would be repeated throughout the entire legion, the auxiliaries, and the camp followers. It would also likely grow and become exaggerated in the telling. He hesitated, then started again and raised his voice to help it carry farther.

"I thank the High Father for his many blessings, including sending us his High Priestess, Amarra. He is first amongst the gods and will always be so." Karus sucked in a breath. "The High Father promised us Romans *an empire without end.* I pledge my life to fulfilling this task, to lead the legion as a shepherd might a flock and protect his people." Karus raised his voice again and hardened his tone. "We cannot go home, but we can create a new empire, a Roman empire. I will give all of my strength ... to my dying breath, to see his will is done in this world ... or the next, wherever our new home will be."

Without even needing to reach for it, the staff flashed with light. The entire parade ground before the palace was lit in pure white brilliance. Karus felt the warmth of the High Father's touch infuse his being, along with his god's love and approval for his actions. Then, in a flash, it was gone, once again wrenched painfully away. He almost sobbed at the loss of contact with the High Father, but instead looked up at Amarra and found comfort in her gaze. There were tears brimming in her eyes. She smiled proudly as she reached down, grasped his elbow, and helped him to his feet.

The bubble of light encasing her had vanished, though her hair was still perfectly white, almost shiny in the growing early morning light. The crystal staff had also lost its glow, completely. In fact, he had to do a double take, for the staff was no longer a staff.

It had transformed back into a spear ... Jupiter's spear ... like the one she'd been handed beneath the ruined temple. Only this one wasn't marble at all but had a well-worn wooden shaft, with a wicked-looking steel head that had been sharpened into a deadly point.

The men gave a thunderous cheer, tearing Karus's gaze away from the spear. Amarra took his hand in hers and squeezed. He turned back and gazed into her eyes as they continued to cheer. In them, he saw a sense of great satisfaction and love. But there was also a sadness lurking within.

"What is it?" Karus asked, leaning closer.

Amarra hesitated, then glanced toward the spear in her hand. "I can no longer heal. That was taken from me. It is now forbidden for me even to make the attempt. Healing is now, I believe, forever beyond my reach."

"Why?" Karus was perplexed.

"The High Father warned me not to squander the power of the staff." Amarra touched her chest. "I didn't… Healing your people was the right thing to do. It had to be done or all would have been lost. I feel it so… why I was given the staff. And I used all that was within, every last bit."

"The staff has no more power?" Karus asked. "Was that why it turned back to a spear?"

"It has no more power to heal," Amarra said, glancing at the weapon in her grasp. She turned her gaze back to him. "This night is a turning point, a forking of the road. There is a different path I must take, a more difficult one to walk. That much I am certain… it was made clear."

"I don't like that one bit." Karus felt himself frown. "And I am not sure I understand."

"Neither do I," Amarra said, "not yet, not fully. But we must trust and have faith. The High Father has a plan for us both."

After all that he'd seen, Karus had no doubts about that.

"It is clear the High Father sent you a message, mistress," Si'Cara said to Amarra, stepping closer.

Amarra glanced at the weapon in her hand before turning her gaze to Si'Cara. She tilted her head slightly to the side. "And what do you think that message is?"

"That he means for you to be a warrior priestess. I would have thought that obvious, what with the staff transforming into a spear."

Karus shared a look with Amarra. He feared Si'Cara was right, and that worried him. He felt a strong desire to protect… to shield the woman he loved from danger. Karus knew that in the end, even if he tried, he would only fail once more, like he'd failed with the refugees. For both he and Amarra seemed to attract trouble almost beyond belief.

"A spear can be a difficult weapon to master," Si'Cara added. "It is fortunate I am quite skilled with one. I will instruct you to use it well."

"I think that might be a good idea," Amarra said. "Yes, I would welcome such training."

"What I will teach," Si'Cara said, "is more than just sticking someone with the pointy end."

"Oh?" Amarra asked, suddenly amused. "Really?"

"Yes." Si'Cara grew serious. "I will teach you to fight with a sword, dagger, and your hands if needed… for all that matters is beating your opponent… not how you do it. And I will not be easy on you, mistress. I will be very hard, for that is the only way to become skilled." Si'Cara paused, eyeing the spear. "And it takes years to properly master any weapon."

"I like you," Karus said to Si'Cara, and then looked to Amarra, "and I approve. Such training will prove invaluable and likely one day save your life."

"Yes," Si'Cara said. "I think so too."

The cheering had died down. Felix separated himself from the crowd of men and approached. Karus had last seen his friend about an hour before, when Amarra had healed him of his wound and of the sickness. He walked perfectly fine and without the limp Ampelius had thought he might have for the remainder of his days. It seemed, Karus realized with another glance to the spear, the legion would continue to have need of the surgeon's services.

"Sir." Felix gave a perfect salute, speaking in a loud tone. It was clear he wanted the men to hear his words. "What are your orders for the legion?"

Karus glanced from the centurion to his men. Though fully restored to health, they looked dirty and ragged, unshaven… nothing like proper soldiers. They stank too, and badly. Still, he loved them just the same, perhaps even more now.

His senior officers were standing about in the crowd, including Pammon, the centurion who had replaced him as senior officer of First Cohort. It was good another friend had survived. He promised himself to never leave the legion again, if he could help it. They were his responsibility and his alone.

"What of discipline?" Flaccus asked, with a glance thrown to Amarra. "For what happened earlier in the palace? That could easily have ended differently."

"There will be no punishment," Amarra said, before Karus could speak. Her words were clear and carried just as well as Felix's had. "The High Father has granted his forgiveness. So too shall we."

"I agree," Karus said, after a moment's consideration. "We will overlook what occurred earlier and speak on it no more."

The men gave another cheer.

"Well then." Flaccus cracked his knuckles eagerly. "I think it's time we got some payback and showed those treacherous bastards in the city the might of Rome."

"We need to teach them why they should never have crossed us," Felix said. This was followed by an angry growl from the men.

Karus could not help but agree. He was itching to see it happen, and now that the entire legion had been healed, nothing would stop him. However, he knew something must be done first, and it was fundamental to the identity of the legion.

"Not yet," Karus said to Flaccus and Felix, his gaze traveling back to the men. He gestured toward them and raised his voice. "You look nothing like proper soldiers. Before we do anything, each of you will shave, bathe, and launder your tunics. This is to be followed by a thorough cleaning of kit. We are legionaries, not barbarian rabble. When we go into battle, we'll do it right. We are Rome." Karus paused a heartbeat. "What are we?"

"Rome!" came the unified shout that echoed off the walls and nearest buildings.

Karus swept his gaze around the circle of men. "After you are presentable and pass a full inspection, we will deal with those who feel they can betray Rome's kindness without recourse. Is that understood?"

"Yes, sir!" came the massed shout.

Karus clapped his hands together loudly. "Then let's get to it. Centurions, see to your men."

Chapter Eleven

"We've managed to secure all four gates, sir," Felix reported as he tapped each one on the map that had been laid out on the main table in Karus's office. "The walls around each gate have also been taken." Felix shot Karus an evil grin. "There's no getting out of the city now, unless someone scales the walls, sir. Given their height, that is a difficult prospect at best."

Considering the map, Karus placed both palms on the table, feeling the coarse grain of the wood. It was close to noon, and the day outside had grown hot. Karus, Delvaris, Felix, and Flaccus were gathered around the table. During his absence, the office had been used to house the sick. Though it had been cleaned two hours before, the room still stank terribly, even with the windows open. From the doorway that led to his headquarters drifted the low drone of many voices as his administrative staff worked.

"That's good news," Karus said after a few silent moments. He was well pleased all four gates had been taken. He'd been concerned that, when they made their move, the refugees would manage to slip out of the city, particularly their leaders. With any luck, they'd now been bottled up, with an escape nearly impossible.

The refugee camp in the city was clearly marked on the map. They had taken a small portion of the south side of the city into their keeping. The streets leading into the camp had been blocked. Flaccus's report on the enemy's position indicated it was moderately well fortified.

"Has there been any resistance?" Karus asked, looking up at Felix. Had there been any fighting, he figured he would have heard by now. But Karus had long since learned to take nothing for granted.

"None whatsoever," Felix said. "As impossible as it sounds, they didn't even bother posting anyone to watch the gates or the walls. In fact, we don't even think they had a lookout on the palace gate. It's entirely possible they were thoroughly unaware we'd marched from the palace, sir … even after we took the gates."

"They certainly know now," Delvaris added and leaned forward, placing a finger on the map where the enemy's camp was located. "Especially after First, Fifth, and Eighth Cohorts, along with the auxiliaries, sealed off the streets leading into their campsite and occupied the surrounding buildings."

"That's right," Felix said, "and the bastards won't be breaking out anytime soon either. We have sufficient strength in place to ensure they don't, sir."

"Did we manage to grab anyone?" Karus asked.

"We've captured twenty-two of their men, and six women, sir," Flaccus said. "They were outside their camp, out scrounging about in the city. My people are questioning them now. We should shortly know the enemy's strength and condition. As soon as any new information is available, I will pass it along."

"Sounds good," Karus said.

"Excuse me, sir."

Karus straightened and looked up toward the door to headquarters. It was Serma, his chief clerk. Serma held his ink-stained hands clasped before him.

"Sorry to interrupt, sir," Serma said. "At your request, Prefect Valens is here to see you."

"Send him right in," Karus said, once again pleased. He had met with his senior officers, the cohort commanders, a little over an hour before. The purpose of that meeting had been to give them their marching orders. That Valens had returned so soon meant the cavalry was prepared and ready to depart.

"Yes, sir." Serma retreated through the doorway, disappearing.

Valens strode into Karus's office a few heartbeats later, the hobnails on his boots clicking loudly against the marble floor. Where legionaries wore sandals, the legion's cavalry had boots. The cavalry prefect, confident as always, snapped to attention and offered a crisp salute. Karus returned it.

"How are your horse soldiers?" Karus asked.

"Me and my boys are assembled and ready to depart, sir," Valens said. "The men are in excellent spirits and eager to be off. We simply await your permission to ride."

Resting a hand on the edge of the table, Karus eyed Valens for a long moment. The man was usually as grim as the ferryman for the dead. And yet, the myriad patchworks of scars across his mutilated face could not hide his enthusiasm to be off.

"You're certain your boys are good?" Karus asked. "There are no lingering effects?"

"None, sir," Valens said. "We're in excellent shape. Heck, I feel as if I've had a full night's sleep… Never felt better, sir. Even the horses are rested and ready." Valens paused. "I am pleased to report your cavalry is prepared for an extended movement. Just give the order. We're ready to go to work, sir."

"All right." Karus motioned Valens closer to the table with the map. The cavalry prefect gave a curt, professional nod to Felix and Flaccus. He then glanced down at the map before looking back up at Karus expectantly.

"I don't like not knowing what's going on outside the city walls," Karus said. "I'm effectively blind and I'd like you to rectify that for me."

"I will, sir," Valens said, with a quick glance at Flaccus. "We would not have returned to the city unless directly ordered to do so, sir."

"Like the rest of the legion, his men became crippled by the disease," Flaccus said, hardening his tone. "I deemed it best to pull them in, as only a few were fit to serve. With the refugees in revolt, we needed every able-bodied man here, just to hold the palace district."

"I'm not blaming either of you." Karus held up his hands before Valens could respond, for the good-natured attitude had slipped from the man. The grimness had returned. "And I am most certainly not going to look back at what could have been done instead. Given our current circumstances, that's simply a waste of time and counterproductive at best. What was done was surely in the best interest of the legion. I have no doubts about that and will not second-guess Flaccus, to whom command fell." Karus paused, sparing each man a look. "I expect you both to comport yourself in a professional manner. I will not tolerate hard feelings or grudges from either of you on this subject. Is that understood?"

"Yes, sir," Valens said.

"Understood clearly, sir," Flaccus said.

They were two of his best. That didn't mean Flaccus and Valens had to like one another, but they had to work together. As professionals, he knew they would do as he asked. Karus eyed them both for a long moment, then glanced back down at the map.

"As I said, the immediate problem for you," Karus said, "is scouting the ground outside the city."

"I'll fix that, sir," Valens said. "Give me a few hours and you will know if there are any threats within twenty miles of the city's walls."

"I'm counting on it," Karus said. "However, I asked you here to give you additional orders, which I am certain you're expecting."

"Yes, sir," Valens said. "I assume this has to do with the allies you mentioned in your briefing with the senior officers from earlier?"

"You assume correct," Karus said and touched the map to the east of the city. "Our new allies should be about two days away, maybe less, marching on this road here." The map on the table didn't show the area more than a couple miles beyond the city walls. He was relying upon Valens's knowledge of the land, which the man had accumulated over the last few weeks of scouting. "They will be slowed by the wagons they're bringing."

Valens leaned forward, studying the road. He looked up after a moment. "I've seen that road, sir… It's in excellent shape and we should make good time. I don't think it will be a problem locating them, and quickly too."

"Good," Karus said. "Once you've found the dwarves, I want you to push with the majority of your strength beyond them and find our real enemy."

"The Horde, sir?" Valens's face clouded over in speculation. "The army of orcs you mentioned? Like the creature we brought back for you to see?"

Karus gave a nod.

"I was hoping you'd want that, sir," Valens said. "It's why I had my men pack extra rations."

"Though you ride instead of march like a real man," Felix said, with the hint of a grin, "no one ever accused you of being stupid."

"The smart ones learn early," Valens said, "that it's better to ride than march, especially if you have to carry your own gear."

"Somehow I never learned," Felix said, "is that it?"

Valens shot Felix a knowing smirk.

"You will need to shadow the enemy as they close in on the city," Karus said, redirecting the conversation back to where he wanted it. He was in no mood for diversions.

"That shouldn't be a problem either, sir," Valens said in a confident tone.

"If practical," Karus said, "and the opportunity presents itself, I would very much like you to ambush the enemy's supply train, along with interdicting any foraging parties you come across. Basically, make yourself a big thorn in their ass, without taking undue losses."

"I believe I can do that, sir," Valens said, suddenly sounding eager. He rubbed his hands together. "This sounds like fun."

"Don't get overenthusiastic," Karus cautioned. He had known the prefect to occasionally bite off more than he could chew. "We cannot replace your horses."

"I will strike only when and where I am confident of success," Valens said, "with an eye toward minimal losses on our end."

"Expect them to have dragons." Though he hoped not, Karus had to assume the enemy had them as well. And he wanted Valens to keep that in mind too.

"Dragons, sir?" Valens said, sounding none too happy about that prospect. "Are you sure, sir?"

"No," Karus said. "However, consider it a strong possibility."

"Yes, sir," Valens said, his enthusiasm giving way to a stony face. "I will keep that in mind."

"Good," Karus said.

"Since they've first shown up, I've been thinking about how to deal with such creatures," Valens said, "or really how to avoid them while still doing my job."

"You have?" Felix sounded surprised.

"Of course," Valens said. "I thought there was the possibility we might run into similar creatures that would prove hostile to our interests. As such, whenever possible, it will mean moving in small groups under cover, or conducting any serious actions or raids at night. Should the enemy have dragons, it might complicate things a little, but I have no doubt my boys are up to the challenge."

"Good thinking," Karus said. "To be clear, I need patrols out in all directions. That said, your primary focus will be to the east and our enemy."

"I understand my mission, sir."

"Very well," Karus said. "I won't keep you any longer. Good luck."

Valens saluted, turned on his heel, and left, his boots clicking loudly on the marble flooring. There was a long silence after the cavalry prefect had gone.

"Though he makes light of it," Felix said, "that man has a hard job to do."

"No more than we," Karus said, expelling a breath.

"Agreed," Flaccus said.

"Right, then." Karus turned back to the map of the city. "Let's focus on the nuts we have to crack... namely digging the refugees out of the city. We also will need to begin preparing the legion to march. That includes moving the supplies we've accumulated out of the palace district and to the gates, where we can better load them onto transport with the least amount of hassle. I see no need to clog the city streets with wagons, especially if we don't have to."

All three of them knew it would be a monumental task.

"I hate to say this, Karus," Felix said, "and I know you won't like it, but... well... since you want to leave Carthum soon after the dwarves arrive, perhaps we should consider just going and not worrying about the refugees."

"Are you serious?" Karus asked. Of all the things Felix could have suggested, he had not expected this. "You mean for us just to pull out?"

"Yes," Felix said. "I think we should consider it as an option."

"You're right," Karus said. "I don't much like the idea."

"Look at it this way. The Horde will deal with the bastards for us," Felix pointed out, "and it's only a matter of time until they get here, right?"

"We need to root them out," Flaccus said firmly, shooting Felix a hard look. "They've a good number of fighters. As we pull out of the city, there's no telling what trouble they might cause or how they may choose to harass us."

The thought of doing what Felix was suggesting had set Karus's blood boiling. Oddly, he found his gaze flicking to the sword in the corner. Karus had left it there, in its scabbard, leaning against the wall. He vividly recalled it encouraging him to kill his own men. He forced himself to calm down and turned his attention back to Felix. He knew, no matter how distasteful, this was potentially a decision that trumped revenge and self-interest.

The wellbeing of the legion came before all other concerns. The rational part of Karus understood, by counseling such an option, Felix was only doing his job. Conversely, the irrational side wanted payback.

"Look," Felix said, "I don't like it either. But any type of assault, no matter how well executed, will see us taking casualties. That'll weaken our strength. Karus, you keep telling us the Horde is the real enemy. And those bastards are just days away. Am I wrong?"

"No, you're not wrong," Karus said. He considered both men for a prolonged moment before turning toward Delvaris. "I've not heard from you yet. Do you have an opinion on the matter?"

The junior tribune appeared surprised by the sudden question posed to him. He shifted his feet, glancing down at the map and then back to Karus. He did not speak.

"Well?" Karus asked when the tribune hesitated a moment more.

"I think we should do as Flaccus suggested," Delvaris said. "I would not want to worry as the legion pulls out of the city." The tribune pointed at the map, toward the enemy's camp. "If the refugees are hungry, as we think they are ... there's no telling what they could attempt. Our supply train might be just too tempting a target, sir. If they hit us, that also will see us taking casualties. I doubt they will ... but just the same, they might even follow, nipping at our heels."

The tribune had made an excellent point. The legion's line of march would be long, and if the refugees followed, they might harass the rearguard. That was, if they had the balls to do so. Karus did not think they would follow. And yet, he knew he could not take that chance. They were a threat and just as much an enemy as the Horde. In short, they needed to be dealt with before the legion left.

"Right then," Karus said, his gaze shifting to Felix as the anger returned. "I agree with Flaccus and Delvaris. The threat is too great to leave them in place. Also, an example needs to be made. The men expect it and I want it... especially for Dio."

"Right then, attack it is." Felix pointed down at the map. "They were able to inflict heavy casualties on us during the previous attempts to force them out. What with the sickness, we also had a smaller force at our command. Now that we have the numbers, it will go differently. Still, I think, any assault could prove costly. Which means it must be planned carefully, with an eye toward minimizing casualties."

"We could burn them out," Flaccus suggested, waving a hand at the map. "Using the dragons, that is. Doing so would make short work of them."

"And no doubt set the city afire," Felix scoffed. "That's just what we need. Imagine trying to move the supplies out of the palace district as the city burns around us."

"I would first create a firebreak," Flaccus said, running a finger around the enemy's camp, "pull down a wide strip of buildings. So much so, the fire has no hope of jumping to the rest of the city. In the unlikely event it does, we can have bucket brigades at the ready. Once the firebreak is completed, send in the dragons."

"What you're suggesting will take time." Felix shook his head. "We need to be readying the legion for a prolonged march, and that doesn't even include prepping the supplies for transport or moving them to the gates. Once the dwarves arrive, we're going to have a difficult enough job just loading all the supply we've accumulated."

"We can do both," Flaccus said. "It's not like we don't have the manpower, not now, with the legion healed. Or we could simply wait until the legion marches. Once we're clear of the city, we burn them all out. Screw the city. Let it all burn. It's not like we're coming back." Flaccus looked to Karus. "Are we coming back?"

"Not if I can help it," Karus said, "and I would not willingly leave any shelter in place for the Horde. I was planning on burning the city, leaving only destruction and devastation behind us."

"Well," Flaccus said, "there you go. Just like a good slinger, we can kill two birds with one stone."

"Once we pull out," Felix said, "there's no guarantee we would get them all with fire. Some would undoubtedly be able to escape into the city itself and, Flaccus, it's a big city, nearly as large as Rome. I also doubt the dragons would want to take the time to burn every single building. They might not even be capable of that. Some of the refugees are bound to get away."

"What about just demanding their surrender?" Delvaris asked.

All three officers looked at the tribune. There was a long moment of silence. Delvaris rushed ahead, filling it.

"We show them overwhelming force and the futility of resistance. As Flaccus said, we have the dragons." Delvaris gestured in the direction of the palace gardens. "The refugees might not realize we're concerned about the city burning. Let's use the dragons as a big stick and threaten to beat them with it."

The moment of silence stretched.

"And if they don't surrender?" Flaccus asked in a quiet tone. "What then?"

"We've lost nothing," Delvaris said, "and we're back where we started. However, if they do surrender, I think it will be easier than forcing our way in, and less costly too. Don't you agree?"

"He makes a very good point," Felix said with a low chuckle. "I like it."

"I think we should try it," Flaccus agreed. "Good suggestion, boy."

Delvaris went red in the face at the sudden praise as both Felix and Flaccus turned their attention to Karus. He gave it some thought, thinking it through. They waited patiently for him.

"Very well," Karus said to Delvaris. "We'll do it your way. I will speak with the dragons. But just the same"—Karus looked meaningfully at the other two senior officers—"I want us to prepare for a direct assault. If they don't surrender, we're gonna hit them with everything we have and do this the hard way, before nightfall too. Is that understood?"

"Yes, sir," Flaccus said.

"It is, sir," Felix said. "I will begin working on plans to do just that."

"Good." Karus scratched an itch on his cheek. "I want to see them within the hour."

"You'll have them." Felix gave a nod.

"Now," Karus said, "I will also want—"

"Excuse me, sir." Serma had come back into the office. "Sorry to bother you."

"Yes?" Karus asked, looking over, wondering on the cause for this new interruption.

"The High Priestess has requested your presence in the gardens, sir," Serma said. "It seems two more dragons have arrived."

"Two more?" Flaccus said.

"Yes, sir," Serma said.

"Kordem and Cyln'Phax did tell me more dragons would be coming to help us," Karus said.

"Well, that's encouraging." Felix's smirk returned and was directed to Karus. "I guess you could say they've just added to our firepower."

"Very funny," Karus said, somewhat amused. He felt a slight lightening of the mood.

"The High Priestess," Serma added, "asked you come right away, sir. Apparently, the dragons bring news of the enemy."

"I will be right there. Thank you."

The clerk withdrew.

"We have a lot to do in the next few days," Karus said, looking between the three officers. "I am afraid we're likely to get little sleep."

"No doubt, sir," Felix said. "It won't be the first time, nor, I suppose, the last I went without rest."

"Once we quit Carthum, do we have any idea on how far we're going to be marching?" Flaccus asked.

"No," Karus said, feeling sudden frustration at the unknown. "And I think it's safe to assume, once we do step off, the enemy will come after us." Karus paused. "Gentlemen, make no mistake, we are their objective, not the city."

"The idea of a pursuit," Felix said, "doesn't sound very appealing to me, especially since it will be us that'll be doing the running."

"I don't like the idea of running either," Karus said. "Perhaps at some point we will be able to turn and fight on our terms. But, right now... we simply have no choice. That said, we'll have plenty of food for the journey. At least in the beginning. With any luck, Valens will have an impact upon the enemy's supply and they'll need to stop or pause their advance after a week or more to bring up additional food stores. That should allow us some breathing room."

"We might even be able to slip away," Delvaris said.

"We can only hope," Felix said, "but we cannot count on that."

"It's a shame we can't bring the enemy to battle," Flaccus said, "defeat them and then march without immediate worry. That would make things a tad simpler."

"I don't see how," Karus said. "They badly outnumber us and, as you heard, it's likely they have their own dragons."

No one said anything to that. Karus felt the urge to move things along. It was time to end the meeting and go see the dragons. He could pick up with them later.

"Right." Karus slapped a gentle hand down on the table and map. "I will be back after I speak with the dragons and learn what they have to say." He looked between Felix and Flaccus. "Have the assault plan ready for me when I return."

"Yes, sir," Felix said. "Flaccus and I will be ready."

With that, Karus made his way to the door and into his headquarters. With no windows and packed with his clerks, a handful of officers, and messengers, the room was hot, almost stifling. The staff did not pause in their work, though the messengers lining the wall snapped to attention as he passed. There was too much that needed doing for his clerks to stand on ceremony, and Karus had issued orders to that effect. They were to ignore his coming and going, unless he said otherwise.

He made his way by the headquarters' guard, who both came to attention as Karus stepped into the corridor beyond. Just a few hours before, the corridor had been a scene of misery, suffering, and death. It had been cleaned, but like his office, it still smelled badly. The stench wasn't going away anytime soon. The rubble from the ruined ceiling had also been moved out of the way for easier passage.

Karus quickly made his way to the exit that led to the palace gardens.

Farther down the corridor stood another pair of guards. These men were guarding the entrance to the great hall, where the legion's standards were kept. That included the Eagle. Karus hesitated, for he had not seen the legion's Eagle since he'd returned. It served as a powerful reminder that they were of Rome. Where the legion went, the honor of Rome went too.

"Later," Karus said to himself, promising to visit the Eagle's shrine and give Jupiter thanks for all that he'd done for the legion.

The light from the two suns was hot against his skin as he stepped out of the palace. The air was warm and humid. Karus felt sweat begin to bead almost immediately on his forehead. He stopped at the top of the stairs that led down into what remained of the palace gardens. Cyln'Phax and Kordem were there, as were two other dragons.

The newcomers were slightly smaller. Both were red in color, like Cyln'Phax. In fact, they seemed almost identical to the larger dragon, as if miniature copies. They lifted their heads, swinging them around to gaze upon him.

Still, though smaller, they were almost unimaginably huge beasts, and between the four of them, the dragons took up much of the garden's available space. There would have been no more room for a fifth dragon.

Amarra and Si'Cara were there, standing before Kordem. None of the other elves were present. They'd been assigned rooms in the palace, along with the Vass. Kol'Cara had placed an elven guard on Ugincalt. Karus had made sure to order an entire century to stand watch over him as well. The Vass was simply an unknown. Until Ugin proved worthy of trust, Karus would take no chances.

With little time to waste, Karus started down the steps. As he approached, Amarra turned and shot him a welcoming smile. He marveled at how beautiful she looked in the sunlight. Her pure white hair was almost radiant under the light of both suns. She didn't have Jupiter's spear. Karus wondered what she'd done with it, but now was not the time to ask.

"You call and he comes," Si'Cara said, amusement dancing in her tone. "You can't ask for more than that in a mate."

"Karus," Amarra said, ignoring the elf as she held her hand out toward the new dragons, "may I introduce Mirdrone and Ketin'Phax."

My daughters, Cyln'Phax said, before Karus could say anything. There was a note of fierce pride in her tone.

"Your daughters?" Karus found himself surprised by that. He had not considered that Cyln'Phax might have children. He looked briefly between the mother and two daughters. "It is an honor to meet you both."

It should be, human, Ketin'Phax said. *It should be.*

Karus had no idea how he knew which dragon spoke in his head, he just did. A few months ago, as the legion's senior centurion, the Ninth's primus pilus, his life had been simple and ordered. Since then, things had become complicated… strange… wild even, to the point where he regularly conversed with dragons and other exotic beings. Karus had even spoken directly with a god. What a difference a matter of months could make.

"You're just like your mother," Karus said, looking over at Ketin'Phax.

More than you know, Karus. Kordem snorted loudly. *More than you can possibly know…*

I will take that as a compliment, Ketin'Phax said, a puff of smoke escaping from her nostrils.

"You brought news?" Karus asked. He had no desire to play verbal games with Cyln'Phax's children. There was too much to be done and little time to do it, especially if he wanted to deal with the refugees before nightfall.

The Horde is three days from the city, Kordem said. *If they keep their current pace, your dwarven friends are just two days out. The advance force of the enemy's army is slowly gaining on them too.*

Feeling as if someone had just gut-punched him, Karus ran a hand through his hair. Once the dwarves arrived, he figured they would need at least two days to load the food and supply the legion had accumulated over the last few weeks.

It all came down to time. And now Karus knew, without a doubt, he was out of time. The enemy was just too close. They would be forced to leave much of the food stores behind.

Worse, with the enemy so close at hand, the Horde would have no difficulty catching up with them when they marched. It would mean a battle, perhaps just a day or two from the city…

That is not all, Cyln'Phax said. *Five wyrms fly with their army.*

There is a good chance they have more, Kordem added.

"Great," Karus said. He would have to alert Valens, now that it had been confirmed. "Just bloody great. I ask you, could it get any worse?"

It might, Cyln'Phax said. *Fortuna seems to have taken a disliking to you.*

Karus resisted a scowl.

My son, Kordem said, *and his mate are providing cover for the dwarves. For the time being, the wyrms are staying clear of them. The enemy does not know how many of our kind are about. We think they do not wish to take the risk of facing us… until they must. That, in and of itself, might be an advantage.*

Six dragons, Karus thought furiously. They now had six dragons with them… against the enemy's five. That was something… at least. But, as Kordem had said, the enemy might have more.

Still, Cyln'Phax said, *we both think it best if my daughters and I fly to the dwarves' aid.*

"You believe they're in danger, then?" Karus asked.

We do, Kordem said. *Our enemy may decide to take the risk and strike, rather than allow the dwarves to join with you Romans.*

That wouldn't be good, Karus thought, for he had hopes of building an alliance with the dwarves. If they eliminated Dennig's warband, it could ruin everything he had hoped to work toward.

I will remain behind with you, Kordem said, *to keep the enemy honest in the unlikely event they decide to strike at Carthum, instead, with a couple of wyrms.*

Before we go, we thought to consult with you and Amarra first. Cyln'Phax sounded incredibly grudging.

"I thank you for that," Karus said and looked to Amarra in question. "What are your thoughts?"

"I think the dwarves need their help," Amarra said, "more than we need theirs right now."

"I am in agreement," Karus said and turned back to Cyln'Phax. "Protect the dwarves if you can. To survive what is coming… we will all need to work together, to form a greater alliance of races. Otherwise, I fear we will all fall to the Horde."

A sort of compact, Kordem said, swinging his head to look at his mate. *Karus, such an alliance has not been attempted for a very long time. It might work, or it might just as well fail. That is a lofty goal for the future, one I think unlikely to bear fruit.*

Regardless, the Horde is coming and is nearly on your doorstep. You must prepare for their arrival, for with the enemy's wyrms… we alone cannot save your legion.

While we deal with the wyrms, Cyln'Phax said, *you will likely need to face the enemy's might with shield and sword.*

Karus had suspected as much.

"What will you do?" Amarra asked Karus.

"I don't know," Karus said. "We're outnumbered on the ground, and greatly too. I fear it will probably mean a fight, sooner rather than later. That the Horde is so close… means it may not be wise to give up the city and its defenses. We may be stuck here longer than I anticipated." Karus glanced at the two new dragons. He turned to Kordem. "How many more of your people are coming?"

We do not know, Kordem said. *The call went out. Those that remain on this world will come. We are sure of that.*

"Do you have any idea on when they will arrive?" Karus asked.

You're asking if they will arrive before the Horde gets here, Kordem said. *Do I have that right?*

Karus gave a nod.

I seriously doubt any will, Kordem said. *My people have scattered to the far winds and corners of Tannis. It will take them time to get to us.*

Karus rubbed at his eyes, feeling intense frustration. "Time is something we've run out of."

It would seem so, Kordem said.

"It never gets any easier," Karus said.

No, Cyln'Phax said, *it most certainly does not.*

Chapter Twelve

The heat of the day was beginning to lessen. At least Karus thought so as a light breeze blew down the wide street. The buildings, mostly warehouses, in this part of the city had been constructed next to one another. They ran the length of both sides of the street, acting like unbroken walls to either side. There were few alleys and side streets within view.

That was likely why the refugees had moved and taken this part of the city for their own. Three streets led into and out of the area where they had settled, and this was one of them. The warehouses along each street were mostly two to three stories in height, which made the refugees' position very defensible and limited avenues for assault.

In his armor and under the direct light of the two suns, Karus was hot and sweaty. It was not a good feeling. He felt like a loaf of bread inside an oven and that he was being baked alive. He also was in a disagreeable mood. The breeze gusted again and was more than welcome. He wiped sweat from his eyes with the back of his forearm.

To his left stood Pammon, the senior centurion for First Cohort and now by default the legion's primus pilus. Pammon had served in Karus's cohort for many years. He was a reliable and steady officer, not to mention a superb combat leader, whom Karus also considered a friend.

Behind them, a few feet back, arranged in six ranks, was Pammon's cohort. Shield bottoms resting on the ground and javelins in hand, the men were grim-faced and silent as they looked on. They stood ready to do their duty.

But what was to come went beyond duty. Karus understood the men wanted revenge and aimed to get it. They were in a murderous mood, one of which Karus had rarely seen the like. Dio had been a popular and beloved officer. The refugees had no idea of the storm they had brewed with his killing.

The legion's temporary field headquarters was in an abandoned tavern just past where Pammon had formed his cohort. Serma, along with Delvaris and a handful of clerks, had set up shop there to help Karus better prepare and coordinate an assault.

The tavern was a run-down, seedy establishment that had likely catered to the extremely poor. It had been well picked over by the time the legion had arrived. However, the tavern did have a large, open common room, along with tables, benches, and stools... nearly everything his clerks could have asked for.

To Karus's front, thirty yards ahead, was a rough-fashioned yet stout-looking wall that cut straight across the street. It had been well-made and would be difficult, but not impossible, to overcome. First Cohort had brought ladders for that effort, which had been stacked out of view, behind the cohort.

Thirty men, standing on a platform behind the wall, manned it. They were all armed with javelins and swords. Undoubtedly, just beyond them and out of sight, additional men waited to mount a defense of the wall when the time came.

"Our weapons?" Karus asked with a slight scowl. He gestured toward the men on the wall and the javelins they carried. Before he'd left for the Fortress of Radiance, Karus had issued orders for the newly formed auxiliary cohort to be armed with the stocks of weapons that had been found throughout the city. That the enemy carried some of the legion's weapons, and potent ones at that, was troubling. He would have to speak to Felix about that.

"Yes, sir," Pammon said. "We armed them, but I don't think we gave them the javelins. They might have just taken them. The blacksmiths were making them in the city and had amassed a good number when we fell back to the palace district. That could have been where they got them from. Heck, I would take a javelin over the long spears the city guard left."

Karus gave an absent nod and rested his hand on his sword hilt. The tingle raced through him. His anger, like a thunderhead about to unleash its might, mounted. He felt terribly bitter about Dio, to the point where he wanted to draw Rarokan and take on the enemy all by himself. Karus almost took a step forward as the hate and fury within him surged.

Only with effort did he restrain himself. Karus took a calming breath and let it out slowly through his teeth. He wondered if the sword was feeding his anger and frustration. At times, when he held it, his anger seemed to have no bounds. He removed his hand and glanced down at the hilt. There was no lessening of the anger, the mighty angst. Karus gave a quiet grunt. Perhaps he was just simply pissed off.

"They're intentionally keeping us waiting," Pammon said. "We've been standing here for at least a half hour. I wish they'd stop dicking around with us and get on with it."

"They're intentionally wasting our time," Karus agreed.

"I tell you," Pammon said, "they're only serving to piss me off, sir."

"Me as well," Karus said. "They believe we're here to negotiate. This delay is really just an attempt to establish a position of strength."

"I see, sir." Pammon glanced over at him. "Will it work?"

"They've miscalculated," Karus said.

It was Pammon's turn to grunt. They fell silent, neither saying anything for a time. Karus looked up. On the rooftops, near the enemy's wall, he could see refugees posted there too. Karus also had men on the roofs, enough that the latest report indicated the enemy were concerned enough to start fortifying their positions up there, hastily working to build a makeshift wall in the event the legionaries came at them over the rooftops.

The other two streets leading into the enemy's camp were sealed off too, as were the rooftops. Felix and Flaccus were commanding and overseeing those efforts. There was simply no way the enemy could break out.

The sky was clear, with only a handful of puffy white clouds. High above, Kordem flew in clear view. The dragon appeared small, like a bird of prey hunting… insignificant, until now, ignored by those below. But there was no mistaking what he was… a dragon.

"How many fighters are in there?" Pammon gestured with his chin toward the enemy's camp. "Did you find out from the prisoners?"

"At least five hundred fighters," Karus said, "maybe as many as six hundred."

"Really?" Pammon looked over at him, eyebrows raised. Sweat beaded the centurion's face. He pulled a small wool towel from behind his armor and wiped at his face with it. "Gods, it's bloody hot."

"It seems," Karus said, "after the recent fighting and kicking out Xresex's people, that's all they've got left. At least, that's what the prisoners told us."

"Any idea on where Xresex and his people went?" Pammon asked, in a mildly interested tone.

"No," Karus said, unhappily. "It's possible they fled the city, or they might have been wiped out. Those of our people doing the questioning barely speak Common. They had to call me in to get detailed answers and, unfortunately, those we had in custody knew little about the Adile."

"Guess I'll soon be learning a new language," Pammon said, "this common tongue."

"You'll need to if you want to communicate with our allies," Karus said. "Pammon, make no mistake... you will need it."

"To communicate with the elves and the dwarves?" Pammon asked.

"Yes. The sooner you learn it the better."

"Yes, sir," Pammon said and turned his gaze back to the enemy. "Why'd they turn on the Adile? Did the prisoners say?"

"It seems," Karus said, "the Adile refused to go back on their word and betray us."

"Well," Pammon said, "that's something, I guess."

"Yep," Karus said. "They were pretty much left alone... that is, until they found a stock of food."

"Any idea on how many women and children are in there?" Pammon asked.

"A little over two thousand noncombatants," Karus said. "And it seems they're short on food. They've begun to go hungry."

"Stupid bastards." Pammon spat on the stone paving. "They should never have crossed us. Had they honored their word, they'd all have full bellies. I hate it when children suffer. I really do."

"I can't disagree with that," Karus said. "Barbarians never seem to miss an opportunity to miss an opportunity."

"Seems that way, sir." Pammon sounded thoroughly disgusted. "They just don't think like the civilized."

There was a clatter behind them. Karus turned to see Amarra making her way through the ranks of men. Behind her trailed a somber-looking Si'Cara. Amarra carried her spear, point upright. She was using it more as a walking staff than anything else. She joined them and gripped his arm briefly in welcome.

"You didn't need to come all the way down here," Karus said to her.

"True," Amarra said, "but I wanted to be here for this, as well as be with you."

"It could get unpleasant," Karus cautioned.

"You need to stop trying to shield me," Amarra said, sounding slightly irritated. Her gaze bored into his. "Just as you have, I've seen the ugly side of the world. I will no longer look away. To do so would be wrong. The only way to improve things and do some good is to take it in with both eyes open… to see things as they really are. Besides, I felt the need to be here."

"The High Father?" Karus asked. "He wanted you to be here?"

"Yes."

"Sir," Pammon said and gestured toward their front. "Something's happening."

Looking around, Karus saw there was movement amongst the enemy. Three men had appeared along the center of the wall. Karus recognized Logex and Ord. He felt an intense wave of dislike wash over him at the sight of them.

The third man, Karus did not know. He carried himself with a natural confidence that spoke of being accustomed to authority. Karus's hand came to rest on the sword hilt again. He found himself intensely disliking this man as well, though he could not find any rational reason for his strong feelings.

"Who is that man there, on the right?" Karus asked Pammon. "Do you know him?"

"That's Garvin," Pammon said. "A real mean bastard. I don't remember his people's name, but he was part of the group we took in after you left. Along with Logex, he was directly involved in the killing of Dio and the fighting that followed."

"You asked to speak with us," Logex called to Karus in an arrogant tone. "Let's get this over with. What do you Romans want?"

Karus felt a stab of annoyance. He badly wanted to end Logex.

Pammon looked over at Karus. "What did he say?"

Amarra translated.

"Cheeky bugger," Pammon said, when she finished. "He knows why we're here. Karus, we need to teach them a lesson they won't soon forget."

"Agreed." Karus turned to Amarra. "Would you continue to translate for Pammon? I would have him follow what goes on."

"I will," Amarra said.

"Don't keep us waiting all day," Logex said, sounding exasperated.

Karus took a step forward.

"Careful, sir," Pammon cautioned. "It's a long toss, but some of them boys over there might be able to use a javelin."

"I'll keep that in mind." Karus stopped, going no closer. He turned back to face Logex.

"Ah, the great leader has returned," Logex said, pretending he had not seen Karus. The man rested his hands on the lip of the barricade. "We all thought you'd run out on your people. And I see you've brought your little witch too. How sweet. From the looks of her, she's good in all the areas that count. I guess that's what matters, especially when the suns set, eh?"

The three laughed nastily amongst themselves. Even a few men on the wall joined in. Though Karus thought most appeared nervous. With the might of First Cohort on display, an overstrength cohort, nearly seven hundred men, they had a right to be.

"Watch your tongue, cur," Si'Cara snapped. "You are speaking of the High Priestess."

"I thought you said she was a witch," Garvin asked and looked over at Logex. The mirth and amusement had gone from the man.

"She is." Logex gestured toward the Romans. "That's what their own people called her. She is but one more pretender, another charlatan peddling a false religion."

Garvin turned back to look on Amarra, his gaze piercing, almost unnaturally so. He did not appear convinced by Logex's argument. In fact, Karus thought he appeared seriously concerned.

"What god?" Garvin asked her. "What god do you serve?"

Karus thought the man's sudden interest odd. What did it matter?

"The High Father," Amarra said, a cold, hostile note in her tone. Surprised, Karus glanced back. Amarra's entire attention was focused on Garvin.

"What is it?" Karus asked, for he sensed something was not quite right. He took a step nearer. "Tell me."

"That man," Amarra said, lowering her voice, "the one named Garvin …"

"Did I hurt the witch's feelings?" Logex asked. His men along the wall laughed at that, enthusiastically. "If you send her over, Karus, I am sure we can comfort her in ways you simply can't."

"What of him?" Karus ignored Logex.

"He is not what he seems," Amarra said.

"What does that mean?" Karus asked, feeling himself frown.

"When I look at him," Amarra said, "I feel a coldness. Perhaps the right word is not cold … but wrong. Yes, that is a better word. I feel wrong and it upsets my stomach, like I've eaten meat that's gone bad. There is something dark about him, evil. I think he is a priest of some kind … or something else … Whatever he is, he's not one friendly to the High Father."

"A dark priest or holy warrior," Si'Cara hissed. The elf had an arrow loosely nocked in her bow. Eyes narrowing, she slowly turned her gaze to Garvin. "He could be very dangerous, if he has *will* and the ability to use it."

Karus was suddenly reminded of the Elantric Warden and her occult power. He went cold at the thought of facing such power again.

"Can you hit him from this distance?" Karus quietly asked Si'Cara.

"Easily," Si'Cara said. "Do you want him dead now?"

"Not yet," Karus said. "They need to hear my terms. Once I have laid them out, his life is forfeit."

"If he so much as twitches before you finish," Si'Cara said, "I will take him down. When you are ready for me to kill him, just say so."

Satisfied, Karus turned back around. He eyed Garvin for a long moment. The man was dressed in a stained and dirty light-brown tunic. He carried a longsword belted and sheathed at his side. That he was potentially a dangerous enemy capable of an unknown power was more than concerning. There was nothing really to mark him as different from the others. That worried Karus.

"Are you going to bore me to death?" Logex asked in an impatient tone.

Amarra continued translating for Pammon.

"No," Karus replied. "I promise, I will keep this short."

"Oh good," Logex said. "I can't tell you how much a relief that is ... I hate long speeches."

Karus had the sense the man was enjoying his moment on stage. Perhaps, he was even playing it up for the benefit of his men ... a false bravado. That would soon change.

"We've sealed you into your camp," Karus said. "You know that. All avenues of escape have been cut off. You're outnumbered, and badly too. There will be no negotiation. You will surrender ... or ... all of you will die."

There was silence from those on the wall. Then, Logex laughed. The laugh seemed louder than it should have been and somewhat forced. Karus noticed several of the men manning the barricade shift uncomfortably, looking to their leaders for reassurance. This time they did not join him.

Saying nothing, Karus simply waited for the man to stop laughing.

"You've already tried to force your way in," Logex said, "and your people failed miserably."

"The legion was sick and understrength," Karus said. "No more. We've recovered."

"I seriously doubt that," Logex said. "I saw thousands fall sick. There's no possible way you could have recovered so quickly."

Garvin leaned over and whispered something to Logex, while he gestured at Amarra. Logex stared for a long moment, then said something back. It seemed when he turned his attention back to Karus, the man had paled slightly.

"It does not matter what you believe," Karus said, before Logex could speak. "I've brought the entire legion to this party." Karus gave a shrug of his shoulders. He turned and glanced back at the legionaries of First Cohort briefly. "But they're not here to dig you out."

"Do you intend to impress us with the show, then?" Ord asked with a nasty chuckle. Logex did not join in the mirth. Neither did Garvin. Both had become grave. "You legionaries do seem to like to impress with all of your spit and polish."

"As I've said, we've sealed you in to keep you from escaping." Karus paused and then raised his voice, addressing the men manning the wall, for they were the ones who really mattered. Several of the enemy on the nearest rooftops had also gathered along the edges and were watching. "Anyone who comes over the wall and surrenders will live," Karus said. "You will be made slaves, even your women and children. But, in the end, you will have your lives. In time, you may even have the opportunity to buy or earn your freedom."

"You would make me a slave?" Ord was clearly incredulous. "I come from a long line of noble warriors. I would never willingly take the yoke. It would be a stain to my ancestors and honor. I would die first."

"The choice I am offering is not for you," Karus said bluntly, "but your people. They can either choose life or… death."

"We'd rather die than live in bondage," Logex snapped back.

"You don't get a say," Karus said. "I'm not here to negotiate. I am simply stating my terms. You, Garvin, and Ord do not get the chance to become slaves. If you surrender, you will be put to death. Resist . . . it does not matter. You three will die this day. I will personally see to that." Karus pointed skyward, toward the clouds. Everyone along the wall looked up. High above, Kordem, great wings outstretched, was flying in a lazy spiral. "I will give you an hour to make up your minds. When the hour is up, the dragon will burn you out . . . all of you. None of my men will be put at risk, but in the end, you will die if you decline my offer of servitude and life."

"You wouldn't dare," Garvin said. "You people follow the teachings of the High Father. He would never condone your actions."

"The High Father," Amarra said, in the same cold tone, "gives all free will. You chose poorly. As such, your people must pay the price for betrayal."

This was followed by silence.

"Had we not a great need for labor," Karus said, "I would simply kill you all. But now . . . you get to choose . . . so choose wisely."

"You're not serious," Logex said, in a horrified tone. The man's voice trembled slightly.

"You're a bastard," Garvin hissed.

"That's true. I can be a real bastard, especially when crossed." Karus hardened his voice. "We are of Rome and when betrayed we do not forgive . . . but seek vengeance." Karus paused, his gaze locking with Garvin's. "Si'Cara, now, if you would."

The arrow was away before Karus could even blink. It flew true, striking Garvin directly through the throat with a sickening sound. Both Logex and Ord looked on in stunned horror. Garvin gazed down in shock at the missile that seemingly had sprouted from his throat. He opened his mouth to scream. Instead, a shocking amount of blood fountained out, pouring down his chest. A heartbeat later, he toppled forward, over the barricade, landing heavily on the paving stones. Garvin twitched, then lay still, while his lifeblood pooled around his body on the street, running like tiny rivers through the spaces between the paving stones.

There was a moment where no one moved. Then common sense and self-preservation took over. Logex and Ord hastily ducked down behind the barricade, along with all the men manning it.

"Good shot," Karus said to Si'Cara, satisfied that the unknown threat the man had represented had been neutralized. He would have liked Garvin to suffer a bit more, but it had been an excellent demonstration for the other two leaders and their followers. Karus's message had been reinforced. Resist and die. He was sure Garvin's death would also be a blow to the morale of his people.

"Thank you," Si'Cara said as she slowly nocked another arrow, while holding her bow loosely and keeping her gaze on the enemy's defensive wall.

"I'd say the parley is over." Pammon clapped his hands together. He eyed Si'Cara for a long moment. "She's a damn fine shot."

"You have one hour!" Karus shouted. "Surrender or die. The choice is yours."

A man on the barricade suddenly stood and raised his javelin to throw at Karus. Si'Cara's bow was up. It once again twanged. Barely a blink of an eye later, the arrow hammered into the man's chest. He gave a clipped cry and fell back and out of sight, landing with a clatter on the other side of the wall.

"One hour!" Karus shouted again and turned his back, moving away from the barricade and toward the men of First Cohort. As he did, the men of his old cohort gave an approving cheer.

Pammon, Si'Cara, and Amarra followed. They made their way through the ranks and to the other side of the formation. There they found Ugin, along with the century Karus had assigned and the rest of the Anagradoom, including Kol'Cara.

The Vass was completely healed of his injuries and looked to be in prime health. The guard detail, with so many watching one individual, suddenly seemed a ludicrous precaution. But then Karus noticed how the elves watched Ugin. It was kind of like how one might warily eye a dangerous animal that had wandered too close.

Several shifted their bows and nocked arrows as Karus drew near. Then he remembered the scores of dead goblins on the hilltop. Ugin hulked over the elves and men of First Cohort, in an almost intimidating manner. The Vass seemed not concerned in the slightest. Perhaps, Karus thought, the massive guard detail wasn't such an overreaction.

"I like how you negotiate," Ugin said to Karus, baring his teeth in what clearly was an amused grin. "If I did not know better, I'd think you might have some Vass blood running through your veins, human."

"What are you doing here?" Karus asked Ugin, deciding to get right to the point. It was too hot out to waste time, and Karus had played enough games for the day.

"I heard there may be fighting." Ugin looked over the heads of the formed-up legionaries of First Cohort, toward the barricade. He turned his gaze back to Karus. It was then

Karus noted Ugin wore not only his armor, but his massive sword. The weapon was strapped to his back. "I came to help."

"You mean to fight with us?" Karus asked, disbelieving. "Really?"

"Well," Ugin said, "not at first. Then…I saw your elf take down the priest of Pattor. So…now I offer my services in the fight to come. Where there is a priest, there are followers. I would help you send them from this world to the next. You will let me help."

"Pattor?" Karus had never heard of such a god.

"It is another name for Castor," Kol'Cara said. "He is worshiped by orcs of this world, goblins, and some humans."

"Pattor, Castor," Ugin said. "Different name, same master. All who follow such a god deserve death."

"How could you tell he was a priest?" Karus asked, curious, for he could not recall the man wearing any religious pendants or sporting markers.

"My people have a natural affinity for such things," Ugin said. "We can spot most priests right off and with some, especially our race enemies, tell which god they belong to. The Great Orttessa has given us this power, so we might carry out her will and purify the land of the unholy."

"Do you know if that's true?" Karus asked Kol'Cara. "Can he truly tell such things?"

"You doubt me?" Ugin demanded, seeming to grow inches as he took a step toward Karus and leaned forward. Bows coming up, several of the elves took an alarmed step toward the Vass. The men of the guard century drew their swords as Karus's hand found his sword hilt.

Kill him, the sword hissed in his mind. *The Vass has* will. *Let me take it.*

Ugin noticed the reaction his move had caused. Grinning, he relaxed slightly, taking a step away from Karus. The elves lowered their bows. Feeling the threat had passed, Karus removed his hand from the magic sword. It was only then that he realized Ugin had been testing his guard's reaction.

Kol'Cara hesitated as he eyed the Vass, then answered Karus's question. "I understand it to be one of their given abilities. Their people can sense servants of gods opposed to their own."

"I would not lie," Ugin said, sounding scandalized.

"No," Si'Cara said, "you'd just mislead, like the rest of your people. Just as you did with the healing potion."

Ugin shrugged his shoulders at that, as if what she had said was no big deal. He looked over at Karus. "So, great leader of men, what now?"

"Now," Karus said, with a glace back toward the barricade, "we wait. They have an hour to decide."

"And then you will burn them out?" Ugin's gaze followed Karus's and then shifted to the dragon high above, flying in slow, lazy spirals. "That sounds like something worth seeing."

"I wish I could burn the bastards to ash," Karus said regretfully. "But we cannot afford to let the city burn. So ... for any that refuse to surrender, it will mean an assault on their position. We will need to overcome them the old-fashioned way, with the sword."

"Now that sounds really interesting." Ugin barred his teeth again, this time in apparent eagerness. "I hope a great number of Pattor's followers decide to resist and fight, for I am coming with you when you attack."

Shouting and raised voices drew their attention back toward the barricade. He looked and saw two men climbing over the wall. They threw down their weapons and approached the legionaries with their hands up.

One of the men suddenly screamed and pitched forward to the ground. A javelin had struck him square in the back. He cried out in agony, flailing, while trying futilely to reach the shaft of the weapon firmly stuck in his back.

Ord stood on the barricade and it was clear he had thrown the weapon. He held out his hand for another javelin. Before Ord could make a second throw, the other man who had made it over the barricade sprinted for the cover of First Cohort. But he need not have bothered. There was the sudden clash of sword on sword, followed by much shouting out of view, behind the enemy's wall. A moment later, Ord disappeared as he turned and climbed down to confront what was clearly an uprising within his own ranks. It was a positive development. The more the refugees killed one another, the less his men had to do.

"Right." Karus turned to Pammon. "Pass along orders to accept the surrender of any that come over the wall and give themselves up here and on the other two streets. Send for Felix and Flaccus. We will meet at my field headquarters in twenty minutes to finalize our plans for the assault. There are bound to be some holdouts and that will require an attack. Understand?"

"Yes, sir." Pammon saluted and moved off.

Karus turned away for his field headquarters. Behind him, the others followed, while Pammon went to carry out his orders.

"Show some courage and resist," Ugin said behind him to the enemy in more of a loud growl than anything else. "Don't all of you give up now."

Chapter Thirteen

"What's the total count now?" Karus asked Delvaris as the tribune stepped up to the table, a battered old thing that was wobbly and literally on its last legs. The surface of the table was stained, pitted, and had been repeatedly carved into by the tavern's patrons. A map of the surrounding city district, nothing more than a rough sketch, had been spread over the table. The map covered up the worst of the carvings, which included several phallic symbols.

It had been almost an hour and a half since Karus had offered his terms to the refugees. Since then, there had been a virtual flood of people surrendering to the legionaries. The door to the tavern was open and Karus could see the shadows spreading across the street outside. Dusk was fast approaching, and he was feeling an impatience to move things along.

Amarra, Felix, Flaccus, Kol'Cara, and Si'Cara were gathered around the table also. A lantern, hanging overhead, provided a dim but serviceable light.

At another table by the fireplace, which had been lit and was heating a pot of tea, two of Karus's clerks worked by candlelight. Sitting on rickety stools, they were bent over a table, busy entering figures on tablets. Serma had left a short while before to return to the main headquarters at the palace.

"Twenty-one hundred and six in total have surrendered so far, sir," Delvaris said, glancing down at a wax tablet that lay on the table. "Of those, four hundred and thirty-eight are men of fighting age. The rest are women and children. All have been thoroughly searched and disarmed. We've broken them up into smaller groups that are easier to manage."

Amarra began translating for the elves, so they could follow along.

"Tell me of the guard you've placed on their fighting men." Though he and the tribune had already discussed how the prisoners should be handled, Karus wanted to be sure the necessary precautions had been taken. When it came to those following his orders, he had long since learned to question everything and assume nothing. Doing so helped ensure no one screwed up, or at least kept the screwing up to a minimum. It was either that, or you tended to get burned by the occasional misunderstanding or lapse.

"Four hundred men have been assigned to the guard detail," Delvaris said. "Elements from Second, Third, and Ninth Cohorts are providing security. Each male prisoner has been secured, with his hands bound. We have broken them up into groups of fifty."

"Good," Karus said.

"Within the next hour," Delvaris continued, "we will begin moving them to the dungeon under the palace. Once they are locked up, it will make guarding them less labor-intensive."

"And the women and children?" Amarra asked. A small note of concern had crept into her voice. "What of them?"

"We've separated the women and children too, mistress," Delvaris said. "They've been organized into groups of no more than one hundred. We're making sure whenever possible to keep family groups together. As soon as the men are secured in the dungeons, we will begin moving the women and children nearer the palace district. Each will be assigned to a building with a guard detail of five men. Once settled, they will be provided rations. Our men have strict orders to harm no one. That said, any resistance or disobedience will be responded to in a harsh manner."

Silence settled upon them, broken only by one of the clerks shifting on his chair as he stretched. The legs of his stool scraped across the wood-planked floor.

"All slaves," Amarra breathed quietly, glancing down at the table. "It is a harsh existence we are condemning so many to."

"Yes, it is," Karus agreed. "Still, it needs to be done. There are just too many prisoners for us to treat them any differently. To do so would potentially compromise our security and safety. I cannot and won't have that."

"It is more than they deserve," Flaccus added grumpily. "I understand our need for labor is great. However, we should seriously consider slaughtering them all for their betrayal, at least their men... thereby reducing our risk. Were we still in Britannia, each would now be lined up to receive an iron collar, in preparation for being shipped back to the markets. There the men would be sold to the mines and plantations, where life expectancy is measured in mere weeks. Some might have gotten lucky and been sold to the gladiatorial schools... not an easy existence either but somewhat better. The educated would have gone to house or administrative work and many of the women to the brothels where they would be whored out to any who had enough coin." He paused a moment, eyeing Amarra. "Mistress, there would be no consideration given to family groups. Those who resist the might of Rome pay for it."

"The empire isn't perfect," Felix said, "but it is where we come from. For those living inside the empire, there was peace for the most part... Roman peace. Disturb that peace and the consequences are severe."

"The empire would have sold the slaves to the highest bidder," Flaccus said, his voice sounding harsh in the confines of the tavern, "and we would have seen a healthy bonus added to our pensions. On this world"—Flaccus tapped an index finger down on the table's surface—"cut off from Rome, the refugees will only be a drain on our food stocks and a potential risk for revolt. They have already turned on us once. I expect them to do so again. As I said, I believe we are being too generous with them. We might want to reconsider that."

Karus resisted a scowl. Flaccus was right. There would be headaches to come. He was sure of it. Even if he cut them loose, they might still cause problems... like joining with the Horde. He had already learned humans worked with the enemy. They had direct evidence of that. Garvin had been a priest of Castor, one of the enemy's gods. How many of those they had taken prisoner were that dark god's followers?

Still, despite all that, he understood the current solution was not a permanent one. It was only a short-term patch at best. He simply did not have the numbers to keep those they had just subjugated in check for long.

Should they kill all the men of fighting age? In a different time and place, had the legate ordered it, Karus would not have batted an eye. Now... he had doubts. Karus knew deep down he would not give such an order, unless he was forced to.

"My people kept slaves." Amarra's gaze had become distant. "The nurse who raised me was one. So were many of the palace servants. Until I found my god, I never gave it much thought. The priests of the High Father told me six out of ten in the city were slaves."

"It is much the same in the empire," Felix said.

"They…" Amarra continued as if she'd not heard the comment, "the priests… opened my eyes to suffering… such as I never imagined. I was shown how brutal life can be for those below my station." Her gaze swung to Flaccus. "The Kingdom of Carthum had mines, farms, workhouses, and brothels too…" Amarra took a breath that shuddered. "And yet… my father… in the end, taught me the greatest lesson of all. He showed me true cruelty, utter heartlessness… the monster within us all." Her tone hardened, gaze becoming piercing as she stared back at the centurion. "Flaccus, I am well aware of how awful life can be."

No one said anything to that. They all knew where she'd been found and who had put her there. Amarra openly bore ugly scars on her wrists and ankles. She never attempted to hide or conceal them. They were a mute testament of her own personal suffering… the weeks of imprisonment, manacled in the dungeon under the palace.

With just enough food to survive until the Horde arrived, she'd been left in complete darkness. Karus felt a stab of anger at what had been done to her. He knew her father, the man responsible, was still out there and wondered if they would ever cross paths. He hoped so… he really did.

"However," Amarra said to Karus, "I find this arrangement acceptable… as a temporary solution. There is a price to be paid, and for these people… this is it."

"Temporary?" Karus asked.

"As you said, Karus," Amarra said, "they should be allowed to earn back their freedom, to redeem themselves… to be forgiven. I expect you to see that such an opportunity is provided...for at some point, we must all work to make a better world."

"A better world?" Flaccus's eyes narrowed as he considered her words. "A Roman world would suit me just fine, mistress."

"Would it?" Amarra asked, locking gazes with the centurion. "Would it really?"

"They will be given an opportunity," Karus said, drawing Amarra's attention back to him before Flaccus could respond. "On that, you have my word. We can discuss how we can make that happen later. Right now, we need to deal with those who have refused to surrender and are holding out."

Amarra inclined her head in agreement, letting the matter drop.

"Has anyone else come across the wall within the last half hour, sir?" Felix asked the tribune. Though he was a youth and a junior tribune, no more than a glorified aide, Delvaris still technically outranked both centurions.

"No," Delvaris replied. "It seems anyone who was going to surrender has done so. The rest apparently want a fight."

"I agree," Flaccus said. "We've given them enough time. We can assume that anyone left is a holdout and has made the decision to resist."

"I would think so too." Felix looked over at Delvaris. "What information have you gathered from the prisoners on those who refused to come over? Anything useful?"

"There has been no time to aggressively question anyone," Delvaris said. "However, Amarra has been exceptionally helpful translating for those who were willing to talk." Delvaris studied the tablet for a long moment, clearly consulting his notes. "There is a tavern at the end of the street." He pointed at the map, which showed the district the refugees had settled in. It wasn't a very detailed drawing, but it was better than no map. The spot he was pointing at was where two of the three roads leading into the district came together. "About here is where the tavern is located. It is a two-story building." He looked up. "Our understanding is there are fifty to sixty men at the most holed up here. They plan on holding to the last man."

"Do they now?" Flaccus said, rubbing his chin as he gazed down at the map. "Do they really?"

Delvaris's expression turned sour. "Apparently, they've made a blood pact to spill as much Roman blood as possible."

"That's just what I want to hear," Flaccus said. "In that case, we will happily give them a helping hand at crossing over into the next life. They'll be the High Father's problem after that."

Amarra frowned slightly at Flaccus but said nothing.

"When the refugees gave up their defensive positions," Karus said, "and began surrendering en masse, I sent scouts over into the district." He pointed toward where the tavern was located. "They've located the building in question. It's not far, perhaps four hundred yards from this spot. After hearing their report, there is no doubt in my mind the position the holdouts have selected will be a tough nut to crack. There are only two doors into the building: a front that opens onto this street here, and one in the back that opens onto this street."

"Any idea on the thickness of the walls?" Felix asked. "How is the building made? Plaster and wood like most of the other structures in the city?"

"It's older," Karus said. "The building is brick construction, with an outer plaster coating. The scouts believe the thickness of the walls to be about a foot."

Felix whistled.

"A veritable fortress, then," Flaccus said.

"It seems that way," Karus said.

"Have you ever seen this tavern, mistress?" Si'Cara asked, looking over at Amarra.

"No," Amarra answered, flushing slightly at the suggestion. "This area was a portion of the city that was not the finest. My father would never have approved of me venturing down there." Amarra glanced around the seedy tavern they were in. "Not to mention here either."

Flaccus looked between Delvaris and Karus. "Is the building attached to another, like the warehouses in this area?"

"No," Delvaris said. "It's free standing. The nearest structure's an aqueduct. It is about fifteen feet distant."

"Windows?" Felix asked.

"None on the first floor," Delvaris answered, glancing down at the tablet again. "Four small windows, with wooden shutters, facing both main streets... enough to get a single man through. None along the side streets."

"Any idea if there is access from the roof?" Flaccus asked.

"No," Delvaris said. "We don't know if there is."

"Well, we've brought ladders with us for assaulting their defensive walls," Flaccus said. "I guess we can bring them along and try the roof... the windows too. We might even want to find some axes, in the event we get men onto the roof. They can chop their way through if need be and enter the building that way."

"However we do it," Karus said, "this is not gonna be pretty. Forcing the building may prove costly, especially if they are determined with no hope. I would like to limit our casualties, if possible."

"When we planned our assault on the district," Felix said, "we thought they might hole up somewhere. It's why we fashioned battering rams. We can use them on the doors of the tavern, knocking them in. While we're at it, men with bows and slings can provide cover for those working the rams, suppressing the windows."

After Amarra translated the last, Kol'Cara cleared his throat, drawing their attention.

"The Anagradoom might just prove helpful to you," Kol'Cara said. "We can put our bows to use and keep the windows clear."

Amarra translated the Common into Latin.

"Are your boys good?" Felix asked, with a skeptical look thrown at the elf.

"They're crack shots," Karus said, not waiting for Amarra to translate.

"All right," Felix said. "This is how I believe we should approach the assault on the building. We keep most of the men back and out of missile range. The rams go in, working to batter down the doors." He looked to Kol'Cara. "Your elves clear the windows, while our boys work the rams. Once we've forced the doors, we then start creating additional openings in the walls themselves, big enough for a man or two to enter at the same time. While we're doing that and fixing their attention, as Flaccus suggested, we send men up ladders to try the roof, from their blind spot in the alley. If there is access to the building from the roof, we begin funneling men in that way. When it comes to the ground level, once we have two additional openings into the building... we begin the assault proper. We use the rest of the ladders and try to force the windows, as well as the two doors and any openings in the wall we've managed to create. If possible, we hit everything simultaneously. That way, the enemy has multiple points to defend. Eventually, with enough pressure, we will see success somewhere and be able to overwhelm them."

"That sounds like as good a plan as any," Flaccus said, looking to Karus.

"I like it," Karus agreed. "We will do as Felix says." He paused and looked from Flaccus to Felix. "Make sure, as you advance up your respective streets, you clear each and every building along the way. I want no surprises or ambushes, and I certainly don't want any of the holdouts to escape. Especially their leaders. When it comes to the assault itself, let's do everything possible to limit our casualties, understand? In the coming days, we're gonna need every sword. They are bottled up and there's nowhere for them to go. We do this right."

"Yes, sir," Flaccus and Felix said in unison.

Karus did not say anything for a long moment as he gathered his thoughts. The next part would be difficult, perhaps more so personally than anything else.

"When I say right," Karus said, "I mean right. We won't put the lives of our men at risk to simply capture their leaders alive. If they choose to fight and are cut down, so be it. That is the end of it. If there is the potential to take Ord or Logex alive, without undue risk, I expect you to take that opportunity. Got that?"

"Understood, sir," Felix said after a slight hesitation. "They need to suffer for what they did, but our boys matter more at this point."

"They do matter more," Karus said, feeling an intense stab of anger at Logex and Ord. Both men should be made to suffer for what they had done. Unfortunately, the realist in Karus knew that was unlikely. They would most probably be cut down in the fight. He looked to Flaccus, who had not spoken. "And you?"

"I don't much like it," Flaccus said, "but I understand. We'll have to settle for their deaths and nothing more."

"Right then," Karus said, and glanced toward the open door that led out to the heavily shadowed street. "We have about an hour of light left." He turned to Delvaris. "I want you to remain and oversee the movement and settling of the prisoners."

"Yes, sir," Delvaris said.

Though he tried to conceal it, the tribune's disappointment was plain. Karus understood Delvaris's youthful need to prove himself. In the days to come, he was certain the tribune would be called to do just that. But today was not that day.

"I will see it done, sir," Delvaris said.

Pleased that Delvaris had not made a show by protesting his orders, Karus turned back to Flaccus and Felix. "I will see you both at the tavern. Now, let's get to it."

Felix and Flaccus came to attention and saluted. Karus returned their salute, and with that, the two senior officers left, heading for their commands.

"I will take my leave as well, sir," Delvaris said. He offered a salute, then also left.

Amarra watched the tribune go and then turned to Karus.

"I am coming with you." Amarra's gaze was firm. From her look, there would be no arguing. Si'Cara, with Kol'Cara by her side, looked on with a curious expression, as if wondering how he'd respond.

"I figured as much," Karus said, surrendering to the inevitable. Then he became concerned. "Is the High Father asking it of you?"

"No," Amarra said. "With Garvin dead, I feel as if the threat has passed, at least the spiritual one. You will still have to deal with those that come from the mundane world."

He wanted to tell her there was nothing mundane about this world she had been born to. It was filled with strange races and fantastical creatures. But he did not voice such thoughts.

"Just make sure you stay back and out of the way." Karus was worried she might not do as asked.

"Protecting me again, are you?" She was teasing him now, with a hint of a smile.

"I'm serious," Karus said, refusing the bait. "You're not a trained fighter. Promise me you will stay well back from the fighting. I have a difficult enough job ahead of me as it is. I do not need to be worrying about your safety."

"I will sit on her," Si'Cara said, with a strong look directed at Amarra, "if I need to. Karus, you have my word on that. The High Priestess has no business going into that tavern with your men making the attack."

Amarra turned an astonished gaze upon Si'Cara. "You would not dare!"

"I am your shield, your protector," Si'Cara said. "As Karus has said, you are untrained. I will do what I feel right to keep you safe, mistress. And that includes sitting on you."

"I would not doubt her resolve in this, mistress," Kol'Cara said. "My sister is strong-willed."

"Thank you." Karus gave Si'Cara a relieved look, then turned his gaze to Amarra expectantly. "I want your word, *mistress*."

"I will remain out of harm's way," Amarra breathed. "I am coming because I cannot bear to remain behind, to worry on your safety. I would rather be there than not."

"I can understand that." Karus felt a smile tug at his lips. He glanced toward the door, feeling the pressure to be off, for surely the assault would likely now be conducted by dusk and continue well on into the darkness. That would bring its own challenges. He looked back. "Let's get this wagon moving, shall we?"

As they emerged from his headquarters, Karus found the street heavily shadowed. The two suns had worked their way down toward the horizon and were no longer visible. The temperature had also begun to noticeably drop, cooling things off. That was a relief in and of itself.

Pammon was waiting with First Cohort, right where Karus had left them. The centurion had moved men up to the enemy's abandoned defensive wall and had taken it into the legion's keeping. The rest stood at ease, or sat on the ground, killing time as they waited for orders. A number glanced his way and knew action was in the offing. Several even stood.

Just outside the doorway, Ugin was waiting. With him were the Anagradoom and the century assigned to guard him. Karus thought it ludicrous so many should guard one. It was a waste of desperately needed manpower. In the days ahead, Karus knew he would not be able to spare even a single legionary to watch the Vass.

"Is it time?" Ugin asked as Pammon spotted him and jogged his way over. Karus waited for the centurion to join him.

"What is the word, sir?" Pammon saluted, an uncomfortable look going to the hulking Vass, who seemed more than annoyed that Karus had ignored him.

"There are about fifty men holed up in a tavern at the end of the street," Karus said and gestured in the direction of the barricade. "We will need the rams and ladders."

"Yes, sir," Pammon said.

Ugin issued a low growl. Karus knew he could not understand Latin.

"As we move up"—Karus pointed down the street at the nearest warehouse—"each building will need to be cleared … no surprises or anyone escaping. We will link up with the other two cohorts at the tavern and coordinate the assault from there." Karus glanced up at the sky, which had turned a bright, almost fiery red. Kordem was still up there, circling. He turned his gaze back to Pammon. "Do you have any questions?"

"No, sir," Pammon said.

"Daylight's burning," Karus said. "Get the men moving before we run out of light."

"Yes, sir." Pammon saluted and moved off, calling his centurions to him.

"I am looking forward to this fight," Ugin said, rubbing both hands together. "There are some that have the will to resist, yes? Tell me it is so." Ugin gestured toward the Anagradoom. "These elves say little. It is as if their tongues have been pulled out."

Karus turned to the Vass and studied him for several heartbeats. "I am not inclined to bring you with us."

"What?" Ugin fairly exploded, turning a number of heads with his outburst. Even though they could not understand the common tongue, it got his human guards' attention too. The Vass's gaze was intense, something akin to a predator eying prey he wanted to eat. "Why not? Why deny me this? I demand you explain yourself."

"Because," Karus said, refusing to back down, "I do not trust you. You will remain here until the assault is over or go back to your quarters in the palace. It is your choice."

"You should take me." Ugin's tone was filled with need, almost primal. "I could be useful."

"Why should I bother?" Karus asked him and pointed his finger at Ugin. "Would you want to go into a fight with someone you don't trust?"

Ugin was silent for a long moment. His jaw flexed and he gave a low growl. "I most certainly would not go into battle with someone I had no faith in."

"There," Karus said. "We can agree on something."

The Vass glanced toward the abandoned barricade as he scratched an itch upon his arm. He seemed to be wrestling internally with something. He looked back to Karus, gaze once again piercing.

"As long as I remain in this city," Ugin said, the words almost grating as they came out, "I give my word to fight as an ally at your side against your enemies. I will do your people no harm." Ugin paused for a long moment. "This is the least I can offer for the saving of my life. All I ask in return is to fight your enemies and mine." Ugin stopped speaking for a heartbeat, as if the next part were difficult. "Is this bargain acceptable to you?"

"Why do you want to fight on our behalf?" Karus wondered on Ugin's true motivations. "It's more than just paying me back for saving your life. Why do you want this so bad?"

"Our race enemies are here," Ugin said, gesturing toward the defensive wall, as if that explained everything.

Karus did not see how he could trust him. Ugin had already misled them once. If given the opportunity, there was no doubt in Karus's mind the Vass would do so again. Was he missing something here? No, Karus knew without a doubt he could not bring Ugin with them. It might even be dangerous to do so.

"You're going to have to settle for disappointment," Karus said.

Ugin's yellow eyes bulged, and his fists flexed as he took a menacing step forward. "I…"

"I believe," Kol'Cara said, hastily stepping forward and placing a hand between the two of them, "that such an offer will be more than acceptable. Don't you agree, Karus?"

Karus blinked, looking over at the elf in nothing short of shock. He was about to vehemently disagree, when Kol'Cara shot him a meaningful look and shook his head ever so slightly.

To their side, a few yards away, Pammon's officer meeting broke up. With centurions shouting orders, the men fell in. Two centuries began advancing toward the wall, while those on it started over to the other side. A century moved for the ladders and the rams, thick wooden poles with handholds nailed to them.

"You can come," Karus said grudgingly to Ugin.

"You seek to insult me?" Ugin demanded, becoming visibly heated again. The veins under his fur along his neck bulged and he took a half step forward toward Karus. "Is that it? Insults, human?"

"I don't understand," Karus said, becoming exasperated. He did not need this headache. He had enough problems on his plate. "You want to fight with us. I just said you could."

"Ugin," Kol'Cara said. "Karus is not of this world and does not understand the ways of the Vass. Until we rescued you, his people had not even heard of yours."

"Ah," Ugin said with sudden understanding. The Vass relaxed a fraction, though his anger and rage clearly simmered just below the surface. "He is ignorant, then."

Si'Cara seemed amused by the comment. Though she buried it well, Karus could read the merriment in her eyes.

"You must formally accept his offer of alliance," Kol'Cara said to Karus, "even if it's a temporary one at that. The Vass do not tolerate half measures. Your commitment to his proposal, or what you and he negotiated, must be complete and without reservation. Do you understand? This is very important to the Vass. They do not react well to people who go back upon their word."

"No, we do not," Ugin said, his yellow-eyed gaze fixed upon Karus.

"Very well," Karus said, feeling none too happy. "I accept your offer, fully and … without reservation."

"That pleases me greatly," Ugin said, looking toward the wall. He was clearly eager to be off. The Vass hesitated and eyed them balefully for a long moment. "If any of you ever tell my people of the terms of this arrangement, I will kill you. That is a promise."

Ugin stepped off in the direction of the wall. The Vass's guards, both human and elven, followed after him. Kol'Cara remained behind, as did Si'Cara. They both shared a look, then turned to gaze on Karus in what appeared to be awe.

"What?" Karus asked them, at a loss. "Tell me what just happened?"

"I believe you just negotiated a fine deal," Kol'Cara said, his gaze following after Ugin. "A very equitable deal, indeed."

"I negotiated nothing," Karus said and gestured at the Vass's back. "I didn't want him to come and I still don't. Now I have no choice."

"That's what made it so effective," Si'Cara said and grinned at him with her needle-like teeth.

Karus scowled, turning his gaze in the direction of Ugin, who was already at the ramshackle wall. Most of the men of First Cohort were climbing over it, with several atop the wall. They reached back to help their comrades up. Ladders were also being passed up.

"Why is this so important?" Karus asked, wondering why they were making such a big deal of it. "Ugin's guard is a complete waste of manpower and the Horde is almost on our doorstep. It would be better to just give him the boot from the city and be done with him."

"No," Si'Cara said, "it wouldn't."

"Doing so," Kol'Cara said, "might cause future problems."

"I don't understand," Karus said, becoming impatient. He glanced over at Amarra. She too looked mystified.

"You wanted to form a coalition of races," Si'Cara said. "Well... he just allied with you."

"I'd hardly call that an alliance," Karus said. "He's only one individual and it's good for as long as we're in the city. Once we leave, if I understand the arrangement correctly, it's done, finished."

"It is a start," Si'Cara said.

"The Horde is coming," Kol'Cara said. "And, though you have not come out and said it, I am thinking we may not be leaving Carthum anytime soon. The walls of the city are just too good to give up. Am I incorrect in my understanding?"

"No," Karus said, "you're spot on, but I've not made that decision yet. We will see what happens when the dwarves get here."

"And Ugin just pledged himself to fight alongside you," Kol'Cara said.

"And he has no idea the Horde is coming," Si'Cara added, with a sudden laugh as she turned her grin on her brother. "No one told him."

"He's just one person," Karus said.

"But he's a Vass," Si'Cara breathed, "and we both think an important one at that. For some strange reason, he seems to respect you enough to take a one-sided deal. I am thinking, if you befriend him, there is the chance that something may grow from it."

Karus resisted a scowl as he glanced at Ugin, who was now atop the wall and gazing down the street. Make Ugin a friend ... a tiger-man? For some reason, Karus thought that unlikely. He pinched the bridge of his nose. Elves, dwarves, goblins, gnomes, orcs, dragons, and now the Vass ... life had become strange indeed.

"You think I got a good deal?" Karus asked ... for he wasn't quite so sure. Ugin was clearly getting something out of the arrangement too. Of that, Karus was certain.

"The best I've ever heard of," Kol'Cara said. "You gave him nothing in return, other than allowing him to fight with your people."

"That's what worries me," Karus said. "I can't help but feel he has motivations other than killing race enemies or fighting with us."

Kol'Cara grew grave and turned his gaze in the direction Ugin had gone. The elf rubbed his jaw speculatively and turned back to Karus. "We will just have to find out what that is, then."

Yep, Karus thought. Ugin was up to something.

Chapter Fourteen

There was a deep *thud* as the battering ram hammered against the tavern's door.

"Again," Centurion Leves roared. "Come on, boys, swing like you mean it."

Grunting with effort, the team of legionaries swung the ram again. It thudded powerfully against the door.

The tavern was a squat, solid, and uninspiring building with a flat roof. As the scouts had said, it was of brick construction. The brick had been plastered over for insulation and then painted. The paint had long since faded to a ghost of what it had once been. Graffiti had been chalked seemingly everywhere within arm's reach.

Large cracks were running through the plaster and it was badly in need of being scraped off and removed. In places, chunks had fallen off or entirely disintegrated, leaving the brick and mortar exposed to the elements.

In the growing darkness, the building was not just uninspiring, it was downright depressing. At least that was what Karus thought as he looked it over once again. Yet, no matter how deteriorated the outer shell appeared, the tavern was no less a fortress than had been described. A strong, determined force defending it would have a serious advantage. Karus understood it would prove a difficult nut to crack and he was bound to lose men in the doing of it.

Several torches had been set for light around the small square before the tavern. With the bulk of First Cohort formed up in ranks behind him, Karus stood about thirty feet from its main entrance and next to a public fountain that had long since stopped flowing. The basin was a simple square pool, five feet by five. It was filled with years of dirt and decay and had clearly stopped functioning long before the city was abandoned.

The fountain itself was a simple block of marble, four feet in height, with a lead pipe sticking out of it. Eight shields had been leaned against the basin's walls.

The men to whom those shields belonged had formed the battering ram team. In the dying light, Centurion Leves stood next to them and began calling out a steady cadence, to which they repeatedly swung the ram, smashing at the door. The rest of the century stood a short distance away, ready with their shields to provide protection should any attack from the windows above materialize.

Each hammer blow made a dull thudding sound as the ram was driven into the stout wood. Despite the degraded look of the building itself, the door seemed solid and well-built. Karus suspected it had been replaced in the last few years and, with the way it was holding up, had possibly even been reinforced too. That spoke directly to the type of people who had once called this seedy district their home.

There was no doubt those inside were doing their best to brace the door as well. This was making the job of the ram party that much more difficult. But that was only to be expected.

The windows on the second floor were, for the most part, empty and dark. A dim flickering light, likely from a candle, glowed from within one. The rest of the windows had not been empty when the attack had begun. The enemy had initially attempted to use the windows to drop rocks and throw burning oil down on the men working at battering away at the doors. The elves had rapidly put a stop to such efforts, almost before the defenders could even get started.

Several of the Anagradoom were positioned both in and atop the adjacent buildings, the closest of which was about twenty feet away. One had even somehow scaled the aqueduct, a towering, arched stone structure that ran over the buildings in this district. Karus's eyes were drawn to the aqueduct, which was at least sixty feet in height.

He spotted the elf perched at the top, a dark, kneeling figure with a bow at the ready, just waiting for a target to show himself. The position allowed the elf to shoot down into the building and at an angle too. Karus would not have wanted to attempt such a climb.

When the assault on the door had begun, the deadly hail of missiles had seen the enemy retreat from the windows and extinguish most of the light. Occasionally, a bow twanged and an arrow would shoot into one of the darkened windows. More often than not, a cry would shortly follow.

Elven eyesight was clearly superior. To Karus, the interior of the building was dark, nearly impenetrable, and inscrutable as could be. He could not even see what they were shooting at. But for the occasional shot and subsequent screams, he would have doubted they were shooting at anything of substance.

Standing with Karus were Ugin and Kol'Cara. Like him, they were watching the ram team steadily batter at the door. In between blows, Karus could occasionally hear the hammering from the ram on the other side of the building as Felix's men worked.

"Your humans," Ugin said, breaking the silence that had grown between them, "er…I think you call them men. Yes, that is it. Your men seem practiced."

"They are well-trained, drilled, and disciplined," Karus said, "if that is what you mean. My men are professional soldiers, second to none. Many will serve the best part of their lives in the legion."

Ugin ran his gaze back along First Century behind them. He was silent for a long moment as he studied the ranks of men before turning back to Karus. In the growing darkness, his yellow eyes reflected the torchlight.

"I will admit," Ugin said, "before this day, I had not seen professional human soldiers. I've only ever encountered conscripts or levies."

"My legion is but one amongst many," Karus said. "Our empire is vast, almost beyond reckoning. We have abundant resources to maintain and support numerous professional armies, such as the one I command."

"I see." Ugin's manner was thoughtful. "Your people have fought many wars, then?"

"Yes," Karus said. "We control most of the known lands on my world, the ones that matter, at any rate."

"Impressive," Ugin said, then gestured toward the tavern. "What did they do to you?"

Karus felt a stab of anger, not at Ugin, but toward Logex, Ord, and the rest of the bastards holding out. He should not be having to deal with this headache. Their actions had forced his hand, and that pissed him off.

"We took them in," Karus said, waving a hand at the tavern. Inside he could hear muffled shouting that sounded like encouragements and someone repeatedly crying in apparent agony. "Their people had been driven out of their lands by the Horde." Karus fell silent for a long moment. "We gave them a place amongst us."

"They turned on you, didn't they?" Ugin's face twisted with what Karus assumed was distaste or perhaps even disgust. "They went back on their word?"

"That's right," Karus said, glancing over. "And now they will pay the price for that."

"My people have a saying," Ugin said. "No good deed goes unrewarded."

"There is much truth in that statement." Karus absorbed that. "So, you trust no one?"

"It is not about trust, but faith…faith in the deals we make and who we negotiate with outside of our own kind. Violate that and we have long memories. Still, we are always…let us say, cautious in any dealing."

Karus did not reply as he thought about the mess he found himself in.

Ugin looked over at him. "Tell me more about what happened."

"We offered them shelter and a chance for safety," Karus said. "In return they were to form a fighting unit under our command. Instead, while I was away, they broke their agreement and murdered some of my people."

"Murdered?" Ugin gave off a low growl as he turned his attention to the tavern. "Did they have cause to do that?"

"No," Karus said, "at least not in my mind. There was a sickness amongst my people. It's gone now. Theirs were completely unaffected. They used it as an excuse and killed some of my boys, including one of my senior officers…a friend."

Ugin was silent for a long moment. "What was his name?"

"Dio."

"How did he die?" Ugin asked, seeming almost hesitant.

Karus did not say anything as the thought of what had been done to Dio struck home again. The pain tore at him.

"If I am to fight at your side," Ugin said, in a tone that was surprisingly soft with feeling, "I would like to know. How did they kill your friend?"

"I was not here when it happened," Karus said, the words coming out in an almost grating manner. "I am told he went to talk and reason with them, to reconsider their actions. They had other ideas and seized him along with his escort. They made demands. When the demands were not met, they slit his throat, along with those of his escort... good boys all."

"Bah," Ugin said, in an irritated tone. "That is no way for a warrior to go."

"He deserved better," Karus said, "but sometimes deserves have nothing to do with it."

"There is no reasoning with such people," Ugin said. "It is always the way with those lacking honor. You do not know what lies in their hearts until they choose to reveal the blackness."

"It was my decision to welcome them." Karus felt a wave of guilt wash over him.

"That does not mean the fault lies completely with you." Ugin gestured toward the tavern. "They bear responsibility as well."

"I am in command," Karus said in a hard tone. "Ultimately, I shoulder that burden."

"That is true." Ugin's eyes narrowed as he considered Karus in the torchlight. "It is as you say, a true leader accepts the burden that comes with command. Doing so shows great heart and develops a sacred trust with your men."

Karus said nothing to that and wondered what kind of a leader Ugin was... for their conversation made him nearly certain the Vass was no common foot soldier. They were silent for a few moments, while Karus's men continued to work on the door. Kol'Cara had said nothing. Karus had the feeling the elf was following their conversation with interest.

"And now," Ugin said after a time, "you will make them, as you say... pay."

"Yes," Karus said through a clenched jaw. "Their leaders are in there, two men, Ord and Logex. They, along with everyone in that tavern, will die this night."

Ugin gave off another growl, his gaze turning toward the tavern. "Ord and Logex... Ord and Logex... you are delivering justice for injustice. There is no finer path to walk. We Vass would do the same, have done the same."

"Sir." A legionary stepped up and came to attention. He saluted.

Karus returned the salute and switched to Latin. "Report."

"Centurion Flaccus reports the ladders in the alleys are up and he's got men on the roof," the legionary said. "There is no roof access. They will begin cutting their way in shortly."

"Very good," Karus said. "Kindly return to Centurion Flaccus and thank him for his report."

"Yes, sir." The legionary saluted, spun, and left, heading back the way he'd come.

"What is it you really want?" Karus asked, switching back to the common tongue and looking over at Ugin. Kol'Cara turned his gaze to the Vass as well, his eyes glittering in the torchlight. "You don't need to fight with us. You don't need to be here. So, I ask you, Ugin... what is it you really want?"

Ugin gave Karus a silent look. "I gave you my reasons."

"Did you?" Karus asked.

"I doubt it," Kol'Cara scoffed, speaking up for the first time. "I seriously doubt that, Vass."

Ugin shot the elf an unhappy look.

Karus decided to push when Ugin did not immediately reply. "Are you being completely honest… honorable even? Why were you on that hill where we found you? I can't help but think it is related to your desire to fight with us, to be here in this city. What is it you are after?"

Ugin blew out a breath that sounded like a hiss as he regarded Karus for several heartbeats, as if weighing what he would say. Finally, he spoke.

"We are searching for something that has been taken from us, stolen," Ugin said, "by someone… who had entered into an arrangement with a brother of my pride. It is a matter of… honor to me and my people."

"You did not find him?" Karus said. "Or it?"

"No," Ugin said, sounding unhappy, his gaze traveling back toward the tavern. "Not yet. We are still searching."

"We?" Kol'Cara asked, cocking his head to the side in a way no human could match.

"*I*"—Ugin corrected himself—"I will keep searching. You saw my brothers on the hill… I will keep looking… until I get that which I want and am entitled to."

Ugin scratched at the fur on his check as he looked toward the tavern. He seemed to be considering something. He turned his gaze back to Karus, clearly on the verge of saying more.

A loud splintering crack drew their attention. The door to the tavern had completely caved in, coming off the hinges and falling to pieces.

Several men had been standing behind the door, clearly attempting to brace it with planks of wood. Two had tumbled to the ground when the door had given way.

As the men with the ram stepped to the side and set it down, Kol'Cara's bow sprang to hand, arrow nocked. He released. The arrow hissed away, smacking into the chest of a man framed in the doorway by the tavern's interior light. He stumbled back and out of sight. A second arrow rapidly followed the first, hammering into the forehead of one of those on the ground as he sat up. The arrow's impact made a cracking sound.

The other man who had been knocked down hastily rolled out of the way as Kol'Cara sent a third arrow hissing into the tavern. It landed where he had just been, arrowhead driving into the wood floor. After that, the rest of the enemy that could be seen quickly stepped out of view.

"Nice work," Ugin said to Kol'Cara. "Very nice work, elf."

Kol'Cara did not reply. His gaze was still fixed on the doorway, an arrow nocked, bow ready.

Ugin drew his massive sword, the blade hissing as it came free from the sheath.

"Where do you think you're going?" Karus asked idly, without looking over. His attention, like the elf's, was still fixed on the tavern. Once the door on the other side was knocked down and a few more holes made, the main assault would start and the real killing would begin.

"I am going to work," Ugin said in a determined tone.

That had not been the response he had been expecting. Karus glanced over and was startled. Ugin was gone. He looked around, wondering where the big Vass had went. Karus could not see him anywhere. It was as if he had just vanished into thin air.

"Where'd he go?" Karus asked, looking over at Kol'Cara.

Eyes narrowed, Kol'Cara was staring toward the doorway into the tavern. After several heartbeats, he pointed. "There he is."

"I don't see him..." Karus trailed off. There was a slight shimmering of the air before the light of the doorway and the hint of an outline of a sword, as well as the Vass himself. It was almost impossible to see him, but he was there, Karus was sure of it. "He can turn invisible?"

"Not completely, no," Kol'Cara said. "Not to elven eyes at any rate. Human eyesight is different, poorer. And he can only maintain it for a short time, maybe a count of thirty at most."

"And you did not think to tell me?" Karus asked.

"It is why we kept such a close watch on him," Kol'Cara said. "I did not want him to slip away. Besides, you had a lot to worry about."

"What about now?" Karus fairly exploded as the distorted air entered the tavern. "Who's watching him now?"

Ugin shimmered into existence just inside the doorframe. His great sword was already swinging toward an unseen enemy. He landed his strike and blood sprayed through the air. The Vass roared like a hungry tiger before he moved deeper into the tavern and was lost from view.

Kol'Cara stepped over to the fountain and leaned his bow against the basin, along with his bundle of arrows. Inside the tavern came the sound of screaming mixed with animalistic roars that set small hairs on the back of Karus's neck on end. The elf drew his sword, an elegant blade that seemed almost too ornate to be practical. Etched runes ran along its length. The blade glinted with torchlight.

"You must be joking," Karus said and gestured toward the tavern. "There are nearly fifty men in there."

"We can't let him fight by himself. It would not be honorable. And you said it yourself, someone has to watch the Vass." Kol'Cara started forward.

Karus felt a wave of intense rage wash over him at Ugin's senseless and thoughtless act. The assault was supposed to be simultaneous, coordinated. He looked around. Pammon was standing with Amarra, Si'Cara, and Tal'Thor.

"Pammon!" Karus shouted to get the centurion's attention. "Send your men in ... right now."

"Yes, sir," Pammon said.

"And get word to Flaccus and Felix," Karus called. "Tell them we've gone in and to get their asses moving. Got that?"

"Yes, sir," Pammon said.

Karus stepped over to the fountain, where the shields of the ram party had been stacked. He grabbed one at random, then drew his sword. He hefted the shield into place and started forward toward the tavern's entrance.

"Karus!" Pammon shouted, clearly alarmed. "What are you doing?"

"Karus!" Amarra called to him, her tone just as alarmed.

He ignored them both and continued up to the door and past the ram party, who were recovering from their efforts. Centurion Leves shot Karus a concerned look and then he was by. Tal'Thor appeared at his side, as did Aven'Terol. Both had their blades drawn. It was clear they had no intention of stopping him. They were grim-faced and determined to go with him into battle. Karus had enough time to give them each a nod of thanks and then he stepped through the doorway and into the tavern.

The common room was lit by several lanterns that hung from the walls and ceiling. The bottom floor of the tavern was one big room with a large fireplace along the back wall that served for heat and cooking. A narrow, steep staircase ran up the left wall to the second floor.

The room was a scene of chaos. Several bodies lay on the floor by the door. One with an arrow and another with a gruesome wound to the chest writhed in agony at his feet. Karus paid them no mind, but he did kick a sword away from the one with the arrow wound.

The room was filled with men and an enraged Vass. It seemed as if everyone was screaming or yelling. Ugin repeatedly swung his massive sword, almost impossibly fast and with terrible force too. It was like he was scything his way through the enemy. Some of the defenders drew back fearfully, while others grimly threw themselves forward and into the attack.

Just behind Ugin, four feet away from Karus, was Kol'Cara. The elf was deftly trading blows with two men. Karus was about to move to help him, when a man came barreling down the stairs to his left. Karus turned, took two steps forward and, putting his shoulder into the move, hammered his shield into the man's body before he could even attempt to slow himself.

The man crashed hard against Karus's shield. The impact landed painfully on his arm and shoulder, which took a good portion of the impact. However painful the blow, Karus knew the man on the receiving end got the worst of it. The air whuffed out of the man's lungs as he bounced off the shield and back onto the stairs, where his head cracked audibly against a step. The sword the man had been holding went clattering past Karus and to the floor.

Recovering, Karus looked over the top of his shield and saw the man he'd hit sprawled on the stairs before him, still and unmoving. Farther up the stairs, another man, this one in leather armor with a sword drawn, had stopped. He eyed Karus coldly for a long moment before continuing down.

It was Ord.

Behind Karus, the clash of steel rang on the air as Tal'Thor and the other elf joined the fight.

"Come on, you bastard!" Karus shouted in Common to Ord.

"Screw you," Ord snarled, still working his way cautiously down the steep staircase, one step at a time.

"I am going to gut you like a fish, you slimy bastard." Holding his shield before him, Karus started up the stairs to meet his enemy. Ord hesitated, and unexpectedly seemed to suddenly lose his resolve to face Karus. He turned and fled back up to the second floor, almost running up the steps, which he took two at a time. Karus continued his steady advance up the stairs. With the windows covered and the tavern surrounded, there was nowhere for Ord to go. Escape was impossible.

Just before he reached the landing at the top of the stairs, a man appeared. Ord gave the man a violent shove. Wearing a chest plate and helm, he made a loud clatter as he tumbled down the stairs toward Karus. Karus dodged to the side, so he wasn't knocked back down the staircase.

As he was about to tumble by, Karus slammed the man into the wall with his shield and pinned him there. It took more effort than he had thought, but Karus did it. He jabbed before his opponent could recover, stabbing the man under his chest plate and down in the bowels. Karus pushed the sword deep, until he felt the inside of the man's hipbone grate against the tip of the sword. Karus gave a savage twist and yanked the blade out, pulling the man's severed intestines with it. Releasing the mortally wounded man, Karus allowed him to slowly tumble the rest of the way down the stairs.

Turning, he looked up toward the landing. Ord was gone. In his place, two determined men waited at the top. One had a sword and the other a dagger. Just as Karus registered the dagger, the man flicked his wrist and threw, aiming for

Karus's head. It was a smooth, well-practiced motion. Karus just barely managed to bring his shield up in time and felt the dagger thud home. The point emerged from the back side of the shield, a half inch from his forearm.

Lowering the shield, Karus continued his advance up the stairs to meet the two men. The one who had thrown the dagger stepped back and away, while the other lunged downward with his sword. Karus deflected the blade to the left and used the side of his shield to pin the man's sword against the wall. At the same time, he stabbed over the top the shield and into the neck of his opponent. The blade ripped the throat open to the bone. A torrent of blood sprayed outward at him. Karus blinked, momentarily blinded, as blood shot into his eyes. He tasted the strong copper tang of it in his mouth.

His opponent fell backward, landing hard, before thrashing and kicking out his last. Karus sensed movement behind and glanced back. Tal'Thor was making his way up the stairs. Aven'Terol had clearly gone to help Ugin and Kol'Cara. Behind Tal'Thor and shouting as they came, legionaries from First Cohort began pouring through the door.

Pleased he wasn't alone, Karus stepped over the man he'd just killed and onto the landing, were he was greeted by an empty hallway. It was not what he had expected. Karus paused, scanning the way ahead. Two grime-covered glass lanterns mounted on the walls by hooks provided a dim light, barely enough to see. From the stairs, the hallway was fifteen feet in length. Karus counted four doors on either side.

"Great," Karus said, for he hated clearing rooms. In his experience, doing so was extremely hazardous.

"They don't seem to want to come out," Tal'Thor said quietly behind him. The elf's voice was barely above a whisper. "We may have to go in after them."

"You think?" Karus glanced back at the elf. Tal'Thor was grinning and seemed as if he were enjoying himself. Shaking his head, Karus took a step forward.

Above, there was the sudden sound of chopping. Dust drifted down from the ceiling. Flaccus's boys were at work, cutting their way through the roof. The fight down in the common room was continuing to rage. Shouts, screams, roars from Ugin, and the harsh clash of steel drifted up the stairs to them.

Tightening his grip on his sword, Karus started down the hallway. The first door to his left was slightly ajar. Using his shield, Karus pushed it open. The room was dark, silent, and small. Nothing stirred. Light from the nearest lamp in the hall showed him it was empty. There was a rope bed without a mattress and some broken furniture… nowhere for someone to hide.

The door to his right burst open. Karus spun as the man who had thrown the dagger at him came charging out, sword raised and screaming a war cry. Tal'Thor was there, his sword moving impossibly fast. Karus's attacker never saw the blade coming, as it landed and bit deeply into his neck with a sickening sound.

Karus twisted aside and out of the way. The attacker's momentum carried him bodily by and into the room that Karus had just been peering into. Before his attacker even hit the floor, he was dead, his head nearly severed from his body.

Once again, blood and gore had sprayed over Karus. With the back of his sword arm, he wiped what he could out of his eyes. Karus found his heart racing as he gazed down at the body. He took a deep breath and let it out slowly, realizing just how close to death he had come.

"I guess you could say," Tal'Thor said, glancing into the room over Karus's shoulder, "he just about lost his head."

"Elf humor?" Karus asked as he turned his gaze down the hallway. He pointed with his sword. "Ord will be in one of the rooms ahead."

"Let us go find him, then," Tal'Thor said. "It's rude for us to keep him waiting. Perhaps the better word is inconsiderate."

"Right." Hefting his shield, Karus moved down the hallway to the next set of doors. Both had been left open. He peeked first into the room on the left. It was empty. On the right side of the hallway, two bodies lay on the floor. They had clearly been shot from the window, each having taken an arrow to the chest. A third man, no more than a boy barely into his teens, was injured and lying on a bed.

He'd also taken an arrow to the chest. The missile had gone clean through and he was struggling to breathe, spitting up blood with each agonized breath. The wheezing of his lungs was a pathetic sound that Karus had heard too many times before. The boy would likely not last an hour.

Anger once again surged in Karus's breast. The dying boy potentially represented the loss of a good soldier…or really the loss of potential…what could have been. Ord, Logex, and Garvin had seen to that. They had led their people to disaster.

"Such a bloody waste," Karus breathed.

"Indeed." Tal'Thor slipped past Karus and into the room. Without hesitation, the elf cut the boy's throat, sawing it open with his sword, nearly to the bone. The youth, eyes going wide, kicked violently as it was done. He gagged as he drowned on his own blood, then went still, eyes fixed and staring in horror at his killer.

Looking grim, the elf returned to Karus's side.

"We elves mourn and detest death," Tal'Thor said, "but that does not mean one should be allowed to needlessly suffer."

"This is a grim business we're in." Karus turned his gaze back down the hall and proceeded to the next set of doors. The door on the left was ajar. Using the point of his sword, he pushed it open. The hinges creaked loudly, almost painfully so.

Empty.

He turned to the door on the right and tried the latch, lifting it. The door was locked from the inside.

Karus glanced down to the last set of doors. In the dim light, he couldn't tell if they were open or closed. He knew there were likely men hiding, waiting to pounce—at least Ord was. He could not proceed until he was sure the locked room was clear. He turned and gave the door a mighty kick. The lock gave and snapped.

The door crashed open. Inside were two men. One was Ord, who immediately launched himself at Karus with a sword, stabbing out and shouting as he came.

Bringing his shield up, Karus easily blocked the man's first strike, which was almost clumsy. Ord's sword cracked against the shield. The blow hurt, the pain radiating up the back side of his forearm, where it rested against the shield. Karus took a step back to gain space and room to fight. He wanted to draw Ord out into the hallway, where there was more room. As he did, two more men emerged from a room at the end of the hall and started for him.

Before they could advance, Karus leaned forward and jabbed a strike at Ord, who had lunged out into the hall for another try at Karus. The tip of Karus's blade stabbed deeply into Ord's hip. Dropping his sword and gripping his damaged hip, Ord cried out and hobbled back into the room.

The men at the end of the hall charged. Karus turned to face them, bringing his shield around and up as he retreated two steps back. Thankfully, the hallway was not large enough for two to fight abreast.

There was just enough room for one, and Karus had a shield. This was his kind of fighting, straightforward and far from fair. There was nothing deadlier than a trained legionary armed with a shield and short sword. He settled into a combat stance, braced himself, and allowed the first man to close. The second was fast on the first's heels.

Thunk.

Ignoring the pain from the strike against his shield, Karus immediately shoved back, taking three quick steps forward and pushing with all his strength. The move was unexpected. Both attackers were close to one another ... too close. With one's momentum going backward and the other forward, they crashed together. Karus gave another powerful shove and both men went down in a tumble of arms and legs.

Pulling his shield aside, he jabbed, stabbing down, taking one squarely in the stomach. He stabbed again for good measure, feeling his blade go deep and through to the floor below, where the point impacted with the wood planking. Mouth open in a silent scream, the mortally wounded man curled up on Karus's blade, gripping it with bloody hands. Karus yanked back, severing fingers as his sword came free. The injured man choked in intense agony, rolled onto his side in a fetal position, and vomited blood onto the floor.

The second attacker had lost his sword and was scooting backward on his butt, attempting to get away. Karus advanced, stepping over his first victim. He jabbed, stabbing the man in the leg before he could scoot farther away and get his feet under him. Wounded, the man cried out as the blade pierced his thigh.

"No," the man screamed in Common. "Please. I want to live."

Ignoring the pleading, Karus drove a second jab into his neck. The man collapsed, dead, his personal story ended on the second floor of a seedy tavern in an abandoned city. Karus felt no regrets about that. He, like the others in this tavern, had earned his fate.

Behind, Tal'Thor finished the first man off.

"A grim business, indeed," Tal'Thor said.

Before Karus could respond, the man who had been in the room with Ord emerged and launched a furious assault, hammering the shield repeatedly with sword strikes. Flecks flew into the air with each strike against the shield. So furious was the assault, that Karus retreated a step. The man came on, moving with him. Stepping carefully back, Karus allowed his attacker to step over the body of the man he had just killed. Once he had, Karus stopped retreating and pushed forward with his shield. So caught up in the attack was his new opponent that he was thrown off balance and he tripped over the body, falling onto his back. Karus pounced on him, stabbing down and into his collar, just above the armor breastplate he wore. A second stab, this one deeper, ended the man's life too.

"That was a little spirited." Karus was breathing heavily. He glanced back at Tal'Thor, who gave him an encouraging nod. Karus once again moved forward and stepped into the room Ord had retreated back into.

He found Ord sitting on the floor, leaning his back against the wall, which was badly stained and in need of painting. Blood formed a growing pool around him. He held a hand to his damaged hip. Face pale, he grimaced in pain as he looked up at Karus.

"You've killed me," Ord said through gritted teeth. "You've killed me, you bastard."

"Where's Logex?" Karus asked. "Tell me and I will make your death quick."

"Piss off," Ord spat. "I'm already dead. It's just a matter of when, now."

Karus glanced back toward the door. Tal'Thor was there, keeping watch. Sounds of the fight below could still be heard as it raged unabated. Overhead, with a crunch, an axe broke through. Karus looked up as part of the ceiling was ripped away and chunks of dislodged roofing tile fell to the floor. In the near darkness, Karus could see someone gazing down into the room from above, but not who.

"Karus," Flaccus called down. "Is that you?"

"Took your bloody time," Karus said and turned his attention back to Ord. He felt an intense stab of anger bubble up. "I gave you a chance and now you will pay."

"You gave us a chance to be your lapdogs." Ord spat bloody spittle at Karus's feet and then groaned in pain. "My people are proud, free, subject to no one."

"Proud they may be," Karus said, "but now you have led them into slavery. Take that thought with you into the next life."

"Get on with it," Ord spat, "and stop wasting my time."

Give him to me, the sword hissed. *He will suffer beyond imagining. Let me take his soul.*

Karus felt his anger toward Ord surge to new levels. The sword burst into flame, blue tongues of fire licking at the air. Karus's loathing for this man was strong. Ord's eyes went wide, and he attempted to draw back, clearly afraid. Needing no further encouragement, Karus stabbed the man in the chest, thrusting hard. The sword went in, as easily as if he were stabbing a sack of hay on the training ground. There was a sizzling sound and the sword hilt grew warm in his hand.

Ord's eyes went dull as the light of life faded from his gaze. His head slumped to the side and he gave a soft sigh as the last gasp of life escaped. Karus drew the blade back. Incredibly, Ord's blood boiled off the burning steel blade. When all the blood was gone, Karus turned his gaze back to the dead man and somehow felt unfulfilled.

The rage slackened. Killing Ord had not made up for Dio's loss. He knew it never would. Till his dying day, Dio's death would be an open wound.

"That is a dread weapon," Tal'Thor said quietly. "Use Rarokan with care, for should you grow too fond of the sword, something terrible may come of it."

"Terrible?" Karus gazed down at the burning sword. There was no reply from the sword. Karus looked to the doorway, but Tal'Thor had already turned and left the room. He was moving down the hall, clearly intent on checking the last two rooms.

"Karus," Flaccus said from above, his head poking through the hole, which had been widened. "Is that Ord?"

"It is," Karus said, glancing down at the body.

"Serves the bastard right," Flaccus said, then eyed Karus's burning sword. "How did you get it to do that?"

Karus did not feel like answering. "Get down here with your men. The fight's not over yet."

"Yes, sir," Flaccus said, pulling his head back. "You men, widen that hole more."

Stepping back out into the hallway, Karus saw that Tal'Thor had finished checking the last two rooms.

"There's no one else," the elf said.

"Logex must be downstairs in the main fight," Karus said and headed back the way they had come, stepping over and around bodies. The wood planking in the hallway was slick with blood and gore. He made sure to step carefully so as to not slip. This was more difficult than it sounded, for his sandals and feet were thoroughly wet. In truth, Karus felt like he had bathed in his opponents' blood, for he was literally covered by it and it was not a comfortable feeling.

When he got to the bottom step of the stairs, he found the fight below petering out. The common room was filled with legionaries. Bodies lay all around. At the center of it was Ugin. The Vass's fur was drenched in blood. When the last man went down, a heartbeat after Karus emerged from the stairs, Ugin leaned his head back and gave a mighty roar of exultation.

Sheathing his sword, Karus scanned the room. Incredibly, he saw only two legionaries down and injured. One had a cut on his forearm and another a stab wound to the leg, which he held with both hands as he rocked on the floor and moaned. Karus had expected their casualties to be far greater and immediately felt a vast wave of relief.

"Pammon," Karus snapped, spotting the centurion. "Get the wounded help. Ord is upstairs. He's dead. Find Logex. He must be down here."

"Yes, sir," Pammon said and turned to two legionaries. "You two, help the wounded to the surgeon."

The two men started forward as Pammon began moving about the room, searching amongst the dead and injured for Logex.

"What?" Karus asked Ugin when he noticed the Vass looking his way. The Vass's gaze was intense, almost suspicious.

"You were upstairs?" Ugin asked him. It sounded more like a statement than a question.

"They're all dead up there," Karus said, "no more for you to kill."

Ugin scowled slightly, then made for the stairs, roughly pushing aside two legionaries who had just made their way down from the roof. Karus wondered why the Vass bothered, but then put it from his mind. He wanted Logex and began checking the wounded and dead. He rolled one man over halfway that he thought had the same build, but was disappointed.

Straightening, Karus glanced around the room. Something was not quite right. The number of holdouts seemed considerably less than the intelligence indicated. He saw no more than twenty refugees.

"He's not here, sir," Pammon said, after a quick search. "The bastard's got away."

Karus felt the intense sting of anger that Logex had somehow escaped.

"He's probably out in the city, sir," Pammon said. "He must have somehow gotten through our cordon."

There was a growl at the stairs. Ugin had come back down. Behind him was Flaccus. The Vass seemed enraged that there were no more to fight.

"Sir," a legionary called for Karus's attention, "over here. Look at this."

A ratty rug was lying near the fireplace. The legionary had pulled it aside, exposing a trap door that had been cut into the wood planking. Pammon stepped forward and pulled a metal ring affixed to the door. With effort, he swung it open, the rusted hinges protesting loudly.

Darkness greeted them, as did a flow of cold air that rushed up and into the room, along with the smell of mold and dust. Karus grabbed a lantern from its hook on the wall and brought it over, shining the light downward. He had expected perhaps a basement.

"A bloody tunnel," Karus said, gazing down into the hole. He could see it was wide enough for a single man and appeared old, ancient even.

"This city seems full of tunnels," Flaccus said. "Everywhere we turn there is a tunnel."

"Was Rome any different?" Pammon said as he straightened.

"We're close to the city wall." Flaccus squatted next to the tunnel entrance and peered into it. "The tunnel moves off in that direction … toward the wall. If I had to guess, this tunnel is likely for smuggling things in or out of the city."

With a sinking feeling in the pit of his stomach, Karus gave a nod. Logex had most certainly escaped. Bloody gods! The man had gotten away.

"You won't find them," a wounded holdout laughed. "Logex has escaped you."

Two legionaries were standing over the man, guarding him. He was sitting up and holding his stomach tightly, which had been ripped completely open. The prisoner was attempting with little success to keep his intestines in. Blood flowed thickly through his fingers, onto his legs, and then to the dirty floor.

"We thought you would burn us with your dragons," the man said, with blood-flecked lips. "But … my god will see you burn instead … in this life or the next. Mark my words. I curse you all."

Karus felt an intense wave of revulsion for the wounded man. It was like he had eaten something foul, and it had turned his stomach. He knew without a doubt this was one of Garvin's followers, a worshipper of a dark god.

"Ah, you found a follower of Pattor," Ugin growled. "This night wasn't a complete waste after all. With his death, this world will become a better place." Ugin strode forward toward the injured prisoner, eyeing him with what seemed like pleasure. "Your evil god won't save you this day."

"I will be saved in the next life, Vass."

"I do not think Pattor will thank you for failing." Ugin glanced around the wrecked common room. He waved his sword and free arm about. "This looks like failure to me, not victory."

The man suddenly appeared uncertain, then grimaced as a wave of pain overcame him. When it passed, he fixed the Vass with his gaze. "Did we fail? Are you so sure?"

The Vass gave a growl to that.

Disgusted by such a man worshipping evil, Karus turned his attention to Pammon. "Take a century. I doubt you will find anything, but see where the tunnel leads. Then collapse it."

"Yes, sir," Pammon said and began moving toward the tunnel. "Second Century, on me."

"I am going too," Ugin said to Karus, turning away from the prisoner and dropping down into the tunnel before anyone could try to stop him. Clearly the Vass would not take no for an answer. Karus did not care. He already knew what they would find—nothing.

If he wanted Logex now, he would have to send cavalry after the man. And Karus knew he could not do that, not now. The Horde was too close, and his cavalry had much more pressing things to do.

The wounded man began to laugh again. The sound of it was harsh. It grated on Karus's nerves. Karus clearly understood those that had remained in the tavern had done it so the others could escape... and to buy them time to get clean away. The thought of it infuriated him.

"What do you want to do with the prisoners?" Flaccus asked, coming up.

Karus looked once more around the common room. There were half a dozen prisoners, all in varying states of injury.

"They had their chance to surrender," Karus said, feeling a terrible exhaustion and weariness settle over him.

"Yes, sir," Flaccus said, "they did."

"Kill them," Karus said. "Kill them all."

"With pleasure." Flaccus drew his sword.

Karus made his way for the door. He wanted some fresh air.

"Your heart will be ripped from your chest and burn in my lord's holy fire," the prisoner shouted at him again. "Just like you would have burned our camp, and families too … mark my words … you will burn, all of you … purified in the fires. Just as this wicked city should burn, so too shall you."

"What did he say, sir?" Flaccus asked.

"It isn't worth translating," Karus said. "He follows a dark god and is filled with hate."

At the door, Karus spared the prisoner one last look, then stepped outside. He found a mass of men waiting. He pushed through them and spotted Amarra with Si'Cara by her side. They were standing next to the defunct fountain. Amarra's hand went to her mouth at the sight of him. Karus leaned the shield against the fountain's basin, returning it where he had found it, a little more battered than it had been.

Under the light of the new moon, he thought Amarra looked wonderful, beautifully radiant with her snow-white dress and hair. She was an image of peace and salvation in stark contrast to Karus, drenched in the blood and gore of vengeance. It brought a weary smile to his lips.

He felt sticky and more than dirty, filthy even. Karus was sure he looked plain dreadful. He wanted nothing more than a hot bath, for he felt even worse than he looked. The excitement from the fight had worn off and the exhaustion was setting in. His body was starting to ache, especially his shield arm from the repeated blows it had taken.

"I am getting too old for this," he said, then looked up at Amarra, who was clearly horrified by his appearance. "None of it's mine."

The relief in her expression was plain.

"Logex escaped with some men," Karus said. "There's a tunnel leading in the direction of the city wall." In truth, Karus felt like he had failed. "I got Ord though. He's dead. That's something, at least."

Amarra said nothing at first, her gaze going in the direction of the city wall. "I am sure Logex will be found. One day, he will pay for what he has done."

Though he wasn't so sure, Karus gave a tired nod. He turned his gaze to the tavern. An intriguing thought occurred to him. He suddenly gave a low chuckle as he thought it through.

"Fire," he breathed to himself and chuckled again. "Perhaps this city should burn after all."

"What?" Amarra asked, a concerned look on her face. "What's funny?"

"I've just had an idea," Karus said. "Well, it's really half of an idea… I will need to speak with my officers to see if it's feasible, but some good may have come from this mess…"

Karus took a step away, his gaze going to the wall. The more he thought on it, the more he liked the idea. The question was… how would Dennig feel about his idea? Not to mention Karus's own officers, for what he was thinking of doing would be risky. No, Karus corrected himself… it would be dangerous.

Chapter Fifteen

Pulling on the reins, Karus slowed his horse, bringing her to a complete stop. In a smooth motion, he dismounted, dropping into the knee-high grass that grew along the roadside. The two suns were almost directly overhead. They beat down on those below with an almost savage intensity that had Karus sweating profusely and once again baking in his armor.

Kol'Cara, who had been riding at Karus's side, also dismounted. The elf calmly surveyed their surroundings and seemed far from impressed.

"Coluuuumn," Prefect Dentatius called, stretching out the middle of the word. The prefect, commanding Karus's escort, was riding next to Optio Bannus, one of Valens's best troop leaders. Bundles of hay, along with a traveling pack, had been secured to the back of the optio's saddle and horse's back, along with empty forage nets. Dentatius raised an open hand in the air above his head. The motion was for the two troops of cavalry that stretched out behind in a column of two abreast. "Haaalt."

With jingling of harnesses, much whinnying, and stamping of hooves, the column of near-forty horsemen pulled up to a stop, and neatly too. Valens's men were well-trained, and it showed in how they handled their mounts.

It had been a good long while since Karus had ridden a horse. They were not his animal of choice. He was an infantry officer and, like most of his breed, believed it was better to march the miles away than ride them.

Extended rides always seemed to play havoc with his back, making him ache for days afterwards. It was the constant jarring that did him in. He took a moment to stretch, doing his best to work out the soreness.

The ride had not been a long one, but he already hurt from the previous night's fight, his shield arm especially, which had become quite bruised. Karus glanced westward in the direction of the city, which was only a short ride away. His gaze shifted over to the road and the long line of captured orc wagons that trundled, creaked, and rattled by, just feet away. They made a heck of a racket.

The dwarves driving the wagons and riding in the beds looked on the legionary cavalry column with what Karus thought a mixed blend of curiosity and borderline hostility. Several of the looks they received were far from friendly.

Most of the wagons, pulled by the six-legged teska, were packed full of wounded. Some had been crammed with stores that had been covered over in tarp or tent canvas.

Very few dwarves were marching. Most were riding. Karus did notice that a small number of skirmishers had been deployed farther out in the rolling grass fields to either side of the road. These provided a protective screen against a potential ambush. Karus approved, for it was what the legion would have done, and it spoke of the professional concern given to the warband's security.

Turning his gaze away from the skirmishers and back to the wagons, Karus wondered how many of Dennig's warband were combat effective. How many were capable of holding a sword? Most of the dwarves he'd seen so far had been injured in some way. It was a troubling sign that worried him. How much strength did Dennig have left?

"My friend," Dennig boomed, holding up a hand in greeting. The dwarf had been marching beside a wagon a few yards farther down the road. It was why Karus had chosen to stop and dismount. Martuke was at Dennig's side, and an escort of warriors, a dozen all told, trailed behind their warchief. Those marching with Dennig appeared hot, sweaty, and tired.

Handing the reins of his horse up to Dentatius, Karus turned to face the warchief as Dennig approached the last few feet. The dwarf's grin was large, though Karus detected a deep weariness mixed with a terrible sorrow in his manner.

"It is good to see you." Dennig held out his hand and they clasped forearms warmly. Dennig drew Karus close and into a bear hug, patting him on the back enthusiastically with powerful blows that, despite his armor, almost knocked the wind out of Karus.

It was as if the two were long lost comrades and had not just seen each other a few days before. Karus understood Dennig was putting on a show for his fellow dwarves. Martuke's expression had soured at the display.

"It is very good to see you," Dennig said again as he pulled away.

"You too, my friend," Karus said, ignoring Martuke and focusing his entire attention upon Dennig. "How are you?"

"Tired," Dennig said, with a note of exhaustion, "and hot. I am more than ready for this blasted march to end."

"I well know the feeling." Karus wiped sweat from his eyes. "Route marches are always brutal when it's bloody hot out."

"Unseasonably so." Dennig glanced over at the wagons passing them by. "My injured are suffering terribly. Every bump and rut on this terrible excuse for a road is a torture session in and of itself. Worse, exposed as they are and under the suns, I am losing warriors by the hour. If I could only get them to shelter…" Dennig heaved a heavy sigh. "But… that does not seem to be in the stars, for the enemy is close."

"We cannot afford to stop to give them a break." There was a pained expression on Martuke's face as he said it. Dennig's second in command glanced upward. Two dragons flew high above, to the point where they were nearly tiny specks in the sky. "The dragons tell us advance elements of the enemy are just ten hours' march behind us, maybe closer."

"They are dogging our heels something fierce," Dennig said. "My rearguard has already had a couple of sharp scraps with their scouts. I've never known the Horde to pursue so hard. They are like a dog that has a bone and, no matter how hard you tug, just won't let go."

Martuke turned, wiping sweat away from his eyes, and stared behind them at the long column of wagons that stretched out into the distance. "They must really want revenge on us for what happened at the town."

"No," Karus said. "That's not it. The enemy is doing their best to catch you. They want to keep us from linking up. Individually, we are much easier to defeat."

Dennig eyed him a long moment before replying. "I agree and I've given this some serious thought. Together we will be stronger."

"Exactly." Karus was pleased Dennig understood.

"I think you're reading into it too much," Martuke said to his warchief, "expecting too much from them."

"Am I?" Dennig asked, suddenly becoming heated. Karus wondered if the two had already had this conversation. He suspected they had. "Am I really?"

Martuke chose not to reply.

"I've pushed my boys as hard as I could." Dennig let go a tired breath as he stared at the nearest wagon, which was full of wounded, as it passed them by. "I've driven them almost to their limit." He looked back at Karus. "Since we left the town, we've only stopped to water the beasts or catch an hour or two of sleep… at most. The teska are on their last legs and we've already had a few collapse from exhaustion. By the Seven Levels, we're in no condition for a fight, not without an extended period of rest."

Valens had provided Karus a report on the dwarves' condition. Karus had not really expected anything different. The dwarven warband had been in poor shape to begin with. A hard march, like the one they'd just undertaken, had only served to wear them down further, even if they were mostly all riding the wagons.

"I never thought I would be grateful to a dragon," Dennig said. "Never in a thousand and one moons would I have guessed." The dwarf gestured vaguely toward the east. "We've seen the enemy's wyrms from a distance, but they don't venture close enough to be a threat." Dennig paused and glanced down at the long grass at their feet before looking back up. "Thank you for sending them, by the way. There is no doubt in my mind that we would not be here without the dragons protecting our march. My Dvergr and I owe you a debt we cannot easily repay." He looked over at Martuke and his tone became hard. "Don't we?"

Martuke's jaw flexed and his eyes narrowed dangerously as he gazed upon his warchief. After several heartbeats, he broke eye contact with Dennig and gave a curt but firm nod. "It is true. We do owe a debt of gratitude."

"Well," Karus said. The tension between the two dwarves was almost so thick you could have cut it with a sword. Another wagon, loudly creaking and groaning, passed them by. Karus waited until it was beyond them. "I've got some good news to share."

Both dwarves looked over to him.

"Good news we can most certainly use," Dennig said, perking up slightly.

"In their rush to catch you," Karus said, "the enemy left much of their supply train unguarded."

"Did they now?" Dennig said. "That sounds like an opportunity."

"My cavalry commander thought so too," Karus said. "Last evening, he hit the train hard."

"They're out of supply then?" Dennig said hopefully.

"Not quite," Karus said. "He was unable to destroy the food stores. What with the enemy's wyrms, there was no time to do that kind of work safely. It was a hit-and-run job." Karus gestured toward the shaggy teska pulling the nearest wagon. "My men were able to slaughter their beasts of burden. According to the report I received this morning, nearly every teska was put to the sword."

"I guess that's almost the same thing as losing their food stores." Dennig brightened considerably. He clapped his hands together. "Their supply train is going nowhere and it's now miles behind their main body. Give it a few days and the bastards pursuing us will go hungry. They won't be able to follow much beyond Carthum."

"We can certainly hope for that," Karus said. "But I think it a risky proposition pushing onward. The enemy is too near for comfort and they outnumber us greatly. With them being so close, we won't have the time we need to load food and water onto the wagons you've secured… or those that my people have managed to build, at least sufficient amounts for both my legion and your boys to feed ourselves longer than a couple of weeks."

"So," Dennig said, "you are not prepared for a march, then?"

Karus shook his head. "Not completely, no."

"Then we will leave you," Martuke said, "and take our chances on the road west... alone, as it should be. The farther we go, the closer we get to safety. The plan was for you to be ready to march when we arrived. You have said you are not. We cannot wait for you to ready your *legion*." Martuke made legion sound like it was a dirty word. "With any luck, when the enemy gets to Carthum, they will stop following us and fix their attention on you humans and the city. At that point, they become your problem and not ours."

Dennig shot Martuke a deeply unhappy look. Karus felt a stab of anger at the selfishness of the dwarf. Was the bastard so blind? Was he so stupid he could not see what was right before him? Karus and the dragons had saved this warband. How utterly ungrateful.

Ugin was right. No good deed went unrewarded. Karus wanted nothing more than to reach out and strangle the bastard. Instead, he calmed himself and focused his attention squarely on Dennig, for it was only the warchief's opinion that really mattered.

"I believe we should hole up in Carthum." Karus brought both hands together before him. "Together we can hold the city."

"You can't be serious." Martuke exploded. "You would have us hunker down in that gods forsaken abandoned place? Let the Horde, with a superior army, come up and seal us in? We just experienced that. You want us to endure another siege?" Martuke turned to Dennig. "Tell me you are not seriously considering this."

"It makes good tactical sense," Karus said. "The walls of Carthum are just too strong for us to pass up. Should we quit the city and march west with you, there is every reason to believe the enemy will rapidly catch up and bring us to battle…before the supply they carry with them on their backs runs out."

Dennig considered Karus for several heartbeats. His eyes narrowed and he reached up a hand and stroked his neatly braided beard.

"You mean to defend the city with or without us," Dennig said, more as a statement than a question. The dwarf glanced in the direction of Carthum. From the top of the gentle rise they stood upon, the buildings in the palace district could be seen in the distance, just barely.

"Yes, I do mean to hold the city," Karus said. "And I'm hoping you will join me. Between your warband and my legion, we should be able to make Carthum a tough nut to crack."

"For what purpose?" Martuke asked, acid in his voice. "For us all to die? We'll be trapped, like fish in a barrel. This is insanity. Our only hope is to keep marching west to the protection of our nearest army, likely General Torga. Even the orcs would have second thoughts about taking on his force."

Dennig snapped his fingers. He pointed a thick finger at Karus and shook it. "You have a plan. I can tell and I think I know what it is."

"A plan to die," Martuke said.

Dennig glanced over at Martuke. "Don't you see? He wants us to hold out long enough for Torga to relieve us."

"What?" Martuke hissed, returning Dennig's gaze. He blinked furiously. "Torga is days from the city, maybe even weeks at this point. You know his objective. It is nowhere near Carthum and he will not be easily diverted. The Thane, with the main army, is likely even farther to the west."

"I'm not so sure," Karus said to Dennig. "When Torga came to Carthum looking for you, he said he was coming back with an army. He as much as told me he would go through us to find you. He seemed quite sincere."

Dennig flashed Karus a weary grin. "Though he is a disagreeable bastard, Torga is a Dvergr of his word. If he said he's coming back, then he will."

"It is dangerous to assume Torga is on his way," Martuke said. "What if he's not ... what then?"

"That is a fair point," Dennig said. "Torga might have decided to complete his mission first and then come look for us."

"If you asked him to come, would he?" Karus asked Dennig. Everything Karus had planned in the last few hours hinged upon this question. If Dennig said no, then ... prepared or not, they would all have to march and take a chance on the road.

"Most definitely," Dennig said. "He would come, especially if he knew my warband was trapped by an orc army. Torga would be Legend-bound to assist us. And he would bring every available warrior he could lay his hands on with him."

"That is what I wanted to hear," Karus said. "Just to be certain, though, we need to send him word. We can get one of your messengers to him quicker than you could."

"How?" Dennig asked. "Would they go by dragon, like we did to get to the Fortress of Radiance and back?"

"No," Karus said. "With the enemy so near, Kordem and Cyln'Phax feel it would be too dangerous for even one of their number to leave us. The wyrms might gain some advantage or show up with more than we've seen to this point. So far, the dragons are the only deterrent holding the wyrms back." Karus turned and pointed back at his horse. "Your messenger will ride a horse and my cavalry will provide an escort to see him safely there."

"Is it hard to learn to ride?" Dennig asked, curiously eyeing Karus's horse, which towered over the dwarves. The animal was happily cropping at the long grass and seemed content, while it feasted, to ignore their conversation.

"I don't think so," Karus said. "It should be fairly easy to learn, but if needed, we can strap your messenger down and one of my men can lead his horse. Believe it or not, these animals can cover quite a lot of ground in a day."

"This course of action is too risky," Martuke said. "We should continue westward. I just don't like it."

"I do." Dennig turned on Martuke, thoroughly irritated. "What's there not to like? Is your objection based on humans in general? Your abhorrence and disdain of them? Or do you find it offensive that they would willingly help us? Tell me, because I am having difficulty understanding your thinking on this matter." Dennig waved a hand at the nearest wagon. "It may have escaped your notice, but we can't go much farther than the city itself. And even if we did, the dragons that provide us protection against the enemy's wyrms would stay with the humans. They owe us no allegiance. We would be vulnerable. Martuke, we are a proud people, myself included, but even I am not afraid to admit we need help."

Martuke, going red in the face, opened his mouth as if to speak. He apparently reconsidered, thinking better, and closed it.

"We have food," Karus said, before more could be said between the two dwarves. "We have shelter and strong defensive walls. The enemy, when they get to the city, will have no siege equipment. It will take them days to get organized to mount a proper assault. That will give Torga time to march our way. We can buy him more time by defending the city, making the enemy pay in blood."

"That's if the messenger finds him quickly enough," Martuke said. "If for some reason they don't, we will be the ones paying in blood."

"Good walls, food, and a roof over our heads. I like it even more," Dennig said, "especially considering our wounded."

"Your boys are tired and need a rest." Karus pointed at the nearest wagon. "You said so yourself. They can get it in the city."

Martuke said something in Dwarven.

"Speak the common tongue," Dennig snapped at his second in command, voice hard with anger and irritation. "Why do you heap dishonor upon him, especially after such a generous offer? Would you turn down the opportunity to save some of our injured? How many will die if we continue westward? The warband will likely even end up being run down like dogs and destroyed by the enemy. Unless I am missing something, there is no Legend in allowing our own to die needlessly. And... I am sorely tired of running."

Martuke turned a hateful glare on his warchief, before shifting his gaze to Karus. "I object to humans in general. That, and the city is ours by right. We had it first. It was never yours to claim."

"You may think that," Karus said, "but we found it abandoned and you weren't there. Right now, Carthum is ours and I mean to keep it that way." Karus softened his tone slightly. "However, you may share it with us."

Martuke bristled and took a step nearer Karus, his hand going to his sword hilt. "I should cut you down for your insolence, human. How dare you claim what is by all rights ours."

"Easy there, friend," Dentatius said in Latin. This was followed by the slow hiss of a sword coming free from the prefect's scabbard. Karus did not move and simply held his ground. He noticed Kol'Cara had unslung his bow and was standing silently off to the side, an arrow nocked and aimed at Martuke's chest.

Dennig's escort moved forward several paces, hands going for their weapons. But no one drew them.

"Are you a fool?" Dennig hissed in outrage at his second in command. "Don't we have enough problems? Do you feel it necessary to create one more for us? We do not need new enemies. We have enough as it is. Now, stand down and behave yourself. That is an order."

Martuke spoke in Dwarven once again, the tone accusatory and directed at Dennig.

"I said," Dennig said, adding menace into his tone, "stand down."

Reluctantly, Martuke released his hand from his sword hilt and took a step back. Dennig turned and said something in Dwarven to his escort. They too relaxed, and with them, Kol'Cara lowered his bow.

Instead of sheathing his sword, Dentatius rested it upon his lap and nudged his horse a couple of steps closer before stopping almost at Karus's side. Martuke scowled unhappily up at the prefect mounted above him. He spoke again in Dwarven to his warchief.

"Tell him what you said in our tongue," Dennig insisted. "Though he probably can guess on his own, I want Karus to understand our feelings about his race and what he is getting into before he takes us in. It is only fair he knows the truth."

Martuke's eyes glinted with extreme dislike as he turned them back to Karus. "I said… we have sunk low indeed, if we must work alongside humans and beg for their protection. This is a sad day, for we lose much Legend."

Karus was silent for a long moment as he considered Martuke's words. He returned the dwarf's gaze with a flinty one of his own. "There has been no begging. Dennig did nothing of the kind. I am simply asking that you join us and fight with us against our common enemy, a temporary compact of sorts. We are in this mess together and in a way partners by simple necessity… nothing more."

"A compact?" Dennig rolled the word over his tongue.

"Kol'Cara and the elves of the Anagradoom have joined with us." Karus gestured toward the elf.

"We have," Kol'Cara said. "It was a long time coming. I personally feel very strongly that our alliance is a necessary one, especially if my people are to survive the coming storm. Sadly, most elves do not yet comprehend the need. I pray that changes before it becomes too late."

Karus glanced over at the elf, slightly surprised by his words. He turned back to Dennig and continued. "Join with us in defense of the city… in defense of ourselves. Let us fight side by side … and"—Karus glanced over at Martuke—"not against one another, for in truth, we are not the enemy of the Dvergr people."

Dennig did not immediately reply. Martuke turned his gaze to his warchief and, like the rest of them, waited.

"It is a gracious offer," Dennig said finally, "more than equitable. I like it. We shall formalize this compact you have proposed."

"You go too far," Martuke said, though there was defeat in his voice. He knew he'd lost. "The Thane will never approve."

"The Thane is not here," Dennig said. "I command and I am only agreeing to join forces and form a temporary alliance. It will last until we are relieved, or the enemy breaks off their siege of the city and we are free to go. I am not binding the Thane to anything, nor would I ever try to. Circumstances dictate a commonsense approach… even if a human was the one to suggest it."

"Once he learns what you've done," Martuke said, "it will mean the end of your tenure as warchief. You should never have led us from Carthum. The fault for everything that has happened since that fateful and ill-conceived decision rests solely at your feet. Though, we all share in the shame."

"That may be so," Dennig said. "I accept responsibility for all that has happened and I most assuredly will answer for it. The Thane is the ultimate authority. If he chooses to remove me from command… then so be it. It means my warband will have survived the storm. My Legend will be more than satisfied, even if I am dismissed from service… in what others consider disgrace." Dennig turned to Karus and drew himself up. "I formally accept on behalf of my warband. We shall fight at your side. Our compact shall last until we are relieved, or the threat is over and we're able to march freely out of the city. Also, should the Thane order me to break our agreement, I will be required to do so. My oath to the Thane supersedes everything else. I assume that is acceptable?"

"It is," Karus said.

"Then," Dennig said, "I swear by my honored ancestors it is so."

Martuke let out a low hiss of disapproval. Karus felt an intense sense of elation. Yes, he and Dennig had already agreed to work together, but now… they had truly formalized it. If they survived the days ahead, and proved they could work together, then perhaps something greater may come from it… something more meaningful. Karus would have to work toward that. But first, he needed to get through the immediate trials that lay in the days ahead.

"Then I suggest," Karus said, "that we send your messenger off as soon as possible. There is no time to waste."

"You mean now?" Dennig asked, glancing at the horses.

"I do," Karus said. "One of my best cavalry troops is provisioned for an extended movement. The sooner we get your messenger on the way, the quicker help will arrive."

"You knew he would accept your offer?" Martuke asked.

"I had hoped," Karus said. "Nothing was certain. I felt it better to be prepared than not."

Dennig turned away, looking around. He spotted a younger dwarf from amongst his escort. Speaking in Dwarven, he called him over.

"Excuse me," Dennig said to Karus, "while I give him his instructions. Martuke, you are with me." With that, the three walked off several paces.

Slinging his bow over his shoulder, Kol'Cara took a step nearer to Karus. The elf did not say anything, but Karus sensed he had something he wanted to share. He looked over at Kol'Cara and raised an eyebrow.

"Your new alliance may not be at all what you expect," Kol'Cara said quietly. "Were I you, I would be cautious."

"How so?" Karus wondered where the elf was going.

"For the most part, dwarves do not like others," Kol'Cara said, with a nod of the chin toward Martuke. "He is the perfect example of that. I believe you recognize this, yes?"

"Dennig seems to be the exception, though," Karus said.

"Yes," Kol'Cara said, "he is a rare dwarf, especially for one in command of a warband."

"Perhaps there are others like him," Karus said.

"Maybe so," Kol'Cara said. "But for most… his people are highly intolerant of outsiders and resistant to change.

Do not expect to find many that are friendly or excited by an alliance with humans, elves … and dragons. Dwarves are a difficult people."

"More so than elves?" Karus asked, looking over.

"In some ways, yes," Kol'Cara said. "Taking them into the city could … cause problems."

"Worse than what we saw with the refugees?"

"Potentially," Kol'Cara said. "That all depends upon how much Dennig is able to control his warriors, how loyal they are to him. By accepting your help, he is weakening himself in the eyes of his people. In a way, it is almost a loss of face. Dwarves look down on other races … as inferior beings. As Martuke said, he feels shame as a result. Expect others to think as he does."

Karus grew silent as he studied Dennig and Martuke speaking with the messenger. He rubbed his jaw, considering them and Kol'Cara's words. After a long moment, he turned back to the elf.

"Soon enough, we will have the Horde on our doorstep," Karus said. "Surely they will put aside such attitudes to survive."

"One would think so," Kol'Cara said, "and I hope that they do … but the dwarven mind is hard to divine. I have no idea how they will behave once you bring them into the city. You must proceed cautiously."

"The headaches never cease," Karus said, "do they?"

"They end when you die," Kol'Cara said. "At least, that is what our philosophers tell us. And truth be told, no one I know of has come back from the dead. So, there is no way to be certain of that either. For all we know, the afterlife could be full of headaches and problems."

"And here I thought you were a philosopher," Karus said, becoming amused.

"Some days I am," Kol'Cara said. "Today, I have chosen to be a realist and your advisor."

"Point taken." Turning his gaze back to the dwarves, Karus rubbed at his jaw. "Dennig and I will just have to make sure that any potential problems are kept to a minimum. To survive the brewing storm, we must all work together."

"Let's hope," Kol'Cara said, his tone full of doubt as Dennig, Martuke, and the messenger began making their way back to them, "that you both are successful."

"This," Dennig said as he returned with Martuke and the younger dwarf, "is Talvan. He is my relative and has already proven himself a brave warrior with great Legend."

Talvan was carrying a heavy pack on his back, though unlike the rest of the dwarves, his armor was brown leather and not plated steel. His right arm was heavily bandaged with what looked like tent canvas. Blood had bled through and stained it a burgundy color.

He appeared tough, resilient, and confident, though was clearly much younger than Dennig and Martuke. His beard was a deep brown and had been tied into a single braid using colored glass beads. The beard reached midway down his chest. He looked curiously at the humans, elves, and horses, before turning his gaze squarely on Karus.

"It is an honor to meet you," Talvan said in Common. His tone was deep and confident. There was no hint of distaste, only respect. "My uncle has told me much of you, Karus. He shared how you saved him from the Elantric Warden and how you both fought the undead together, then the elves and the Horde. Such actions speak not only of your courage, but also of your Legend."

"It is an honor to meet you as well," Karus said, "and I am sure Dennig exaggerated some in the telling."

"Those only serve to make the stories better," Talvan said. "But I think with you, not so much. It is not every human who commands elves, dragons, and fights the undead."

"He thinks you command me." Kol'Cara smirked, thoroughly amused. "I think he has a lot to learn about alliances."

Karus gave a grunt and then turned, looking back. "Optio Bannus, on me, if you would."

"Sir," Bannus said, dismounting and coming forward. He snapped to attention. Standing a little over five feet in height and slightly bow-legged, the optio was a man with fifteen years of service behind him. The previous year, he had transferred from Second Cohort to the auxiliary cavalry. Karus knew him to be a determined and steady man. He had proven to be a solid leader and was respected by his peers for his coolness in combat and levelheadedness. More important to Karus, Valens spoke highly of him and considered him one of his finest combat leaders. It was only a matter of time until Bannus was promoted to cavalry prefect.

"Talvan," Karus said, "Bannus will command your escort. He will make sure you get to where you need to go. He does not speak the common tongue, nor do his men. Sadly, I am the only one of my people who does. You both will just have to make do, communication-wise." Karus paused. "If need be, they will defend you with their lives to see you to your people."

The young dwarf looked at the optio, who was still at attention. The last bit seemed to startle him, for he shifted his stance slightly. "I understand. Hopefully, it will not come to that."

"I hope so too," Karus said and then suddenly could not help himself. "When you see him, would you pass on a message to Torga for me?"

"The general?" Talvan asked.

"Yes," Karus said, with a glance toward Dennig, who was looking on curiously, clearly wondering on the message too. "Tell him I found his missing boys, including Shoega. If he wants them, he can have them. But he must come with his army. Make sure he gets that last part... to bring his army, as he threatened to do."

"I can't tell the general that," Talvan said, with a nervous look thrown to his uncle. He seemed scandalized by the very idea of doing so. "It would insult him to his core... a human demanding that he comes? That's unheard of!"

"You can and will," Dennig said, chuckling, then looked to Karus, mirth dancing in his eyes. "I enjoy your humor, my friend. With any luck, Torga will too. It will be either that, or he will want blood. When he gets to Carthum, I think it will be interesting to find out."

"Are you certain, sir?" Talvan asked. "I am to tell the general that?"

"Today has seen a lot of firsts." Dennig turned to Talvan. "Consider it an order from me. Deliver the message I gave you and Karus's too. Insist upon personally seeing Torga. Do not give it to any of his subordinates first. I want politics kept to a minimum. Deliver the message only to the general. Is that understood?"

"Yes, sir," Talvan said. "It shall be as you command."

"Bannus," Karus said, switching to Latin. "This is Talvan. He does not speak Latin. You will see him to his people. Once you do, return to us. Understand?"

"I do, sir," Bannus said.

"If he doesn't make it, and their people do not march to our aid, the legion will be crushed by our enemy. Got me on this? Whatever you do and at all costs... you must get him to his people."

"I will see him there safely," Bannus said. "I won't let you or the legion down, sir."

"Good. I knew I could count on you," Karus said and turned back to Talvan. "You do know the way, right?"

"More or less," Talvan said.

"That doesn't exactly fill me with confidence, son," Karus said.

"When we marched for Carthum some weeks ago, Torga's army was on the move," Dennig explained. "Have no fear. If the general is marching to Carthum, Talvan will find the general sooner than if he has to go looking for him. And if he's not headed for Carthum, we know where Torga's army was headed before you met him, which should make locating him easier."

Karus gave a nod of understanding.

"Talvan is a trained pioneer," Dennig continued. "He is what you would call a scout. Either way, he will find Torga and bring him to Carthum."

"And if Torga is too far away to come in time to save us?" Martuke asked. "Have you considered that?"

"Then we will find ourselves in a tight spot." Dennig glanced to Karus. "But… we won't be alone."

"No, you won't," Karus affirmed and then looked over at the optio, switching to Latin. "Bannus… Talvan knows the way and he's good to go. Time to get moving."

"Yes, sir," Bannus said, saluted, and then beckoned to the dwarf. "Come this way, friend. I have a mount waiting, a nice, calm mare. I think you will like her."

Karus watched them move down the line of horses toward where Bannus's troop was located and a spare horse waited at the end of the column.

"Will you march with me for a bit, my friend?" Dennig asked, eyeing the road ahead and the wagons, which continued to roll and creak by.

Karus glanced over at his horse, eager to return to the city.

"You want to get back?" Dennig asked. "Don't you?"

"I do," Karus said. "There is much to be done before the enemy gets here. That said, I will spare you a half hour. Despite the heat, I believe it will be good to stretch my legs and get some marching in."

"Good," Dennig said enthusiastically. "We need to discuss how to keep our two peoples from killing one another once we get to the city. I would rather see our aggression directed toward the enemy and not inward."

Kol'Cara shot Karus a knowing look as Dennig started walking. There was a *told you so* in his gaze.

"I believe that might be worth discussing," Karus said and followed after his friend. "Let's talk about that."

Chapter Sixteen

"They put on an impressive show," Dennig said to Karus, without looking over. The Horde had arrived and the enemy's army, on the east road, stretched out into the distance before them. "Do they not?"

Resting his hands upon the stone of the city wall as he stared out at the enemy army, Karus could not help but agree. The stone had been warmed by the first of the two morning suns, which had risen a little over an hour before. In his face, the sun half blinded him. The city behind him on the other side of the wall was still steeped heavily in shadows. In another half hour that would change as the first sun climbed higher in the sky.

Promising yet another day of brutal heat, the air was already warm and humid. In his armor, Karus was sweating, hot, and uncomfortable. He was tired of the heat and more than ready for a cooling down.

Both he and Dennig were standing upon the east wall, a few yards from the gatehouse. Kol'Cara was a few feet away, also gazing out at the enemy. Since they had arrived, the elf had fallen into a sullen, almost troubled silence. Karus's legionary escort waited back by the gatehouse, where he had left them.

A commotion to his left drew his attention toward the gatehouse. The sentries were being changed out, with their replacement formed up in a line. Dwarves manned this portion of the wall. What looked like an officer was addressing them, clearly giving the replacements their orders.

Both he and Dennig had thought it a good idea to give the dwarves a part of the city to defend. Dennig had specifically requested the honor of holding the section of wall around the east gate. The dwarf had explained he wanted the enemy, when they arrived, to see his warriors manning the city's battlements, along with the warband's standards. Those had been mounted along the wall. The fabric of the nearest standards fluttered and flapped whenever the wind gusted. It was a show of defiance, one of which Karus approved.

By entrusting the defense of a critical portion of the wall to the dwarves, Karus was showing his faith in his new allies. At least, he hoped so. There was no telling just how the dwarves would take it. They were an alien race and he could not assume their thought process would align with his.

Already, there had been several disagreements and misunderstandings. Mostly, these had been caused by the inability to communicate effectively, other than through hand gestures.

One such instance involved the movement of dwarven wounded to the palace. It had almost come to blows. Swords had even been drawn before officers on both sides had taken control. Karus keenly recognized the sooner his people learned the common tongue, the better.

When he failed to answer, Denning looked over. The dwarf's expression was expectant. He pointed out toward the enemy. "You don't think them impressive?"

"It's not that." Karus refocused his thoughts on the present. "I just wish they had not gone to the trouble of putting on such a show for our mutual benefit."

Dennig gave a good-natured chuckle that trailed off as they both went back to silently studying the enemy. The might and raw power put on full display by the Horde was indeed impressive.

In all his years, Karus had not seen the like. He could easily understand why the enemy were slowly overrunning this world. The Horde was highly organized, disciplined, and clearly had vast reserves of…manpower? Or was it orcpower? Or both? For some humans willingly served alongside the enemy and worshipped their dark gods.

Back in Britannia, rarely had more than two legions worked together at any one time. And when they had marched as a combined army, he had thought that a terribly impressive thing to see.

Both legions, along with their auxiliary cohorts and local allies, had numbered a little over thirty-five thousand fighting men. The Horde army before him, Karus conceded, was altogether different, grander.

The first of the enemy's formations had begun arriving shortly before dawn. These had moved to a position a little over two thousand yards from the city and were now actively engaged in building an encampment centered around a small treeless hill. Fenced in, with high stone walls, the area looked to have once been a field for grazing animals.

At least seven to eight thousand orcs had been set to digging a trench and building a turf wall, while several hundred more pitched tents. As Karus studied the enemy, he even spotted what he thought were teams of engineers, marking out sections of the encampment yet to be developed. These were planting small white marker flags in the ground.

It was all very professional and organized. Karus found it eerily similar to how the legion went about setting up a fortified camp. Of course, there were differences, but the professional soldier in him was deeply impressed all the same.

Within mere hours, probably before the onset of dusk, the fortified encampment would be complete. From the scale of what they were working on, the camp itself would be huge.

Beyond the enemy's budding encampment, the nearest farms were either in flames or smoking, smoldering ruins, dozens of them. Karus had ordered Valens to burn any structure within ten miles of the city. The evidence of that effort were not only the fires, but the thick columns of smoke dotting the horizon. Karus had wanted to leave nothing for the enemy to use, especially if it could assist them with their assault on the city walls.

From personal experience, he well knew buildings could easily be taken apart to fashion battering rams and scaling ladders. Hence one of the reasons the farms had to go. He wished there had been time to do more, leave less for the enemy. But wishes were often like dreams, carrying little substance.

"Excuse me, sir." A legionary had come up and was standing to attention. Bathed by the rising sunlight, the messenger's armor glinted, especially the helmet. The man was sweating, and his cheeks flushed. He had likely jogged from the palace district. He offered Karus a crisp salute and then held out a sealed dispatch.

Karus took the dispatch, opened it, and quickly scanned the contents. It was a report from headquarters, which really was not a surprise. He recognized the neat scrawl. Delvaris had penned it himself, which meant the clerks were incredibly busy. Tucking the dispatch behind his armor, Karus looked up at the legionary.

"Thank you. I will not have a reply. Report back to headquarters. You are dismissed."

The legionary saluted again. With that, he turned on his heal and left. Karus watched him go before moving back to the wall to continue studying the enemy.

"Anything interesting?" Dennig asked, glancing over.

"Enemy scouts have been reported surveying the west and north sides of the city wall. Nothing yet from the south side."

"They're dragging ass," Dennig said. "I would have had warriors on each side of the city by now."

"Give them time. It's a big city." Karus paused to suck in a breath. "The wagons also seem to have gotten away and are now seven miles to the west. There is no sign the enemy intends to pursue them. The cavalry has reformed and, as ordered, is providing a screen. Once the wagons are twenty miles out and safe, the cavalry will turn back to harry the enemy… any way they can. It does not seem as if the enemy are at all interested in chasing down the wagons."

"It is possible," Dennig said, "since they set out at night, the enemy simply does not yet know that the wagons continued on westward. Then again, there is not much worth chasing, seeing as how we unloaded them first. I'm betting it's the latter."

"That would be nice," Karus said. "We need something to go our way."

"I must admit, I am still somewhat troubled by sending the wagons onward," Dennig said. "We're going to need them if we survive this. There's a lot to haul away. That's one of the reasons the Thane sent me to Carthum, to salvage what I could. It would be a shame if one of the enemy's wyrms destroyed all of the transport."

"It is a risk, for sure," Karus said. "But, with what I have planned, they can't be kept in the city. You know that. Besides, Kordem is flying cover over the wagons."

Dennig ran a hand through his tightly braided beard and let out a long breath. "You're right. They had to go. There was nothing else we could do."

"If this works out and Torga relieves us," Karus said, "we will have some breathing room and the wagons can return."

"True. That also would be nice. And it may keep the Thane's wrath at bay."

Karus turned his gaze skyward. Only a handful of white, puffy clouds scudded lazily across an almost brilliant blue sky. From the top of the wall, he figured he could see perhaps twenty to thirty miles, maybe more.

The enemy's line of march was organized into block-like formations of several hundred each. It stretched out for as far as the eye could see to the east. The army had kicked up a large cloud of dust from the road, which the wind was carrying to the north. Any time an army moved, especially in dry weather, there was always the choking, ever-present dust.

Six of the enemy's wyrms flew off in the distance, far enough away that they appeared like a flock of birds…yet the massive creatures were still near enough that they could easily protect the soldiers on the ground. At least that was what Kordem had told him before he'd left to watch over the wagons.

Scanning the sky, Karus spotted Cyln'Phax and one of her children circling incredibly high over the city. The fact that they were there providing cover was a great comfort to Karus.

The two sets of dragons were cautiously watching one another. They were playing a deadly game. When one side made a move, the other side would undoubtedly strike. Karus did not know how such a confrontation would go . . . or who would come out on top.

There was one thing he did understand all too well. If his dragons lost, the legion was most likely done. The wyrms would burn the city and his boys along with it. Then the orcs would come in to finish off anyone who survived the conflagration. That thought alone frightened Karus, for he had no control of anything when it came to the dragons.

The only solution they had managed to come up with in short order, for a semblance of protection, were legionary bolt throwers, a handful of which had been mounted on the walls and throughout the city. These had been modified to shoot skyward. Privately, Karus had little faith that they would make a difference. He had, after all, seen the raw power dragons were capable of unleashing. Not much could withstand such an onslaught.

The dwarves had brought two larger bolt throwers with them. They called these "dragon killers." Both machines had been disassembled and moved to the palace district. In the hours ahead, they would be put back together and mounted on the walls by the palace.

"You were right," Dennig said.

"About what?" Karus asked.

The dwarf pointed toward a formation of several hundred orcs. They were being guided off the road and into the enemy's encampment. He had a feeling he knew where Dennig was headed. Behind the formation followed ten heavily loaded teska.

"Had we continued on westward, that teska train tells me the enemy's main body had sufficient food stores with them to run us down," Dennig said. "I've been watching and each new formation that comes up seems to have a similar train."

"I do not enjoy being right." That the enemy had some transport left meant after they finished constructing their encampment, they could send the teska back to retrieve food from the main supply train Valens had crippled. Karus found that thought downright depressing.

"Martuke won't enjoy you being right, either." Dennig gave a harsh laugh and then patted the stone battlement. The stone was old, ancient even, and had been smoothed by years of exposure to the weather. "I, however, am grateful for the protection of these walls. They are solid and tall. The enemy has their work cut out for them."

Karus scratched an itch upon his cheek. He was starting to sweat buckets. The heat of the day had increased. The second sun was just beginning to peek over the horizon. He found the heat was making him thirsty. He took his canteen from his harness and unstopped it before holding it out to Dennig. The dwarf took a generous swig.

"Thank you." Dennig wiped his lips with the back of his arm, before handing the canteen back.

Karus tipped the canteen and drank several swallows of warm water before returning it to his harness.

They both became silent for a time, each lost to his own thoughts. The full magnitude of the Horde's army, so close, was disturbing. Karus had his plans for defense of the city, and until he'd joined Dennig on the wall, he had felt quite good about them. Now... not so much.

Before any action, he had always suffered from doubt. A good leader questioned himself relentlessly, especially when it came to the planning of a fight. In combat, nothing ever went exactly to plan. Something always tended to go wrong. It was why the legion promoted men who could, under incredible stress, assess a problem, think of a solution, and then react accordingly. That took years of experience, hard service, and training to develop. It could not happen overnight and was another reason why Roman legions were second to none.

Still, the better you planned, the more prepared you were going into a fight, the greater the chance a commander had for the desired outcome to be achieved. Yet no matter how much you prepared, that did not always guarantee success or that things would swing your way. As the saying went, the enemy always got a vote... perhaps even the last word, which was never desirable.

After seeing the enemy up close, Karus was no longer so certain he had made the right decision by holing up in Carthum. In fact, he was becoming concerned he had made the wrong decision. But now, the time for second-guessing was over. He was committed to a defense of the city.

Once the enemy got organized, Karus was not at all sure he would be able to hold out long enough for Torga to reach them. Worse, he had no idea how long it would take for the dwarven general to bring his army to Carthum. That was, if he came at all. Karus found it a slim comfort that Dennig was convinced Torga would bring his army.

Still, even without the prospect of Torga's army and knowing what he knew now, Karus suspected he might have elected to remain in the city anyway. There were serious advantages to the defensive nature of the walls and stockpiles of food they had accumulated. Making your enemy struggle to simply get at you was a serious positive in Karus's book. And struggle they would.

"We have good defenses here," Karus said, almost to himself. "Very good defenses."

"The walls are strong." Dennig waved a hand at the enemy. "The bastards will need time to settle in, construct siege equipment, scaling ladders, and just generally prepare for an assault. That all takes time. And you have gone and kindly burned the closest building supplies for such an effort. I am thinking we will have a few days before the fun begins... which is good for us. It gives our boys more time to prepare a hot welcome for our new guests."

"There's a whole forest out there, just a few miles away." Karus gestured vaguely with a hand. "Plenty of building material for them there."

After having been transported to this world, Karus well recalled the dark and forbidding forest the legion had marched through. The trees had been virtual giants compared to the ones they had known back in Britannia or the rest of the empire. Under the shade of the forest's canopy, he had felt small and insignificant.

Then there had been the feeling of being watched. It had been ever present, and was almost unnerving, especially with the repeated reports of spotting people high up in the canopy. He had since learned that the forest was settled by elves, who lived and built their homes in the trees themselves. If he had not seen such things himself, he would scarcely believe it possible.

"It will take a little effort," Karus continued, "but in short order, they will have all the construction material they'll need."

"That's elven land," Dennig said. "I doubt very much the elves will look kindly upon orcs harvesting their precious trees. The enemy will know this. There is a strong chance they will avoid the forest altogether and scavenge what they need from farther afield."

"I hope you are right," Karus said, though he personally doubted it. Short on food, the enemy commander would take the risk. A protracted siege was not in his best interest, even with a small train of teska shuttling back food. He would want to get at the city as quickly as possible and overcome the defenders before his food ran short and his warriors grew hungry.

"I know I am right," Dennig said firmly. "The elves are fanatical about their trees. I've heard it said they even talk to them. Can you imagine such a thing? Talking to a tree…a daft thing to do." The dwarf laughed. "It must be a one-sided conversation, like talking to yourself…" Dennig paused, as if considering something. "Though to be perfectly honest, I talk to myself all the time." He shook his head, as if he were reconsidering. "So maybe it's not so crazy after all."

Karus turned toward Kol'Cara, who stood a few feet away. The elf was still gazing out through the battlements at the enemy. Since they had arrived, he had been oddly silent.

"What do you think?" Karus asked the elf.

"About what?" Kol'Cara looked over as the wind gusted lightly, bringing with it a modicum of relief from the growing heat. "Talking to the trees? Yes…we occasionally do that. There is much to be gained from listening to the voice of the forest."

"Hah!" Dennig slapped the stone of the wall. "See? I knew it had to be true. I just knew it. You can't make up something like that."

Karus refused to be put off. "Do you think they will do it, risk going to the forest?"

"Despite any misgivings about trespassing upon elven lands, I think it a strong possibility." As he spoke, a sad note had crept into Kol'Cara's voice. "You should expect them to take down ancient trees that should be left to finish out their lives."

"It's your people's land," Karus said. "Won't they try to stop the enemy from doing just that?"

"I told you," Kol'Cara said, "we of the Anagradoom stand apart. We no longer have a people."

"You know what he means, elf," Dennig said. "You people can never just answer a simple question, can you? Whether you call them yours or not, they are still your kind. So, will they defend their trees or stand by while the orcs cut half the forest down?"

Kol'Cara shifted his gaze back to the enemy and fell silent. Just when Karus thought he might not answer, the elf looked back at them.

"Our enemy may succeed in taking a few trees," Kol'Cara said, "but it will not be tolerated for long, no more than a day or two. The trees will cry out. After that, the rangers should begin making their feelings known on the matter."

"Will they come to help?" Karus wished he had thought to ask before now. "We might be able to sneak one of your people out of the city before the enemy tightens the noose. If you asked, that is... would the elves in that forest come to help?"

"I don't know if they will," Kol'Cara said. "However, there is no need for such action."

"Why not?" Dennig asked.

"I have already sent word and requested their assistance," Kol'Cara said, as if he were simply commenting on the weather. "We shall just have to wait and see if they are so inclined to come to our defense."

Karus blinked, not sure he had heard correctly. "What? You did what? Why didn't you say so before now?"

"There was no point in getting your hopes up." Kol'Cara cocked his head to the side. "When it became clear you intended to hold the city, I sent Miron'Teh over the wall and into the forest. He left around the time of the assault on the tavern and… has yet to return."

"What assault?" Dennig looked to Karus. "What happened? What is he talking about?"

"We had some locals we'd taken in," Karus said. "A band of refugees who had lost their land. We gave them shelter and protection. They decided to cause trouble and killed some of my men. When I got back, I was forced to deal with it. The matter has been handled and they no longer pose a problem."

Dennig seemed intrigued and on the verge of asking additional questions, but Karus had already turned his attention back to Kol'Cara. "Is that a good sign or not?"

"That Miron'Teh has yet to return?"

Karus gave a nod.

"Neither," Kol'Cara said. "It will take him several days to reach the nearest settlement and make contact."

"What of the rangers you mentioned?" Karus asked. "The ones that will make their feelings felt. Will they help?"

"Those will be individuals," Kol'Cara said, "no more than four or five, perhaps even a ranger team. They will be unable to help, beyond making the orcs pay in blood for every tree they take. And they will make them pay dearly. What I asked for was something more substantial."

"Substantial?" Karus asked. "As in soldiers?"

"Yes." Kol'Cara gave a slow nod. "They will either come, or they won't."

"That's not helpful," Dennig groused. "Knowing elves, they won't come at all, and just for spite, too. They would rather talk to trees or admire a pretty flower than lift a finger to help. All the while, we do the fighting and dying. Why should things change now?"

Expression neutral, Kol'Cara said nothing.

The dwarf made a snorting sound and turned away.

Karus privately suspected Dennig was correct. He knew in his heart the elves would not be coming. After what had happened with the Elantric Warden, Kol'Cara's people would be in turmoil. Many would blame Karus for the warden's death.

Kol'Cara seemed to read his mind, for the elf gave a knowing nod. It was filled with what Karus took to be regret. The elf turned his attention back out to the enemy. He clearly wished to speak no more on the matter.

Feeling far from satisfied by the exchange, Karus ran his gaze around the wall upon which they stood. There were dwarves posted every thirty feet. Behind him, in the nearest buildings, were billeted around five hundred more, ready to be called to action at a moment's notice.

Dennig had another four hundred walking wounded caring for the injured, who, if need be, when the time came, would be formed into a reserve force. And Karus had no illusions about that. The need would come, likely sooner rather than later. Karus's thoughts shifted to Dennig's wounded and how badly the warband had suffered.

"We've got your injured settled into the palace district," Karus said. "I've assigned a couple of centuries to help your boys care for them. My surgeon and his doctors are assisting too. Some of our civilians have volunteered as well."

"I know," Dennig said. "Thank you for that. I appreciate your efforts."

"There is no need to thank me," Karus said. "I would have expected the same from you."

"My people would not have so willingly reciprocated," Dennig said. "Nor would we have been so generous. You understand that, right?"

"I don't like the thought of it, but yes, I do understand," Karus said. "There is not much love for us."

"We were betrayed too many times, by outsiders"—Dennig paused—"or it could just be that my people are a stiff-necked race. Regardless, we do not like outsiders, let alone being indebted to them."

"Perhaps we can change such feelings," Karus said, "build a bridge between our two peoples. Maybe... it even starts here in Carthum, with us."

Dennig looked over at him. At first, he said nothing. Then he shook his head slightly. "I count you a friend, but I would not plan on that ever happening. Trust me on this. There is no chance for such a thing, ever."

"Are you so certain," Karus said, "that you don't even want to try?"

Instead of replying to Karus's question, Dennig stiffened as his gaze was drawn toward the gatehouse.

"What is that doing here?" Dennig's tone was cold, hard, and tinged with hostility.

Karus followed his gaze and saw Ugin approaching. Six of the Anagradoom trailed after him. With the enemy on the city's doorstep, Karus had need of every man. He had released the century guarding Ugin to return to their normal duties.

It was a risk, but he felt he had no choice. Kol'Cara, however, had insisted a small team of his Anagradoom watch the Vass every moment, day or night. The rest, when the fighting came, would be glued to Karus.

The dwarves on the wall stared in horror at Ugin—or was it loathing? Karus wasn't sure which, but they seemed stunned by the Vass's appearance in their midst.

"What is he doing here?" Dennig asked Karus as Ugin joined them. Before Karus could answer, the dwarf fixed an unfriendly gaze that simmered with heat on the Vass. "Ugincalt, it is *so* good to see you again."

Dennig's tone dripped with acid.

"As welcoming as ever," Ugin said. "That's why I like you, Shoega. Though I willingly admit, I did not expect to find you here in Carthum… with these humans." The Vass looked over at Karus. "I am impressed. You keep the most interesting company, Karus, and continually surprise."

"I take it you are both acquainted," Karus said, more as a statement than a question.

"Aye." There was a hard note in Dennig's voice. He seemed genuinely displeased to have discovered Ugin in the city. "I am well acquainted with Ugincalt, Knight of the Vass and Lord Commander of the Death Watch. He and I have had past dealings."

Though the titles meant nothing to Karus, the elves seemed stunned by the revelation. He had never seen them look so surprised. Almost nothing could get a rise out of them, and yet this had. Two of the Anagradoom that had been trailing Ugin took a step back, hands going to their weapons. They did not draw them though. Their gazes were fixed upon Ugin, intensely so… as if they expected him to attack at any moment.

Ugin spared the two elves a disdainful look that spoke volumes.

"So"—Dennig pointed a finger at Ugin—"I ask again, my friend… what is he doing here?"

"Karus and I have an arrangement," Ugin answered in a growl.

"What sort of an arrangement?" Dennig asked suspiciously, glancing over at Karus.

"I have pledged myself to fight at his side," Ugin said simply.

"Really?" Dennig asked. "What do you get out of it?"

Instead of responding, Ugin's gaze slid over the top of the wall to the enemy and then back to Karus. The Vass's gaze was intense. "You neglected to mention a Horde army was coming. Once I heard, I decided to come looking for you, Karus. Would you care to explain how such a detail could slip your mind?"

There was a terrible burning menace in those words, an undeniable threat. Karus itched to draw his sword and defend himself, for he could sense the Vass's anger and urge to draw blood. Ugin seemed almost hungry to do so.

Instead of reacting, Karus restrained himself. He judged such an attack unlikely. Should Ugin try anything, Karus knew the Vass would end up paying with his own life. For surely the elves would kill him. Then again, Ugin might kill Karus first, before they could take him down.

"You might recall, it was you who insisted on our deal," Karus said. "I wanted no part of it and you did not ask me about the Horde."

Karus felt his anger stir at the Vass. He had been forced into accepting Ugin's help and had not appreciated that. Karus did not enjoy being forced to do things he thought risky or questionable.

"That still does not excuse such an omission," Ugin growled.

"Had you bothered or thought to ask…" Karus's anger surged to new levels. He felt no fear toward the large tiger-man, only a growing rage. Where it came from, Karus had no idea. "I would have told you of the enemy marching on the city. Besides, you seemed so bloody eager to get in on the fight at the tavern too. Why would I spoil a good thing after it was so freely offered?"

His fur standing on edge, Ugin leaned forward slightly and flexed both hands into fists. Karus could hear the joints in his hands crack and the Vass's black armor creak. Ugin's gaze was intense and bored in on Karus. They stared at each other for several long moments. Then the Vass leaned back. The tension abruptly left him as he bared his teeth at Karus. He made a chuffing sound that could have been laughter. It grew into a deep belly laugh.

"Long has it been," Ugin said, "since anyone challenged me as openly as you do. With each passing day, I become more convinced you are part Vass. For a human, you are quite cunning and frustrating... You roped me into fighting the Horde. Well played... well played."

Karus felt some of the anger begin to drain away from him.

"If you want me to release you from our bargain," Karus said, "I will."

"What?" The Vass seemed taken aback.

"There is still time for you to leave," Karus said. "If you want to."

"I gave my word," Ugin said. "I will not back out now. You are stuck with me. My honor would be tarnished if I cut and ran now with the enemy just over there."

"Oh really?" Dennig scoffed.

"I am staying," Ugin said, "and that's my last word on the matter."

"Where are your protectors?" Kol'Cara asked, drawing the Vass's attention.

Ugin hesitated a moment, then made a show of slowly gazing around them. "Obviously, not here."

"Are they in the city?" Kol'Cara pressed. "Don't toy with me, Ugin, not today."

Ugin did not reply, but his jawline flexed, ever so slightly.

"I hate to admit it, but the elf has a point," Dennig said. "Your escort seems to be lacking. A Knight of the Vass always has protection. Why are you alone? Where are they hiding?"

"I don't see any," Ugin said, "so it must be just me."

"How ironic," Dennig said, with a glance to Karus.

Ugin gave another chuffing laugh.

"When we found him," Karus said, "there were two other Vass that had been killed. Perhaps his escort is dead. We did find him near death. You would think, if others lived, they would have rendered him assistance."

"A Knight of the Vass," Kol'Cara said, in an icy tone, "usually travels with no less than twelve protectors. The number is mandated by their goddess. So, there are ten more that are missing. They could be somewhere in the city, and that does not count the servants of the Death Watch."

"For what purpose?" Karus asked. "Why would they be out there hiding?"

"That is a good question," Kol'Cara said, his gaze fixed on Ugin.

"If they were here," Ugin said, "they would not be hiding. Vass don't *hide*."

"I don't even know what a Knight of the Vass is," Karus said, "let alone a Lord Commander… Care to explain?"

"Amongst his kind, he is a warrior of some renown," Dennig said. "He has won the favor of his god. She has blessed him with gifts other mortals can only dream about. Not only does he have protectors—think overly fanatical guards— but there is a religious faction or sect amongst his people that he leads too. All of them would willingly lay down their lives for him. Ugin is a nightmare to those he names his enemies."

"That is true," Ugin said in simple agreement.

"Where are they?" Kol'Cara asked again, taking a step closer. "Tell me."

Ugin grinned at the elf in challenge. "Or what?"

"Don't test me," Kol'Cara said.

"We're on the same side," Karus said, stepping between the two before things could escalate.

"Are we?" Kol'Cara said. "Are we really?"

"For the moment," Karus said, "we are."

Kol'Cara's eyes shifted to Karus's. The elf gave a nod and took a step back.

"I don't trust him," Dennig said.

"Now you are being unkind," Ugin said. "Our past dealings proved beneficial to you. I delivered on my end. More importantly, I kept my word."

Dennig shot the Vass a pained look. "I believe you got more out of the bargain than I did..."

"Possibly."

"You know," Dennig said, "the Thane almost removed me from command because of our dealings."

"The politics of dwarves do not concern me. You got what you wanted, and I got"—Ugin barred his teeth at Dennig—"what I desired. Just because you got what you wanted, doesn't mean it will make you happy."

Dennig gave a grimace and turned to Karus. His expression was sour. "Striking a bargain with him was extremely unwise."

"He has agreed to fight at our side and against our enemies," Karus said.

"While in the city," Ugin pointed out. "Once we both leave, our deal is done, concluded... finished. Just so they understand and there are no questions later."

"I'd still have him watched like a hawk," Dennig said. "A bargain made with a Vass typically comes back to bite. You can take my word on it."

"We are watching him," Kol'Cara said, "and if he so much as steps out of line, we will end him."

"I'd like to see you try," Ugin said.

"Easy." Karus held a hand out to each of them. "We don't need to fight amongst ourselves... not now."

Dennig expelled a heated breath. "I never thought I would see the day. Humans, elves, and now a Vass." He looked toward the heavens. "Thulla, just what have I gotten myself into?"

Shaking his head, Dennig returned to his position by the wall and gazed outward. Ugin moved to the battlement on the dwarf's right. As he did, Kol'Cara's veiled eyes followed him. In them was a dangerous glint. Karus had the impression the elf was weighing whether to attempt to kill Ugin outright, here and now.

Before he could say or do anything to dissuade him, Kol'Cara looked to those Anagradoom that had accompanied the Vass. He did something with his fingers that Karus realized was a form of communication. Message sent, he returned to his position at the wall and resumed his vigil, gazing outward at the enemy. The Anagradoom guard spread out, eyes on the Vass. Though they seemed watchful, gone was the coiled tension.

Karus blew out a relieved breath. Why couldn't things ever be simple? Fortuna simply loved screwing with him.

"That is a big army out there," Ugin said, "very big."

"You think?" Dennig said. "Perhaps it will test even your people's thirst for blood?"

"This will prove a true test of the warrior's spirit." Ugin leaned on the stone, almost eagerly staring out at the enemy army. "The goddess will be well-pleased with the severed souls I send her … for I will kill many race enemies before this is all over."

"It's going to be a bastard of a fight," Dennig said, "that's for sure."

Frustrated, Karus turned around and walked over to the other side of the wall, more to get some space to think. He rubbed the back of his neck as he gazed out over the heavily shadowed city. Toward the palace, there was a light cloud of dust rising into the air.

The morning sunlight had given the dust an almost orange glow. His men were busy tearing down a line of buildings. He had ordered that the city be pushed back by five hundred yards from the walls surrounding the palace district. The work was proceeding rapidly and Karus had been well pleased with the last report on their progress. If things remained on schedule, in two days' time, the work would be complete.

When it came time to fall back upon the safety of the palace district's walls, there would be no ready cover for anyone attempting to assault them. Any enemy units attacking the palace district walls would be exposed to a veritable killing field. That would make defense a little easier.

His men were also hard at it, blocking streets and key choke points throughout the city. They were actively building makeshift walls and defensive positions, even digging deep trenches filled with wooden spikes across main roads.

The fighting would eventually move from the outer walls to the city itself. There was simply too much wall to properly defend and, despite the legion's size, not enough men and dwarves to hold it for an extended period.

After a few determined assaults, at some point, part of the wall would be overcome. The enemy would eventually gain a foothold and expand upon it. Then a determined and stubborn fight through the city would follow, moving back toward the palace.

When they finally fell back to the safety of the palace district, the walls there would be much easier to hold. This was due simply to there being much less actual wall to defend.

How long they would manage to hold the city walls was anyone's guess. The longer, obviously, the better. Though there was something Karus was certain about… the cost in blood for the enemy would be high, especially with all that he and his senior officers had planned. To overcome his defense of the city, the Horde would pay dearly. At least, he hoped so. He reminded himself the enemy always had a say.

Karus went back to his original spot next to Dennig. Multiple enemy formations had stacked up. Each new unit was met by a guide, given instruction, and then led off the road into the growing encampment. With the size of the enemy's army, Karus suspected new formations would still be arriving well into the next day.

Watching them, he felt ill. Despite all that he had planned, and was preparing to do to defend the city, there was no doubt in his mind… the enemy had plenty of blood to spare in the taking of Carthum.

The legion did not.

Chapter Seventeen

"It was an exhaustive search, but I believe we have found every single cask, amphora, bucket, and whatever else there was in the city, sir." Centurion Macrinus of Third Cohort sounded tired, weary even. "We've concentrated nearly everything capable of holding water here in the palace district."

Karus gave a nod of understanding as he gazed around the table in his office. Senior Centurions Felix, Flaccus, Macrinus, and Arrens had joined him for this morning meeting, Tribune Delvaris also. They all looked tired and worn.

Seven days had passed since the enemy army had arrived. There had yet to be an assault upon the walls. The enemy had improved their encampment, and then set about sealing the defenders into the city with a series of siege works erected around each gate. While the enemy worked, the legion and dwarves prepared the city for a determined defense.

The map that had been unfolded on the table was an extremely detailed representation of the city. While Karus had journeyed to the Fortress of Radiance, Serma had found it in one of the palace cellars, amongst several other old maps. He had said the room where he had made his discovery had looked like an archive.

The parchment had turned yellow with age and the map itself was outdated, but for the most part it gave them an accurate detailing of Carthum. In planning the defense of the city, it had proved an invaluable tool.

"Not counting the deep wells here in the palace, sir," Macrinus continued. "We're using the aqueducts to fill everything we can. I have drafted camp followers to help with the work and speed things up. We should have plenty of water when the time comes to give up the city. Let's just say we are not gonna be running out anytime soon. That is for sure."

"Give up the city," Flaccus groused and then snorted. "We will spill much of their blood before that happens"—the centurion paused and looked to Karus—"and even more after."

"That is the plan," Karus said and, desiring to stay on topic, turned back to Macrinus. "And what of the water sources in the city? How is that work progressing?"

"We've already begun spiking, poisoning, and/or salting the wells," Macrinus said. "The city's sewage system is old and poorly maintained. Most of the wells we found were already polluted and fouled from leaking sewage. They seem to predate the aqueducts. It is doubtful many were used by the populace. Still, we are dealing with the wells just the same. When it comes to the aqueduct-fed fountains, the holding basins are being destroyed... except for the ones our boys are currently using. When it's time, those fountains will be wrecked too. The aqueducts themselves will be a little trickier."

"How so?" Karus asked.

Macrinus gestured toward the map. "Since they arrive in the city from underground channels and pipes, they are still gonna deliver water no matter what we do. Instead of going into a basin or letting them spill out into the street, we're diverting as many as we can into the city's sewers. I have some of the engineers helping with that."

"I see," Karus said.

"We have no way to stop the flow from the source." Macrinus gave a shrug of his shoulders. "With a little effort, if they know how... the enemy will be able to repair them and, in a few days, get clean, drinkable water."

"I just need them disabled is all... for a little while," Karus said. "That can be done, right?"

"Yes, sir, it can," Macrinus said. "I've got two hundred boys on it."

"Very good." Karus turned to Centurion Arrens of Eighth Cohort. "Tell me of the oil stocks that have been accumulated and what you've accomplished so far. I'd very much like an update, for as you well know, it is critical to our plans."

"Yes, sir," Arrens said. "We've scoured the city for oils of any type that will burn. When Carthum was abandoned, the inhabitants left a surprising amount behind. It seems they couldn't bring it all with them. We found two entire warehouses that were full of what we think is lamp oil." Arrens leaned forward toward the map of the city. "As directed, we have moved sufficient supplies for our own use here, to the palace district. We have enough to last more than a month, longer if we ration and cut back on the number of lamps being used. We found plenty of tallow candles and I'd recommend using them instead."

"That can be easily done," Karus said and looked to Delvaris. "See that it happens."

"Yes, sir," Delvaris said.

"Continue," Karus said to Arrens.

"Large quantities, several thousand amphorae and casks of oil, have been distributed to the cohorts manning the city walls, as well as any pitch or tar that could be found." Arrens leaned forward, pointing at the map. "These buildings here, here, here, and here, sir, by each gatehouse, have been set aside as depots to resupply the defenders on the wall if they run low."

"How far back are those buildings from the wall?" Karus asked. "The enemy has been constructing artillery. That last thing we need, while we're trying to hold the walls, is for a fire breaking out in the city and those buildings going up. Should that happen, it could well prove catastrophic, as any fire would likely spread, and quickly too."

"They're a good ways back, sir," Arrens said. "Each one's at least five hundred yards from the wall. There is some risk, but the distance helps minimize it."

"I worked with Arrens on this, sir," Felix said. "We both selected the buildings in question. If we put the depots too far back, we run the risk of complicating and weakening our defense of the walls. More men will need to be sent in relays to fetch what they need on the wall. Set the depot too far back and it's basically useless… too near and it becomes a risk. This is the best solution."

"I understand," Karus said. Though he did not like the idea of the depots being so near, the argument was sound. Holding the walls was the priority. Karus idly tapped an index finger on the wood of the tabletop as he thought it through. "It seems it is a risk we must take. Arrens, please continue."

"As directed, these seven buildings, mostly apartment blocks, on the main streets"—Arrens touched the positions on the map closer to the palace district—"have been set aside for the overflow…" Arrens smirked slightly and then chuckled at his own joke. No one else in the room laughed or seemed amused. Suddenly uncomfortable, Arrens cleared his throat. "All seven have been packed full of various types of oil, sir, along with the excess pitch and a strange black powder we found that burns intensely when lit. It smells too. Since the designated buildings are full, we've begun storing the excess oil, pitch, and powder in the surrounding buildings."

"Black powder?" Karus asked. "It burns?"

"Yes, sir," Arrens said. "The blacksmiths think it's used in the forges somehow, but have no idea on how to work it yet. It seems to be dangerous stuff, sir. It burned one of the smiths when he experimented with it. Not too badly. Ampelius says he will recover. Anyway, we found a substantial supply of the powder, so I thought it best to put it with the rest."

"Good thinking," Karus said, extremely pleased. "How much more time do you need to complete the job?"

"We're about done, sir," Arrens said. "There's not much left for us to move. Before sundown, my men will be available for reassignment."

"Right," Karus said. "Your boys have been working hard. We will give them a break from labor, with a day or two on the walls."

"They could use it, sir," Arrens said. "Hopefully, they will be quiet days."

"Delvaris," Karus said, "when we're done, see that appropriate orders are cut."

"I will, sir," Delvaris said.

"Felix," Karus said, "how are preparations going on your end?"

"We've finished work on the six main streets that lead to the palace district, sir. On each street, there are five lines of defense, with each one blocked by a trench and backed up with a defended wall." Felix leaned forward and pointed to several positions that had been marked on the map in a charcoal pencil. "The adjacent buildings around each position have been filled with dirt, at least their ground floors, to keep the enemy from easily flanking. In the event something unexpected happens, initially these positions will be manned at all times by a century of men. When the enemy gets into the city and the horn call is sounded to give up the walls, the cohorts have been issued orders to withdraw to their respective defensive positions. Each position will be held by an entire cohort and in some instances, such as the main avenue leading to the palace, by more than one."

"I would not want to be the ones asked to assault those defensive lines," Flaccus said. "I've seen them, and they are plain mean, just nasty."

"What about the secondary streets?" Karus asked. "What have you done with them?"

"We've begun working on those," Felix said. "Mainly just blocking any side streets or alleys with whatever we can, piles of furniture or trash. The city is just too large to fortify them all and we don't have the manpower to hold them, if we did. The back streets are really a confusing maze, more rabbit warren than anything else. It is easy to get turned around. That should also help us. However, each defensive position will have several centuries watching and blocking the nearest alleys and side streets." Felix paused, almost dramatically. "Eventually, the enemy will work their way around in strength and threaten to flank. At that point, the main defensive position will be given up and the defenders will fall back in good order to the next line and so on, until there is nowhere to fall back to but the safety of the palace district walls. The goal is to delay and bleed the enemy and reduce their numbers. Once in the city, it should take them a day or more likely two … hopefully three, to overcome our defenses and force us into the palace district."

"And the rooftops surrounding the defensive positions?" Karus asked. "What of them?"

"We're in the process of securing those as well," Felix said. "We won't make it easy on them, sir. We've managed to build walkways linking several buildings around each defensive position. Teams of archers and men with javelins will be working the rooftops, raining death down on the enemy."

Karus was silent for several heartbeats. He was liking everything he was hearing … Real progress had been made, and yet he found himself somewhat unsettled. He had the feeling they were overlooking something … vital. Though he had no idea what that was … it nagged at him and had kept him up at night.

He had not expressed this to his officers. They need not learn of his concerns and doubts. That might weaken their resolve. What they needed from him was strength, professional confidence, and that was what they were getting. Karus dearly wished Dio was here, for if there was anyone he could confide in, it would have been his old friend. Felix was a close friend, but their relationship was not the same, not as close. He didn't feel he could be as open with Felix. When Dio had died, Karus had lost something that would likely never be regained.

"I would like a tour." Karus had last seen the defensive positions two days prior. He had been more focused on walking the walls, checking to make certain the proper preparations had been made, for that was where the enemy would strike first. Though his senior officers were professionals, Karus had long since learned to take nothing for granted.

He had put in years of service to the empire. In that time, Karus had experienced more than many of his senior officers when it came to sieges and the breaking of them. His inspection tours served to confirm that things were being done properly, but also to make certain everything that could be done was.

Occasionally, Karus spotted things others had missed, overlooked, or found something that could be handled a different way, and better too. But for the most part, he had been well satisfied with all that he'd seen. His senior cohort commanders were seasoned men, well-trained and extremely competent. When it came to killing others in a systematic way, there was no one better than a legionary centurion.

"Yes, sir," Felix said. "I believe you will be pleased with all that has been accomplished. How detailed do you want the tour to be?"

"I would like to see each main defensive line," Karus said, "and get a proper sense for them. A thorough walkthrough."

"That will take about three hours, sir," Felix said.

"Have any more tunnels been discovered?" Karus asked.

"No, sir," Felix said. "We're still searching and have regular patrols out, sweeping the city. But, sir, it is a big city."

Feeling slightly dissatisfied, Karus gave an understanding nod.

"Flaccus." Karus turned to the centurion. "Any movement from the enemy?"

"Not much has changed from the report I gave in our meeting last night, sir," Flaccus said. "They have continued to bring up siege ladders to within three hundred yards of the city walls on all fronts. They're not even bothering to hide them from us, and there are a lot of ladders, sir. The green bastards have been busy."

"With their numbers," Felix said, "they don't need to hide their work. We know they will have to assault the walls. There is no surprise in that. The question now is ... when?"

"True," Karus said and nodded for Flaccus to continue.

"As to their artillery, they have four machines that are nearing completion and another six in partial states of construction. It looks like they sent teska back to their disabled supply train and moved the equipment forward in pieces. Give it a day or two and the buggers will begin lobbing rocks at us. Beyond that, they seem intent on continuing to work on the defenses, sealing in each gate. We will not be getting out anytime soon. That is for certain. I would not even want to try at this point."

"We don't want to get out," Felix said. "We want to keep them out ... at least for a time."

"We have noticed a slight concentration toward the north wall," Delvaris said, speaking up. "Reports have come in this morning on it, a growing of their numbers."

"How slight?" Karus asked. This was the first he had heard of it.

"They've moved at least three thousand additional orcs up," Delvaris said. "Flaccus and I discussed it. We don't know why or what they are up to ... but they are there."

"That's right," Flaccus said. "It does not seem to be enough for a proper assault, sir. They're going to need far greater numbers to make a good attempt of it. They could be there for added labor, but we have yet to see them get to work. When I left for this meeting they were still in formation and seemed to be waiting for orders."

"Where are they formed up?" Karus asked, glancing down at the map. "And how many orcs are there facing the north wall in total?"

"Here," Flaccus said and touched the left side of the north wall on the map. "About five hundred yards from the wall and the addition of this new formation would make it around thirteen thousand, maybe a few more or less. It's hard to get an accurate count."

Karus tried to recall what the ground looked like there before the wall. Something nagged at him. "Wasn't there a compound located nearby?"

"It's been razed sir," Flaccus said, "and it was a plantation. There was a large bunkhouse, a barn, and several other buildings. There's nothing but ash there now. Valens saw to that."

"Well," Karus said, "keep an eye on them."

"Of course, sir," Flaccus said.

"We've also spotted several dozen humans among the orcs, sir," Delvaris said.

That sent an uncomfortable ripple about the room. The thought of humans working with such creatures seemed unnatural.

"Before the north wall?" Karus asked.

"No, sir," Delvaris said, "near their main encampment."

Karus was silent a moment as he considered this new information. Was it Logex and his people? Or had they simply legged it? Karus suspected it was the latter.

"We knew humans of this world work with the enemy," Karus said. "Keep in mind, they are the enemy, just the same as if they were orcs. Don't expect them to think like us. Look at what the bloody refugees did."

"The barbarian mind," Flaccus said. "Idiots."

"The enemy might be preparing to test our defenses on the north wall in some way," Felix said, "see how prepared and determined we are."

"It could be that," Arrens said. "Their commander might want to learn how we're going to defend the city... see what weapons we have at our disposal, that sort of thing."

Looking down at the map and the north wall, Karus considered what his officers had said. All of the weapons they had to repel an assault—rocks, heated sand, boiling water, pitch, oil, arrows, slings, spears, javelins, bolt throwers, and ultimately swords and shields—were fairly standard. The enemy would expect such weapons.

"It is more likely," Karus said, "that their first assault or two will simply be probing in nature. Like Arrens said, the enemy general might just want to see how we're going to defend the city... how tenacious we will be."

"Should we hold something back, then?" Flaccus asked. "Save the oil and pitch? If they attack, that is? Make it seem like we're weaker than we actually are? Lull them into a false sense of confidence...?"

"I don't think so," Karus said. "If an attack comes, it will likely be to test our strength and will to resist. We won't play games when it comes to that. Doing so might cost lives and I will not have it. We give it our all. I want that understood. There is to be no holding back. They attack, we punish them and murder as many as we can. That is our goal."

"Perhaps we should consider reinforcing the north wall," Felix said, "sending two or three more centuries as reserves might give the senior centurion there some backbone."

"Backbone?" Flaccus bristled. His cohort was one of two holding the north wall, and command for that wall was in Flaccus's hands. The centurion's face flushed with anger. "You think I need backbone?"

"I am just teasing," Felix said and held his hands up. Arrens and Macrinus shared an amused look. Karus, however, was still focused on the problem of the enemy increasing their strength on the north side.

"How many men do we have there, now?" Karus asked. "How many men hold the north wall?"

"Nine hundred and fifty-four, as of this morning," Flaccus said, without hesitation. "First Cohort is there too, along with an auxiliary cohort in reserve, three hundred and eighty more, mostly light infantry with bows and slings."

"The First Nervorium?" Karus asked, recalling the dispositions from the previous night's meeting. To give a break from either hard labor or sentry duty, several of the legionary cohorts and auxiliaries had been rotated around.

Standing units up for extended periods of time on the walls was taxing on the men, even if all they were doing was watching the enemy. It was something every centurion had learned. You could not remain on alert forever and maintain an edge.

Fatigue would inevitably set in and that was when mistakes were likely to be made. Vital things could be overlooked or, worse, men slacking off when it came to duty. Hence, every other day, units posted to the wall were rotated off for a break.

"Yes, sir," Flaccus said. "Otho's boys are the ready reserve."

Karus took Felix's suggestion seriously, even though it had been made as a half jest. "If they go for the walls, it will take time for them to make any progress. That is, if they can. I expect we will be able to shift reserves to where they are needed, when they're required and not before. Felix, I don't want to shuffle our dispositions around too much. Marching men from one side of the city to the other and then back again in full kit will be tiring, especially in this brutal heat. We need our boys fresh for when the action begins."

"Yes, sir," Felix said.

"And it could begin at any time," Delvaris said.

Karus gave the tribune a nod, then looked down at the oversized map of the city. He hated meetings, as they sometimes tended to drag on needlessly. This was his third of the day. His days seemed to be consumed by them.

Welcome to command, Karus thought to himself.

The day had started with the legion's chief engineer and after that had been a meeting with Dennig and Martuke. Dennig's second in command had been as tiresome and querulous as usual. That had made the meeting with the dwarves almost painful to bear. Karus had found it difficult to keep his temper, but he had. Meetings, like this one, were necessary, especially if things were to be done right, and so Karus put up with them. He had made it a point to regularly meet with all of his senior officers in small groups, like this meeting.

He gazed around the table. There was likely more that could be discussed, but Karus had tired of it. There were things he wanted to get done before his tour with Felix. If he continued with the meeting, he doubted he would have time for them.

"Is there anything more that's pressing?" Karus asked.

No one replied. Karus glanced down at the map again, wondering if he'd forgotten anything he had wanted to address. His eyes were drawn to the oil depots marked out on the map by each gate. An idea hit him.

"Flaccus," Karus said, looking up, "send me ten picked men, including Optio Divius and his partner in crime, Lanza. They will officially be on detached duty. I have a job for them, and I want to pass on my orders personally."

"Yes, sir," Flaccus said.

Karus could tell the centurion wanted to ask what he had in store for both men. Before he could, Karus addressed those gathered at the table.

"Good work, gentlemen. I appreciate your efforts and I won't keep you any longer from your duties. Once the sun sets, I plan on holding a senior officer meeting, around eight bells tonight. There will be food served. If anything changes, I will alert you. Dismissed."

The officers came to attention, saluted, and then left, filing out of the room and into his headquarters. Felix, however, remained behind. Karus looked over at the centurion and arched an eyebrow, curious.

"Tell me you are uncomfortable with the enemy's inaction, too," Felix said.

"They've been relatively busy building defenses. I would not call them inactive. From the scope of their works, I'd say industrious is a more appropriate way of describing them."

"You know what I mean," Felix said.

Karus was silent for a moment as he considered his friend. Felix looked tired, like he had not gotten a good night's sleep for several days. All of his senior officers were tired, run-down even. They were burning the candle at both ends to prepare for the enemy's inevitable attack.

Despite keeping busy, the stress of waiting on the enemy, day after day, was beginning to take a toll on everyone. Karus himself had only managed three hours of restless sleep during the night.

"We knew it would take time for them to become organized," Karus said. "After all, Valens did cripple their supply train." Karus paused, sucked in a breath, and then let it out slowly. "But yes, I am uncomfortable with the inaction as well. I had expected something before now… even if it was only a parley to talk."

"They're up to something," Felix said. "It's a gut feeling, but I just know it."

Karus gave a slow nod. "I think so too. The question remains… what are they up to?"

"That, I don't know."

Karus knuckled the table, rapping it lightly. He keenly felt the frustration of not knowing.

"Regardless," Karus said, "the longer they delay, the better for us."

"Agreed," Felix said. "I just wish Dennig's people would hurry up and get here to relieve us."

"Me too." Karus gave the enemy's inaction a moment's more thought before looking back up. "Give me two hours. I will meet you at the palace steps for that tour. It will be good to stretch my legs, but there are some things I need to attend to first."

"Yes, sir." Felix drew himself up to attention, saluted, and left.

Alone in his office, Karus returned his gaze to the map of the city. He scanned it, studying the defensive lines, strong points, corridors designed to funnel the enemy into his killing grounds. There were dozens of additional notations on the map, some made by his own hand and others by his clerks or Delvaris.

They marked the positions of centuries and cohorts, already positioned within the city. The dwarven dispositions too were noted. The notes also indicated all fountains and paths of the aqueducts. The city's sewers were also marked. His men would be using some of them to move about the city. Others had been caved in to deny the enemy their use.

With each day that passed, the enemy was giving him time to improve his defenses, to better prepare a hot reception. With all that was being done, Karus was well pleased with the legion's progress.

So, why did he feel unsettled? He glanced in the direction of the doorway that led to his headquarters. The noise and hubbub from activity drifted into the office. Felix was right. The enemy was up to something.

"Right," Karus said, "time to get a move-on."

He stepped over to the corner of his office, where he had left the sword. He picked up the weapon by the scabbard and slipped the harness over his head and shoulder, settling it comfortably into place. His hand found the hilt. The welcoming tingle raced up his arm.

He spared one more look at the map, turned away, and stepped out of his office. Headquarters was crowded and hot from the press of bodies, almost uncomfortably so. With all that the legion was doing, it was a beehive of activity as reports were received, information recorded and analyzed, reports generated, and orders cut. Even with the shutters to the windows thrown open, the room smelled strongly of sweat, lamp oil, tallow from candles, and ink.

Delvaris was seated at a table, reading through a stack of reports written on wax tablets. If there was anything that required Karus's personal attention, Delvaris or Serma would make certain the matter was brought immediately before him.

A messenger took a dispatch from one of the clerks and immediately made for the exit. The clerk bent back over the table and, using a stylus, began writing. Headquarters was the heartbeat of the legion, and it showed.

"Serma," Karus called as he walked after the messenger toward the doorway that led out to the rest of the palace. He stopped, looking back over at the clerk.

"Sir?" The clerk set his stylus down and stood, respectfully. "How may I help you?"

"If you have need of me," Karus said, "I am headed to the gardens."

"Thank you, sir," Serma said.

The two guards crisply snapped to attention as he stepped out of his headquarters. The corridor that ran the length of the main floor of the palace was cooler. Karus found his personal escort, four legionaries from First Cohort, waiting. They immediately fell in behind him as he started forward.

Two messengers hurrying the opposite way stopped, came to attention against the wall, and saluted. Their faces were flushed and they were sweating. It was yet another brutally hot day. At least the palace mostly remained cool. Whoever had built it clearly knew what they were doing.

Karus gave them a nod and passed by. A few feet beyond, he found himself hesitating at the entrance to the gardens, hand on the frame of the open doorway. Si'Cara was out there, training Amarra. He wanted to visit with Amarra, even if it was for a short time. He found her presence refreshing and a break from the headaches of command.

Other than to spend the nights with her, he had not seen her much over the last few days. And then, she was exhausted almost beyond measure, immediately turning in and going to sleep. Si'Cara, good to her word, was being a hard taskmaster when it came to the High Priestess's training. The elf trained Amarra until she was ready to drop. Karus thought that a good thing and approved.

Still hesitating, he almost stepped outside... but, Karus thought, there was something else that needed doing first. He turned and made his way farther down the corridor. The guards at the entrance to the palace's great hall snapped to attention as he neared.

"Wait here," Karus told his escort as he entered what had once been the seat of Carthum's power, the throne room of the king. The hobnails on his sandals clacked hollowly upon the marble floor as he strode down the hall.

He ignored the captured standards and trophies of war with which, over the centuries, the kings of Carthum had decorated the hall. His eyes were fixed on the legion's Eagle, which was closely guarded by four legionaries.

The Eagle had been placed upon a raised dais, where the king's throne had once sat. Until the enemy had arrived, the Eagle had been surrounded by the collective standards of the legion. Each cohort and century had placed their standards here.

They had since been removed and returned to their respective units. The men would be heartened by their presence and would fight harder as a result. They always did, for there was collective pride and honor contained within each. It also helped that the standard-bearers were the ones to keep track of the books, including the men's pay and pensions. If the men would not fight for pride and honor, they'd sure as shit fight for their savings.

Only the Eagle remained, a solitary reminder of the legion's honor, and by extension that of the empire. Also, Karus thought, in a manner of speaking…the Eagle touched on Jupiter himself. The Eagle was not just a symbol, but a representation of the divine. The Eagle shrine was a holy place that legionaries of all ranks were permitted to visit, offer devotion, or simply pray.

He stopped, studying the Eagle for a heartbeat, then shifted his gaze to the Eagle guard.

"Leave me with the Eagle."

"Yes, sir," one of the legionaries, an optio, said. "Come on, lads. Let's give the camp prefect some privacy."

Karus waited for them to leave the great hall. Once they had, he stepped up onto the dais. Karus found his heart had started beating a little faster. The Eagle had always held special meaning to him, beyond simply being an inspiration. The emperor himself had held the standard with his own hands and presented it to the legion. It was a ceremony that dated back to the founding of the empire and the first emperor. Karus stared at the Eagle for a long moment before dropping down to a knee and bowing his head.

"Jupiter." Karus cleared his throat. "High Father ... I do not have a proper sacrifice for you. There was no time to find one. Until I do, I thank you with all of my heart for your many blessings. I thank you for healing my boys from the sickness. I thank you for my life and the honor to lead the legion. I thank you for your trust in me." Karus paused as he gathered his thoughts for what would come next. "All that said, we are in a difficult position and could use some divine help. I humbly ask you lend me the strength, if you would, to see the legion through the days ahead. I fear they will be filled with trial and hardship. Help me lead your faithful to victory over our enemies." Karus felt a righteous anger toward the Horde grow within his breast. "Help me show them the might of Rome. Great god, I ask that you bless and assist us in killing our enemies, preferably by the tens of thousands. Help us murder those unholy bastards and send them on from this life to the next. Lend us the strength to see your will done in this world and we will do it."

There was no answer. He had not really expected one. He reached out toward the Eagle and gripped the polished wood of the shaft. Head bowed, he held it for a long moment, seeking … longing for a closer connection with his god. Releasing the shaft, he leaned back.

Gazing up at the polished gold-painted Eagle, Karus felt better. Yes, it had been good to come here. His visit had been long overdue. He climbed back to his feet and noticed that his joints no longer ached like they had. In fact, he could not remember them aching for several days now. Had Jupiter graced him with additional strength? Karus hoped so.

"I have a job to do," Karus said in a hard tone, his voice echoing off the walls of the great hall. "I will see it through to the end. On that, great lord, I swear."

He spared one more look at the Eagle, then, cloak swirling, swung around and returned the way he had come. The six guards, all standing outside the great hall's entrance, came to attention. So too did his escort.

"Resume your posts." Karus turned in the direction of the palace gardens and started back down the corridor.

"Yes, sir," the optio of the Eagle guard said as Karus's own honor guard followed after him.

Karus made his way rapidly back down the corridor and out to the palace gardens. He stopped on the steps. The day was bright, hot, and humid. So much so, he already felt sweat begin to bead on his forehead.

The dragons were gone. The evidence that they had used the space as their temporary home was in plain sight. When the legion had arrived in Carthum, the gardens had simply been neglected and overgrown. Since then, they had been thoroughly damaged, destroyed even. Pottery had been shattered and dirt strewn about the courtyard. Flowers, torn up from their beds, lay dried and gnarled across the few pathways that had not been ripped up. The beauty that had once graced this place was no more.

"Ouch," came a cry to his left. This was followed almost immediately by a grunt and clatter.

Si'Cara was standing over Amarra, who had clearly just been knocked on her ass. Amarra was holding her stomach with a hand. Si'Cara held a long wooden staff, which, with a practiced ease, she swung around in a flourish, and placed the butt in the dirt. Amarra's staff lay discarded next to her.

Amarra was wearing a plain, loose-fitting, brown dress. And her white hair had been tightly bound into a single braid. She was sweaty and red in the face. There was an angry look from her that blazed up at Si'Cara.

"That," Amarra said, outrage in her voice, "was unfair."

"Get accustomed to it," Si'Cara said calmly and tapped the butt of her staff in the dirt. "Life is unfair. Perhaps I was mistaken, but I thought you knew this already. When an orc comes for you, he will do whatever he must to kill you, mistress. You must do the same to him. It is better you take his life than the other way around."

Si'Cara held out a hand and helped Amarra to her feet. Dusting off her hands, Amarra bent down and picked up her staff.

"You're beating me up good," Amarra said, and brought her staff up into a defensive position. "I can take more."

"And I can do a lot worse," Si'Cara said. "Trust me. I am taking it easy on you."

"I find that hard to believe."

"With practice and gained skill, and a few more lumps to chalk up to experience ... you will come to learn the truth in my words," Si'Cara said with a grin. "Now, let me show you what I did."

Karus stood where he was and watched as Si'Cara demonstrated what she had just done and then slowly walked

Amarra through the movement. She offered pointers as Amarra attempted to repeat it.

She sought to understand and learn, asking questions as she walked her way through the movement again under Si'Cara's experienced gaze. Karus felt a sudden warmth toward Amarra. There was a fierce determination there to be better at anything she did. That was one of the things he loved, her unyielding determination.

For the last week, Si'Cara had worked Amarra literally from suns-up to suns-down. Each night, Amarra had come back to the room they shared exhausted, battered, and bruised. However, in the morning she stiffly rolled out of bed, eager for more.

"Sir."

Karus turned to find Delvaris behind him. Immediately, the warmth he had felt vanished. It was like a cloud had covered both suns, and with it, a cold feeling slithered down his spine. If it had been a regular update, a messenger would have been sent. Something had clearly happened.

"The enemy has launched an assault against a portion of the north wall, sir," Delvaris reported. "I have no other details. The message was terse and came in from one of Flaccus's subordinates. Centurion Flaccus had already left the palace when the news arrived. It was too late to catch him. I imagine he will learn soon enough when he returns to his command."

"It's begun," Karus said.

"Seems that way, sir."

Karus was silent for a moment. It took at least a half hour for a messenger to reach headquarters from the north wall. That meant the attack had been going on for that long at least, maybe longer. The fight had started and he'd remained ignorant of that fact. He felt an intense wave of frustration at not knowing how things were going. Remembering that his officers were trained professionals, he calmed himself and thought of the larger picture.

"Any word from the other walls?" Karus asked.

"No, sir," Delvaris said.

"Sound the alarm, then send messengers to the other walls," Karus ordered. "Alert them to the attack on the north and tell them to be prepared to be hit as well. Instruct them to inform us if the enemy facing their commands so much as sneezes. Got that?"

"Yes, sir," Delvaris said.

"I am going to the north wall."

"I thought you might be, sir," Delvaris said.

Without Amarra and Si'Cara ever having known he had been there, Karus moved past Delvaris and back into the corridor and the shade. Amarra was better off training with Si'Cara and away from the action. She'd be safer that way, for in Karus's opinion, she had no business being near the fighting. That was his job.

He found four elves, including Kol'Cara, waiting along with his legionary escort. Delvaris had likely summoned the elves.

"Let's go," Karus said to them and started down the corridor. He wanted to see the action for himself.

Chapter Eighteen

The sky was clouding over, blocking the two suns entirely. Despite the break from the sunlight, the cloud cover did nothing to lessen the brutal afternoon heat. Boiling and baking away in his armor, Karus stood upon the south wall, his gaze fixed upon the enemy.

He had just arrived a short while before and was watching the enemy attempt to overcome the legion's hold of the wall. At his side was Centurion Varno, of Seventh Cohort, whose men were directly engaged in the fight. Kol'Cara was with them. The elf was studying the enemy. He seemed almost brooding in his silence.

They were on a portion of the wall that jutted out from the main wall by a few feet and were only yards from the fight. The perch was also slightly raised and gave them a unique view of the entire battle, which encompassed a small section of the south wall, about a hundred yards in length.

Mixed with the clash of arms, there was shouting, cursing, officers screaming orders and encouragements, the animalistic roars of the enemy, and cries of the injured. They were so close, Karus could smell the sweet stench of blood on the air and taste it on his tongue.

Only the north and the south walls had been tested by the enemy so far. Karus had spent a good portion of the day on the north wall with Flaccus before making his way through the city to see the action in the south.

"We're holding good, sir." Varno's eyes were on the fighting, studying it. He was cool, collected, and in control and had been when Karus had arrived, just like a good officer should be. Karus could sense the desire in the man to get back to the fight and his men. He could well understand the feeling, but Karus was not ready to let him go yet. Varno's junior officers could handle things for a short while.

"This is their third attempt at forcing the wall?" Karus asked.

"Yes, sir," Varno said. "It is. My boys are holding good."

From what he was seeing, Karus could not disagree with his centurion. Varno's boys were holding. In fact, they were doing better than that. Seventh Cohort was having no difficulty at all defending the wall. The noise the fight generated was loud, cacophonous even, but Karus had heard noisier battles.

The enemy had thrown at least five thousand orcs with over a hundred scaling ladders forward to attack. They had no artillery support or even, for that matter, any light infantry with bows or slings to give them covering fire.

The orcs simply ran up in ladder teams, shouting as they came with great enthusiasm and energy. The ladders were thrown up against the wall and they began climbing.

As the enemy climbed, the men above threw rocks and broken pieces of stone and masonry down on their heads. They tossed sand, baked near the melting point, over the wall, along with buckets of boiling oil and water. The oil was particularly nasty, because it got under the armor and burned whatever skin it touched. A handful of auxiliaries armed with bows moved along the wall and shot arrows down at the orcs, more of a harassing fire than anything else.

The fighting at the top of the wall was ugly, brutal, and unforgiving. Teams of legionaries worked together to dislodge the enemy ladders. They used long poles, shields, and their bare hands to push them off the wall and away. While their fellows climbed, hundreds of orcs on the ground struggled mightily to keep the ladders in place.

Time and time again, the legionaries won the struggle, throwing ladders thick with the enemy back and off the wall. These crashed to the ground, outright killing or seriously injuring those unfortunates who had been clinging to the ladders.

Several who had been waiting their turns below were not quick enough to get out of the way. Karus had seen a number crushed as their fellows came down atop them. The few orcs who managed to make it to the top of the ladder and wall found short swords, shields, and grim-faced men waiting for them. They had no chance of making it off the ladders and over the wall.

It was an unequal fight, one balanced heavily in the legion's favor. The story had been the same on the north wall. Karus did not understand the enemy's thinking. Just beyond the assault waited another ten thousand orcs. These had been employed in constructing siege works, the purpose of which was to seal the gate in so the defenders in the city had no hope of sallying forth. Those works consisted of three deep trenches, backed up by a steep-faced earthen wall.

Instead of supporting their fellows, these orcs stood on their newly constructed wall and simply watched the attackers make what Karus considered a futile assault.

For the life of him, he could not think of what the enemy was doing or hoping to accomplish with their attack. It must be a test of some kind or a distraction, for his men were slaughtering the orcs with near ease.

Frustrated, Karus stepped up to the edge of the wall. The stone of the battlement, under the direct light of the two suns, almost burned to the touch. Karus rested his palms upon it. He barely noticed the heat as an unconscious man was hurriedly carried by on a litter. The legionary had taken a savage cut that ran from his lower cheek to the bridge of his nose. Exposed cartilage and bone could be seen.

As the litter party hurried toward the gatehouse to find a surgeon, they left a trail of splotchy blood behind them. It had not been the worst wound Karus had ever seen, but it pained him no less seeing one of his men in such a state. He never enjoyed seeing his men injured or suffering.

"Gods." Varno shook his head at the sight of the injured man. "I'll never get used to this side of the job. Fucking Fortuna, Kenvaanes is one of my best men. He was on track to be promoted to optio once a vacancy opened. If he survives, he's gonna be seriously disfigured."

"Any idea on how many casualties you've taken so far?" Karus asked, glancing over. He had seen many a promising man die before his time or become permanently disabled. It never got any easier.

"If I had to guess, about ten," Varno said as he expelled a slow breath. "Besides Kenvaanes, none have been serious wounds so far. Light injuries only, cuts and smashed fingers mostly."

A man a few yards to their right stepped up to the wall with a javelin. In a smooth motion and grunting with the effort, he threw the heavy weapon at an orc hanging on the side of the nearest ladder. The orc was waving his sword in the air with one hand, pointing it up at the legionaries above while yelling at those below, seeming to encourage them onward.

The javelin flew true and took the creature in the side, punching right through the leather armor. So powerful had the missile been thrown that he was snatched from the ladder. He fell to the ground thirty feet below and, still gripping his sword, moved no more.

"Good throw, Jaxus," Varno shouted to the legionary.

"Thank you, sir," Jaxus said, after he'd surveyed his handiwork. "Centurion Kellon asked me to take him out, sir. Thought he might be an officer."

Karus turned his gaze skyward. He spotted Cyln'Phax as she circled above. He could see none of the other dragons, but he knew they were nearby. A moment later, the red dragon disappeared into the clouds and was lost from sight.

He shifted his gaze outward to the fields before the city, searching for wyrms. He saw one had landed perhaps a half mile away. The dragon appeared small, but he knew that was only an illusion created by the distance. Though much smaller than taltalum, the wyrms were still huge and deadly.

Some type of camp had been erected around the creature. Karus could make out tents and smaller figures moving about. He supposed they were tending to the wyrm's needs, whatever that entailed.

Movement caught his eye, and he spotted another wyrm. This one was swooping down from the sky in a leisurely glide toward the ground and the camp. Wings outstretched and wobbling slightly on the wind, the creature was coming in for a landing. Watching the dragon, Karus was reminded of geese he had seen back in Britannia as they came in to land on a pond.

Interestingly, a figure rode on the wyrm's back. Karus wondered if it was someone important or just how the dragon was controlled. Cyln'Phax had told him repeatedly that wyrms were no smarter than horses and needed control.

As the creature neared the ground, it began flapping mightily, slowing its speed to a near hover. Almost gently, it landed behind the wyrm already on the ground.

"At least the dragons have not attacked us," Varno said, having clearly followed Karus's gaze. "That's something at any rate."

"Agreed," Karus said, "and with ours flying cover, that's not likely to happen."

"I hope you're right, sir," Varno said. "Those beasts are unnatural. I am sure glad we never had to face anything like that back in Britannia. I'll take the Celts any day."

Grunting his agreement, Karus turned his gaze back to the fighting. He watched it for a time. The battle's outcome was a foregone conclusion. The wall would remain in the legion's hands.

"Have you called up the reserve cohort yet?" Karus asked. He knew Varno had not. But still out of courtesy he posed it as a question.

"Not entirely, sir." Varno shifted almost uncomfortably at the suggestion. Karus knew Varno now felt compelled to defend his actions. "I have a section or two with bows," Varno explained, "but nothing more. There seemed no point. The enemy's assault is on the light side. Should they push those others out there forward, I will have fatigued our reserves for no good reason. I would prefer to save them, sir, until we really need them."

Karus considered the centurion's thinking, his gaze shifting back to the other orcs who were watching the fight. Most were standing on the new wall to get a better view of the assault. Many still held shovels or pickaxes. They were not formed up and stood loosely about.

There was, in Karus's estimation, simply no way in the short term they could be organized sufficiently and brought forward to attack or reinforce. He judged they would need at least half an hour to a full hour to get their act together. By then, the fight at the wall would likely be over … sooner if Karus had anything to say about it. Varno's decision to withhold his reserve had been prudent and well thought out. Karus could not and would not fault him for that.

"The Second Vasconum CR is your reserve, right?" Karus asked. When they had left their garrison at Eboracum in Britannia, the CR had originally been an overstrength light infantry cohort, one with a long and prestigious history, dating all the way back to the days of Caesar and Pompey. After fighting the Celts in the final battle before they had been magically transported to this world, the formation had been whittled down to a few hundred. It was commanded by Varno's brother, Gordian.

Varno and Gordian had enlisted together more than fifteen years prior. They were some of his best officers. More important to Karus, the two men worked well together, which was one of the reasons why the CR was Varno's immediate reserve and fire brigade.

"They are, sir," Varno confirmed. "They can be up on the wall in short order."

"Right then," Karus said, "order up your brother's cohort. Make sure they bring enough javelins for five tosses, understand?"

"Five? That will eat into our ready supply, sir." Varno pointed down the wall. "We have only five thousand of the weapons for the defense of the entire southern wall. I was trying to conserve them for when we need them."

Given the lack of the enemy's efforts against the wall, that was only sensible. But Karus had different ideas. The enemy had no idea how many javelins the legion had, and he wanted to set an example. By throwing forward an unsupported force in a confined area, the enemy had made a mistake and he wanted to make them pay for it.

"The enemy is before us." Karus waved toward the assault. "They are concentrated in one confined area and likely won't be again." He pointed down at the lines of orcs waiting to go up the ladders. "Not like this. A real assault against this wall will see them spread out along its entire length, thereby thinning our numbers. That will increase their chances of gaining a foothold and make it more difficult for us to hold them back. When the enemy get serious, they will also bring up infantry with bows and slings, maybe even some light artillery, bolt throwers and such, if they have them." Karus paused, his gaze sweeping the enemy. He felt his anger begin to mount. "This attack upon your position cannot go on for much longer. Do you disagree?"

"No, sir," Varno said, "I do not."

"I intend to use it as an opportunity to kill as many as I can, while I can. That will mean the less we face later, and we will educate our enemy on how dangerous we can be. Understand me on this matter?"

"Yes, sir," Varno said. "I do."

"Good," Karus said. "Then kindly see that your brother brings up his cohort."

"I will, sir." Varno saluted and moved off to give the appropriate orders to one of his legionaries, who dashed toward the nearest stairs. The centurion returned a few moments later. "If you will excuse me, sir. I'd like to return to the fight and my men."

Karus gave the man a curt nod of approval and Varno left. Kol'Cara moved closer to Karus. For a time, neither said anything. They just watched as the legion murdered the enemy.

"You're concerned about the nature of this assault," Kol'Cara said. It was not a question.

"I always worry when it comes to a fight."

"But this is different, no?" Kol'Cara asked.

Karus waved a hand at the enemy. "This attack, and the other one against the north wall, makes no tactical sense. For all intents and purposes, the enemy is allowing me the opportunity to slaughter their warriors."

"Yes," Kol'Cara said, "they seem to be doing just that."

"It is a waste of good infantry."

"But you are killing them," Kol'Cara said. "Is not that what soldiers are supposed to do? Kill the enemy, preferably before they kill you?"

"Don't get me wrong," Karus said. "I will happily murder them in a one-sided fight all day long. But I still disapprove of my opponent's methods. There is nothing baser in my opinion than to waste good soldiers for no reason. A sacred trust exists between leadership and the rank and file. A commander should never, under any circumstances, *ever* violate that trust."

Kol'Cara turned his timeless gaze on Karus, who was suddenly struck by how alien the elf's eyes were. He at times forgot that the elf was not human. It was yet another reminder of the strange land the legion had been brought to. Life had taken a fantastical turn. Karus understood it would never be the same for him and his people. What they had once considered normal was now forever lost to them.

"It is important to remember," Kol'Cara said, "there is a reason for every decision. We just do not know what their reasoning is, or we are not seeing it….think perspective."

"Perspective?" Karus asked.

"Yes," Kol'Cara said. "It is all about one's perspective. The enemy general's view of the situation is different than our own."

"True," Karus said, thinking the elf very correct. "We're just not seeing it…"

Kol'Cara inclined his head slightly, then raised an eyebrow. "Perhaps they seek only to distract."

"That's what I am afraid of." Karus looked over at the elf. "But from what?"

"I do not know," Kol'Cara admitted. "Have you considered there might be additional tunnels into the city? And that the enemy knows about them?"

"We have," Karus said. "It's why there are roving patrols out, moving throughout the city, randomly checking buildings." Karus expelled a heated breath. "As soon as I saw the attack against the north wall this morning, and the lack of effort on the enemy's part, I doubled the patrols. The problem is…Carthum is a big damn city. It is easy to miss something." Karus smacked the stone of the battlement lightly with his palm. "You could hide a cohort in some of the larger buildings and no one would ever know, unless they went inside and searched."

"You brought the tunnel down under the tavern?" Kol'Cara asked.

"We did," Karus said. "I personally checked the work. It won't be easily opened either. Even if they manage to discover a tunnel we don't know about, they still will have to contend with our defensive positions throughout the city. They're not going to get far before bumping into someone, and then the alarm will be sounded."

"That is a comfort," Kol'Cara said. "Let us hope they are ignorant that such tunnels might exist."

"They'd have to find one first," Karus said, thinking of the small group of orcs they had caught weeks ago in the city. Before their deaths, those had scaled the city wall. Had they known of a tunnel they would have surely used it to avoid detection.

Behind them, men from the CR began to pound their way up the stairs and past. Each man carried five javelins. With officers shouting, the CR moved out behind the men of Seventh Cohort, who were fighting back against the enemy's attempt to scale and overcome the wall.

"Sir." Gordian Varno, prefect of the CR, gave Karus a salute as he came up. Gordian was five years older than his brother. He was a tall man, fit, and hard-looking, with a square jaw and piercing blue eyes. Though you could not tell due to his helmet, he was almost completely bald and looked nothing like his brother.

Despite being assigned to leading auxiliaries, he wore legionary armor. Prior to taking command of the CR, he had been a centurion in Second Legion.

"Gord," Karus said, "good to see you."

"You too, sir." Gordian went to the wall and looked over at the enemy making their assault. He studied them for a long moment and gave a low whistle before his gaze traveled to the legionaries holding the wall. "A nice day for a fight, sir, good and hot for the enemy."

"See if you can make it hotter for them," Karus said, "will you?"

"We'll make it scalding, sir," the prefect said, with a grim smile.

"That's what I am counting on." Karus genuinely liked Gord. He was a professional soldier, through and through. "As soon as your boys are in position, you can start tossing javelins at will. Before they call off the assault, I want to kill or injure as many of the bastards as we can."

"Very good, sir. I will get right to work." With that, the prefect moved off, shouting to his men, who were still pounding their way up the stairs. "Move your collective asses, you maggots. Officers, I want your men in position yesterday. Come on ... move it, boys. The enemy's waiting on us."

Karus watched as Gord got his men slotted into position, junior officers working to dress the men, one next to another. The space on the wall was large enough for them to group up in ranks to the flanks of the main fighting for a concerted toss. Gord also positioned a thin line of men directly behind those holding the wall. The extra javelins were set to the right of each auxiliary, at their feet, with the iron heads of the weapons pointed toward the enemy.

"Prepare to toss!" Gord shouted at the top of his lungs. His men to the sides stepped up closer to the wall. Those behind the fighting prepared to throw over the heads of the men to their front by taking a step backward and hefting the heavy missiles. "Make it a good throw, boys. Let's show the legionaries how javelin work's properly done. I expect you to make Daddy proud." Gord paused for several heartbeats. "Release!"

An iron-tipped wave, carrying with it injury and death, arced up into the air. All told, over three hundred of the deadly missiles were thrown at the enemy. There was a loud clatter as the weighted javelins hammered home, punching through armor, skin, muscle, and bone.

A shocking number of screams followed, a testament to the effectiveness of the toss. Dozens on the ground had been hit. The men of the CR had been good soldiers before Gord had taken command. After, they had become even better. His men loved him, and had nicknamed him Daddy, because he went out of his way to look after them. But that did not mean he coddled them. Gord was a harsh disciplinarian, but also fair in the meting out of justice. The men respected that, for not all officers were as evenhanded.

"Second toss," Gord roared. "Ready yourselves. Let's go, boys ... be quick about it."

The men picked up the next javelin and prepared for the toss.

Gord took a long moment to look to the left and then the right, studying his men. Apparently satisfied that all was ready, he shouted, "Release."

A second wave of javelins flew up before plunging inevitably downward. There was an ear-ringing clatter, followed by screams, shouts, and cries of agony. The intensity of the fighting on the wall slackened noticeably. The defenders were able to easily shove several ladders back and off the wall. More ladders followed a heartbeat later, crashing to the ground.

"Smartly done, boys," Gord shouted. "Ready yourselves for another toss. Let's show them some more love, shall we?"

The prefect waited, almost patiently, till his boys were prepared. Only someone like Karus, who knew Gord well enough, could spot the signs of excitement, barely contained nervous energy, and impatience, as the prefect stepped up to the edge of the wall and peered over the side. The big man hesitated a moment as he surveyed his cohort's handiwork. Gord grinned broadly, then shouted, "You beautiful bastards! Give 'em another ... Release."

The third wave of death rose up, flying outward, before cresting and crashing home in a devastating volley. Much of the enemy's effort had ground to a halt. After this last toss, it all but stopped. The enemy at the base of the ladders appeared badly shaken and disorganized. One after another, ladders were shoved off the wall, until only two remained.

An orc at the top of one, to avoid being run through by a short sword, slashed his sword wildly about at the legionaries. For several moments, he managed to keep the swords at bay. However, his efforts were in vain.

Almost simultaneously, several legionaries jabbed at him. As he dodged and blocked, one strike connected, stabbing him through the eye socket. He stiffened and fell, tumbling limply down the ladder, taking the next two orcs with him to the ground. The ladder followed him down a few heartbeats later as the legionaries shoved it off the wall with long poles.

"Excellent toss," Gord shouted at his men. "A very nice throw, boys. Ready yourselves for the next toss."

A horn sounded, three long blasts. With it, the orcs began to draw back from the wall. Karus felt a sense of triumph and elation wash over him. The enemy was calling off the assault. At the same time, the keen sense of victory was mixed with frustration. The enemy would soon be out of his reach, and that irritated him immensely. Karus wanted to hurt them some more.

"Should I hit them one more time, sir?" Gord shouted at Karus as the horn call sounded yet again, for he had seen them pulling back too.

"If you would," Karus called back, "give them a parting gift. Let them know what's waiting for them when they return."

"Right, boys, make your final throw count," Gord shouted and then checked to make sure all were ready. "Release."

Karus watched the javelins fly outward. They landed amongst the withdrawing orcs. Dozens more of the enemy were hit. What had started as an orderly pullback rapidly became a rout. This last toss had hurt, and badly too. Added to the previous throws, hundreds of the enemy were down, dead, and injured. On the grander scale, when compared to the entirety of the enemy army, it was a minor victory, but he'd take it just the same.

The men gave an enthusiastic cheer.

KARUS.

A scream, like a hammer forging iron, slammed his mind. It was so powerful, he was rocked by it and stumbled backward. He staggered like he was drunk, almost falling to his knees. Kol'Cara grabbed his arm to keep him upright.

"Are you injured?" Kol'Cara asked in alarm. "Have you been hit?"

Karus, the shout came again. This time it was not as powerful, but it was urgent and filled with what he thought was desperation. Or was it fear, mixed with a terrible dread? He recognized it as Cyln'Phax. *We must leave.*

"What?" Karus asked, still staggered by the intensity of her call. "Leave?"

Almost frantic, Kol'Cara began scanning Karus, checking for wounds. Ignoring the elf's efforts, Karus looked directly up, for he sensed that was where the call was coming from.

Cyln'Phax emerged from the clouds, her wings tucked back and close to her body. She was pointed straight down at the ground, plummeting earthward like a rock, seeming to dive right at them.

Seeing Karus's gaze, Kol'Cara looked up and said something in Elven, likely a curse. Several men on the wall spotted her and shouted out a warning. The cheer died out, with nearly every eye looking up.

Recovering himself, Karus shook Kol'Cara off as Cyln'Phax twisted her body around. Just when it seemed like the dragon would hit the wall, crashing into them, she extended her wings and pulled out of her dive. For a long moment, Cyln'Phax seemed to hang right over them, then she flashed by, moving over the city, heading in a westward direction. Her passage created a powerful gust of wind that almost knocked several men from the wall and staggered Karus again.

Noctalum! she shouted at him. *There are too many. We must go. I don't... I don't know when we will be back... I am sorry... but... you are on your own...*

Then she was gone from view and the connection between them was severed. Karus did not know how he knew, he just did. There would be no more speaking with her. A deep, malevolent roar filled the air. It seemed to shake the wall and was so loud, Karus felt it in his chest.

"Oh, shit," Karus said, eyes going skyward again. With dread, he knew what he would find.

A gray and black dragon, a noctalum, had emerged from the clouds over the city. Clearly in pursuit of the red dragon, the monster was diving in the direction Cyln'Phax had gone.

Two more of the great beasts appeared, diving down on the wyrms out in the field. Both animals had taken to the air and were desperately beating their wings, attempting to flee.

Behind Karus and to the north, there came other somewhat muffled roars from somewhere in the direction of the city and out of sight. Karus wondered how many of the massive dragons were out there. The thought of it made his blood run cold.

The two noctalum to their front were rapidly gaining on the wyrms. Karus watched in awe as one of the dragons caught up with a wyrm. Claws outstretched, it reached out with its forelegs and latched onto one of the smaller dragon's wings.

Almost with ease, the big dragon tore the wing apart, then released its hold. Screaming in agony, the injured wyrm lost control and crashed into the ground with tremendous force, kicking up an incredible shower of dirt. Karus could feel the impact through his sandals as the wall itself seemed to tremble.

The noctalum banked to the right and began beating at the air with its massive wings as it worked to catch up with its companion, who was chasing the last wyrm in view.

Desperate, the wyrm weaved wildly to the left and then right, attempting to evade the hunter, who was steadily gaining on its prey. It reminded Karus of watching a hawk hunt a pigeon. The wyrm's attempts at evasion did not work. The noctalum caught it firmly with its claws. As it latched on, the bigger dragon bathed the wyrm in a stream of fire so bright, it was equal to the intensity of a sun.

The wyrm screamed horribly, a piercing sound that grated at the ears. The scream was abruptly cut off and the wyrm fell limp. A mere heartbeat later, the noctalum released the burning wyrm. It too crashed to the ground, landing with a deep *thud* and throwing up a great geyser of dirt high into the air.

The noctalum let out a truly monstrous roar of what Karus took to be satisfaction. As one, both of the gray and black dragons swung around toward the city.

"Gods," Karus breathed. The dragons were coming for the legion. They drew closer, then, almost leisurely, both began pumping their wings, each flap taking them high and higher. He watched as they climbed skyward, swinging away from the city before heading in a westward direction and into the clouds. A moment later, they were gone from view.

Silence followed as every man on the wall stared skyward in shock. The enemy below seemed just as stunned. It was as if even the wind had stilled. There was not a sound, nor a breath on the air.

The silence did not last long. The enemy's horn blew again. Those below, who had been stunned to immobility by what had happened, continued their flight to safety and out of javelin range.

"Do you think they are coming back?" Karus asked Kol'Cara.

"I don't know," the elf said in a quiet voice. "The noctalum on this world have been hunting other dragons since before I went into stasis. It is not known why they do it. I think there is a good chance they will ignore us, as we lesser races are generally beneath their notice."

"Lesser races?" Karus asked.

"At least...we can hope they do," Kol'Cara said. "It is not wise to draw their attention, for they are an unforgiving people that even we elves do our best to avoid."

Karus was heartened by that, but at the same time was deeply concerned for Cyln'Phax, Kordem, and their children. He hoped they got away. A worrying thought struck him. What would happen if the enemy's wyrms came back first? For surely some of the enemy's dragons would survive the noctalum's attack and escape.

"Where is the camp prefect?" a voice called urgently from behind them. "Where is he?"

"Over there," someone shouted.

Karus turned and saw an out-of-breath messenger approaching. The man's face was flushed from jogging in the brutal heat. He came to attention, saluted crisply, and passed over his message.

Opening it, Karus read. He closed his eyes in frustration.

"What is it?" Kol'Cara asked.

"The enemy is hitting the entirety of the east wall … in force. They marched out of their camp and attacked." Karus bit the words out. He felt his anger mount. Why had word not reached him about that sooner? The moment the enemy had marched, he should have been alerted. He turned to the messenger. "Do you know how long the attack has been going on?"

"About an hour, sir." The messenger was breathing heavily. "It's hot and hard fighting. Tribune Delvaris told me to tell you that, sir. He asked that you come immediately."

Karus crumpled the message, thoroughly disgusted. Someone had screwed up, for the enemy marching that many orcs forward and forming them up for an assault would have taken some time. By all rights, he should be at the east wall, commanding the efforts, and not here, where the fighting was essentially irrelevant. Karus turned his attention back to Kol'Cara.

"It seems they've thrown in at least twenty-five thousand warriors, maybe more, against us. Reinforcements are being sent from the west wall to strengthen our defense." Karus glanced out at the retreating enemy. "I guess we have our answer now. The attack on the north and south walls was only a distraction, as we had thought. The real assault has begun."

Chapter Nineteen

"This way, sir," the legionary guide said as he turned onto a side street. The buildings seemed to crowd in on them. This area was one of the poorer districts in the city and the evidence of that was all around. The buildings had a decayed and frayed look to them, as if basic maintenance had been an afterthought.

It was late afternoon and the street was heavily shadowed, presaging the near onset of dusk. Kol'Cara walked at his side. Two other elves, Joron'Tas and Kelus'Su, and four legionaries followed a few steps behind.

They had picked up their guide at the last defensive position they had passed, where Karus had found himself briefly detained by the centurion in command. He had wanted an update on what Karus knew about the attack on the city walls, which was not much.

Their guide led them another hundred yards down the street and finally onto a wider boulevard, with a small square just ahead. They passed through the square and were led up to a squat two-story building that was sandwiched between two warehouses. At the far end of the street, the east wall was finally in view, seventy yards away. Karus could hear the fighting, somewhat muted, but raging all the same.

On the wall itself, there were figures moving about. He wanted to get up there, to eyeball the situation personally, but first had decided to stop by the dwarven headquarters and get an update on the larger picture of what was going on. That way, when he did see the fighting, he would be better informed and guarded against making assumptions based upon incomplete information.

Armor jingling, a century of men carrying javelins and shields overtook them, jogging past toward the wall. The centurion in command, jogging to the side of the formation, offered a salute on the move. Karus returned the salute.

"This is where I will leave you, sir." Their legionary guide opened the door to the building he had led them to.

"Thank you," Karus said. "You may return to your century."

"Yes, sir." The legionary saluted and left.

Karus was about to enter the building when he thought he heard shouting behind them. It died off rapidly. He paused and looked back.

"What?" Kol'Cara asked, glancing in the direction Karus was looking.

"It's nothing," Karus said, deciding he had only heard an echo from the wall, a trick of sound... nothing more.

The elf scowled slightly, scanned the street, then said something in Elven to the other two elves. Without hesitation, both moved away in the direction they'd just come. Karus's legionary escort watched them go in question. Karus turned his gaze to the elf.

"Just to be sure it was nothing," Kol'Cara said.

Karus gave a nod and turned away, stepping into the dwarven headquarters. He was followed a moment later by Kol'Cara and the escort of legionaries.

The building had once been occupied by a leather maker. It smelled terrible, almost bad enough to make the eyes water. Scraps of leather littered the floor. The tanning vats, having long since dried, had been moved and stacked against the walls, along with the racks that had been used for curing.

Since there were no windows, Karus wondered if they had tanned inside, which seemed almost inconceivable to him. It was more likely they had done it out on the street.

Three clerks sat at a large table. None looked up as he entered. They were hunched over wax tablets and writing furiously with ornate metal styluses.

The heat of the room made the stench worse. It was lit only by a handful of oil lamps, which barely provided adequate light. Martuke was standing by a table, giving instruction to a fourth clerk, who was writing as Martuke dictated. Dennig was nowhere to be seen.

Martuke glanced up and spotted Karus. He frowned slightly as recognition set in. Karus noticed that the dwarf's armor was covered in a spattering of dried green blood, orc blood. He had clearly been up on the wall and in the thick of things.

A bucket by the door held fresh water. As Karus and Kol'Cara moved over to Martuke, one of his legionaries took the ladle, dipped it, and drank.

"Messages were sent to you the moment the enemy began to march from their camp," Martuke said by way of greeting. "It is about time you decided to come to where the action is."

"I never received those dispatches," Karus said, wondering what had happened to the messengers. Had they gotten lost in the city? That seemed difficult to believe. "The only messenger that found me told me the attack was well underway."

Martuke gave a disbelieving grunt and said something more in Dwarven to the clerk, who continued to write. Then

Martuke turned to face Karus fully. The intense dislike in his gaze was more than evident.

"Where is Dennig?" Karus asked.

"Shoega is on the wall," Martuke said.

With the fighting, Karus figured he would have been there. It only made sense.

"He is exactly where he should be," Martuke continued with disdain, "leading our warriors in battle."

Karus did not like the bastard's implication. He felt his ire toward the dwarf rise. It took a surprising effort, but Karus managed to contain himself from responding. He needed the dwarves and had enough headaches as it was, especially with his legion in battle and the city's walls under assault. He took a calming breath, glanced around the large room. There was a door opposite the one he had entered and a staircase that led to the second floor.

"Before I go up to the wall," Karus said, "can you give me an update on the tactical situation? I have been at the fight on the southern wall."

Martuke eyed him for a long moment. He appeared as if he might refuse, then apparently reconsidered.

"This way."

The dwarf led him over to a long table. A map had been spread out on the table. A small clay lamp, formed in the shape of a teska, lay on the tabletop. The map turned out to be a rough sketch of the section of the city wall the dwarves were charged with holding. It showed a little beyond their position too. Karus recognized it as a camp scribe copy, most likely provided by the legion since there were notes in Latin. The dwarf rested a palm upon the map.

"The enemy has thrown around forty thousand against the east wall. That is only an estimate, but one I think accurate. Needless to say, the fighting is difficult. Your Eighth

Cohort is to our right, here." Martuke touched the map. "So is the Ninth, along with one of your auxiliary formations. I don't recall their name. To our left is the Tenth. All along the wall, the enemy are pressing, but their main thrust, or really their strength, is here, against our position, and here facing the Tenth." Martuke paused and glanced up. "I understand more of your legionaries are on their way, as well as another auxiliary cohort."

Karus thought that good news. Someone had made the decision to call for help.

"The enemy is pressing us hard," Martuke continued. "So far, we are holding and killing them in great numbers. They are also bringing up more warriors, perhaps another twenty thousand. Those are forming up here." Martuke touched a point to the front of the east wall's gate, then rubbed at his eyes, which were bloodshot. Only then did Karus recognize the weary exhaustion that battle brought on.

Seeming to deflate, Martuke let out a long tired breath. "As I said, we're holding for the moment. However, unless you order more men up, beyond what are already on their way... within two or three hours, our warriors and your legionaries will start to become fatigued. They will need replacement and rest. That is where the real threat lies... in exhaustion. Without help and sufficient reinforcement, I doubt we will be able to hold through the night."

Karus took a moment to absorb that. It was not good news, but also not unexpected. He had understood, when the enemy hit them in earnest, things would not be so easy. Martuke's briefing only reinforced that feeling.

"The enemy's assault, for lack of a better word," Martuke said, "is furious. They have thrown their best at us."

"You don't think they will call off the attack once darkness comes?" Karus asked, knowing it was incredibly difficult to coordinate an assault, let alone fight, once it became dark. With the cloud cover overhead, there would be little to no moonlight. He could not imagine what a major assault would be like on a fortified city in the dark. Whenever possible, most commanders he had known avoided night actions, himself included.

"No," Martuke said. "I do not think they will…."

The door opened on the other side of the building. Ducking through the doorway, Ugin stepped into the room. He spotted Karus, bared his teeth in a pleased grin, and started over as one of the two elves of his escort behind him closed the door.

"This place stinks like an orc's hovel," Ugin said. The Vass had to hunch his shoulders slightly to keep his head from hitting the ceiling beams.

"It does," Martuke agreed.

"You could not have chosen a better headquarters?" Ugin asked, glancing around in disgust. "There is an entire city of empty buildings out there."

"Shoega always chooses the worst locations for his headquarters," Martuke said, with an unfriendly look thrown to the Vass. "He does not want his officers lingering too long here or becoming comfortable. Their place is with their units."

"I guess that makes sense," Ugin said and then turned to Karus. "I was hoping to get some information before I went up to the wall. I did not expect to find you here. This, I must admit, is a pleasant surprise, for no one could find you."

"I am gathering that," Karus said, feeling intense frustration. Normally this kind of thing did not happen. Why they couldn't find him was beyond Karus. "Something must have happened to the messengers," Karus said. "They got lost or…"

"Something," Ugin said with a shrug. "Well . . . it does not matter. I have found you and come to fight, as our bargain dictates."

"I think we're gonna need that sword of yours," Karus said.

The door through which Ugin had come opened again and a grim-faced dwarven warrior entered. He walked up to Martuke, stood to attention, and said something in Dwarven. Martuke gave an unhappy nod and replied tersely. The dwarf spun on his heel and left.

Running a hand through his beard, Martuke watched him leave. The dwarf blew out a long breath before turning to one of the clerks. He snapped out what sounded like an order. The clerk gave a nod, set his stylus down, and pushed back his stool, standing. He started for the door Karus had entered through. Stopping their work, the other two clerks set their styluses down and moved over to where their swords had been leaned against the wall, next to their packs.

"What's going on?" Karus asked.

"The warchief has ordered the rest of our reserves, about a hundred, to be sent into the fight," Martuke said. "I will be going with them, as will the clerks."

That told Karus how difficult things were becoming. He felt the intense need to get to the wall to eyeball the battle for himself and regain touch with the legion. He needed to begin exerting some control over events before they overtook him and things spun out of control.

Martuke said something to the clerk who was headed for the door. Hand on the latch, the clerk turned and started to reply. As he did, the door burst open, knocking him roughly backward several steps. It was one of the elves, Joron'Tas. He had his sword out, and it was stained with green blood. He shouted something in Elven to Kol'Cara.

There were shouts of alarm outside, followed by the ring of steel on steel. Joron'Tas glanced behind him, then made to step inside but was instead thrown forward. An arrow had hammered square into his back. The tip had emerged from his chest. He vomited blood and, curling up, rocked on the dirty wooden floor amidst the scraps of discarded leather.

Kelus'Su appeared at the door. His bow was in his hands, and he fired an arrow back through the door. There was an answering cry of pain. He hastily stepped out of the way of the doorway and dropped his bow in favor of his sword, which he drew in one smooth motion.

"Arm yourselves!" Kol'Cara shouted as he drew his sword.

Karus's hand was already on Rarokan. As he drew the weapon, the tingle was a welcome friend. The clerks went for their weapons. Martuke yanked his sword out, just as an orc burst through the door. It was huge, hulking, and powerfully muscled, fearsome-looking. The creature had a stone hammer and smashed it down on the injured Joron'Tas, killing him.

Screaming in rage, Kelus'Su slashed the orc in the side of the neck, nearly severing the head from the body, instantly felling him. Another orc charged through the doorway, rushing past Kelus'Su and at the surprised clerk who had been knocked backward by the door opening. He had not even managed to get his sword out yet. Snarling, the orc fell upon him, cutting him brutally across the face. The dwarf went down in a spray of blood.

Two more orcs, each carrying swords, rushed into the building, one being engaged immediately by Kelus'Su. Great sword out, Ugin shouted something in his own language and launched himself at one of the orcs. Inside the confines of the walls, the clash of steel rang out jarringly, hurting the ears. Three more orcs pushed their way into the building. Martuke attacked the nearest orc, taking a powerful blow on his sword that sent sparks flying. A heartbeat later, the rest of the clerks joined him in the fight, as did the legionaries. The long table was in between Karus and the fight. He and Kol'Cara began hastily moving around it toward the action.

As if he were parrying a child, Martuke turned away the enemy's blade. He smashed his fist into the orc's face. The creature's head snapped back and he stumbled a step. Then, lightning-fast, the dwarf brought his sword back and slammed the hilt into the orc's jaw from the side. There was a popping sound and the creature collapsed, losing his sword. Without hesitation, Martuke reversed his blade and stabbed downward, powerfully punching his sword right through the orc's breastplate with a loud cracking sound.

The dwarf let out a howl of exultation at his kill. It was cut off as an orc blade swung down onto his shoulder armor with a heavy *clunk*. Martuke took a step back, staggering slightly. He recovered bringing his sword up, skillfully blocking the next attack, even as additional enemy warriors entered through the door.

Karus raised his sword to block as an orc rushed him, but an ornate dagger appeared, as if by magic, in the orc's forehead. The creature crashed to the floor at his feet, sword skittering away across the floorboards. Karus glanced over and saw Kol'Cara had thrown the blade. He nodded his thanks and started to move forward to help but found himself restrained by the elf, who grabbed at his arm.

"We must go!" Kol'Cara shouted at him over the noise as the battle raged before them. The elf pointed toward the fight. "There are too many. We must leave now."

Even as he said this, more enemy warriors had entered. Where before the room had seemed spacious, now it was crowded. There was no telling how many were out on the street beyond. With the numbers pouring into the building, he figured it was a good amount. Kol'Cara was right. They needed to get out of here, and before it was too late.

"Fall back!" Karus shouted as he and Kol'Cara made for the other door. "Fall back!"

Martuke ignored him as he fought, almost shoulder to shoulder with two of the legionaries of Karus's escort. One of the clerks was cut down as a powerfully wielded blade severed his leg. He screamed horribly, until an orc silenced him. Ugin finished his opponent by backhanding him to the ground, then running him through the neck to make sure he did not get up. One of Karus's men dropped next as he tried to fall back to the other door. The orc raised his blade to finish the man.

"No!" the legionary shouted, holding a hand up to ward off the blow. It did no good. The blade stabbed down, through his forearm and into his collar. The orc drove it deep into his core, killing him.

"Ugin," Karus shouted, "Martuke ... time to go."

The Vass glanced around, spotted them by the door, and with the two elves of his escort, began backing toward them as he fended off three of the enemy with his big sword. Martuke, seemingly lost to the fight, stabbed another enemy in the side. Before he could pull back the blade to finish his opponent, a sword strike slashed his arm, opening a wound that exposed the bone and rendering it useless. He grunted in pain, his sword clattering to the floor from nerveless fingers.

The dwarf fell back, looking wildly about for help. There was none, for he was now cut off. Karus saw realization sink home as their eyes briefly met. In a heartbeat, a hard look of resolve steeled across Martuke's face.

"Go!" Martuke shouted at them as he drew his dagger with his uninjured hand and threw himself forward again. He plunged the blade into the neck of the orc that had struck him. Martuke's momentum took them both to the floor. A breath later, the dwarf was hit by a stone war hammer. The weapon caved the right side of his head in. He died atop the orc he'd stabbed and killed, almost in the end seeming to embrace his enemy.

"Gods," Karus hissed as another of his men was cut down. Then, having backed through the door, he was outside on the street. The scene he found was one of chaos. Dwarves and legionaries were all mixed up, fighting the enemy in a wild, disorganized melee. The sound of the fight echoed off the walls of the buildings, and the stone paving was already slick with blood. Bodies lay haphazardly scattered about.

Somehow the enemy had gotten into the city, and not just a few. Kol'Cara and the elves came out next. Ugin growled as he emerged. It was a deep, menacing sound. The Vass lunged, stabbing back through the doorway, and took an orc, who had been attempting to follow, in the stomach.

The Vass's sword had begun to blur with what looked like a swirling darkness. It took Karus a moment to realize the blade was burning with black flame. Ugin stabbed back into the doorway again at another orc, causing it to jump out of the way.

Karus had no more time for thought, as he was attacked himself. He crossed swords with a hulking orc and blocked a wild strike at his head. The creature wielded a curved sort of longsword and wore a mail shirt with a rough-looking helm. The blow stung his hand terribly, and with it, Karus's anger flared.

Kill it, the sword hissed in his mind. *Kill them all and we will grow in strength. Together… we will become powerful beyond imagining. Wield me.*

As he blocked another strike, Karus felt his rage reach new levels. With not a little effort, he forced the enemy's blade away before twisting and stepping in close. He aimed a strike for the right leg, which the creature had put forward as it lunged at him.

The tip of Karus's sword bit into the orc's leg, perhaps only an inch. The hilt grew warm in his hand and his enemy dropped, going completely limp, like a puppet whose strings had been cut.

The sword exploded into blue fire. In the heavily shadowed street, it seemed brilliant in its intensity, casting a blue glow on any who drew near. Karus welcomed the fire, for with it came more anger and rage. It seemed to empower him, make him stronger, faster, and deadlier. What soldier wouldn't want that?

More, the sword hissed. *I need more. Feed me. Together we become one and grow powerful.*

The nearest orc, who had been making for Karus, came to a stop. It stared at the fiery sword in what was clear surprise tinged with wariness. It took a step back before snarling something at him in its own language. Feeling energized, Karus decided not to give his new opponent a chance to recover from its surprise.

He attacked. His opponent skillfully countered. Karus barely felt their swords connect. They engaged in a series of strikes and counterstrikes before he saw an opening and jabbed, aiming for the orc's groin. The creature saw the blade coming. The creature dodged nimbly to the side while blocking and knocked Karus's blade upward slightly so that it impacted with the orc's armor.

Like he was cutting into parchment, the blade sliced right through the armor. He felt the tip of the sword bite into the flesh of the stomach, and with that, the orc collapsed, like the previous one.

Karus stared down at his deceased opponent for a long moment. The hilt of his sword was almost burning hot in his hand. The fire running along the blade was brighter too. Power radiated from the weapon and into him. He could feel it... he could feel the sword's insatiable thirst and hunger. Time seemed to slow and the fight around him quieted a tad.

"Come on." Kol'Cara grabbed at Karus's shoulder, pulling him back and breaking the spell. "We have got to go."

"No." Resisting, Karus did not want to leave. His blood was up. He wanted to kill and there were a lot of enemies here that needed killing.

I want them all... need them... feed me...

"If we stay," the elf shouted, shaking him roughly, "we die."

The words penetrated. Karus blinked, the rage draining away. Serious concern replaced it. He had almost lost himself to the bloodlust, something that was unforgivable in a commander. He glanced around quickly and saw a scene of utter confusion about them. There were orcs seemingly everywhere, and mixed in were a handful of dwarves and legionaries battling desperately for their lives. The odds were most definitely not in their favor.

"This way." Kol'Cara pointed toward the wall. "Ugin, we are leaving!"

Karus began backing up. A few feet away, Ugin slashed with his sword, neatly slicing through the throat of an enemy. The Vass reached out and grabbed his opponent, pulling him close so that they were face to face. The orc was choking on his own blood as he died, and Ugin seemed to be relishing the moment.

"Ugin!" Karus shouted again.

The Vass looked around and spotted them. He dropped the orc he'd been holding and began backing up as well. Several orcs closed in on him. He let loose an animalistic roar that set the small hairs on Karus's neck on end and for a moment drowned out the sounds of fighting.

The black fire on his sword grew, flames licking violently at the air, stretching out almost a half foot from the blade. The orcs before him seemed to hesitate as they reconsidered the wisdom of challenging the enraged Vass. They turned, almost as one, and threw themselves on the nearest dwarves and isolated humans.

Dozens more orcs rounded the corner of the building and joined the fight, pressing their way forward in a line six across. They wore matching armor and carried large rectangular shields, and Karus recognized them as heavy infantry. They also had an officer directing them, who marched to the formation's side with a standard-bearer. The standard featured a green clenched fist set on a black field of fabric.

The orcs fighting around them wore only mail shirts, which told Karus they were light infantry. In moments, the few defenders left in the street would be overwhelmed. He was sure of it.

"Run!" Karus shouted.

With that, they turned and ran for the stairs to the city wall. Behind them, there was a shout of outrage. Karus glanced back and saw a dozen orcs charging after them and gaining. He pushed himself for all he was worth.

Ahead, dwarven warriors were streaming down the stairs from the city wall to the ground. Someone above had clearly seen the fighting and sent help. Kol'Cara and Kelus'Su ran with them, as did Ugin. Karus glanced back around again. He had no idea what had happened to the rest of his escort or the other elves. He looked back again and saw the last of the defenders had been cut down. Almost all the enemy, it seemed, was after them... all except the organized formation of heavy infantry. They kept to their ranks and a steady pace forward.

A dwarven officer stood a few yards from the bottom of the stairs. As they were coming down to the street, he was shouting orders at his warriors and was working to form a line of battle. There were already two dozen lined up into a single rank. The line made space so that Karus and company could pass through their ranks. Once through, they closed up ranks and raised their shields, while bracing themselves. A heartbeat later, the enemy slammed into the scratch line with force and a tremendous crash.

The line wavered a moment, threatening to collapse, with some of the dwarves being forced to take a step back. The officer shouted and the dwarves, throwing their shoulders into it and grunting with effort, pushed back with their shields. The enemy gave and the line came back together again, shields interlocking. It was an impressive performance.

The officer called out an order. The shields parted and swords stabbed out. The agonized cries of the enemy answered. The line had stabilized. More dwarves joined it and the line expanded its length and depth. Within a few heartbeats there were two ranks, then three, with more than fifty dwarves filling the formation out and still more pounded down the stairs.

The dwarven officer shouted again and his line took two steps forward, forcing back the orcs hammering away at the shields. It also served to make room for those newly arriving to join the formation, making it longer and adding depth through additional ranks. A second officer arrived and took over from the first. The intensity of sound from the struggle grew by the moment.

Beyond the mass of orcs attacking the dwarven shield wall, Karus saw the orc officer with the heavy infantry had stopped his formation twenty yards away from the fight. He was calmly and deliberately reorganizing his ranks into a longer line to match the one the dwarves had made. It was orderly and well-executed.

Karus looked toward the wall. The stairs were choked with dwarves coming down to join the fight. There would be no going up. Forty yards away to his right, another stone staircase was also full of dwarves coming down. Karus looked to the left, toward the gatehouse. It was three hundred yards off. There were hundreds of the enemy already there, battling against a few dozen dwarves. More dwarves were coming down from the wall and emerging from the gatehouse to help hold the gate.

Breathing heavily from the run, Karus sheathed his sword and leaned his hands upon his knees, then straightened and studied the fight by the gate. If the dwarves failed to hold, the enemy would gain control of the gate. They would seek to open it so that the rest of their army could enter the city. A volley of arrows rained down from above. A handful of javelins followed. Dozens of the enemy went down.

Shaking his head, Karus understood they were in a real bind. There had clearly been more tunnels into the city. There was no doubt in his mind about that. He wondered how the enemy had found them so quickly, then forced that thought aside. It was irrelevant now. The enemy was here. His energies were better spent on trying to fix this mess. If he could get some strength into position, some organization, a cohort or two, he would be able to turn things around and push the enemy back. But first, he had to find his men.

A horn blew from the top of the wall.

"No." Karus froze, ice seeming to form in his veins. It was the call to give up the walls and fall back to the defenses within the city. "No … no … no!"

Another horn sounded in the distance, answering the first. He looked back on the enemy and shook his head in utter dismay. He could not believe how quickly everything had fallen apart … was falling apart. There were hundreds of orcs in the city, maybe even thousands. He had lost control. With the horn call, they were giving up the walls … sooner than he had expected … could have dreamed possible. It also meant the city gates would be abandoned.

Had Dennig made that decision?

Karus's anger blazed white-hot. The sword flared into brilliance. His plans were falling apart. He had to somehow gain control of the situation. But that required getting back to his men. He saw Kol'Cara staring at him. So too was Ugin. The Vass's eyes were on the sword.

"We're not doing any good here. I have to get back to the legion," Karus told Kol'Cara. "I need to exert some control before this becomes a true disaster. I've been out of contact too long."

"If I recall"—Kol'Cara pointed down a side street to their left—"there is a defensive position about four hundred yards that way, along one of the main avenues. I believe we can take backstreets to get there."

It sounded good, more than good. Once there, he could begin getting a handle on things, reconnect with the legion, take command, and coordinate the city's defense. More important, since it was the nearest defensive position, reinforcement would be flowing in as men and dwarves retired to it from the city walls. They would be able to begin checking the enemy's taking of the city… at least for a time.

Since the walls were being given up, there would be no retaking them. The enemy's strength in numbers was just too great. His secondary plans would go into effect and that would involve bleeding his enemy and making the taking of the city a true meat grinder.

"Right," Karus said. "Let's go."

They jogged behind the dwarven line, which was holding back the orcs. With every passing moment, more dwarves joined the growing defense. However, the same was happening on the enemy's side. It was shaping up to be a serious fight, especially when the enemy's heavy infantry pushed forward.

Karus followed after Kol'Cara as they ran along the wall and beyond the fighting. Within moments, the fight was fully behind them. They turned onto the side street. There was no pursuit. The enemy was too focused on the dwarves to worry about a handful of individuals fleeing.

Despite the darkening shadows of the city, the heat was still brutal, oppressive even. Slowing to a jog, Karus found himself once again breathing heavily and sweating like a pig. It was just the four of them now: two elves, one Vass, and Karus.

The sounds of fighting could still be heard, but the farther they traveled down the street, the more muffled it became. After four hundred yards, the city around them became still, abandoned, and seemingly dead. It was eerie, for he kept expecting the enemy to emerge from one of the numerous dark alleys or doorways they passed.

The street did not lead them straight to the defensive position. Unexpectedly, it curved around and started going in the opposite direction than they wanted.

"I think if we cut through here," Kol'Cara said as they came to a stop, "it might take us closer to where we need to go."

As he gazed into the dark alley, Karus found himself sucking serious wind. Running in armor was never easy and was always exhausting.

"This is not the time, I think, to become lost," Karus said to the elf between heavy breaths. "Are you sure?"

"Yes," Kol'Cara said. "I am."

Karus wondered how, for the elf was relatively new to the city. But he seemed certain, and Karus decided to trust him. Besides, it seemed the right direction to Karus as well. There was a shout behind them, that snapped their heads around. It was followed by the clash of weapons. At the far end of the street a fight had broken out.

"Right," Karus said, "the alley it is. In we go."

Hastily, he started forward. The alley was very narrow. Karus had to turn sideways to keep his armor from scraping against the walls and making unwanted noise. It was filled with trash and years of debris no one had bothered to pick up. The alley smelled strongly of decay.

They moved along quickly, doing their best to make as little noise as possible, and came to another street. Peering around the corner, Karus looked to the left and then right. He saw no one. Directly ahead was another alley. He could see a street at the far end and a matching alley across from that one.

"I think that street there," Karus said, trying to remember the layout of the city, "at the end of the next alley, might be the one we want."

Looking back, he saw Kol'Cara, who was just behind him, give a nod of agreement. "It does look broader, like a main way. I believe you are correct."

There was the sound of more fighting behind them, louder this time. That meant it was closer.

"I'd say moving forward is as good a decision as any," Ugin said, "especially if we don't want to be caught."

"Right." Karus made his way quickly across the street to the next alley. No shouts of alarm came. He breathed out a breath of relief as he stepped back into the shadows. This alley was choked with what seemed like ages of debris. It was very dark, as the buildings to either side were three stories and seemed to be apartment tenements of some sort.

After tripping and almost falling on his face over a discarded amphora that had been broken in two, Karus drew his sword. It seemed to know what he wanted and flared to life. He held it before him for light as he continued forward, careful not to trip over the discarded trash and debris.

They came to the end of the alley and, sure enough, found it was a main street. Several defensive positions would be located along its length. Karus was certain.

At the corner, he looked to his right and saw orcs. More than a dozen of them about forty yards away. They seemed to be milling around, doing a whole lot of nothing. He pulled his head back and sheathed his sword to keep its light from alerting the enemy to their presence. He looked back and pointed to his eyes with two fingers and then in the direction he'd seen the orcs. Kol'Cara gave a nod. Ugin clamped his jaw firmly shut and tightened his hold on his sword, which was still burning with black fire.

Karus peered quickly to the left and saw one of the defensive positions, about a hundred yards distant. It was likely why the orcs were doing nothing. He could see legionaries manning the wall, which was an immense relief.

To get to safety, they would have to make a dash, cross the defensive trench, and then climb the wall. The legionaries holding it would have javelins and could provide them with cover. The tricky part would be reaching the position before the enemy caught up to them.

"How do you feel about running?" Karus asked, quietly. He was already tired but there was no question in his mind about making the attempt. "The defensive position is about one hundred yards off. The orcs are closer and there are a lot of them."

"We're gonna have to run for it," Ugin said, without hesitation. "I don't want to be caught by them."

"They might make a pelt out of you," Kol'Cara said, "for a cold night."

"That's not funny," Ugin hissed back.

"I was not joking." Kol'Cara squeezed by Karus and peered around the corner at the orcs.

"You'd make a nice throw blanket," Kelus'Su said from behind the Vass. "I am sure all that fur keeps you very warm in the winter. I mean, why even bother wearing clothes when you've got fur? I just don't understand you Vass."

"I shouldn't have to put up with this," Ugin said to Karus.

"It's going to be a race," Kol'Cara said.

"Yep," Karus said. "It's gonna be a race all right."

"What are we waiting for?" Ugin asked. "Or are we just dragging our feet so the elves can continue to insult me?"

Ugin shot Kelus'Su a look that said blood would be spilled if he spoke another word.

"Let's go," Karus said to Kol'Cara and patted him on the shoulder. The elf stepped out onto the street. Karus followed and was about to break out into a run when a half dozen orcs emerged from an alley a building down toward the defensive position, on the other side of the street. The orcs came to a stop, looking just as surprised as Karus felt. Ugin shouted out a war cry and, shoving past Karus, charged them.

"Bloody gods." Karus drew his sword and followed. Kol'Cara was at his side, as was Kelus'Su. They were amongst the orcs before the enemy could fully prepare themselves. Screaming, Karus drove his sword deep into the side of a startled orc. The chainmail armor posed almost no resistance whatsoever. He felt the blade scrape against the bone of the ribcage as it went in. The creature died instantly.

Ignoring the warmth from the sword hilt, he shoved the orc aside and attacked the next. Their swords met and Karus felt the pain of the blow communicated to his hand.

To his right, Ugin was a veritable demon, battling his opponent furiously, all the while growling and snarling. Kol'Cara and the other elf were a blur of motion. They were unbelievably quick.

Behind them, shouts from the other group told Karus they were on their way to join the fight. He fought harder and managed to sneak in a quick strike to the neck, which only grazed his opponent. Surprisingly, this did not immediately kill. Pain in its eyes, it stumbled backward.

He was about to push the attack home when he was tackled from behind. Karus went down, landing hard on his right arm. He lost his sword as his helmet connected with the stone paving. His attacker landed on top of him. It was almost impossibly heavy.

Without hesitation, though he was slightly dazed... it was probably instinct alone, Karus pulled his dagger out and plunged it into the arm of the orc. The creature screamed and scrambled off, tearing the dagger from his grip.

Groaning, Karus rolled onto all fours to see the orc he'd stabbed pull itself to its feet. His dagger was still lodged in its right bicep, but it too had lost its own weapon. Rarokan lay at its feet. Eyes on Karus, it bent down for the sword, baring its tusks at him.

"No!" Karus shouted and dragged himself to his feet, prepared to charge the creature.

As the orc's hand closed on the grip of the weapon, there was a brilliant flash and a snapping sound that kicked the dust from the street up into the air around them. Encased in blue light, the orc opened its mouth to scream, but nothing came out. Distracted, the other orcs took a step back. Before they could recover, Ugin, Kol'Cara, and Kelus'Su pressed their attack, finishing off the last of the orcs.

The orc holding Rarokan collapsed to the ground and, with it, the light faded. Karus's right arm throbbed and hurt terribly. He hastily went for his sword. The orc looked to have been burned all over its body. Its skin had turned black. The sickening stench of charred flesh was strong in his nose. Not only did he need a weapon, but he would not leave Rarokan to the enemy. He pried open the orc's hand. The charred skin sloughed away from the bone as he retrieved his sword.

He heard pounding feet and turned. The orcs from farther down the street were almost upon them. Karus felt a sinking feeling deep in his gut. There were just too many to fight. He glanced back toward the defensive position a little less than a hundred yards distant. No help would be coming from that avenue. Not in time, anyway.

There was no longer the opportunity to run. He knew in his heart it was over. He thought of Amarra, wishing regretfully he'd had a chance to say goodbye. Karus recalled the man he'd killed in the tavern. Like him, Karus's personal story would end in an abandoned city that soon no one would remember. The thought of such a useless death angered him mightily.

Karus sucked in a breath of the hot, humid air and decided he truly hated Carthum. He turned to face the enemy. If he was to die this day, he'd sell his life dearly. They would pay in blood before they took his own. He braced himself as they closed the last few yards.

"Let's make them pay for our lives," Karus said.

"We won't need to." Ugin's tone was a quiet one. "They're already dead. They just don't know it yet."

Karus blinked and took a startled step back. The air before him seemed to shimmer. Where a moment before there had been nothing but empty air now stood eight armored and hulking Vass with their great swords out. One of the Vass shouted something out in a guttural tongue and the others in unison answered with what sounded like a single word. The orcs stopped, some almost skidding to a halt. One tripped and fell, losing his stone-headed hammer.

The Vass did not give them time to think. They rushed forward, great swords carving through the enemy as if they were scything wheat. The orcs for their part seemed frightened almost beyond reasoning. Several squealed like pigs in their fright. They were barely able to mount a defense. Karus had never seen anything like it.

The Vass were incredibly efficient in their killing, their movements graceful and yet at the same time ferocious, brutal, and without mercy. Watching them tear the orcs apart, Karus suddenly understood why the Vass were so feared.

What would an army of these creatures be capable of? Who could stop them?

A few moments later, it was all over. Blood, body parts, and the dead lay strewn across the street. The last orcs threw down their weapons, turned, and fled before the Vass could reach them. One of the Vass took two steps forward and held forth a hand, palm out, toward one of the running orcs. A blue dart of light flashed out. It smacked into the orc's back with a crack. The creature went crashing down to the street. It did not get up.

There was a long moment of silence where no one said anything.

"I guess," Kol'Cara said, breathing heavily as he looked over at Ugin, "we found your protectors."

Ugin bared his teeth at the elf. "They were never lost."

Exhausted and arm hurting something fierce, sucking at the air, Karus let his sword tip rest on the stone paving of the street. He stared for a long moment at the newcomers, Ugin's Vass protectors, and shook his head in disbelief. Incredibly, they would live. That was a sweet thought. He suddenly realized he was terribly thirsty. He checked his canteen, which was secured to his harness. It was empty. Karus glanced up at the darkening sky. He sucked in a deep breath of the humid air and turned toward the defensive position. He started moving, then paused and looked back at Ugin and the two elves. Beyond them were Ugin's protectors, who were poking amongst the enemy, making sure they were dead.

"Are you coming?" Karus asked. "We're not done yet. There's work still to be done and a city's defense to be managed."

Chapter Twenty

The sound of the fighting as it echoed off the walls of the buildings along the street was near deafening. It battered painfully at the ears. The enemy was doing their level best to assault one of the legion's main defensive positions.

Both suns had long since set and night had come full on. The moon was hidden behind a layer of clouds. For the most part, though, it was bright enough that it shone through a bit, giving the defenders some light to work with.

Karus was standing back and away from the struggle, watching as Fourth Cohort worked to keep the enemy from gaining purchase on the wall they were holding.

The legion's position cut clear across the street, a main avenue that led directly to the palace district. The wall the legionaries were defending was constructed of dirt, piled to a height of seven feet. It had a wooden-planked barricade for protection that added another three feet. A wide area behind the barricade had been packed down and made smooth for the defenders to stand upon and fight.

From his position a few yards behind the wall, Karus could not see the trench he knew had been dug ten feet down to its front. The trench had steep, angled walls that were designed to be difficult to climb. At the bottom, sharpened stakes waited for the enemy.

The defensive position was formidable. Yet, despite the depth of the trench and height of the wall, the enemy doggedly fought the legionaries at the barricade. Before working to scale the wall itself, they had thrown stools, furniture, garbage, doors that had been ripped off their hinges… whatever they could easily lay their hands upon and move… it all went into the trench. In a surprisingly short time, the trench had been mostly filled in, so that the enemy could better get at the defenders. It had been a crude tactic, but it worked.

The assault had been underway for a little over a half hour. A good number of the enemy had been injured or killed in that time. Karus understood those orcs now assaulting the barricade stood upon the bodies of those who had preceded them, whether they still drew breath or not. The enemy seemed to care little for their combat casualties. Karus found their single-minded focus somewhat disturbing.

The defenders used their shields to push back against the enemy, blocking attacks while stabbing with their short swords. Men behind the front line that manned the wall reached over their heads and jabbed out at the enemy with javelins.

It was ugly and brutal fighting. Both sides were highly motivated, well-trained, and disciplined. Both sides also wanted the wall. It was an epic fight over who would be king of the hill. Unlike a child's game, there was no mercy, no thought of quarter. It boiled down to kill… or be killed.

Above, on the rooftops, going down the street past the defensive position, dozens of auxiliaries shot arrows or threw javelins down upon the enemy in the street below, which had become an avenue of death. Blood slicked the paving stones and ran down the gutters in small rivers.

The enemy had yet to find a way up to the rooftops to try to dislodge them. But there was no doubt in Karus's mind they were working on doing just that. When he had gone up to the wall to look over a short while before, he had seen orcs thick on the street beyond the trench, holding their shields up over their heads as protection against the deadly rain. Others, armed with bows, shot back up at their tormentors. The legion had created the perfect killing ground and it showed. Still, the enemy came on, weathering the storm and desiring greatly to become crowned king of the hill.

Sword and shield out, Felix moved on the wall behind his men, pacing slowly from one side of the wall to the other and then back again. He was clearly shouting encouragements and orders. Over the cacophonous wash of sound, Karus could not hear what he said. But Karus had walked in Felix's sandals more than once and well knew what the centurion was doing. Occasionally, Felix would stop and stab at an enemy, dealing with an issue one of his men could not or had missed. He was the consummate professional centurion, leading by example and lending his strength of will for his men to lean upon.

Along the narrow and twisting confines of the side streets and alleys that branched off from this main avenue, Karus understood that the fighting was more intense, personal even. The nearest of those streets had been thoroughly blocked, but beyond them, there were few defenses other than a handful of centuries that had been posted and spread out in an effort to slow the enemy.

When encountering an enemy in those tight quarters, it frequently came down to a legionary's shield and sword and the comrade standing next to him, sometimes even daggers and fists. From the reports he had received, as the enemy sought and pushed to get around the main defensive positions, the fighting was also house to house, building to building.

The legion's manpower was not as great as the enemy's. This meant the centurions leading their men out on the city's backstreets had to fight smart. They used the narrow confines of the side streets or alleys to their advantage and whenever possible ambushed the enemy.

Ugin and his protectors had gone off on the right side to help keep the enemy from flanking the current position. As the fighting raged from backstreet to backstreet, and house to house, he suspected they were proving to be pure terrors for the enemy, especially with the Vass's ability to briefly turn invisible and mask themselves from eyesight.

The enemy had already flanked two of the defensive lines. This had compelled Karus to, twice now, order a city-wide pullback to the next set of defensive lines. Both instances had come surprisingly quick and in rapid succession.

Once the main city walls had been given up, it was clear the enemy general had poured the majority of his army into the city. The enemy had vast reserves and they were now using them to their advantage. The Horde was steadily overrunning the city and outflanking his defenses, much faster than he had expected. That seriously worried him.

Karus's arm throbbed from when the orc had tackled him. He flexed his fingers and had no problem doing that, so he figured it wasn't broken. But the pain radiating from his right shoulder to his forearm was no less intense. He had clearly damaged it.

"Are you all right?" Kol'Cara asked, stepping nearer so that he could be heard over the noise of the fight. "Your arm…"

Karus glanced over at the elf and nodded. "It just hurts is all. Bloody orc tackling me … I never saw him coming. It was a stupid thing to happen. Don't worry about it. Given time, I'll be fine."

"If you say so," Kol'Cara said, sounding far from convinced. Six Anagradoom stood a few feet back, watchful. Each had a bow at the ready, an arrow loosely in hand. They had appeared shortly after Karus, Kol'Cara, and Kelus'Su had arrived at the defensive position. Karus had no idea how they had known to find them there, but they had.

Though his field headquarters was a couple hundred yards back in a small tavern, four messengers waited a few feet away. Karus had taken them from the Fourth. They were his runners that kept him connected with headquarters and, by extension, with the entire fight for the city.

"What do you think?" Karus asked, pointing to the fighting with his good hand.

"I think they are determined," Kol'Cara said, "to overcome your wall."

Karus shot the elf a look that said, *Oh really* … In response to that, Kol'Cara's gaze shifted to the wall and back again. He eyed Karus for a long moment before speaking.

"The enemy is doing an excellent job of moving through the city and getting behind your defensive positions. I think if it continues at this pace, we will be back at the palace before sunrise. I also *think* you already know this to be true. So, why bother asking?"

Karus eyed the elf for several heartbeats and gave a nod. Kol'Cara's assessment matched his own. He was feeling intense frustration and it had come out in asking a question, the answer to which he already knew. Karus needed to hold out for as long as possible before giving up each defensive line … to delay and make any gains in the city exceedingly costly for the enemy, all the while keeping his own losses to a minimum. The defenses the legion had built should have seen to that. The more of the enemy he killed now, the less he would face later. That's what he had planned to do. Unfortunately, it wasn't playing out that way.

The problem was the choke points, his defensive positions. They were being turned all too quickly and in great force too. It meant his killing grounds were not being given time to adequately develop to the point where they could murder the enemy in large numbers. Karus rubbed at his jaw, feeling the stubble, and grimaced at the pain in his shoulder, which stabbed intensely. He had inadvertently used his right hand.

"Gods," Karus breathed as the pain subsided.

Two camp followers, both women, were bringing a man lying on a stretcher back toward the aid station. They were heading in the direction of the palace district, where the surgeons and medics had set up shop.

Many of the camp followers had volunteered to help with the injured. All of them had loved ones in the ranks, and when asked to help, many had jumped at the opportunity. It meant the chance of wounded being left on the battlefield was greatly reduced. There were times when a cohort was forced to leave the wounded behind. It did not occur often, but it did happen, especially in a fight like this one... a delaying action.

The injured man being carried off had taken a vicious wound to the calf. A bloodied tourniquet had been tied around his left thigh and he held his leg with a hand that shook, moaning loudly with each step of the stretcher-bearers. His young face was pale as a sheet of fresh snow. He had clearly lost a lot of blood. Karus wondered if he would survive the trip. He hoped he would.

Karus turned his attention back to the fight, just as an auxiliary on one of the rooftops was hit by an arrow in the chest. He stiffened, dropped his bow, and fell down upon the enemy on the street below. A heartbeat later, another fell. Watching his men die and become injured was always painful. Karus hated it, hated having to order his men into battle. But this was necessary. A good commander did what was required.

Felix turned and called out an order. A heartbeat later, a wave of javelins arced up over the struggle at the wall. The wave plunged down out of sight and into the enemy massed on the other side. A clatter mixed with a multitude of screams followed. The fighting on the wall did not slacken. The intensity of the struggle continued unabated, as if the toss had never happened.

"Excuse me, sir."

Karus turned to find a messenger from headquarters. The man saluted and handed over a dispatch. He opened it and scanned the contents, nodded his thanks.

"Dismissed," Karus said.

The messenger saluted smartly and returned the way he had come. Turning his attention back to the fight, Karus crumpled the dispatch and dropped it.

"Anything interesting?" Kol'Cara asked.

"One of the defensive positions on the west side of the city was flanked. The defenders fell back to the next line," Karus said. "They are under a great deal of pressure over there... possibly more than we are here."

"There are some advantages," Kol'Cara said, "to the enemy making a rapid conquest of the city."

"Oh?" Karus looked over, curious to get the elf's thinking. "Such as?"

"They will not have time to properly search the city," Kol'Cara replied. "Won't that help move your overall plan forward a little?"

"Possibly," Karus conceded, considering the elf's words. "It might...just...do that."

His head snapped around as the fighting to his front seemed to surge in its intensity. The enemy was making a titanic effort at overcoming the wall, a real concerted push. Several men were knocked violently back from the line. They did not immediately return to their positions. Whether they were injured or not, in the darkness, Karus could not tell. He suspected they had been.

Felix called more men from his reserve forward as an orc clambered over the barricade and onto the wall, barely two feet from him, where a gap had formed. The orc made to bring his sword around to strike. Karus's friend turned and, without missing a beat, lunged and stabbed his sword through the creature's mouth.

It toppled backward over the barricade and down the way it had come. Then the men of the reserve were there, filling in the gaps and stabilizing the defense of the wall. Fourth Cohort was holding and would continue to hold for as long as needed. That was clear. Though Karus was only too aware that he was losing men he could ill afford to replace. He was buying time with the lives of his men and that was always an uncomfortable feeling.

"Sir."

Karus turned to find a legionary standing behind him at attention. This wasn't a messenger from headquarters. It was one of Felix's men. His rank marked him as an optio. Though Karus recognized him, he did not know his name. He was injured and had received a fairly deep cut on the forearm. It was a fresh wound and bled freely, but not overly much. The blood dripped from his fingers onto the paving stones at his feet.

"The aid station is down the street, legionary," Karus said, wondering if the man was confused. Perhaps he'd also taken a hit to the head, but Karus did not see any damage to his helmet. He pointed in the direction the optio should go. "That way, toward the palace district. Someone can help you there."

"I am not here for that, sir," the legionary said, glancing down at his arm. "I've had worse. My centurion sent me to report to Centurion Felix, but I saw you, sir. I hope you don't mind. Centurion Felix seems a little busy, sir."

"Not at all," Karus said, wondering what bad news the man brought. "Continue."

"Yes, sir," the optio said. "The enemy has pushed up a side street off to the left about two hundred yards." He pointed in the direction with his injured and bleeding arm. "My centurion said they will be able to flank behind this defensive position in less than a quarter hour. He has a section of men slowing them down, sir. It is his recommendation we pull back to the next line, as soon as possible. There are too many of the enemy, sir, moving along the side streets and alleys. And… there are simply too few of us, sir."

Karus felt his stomach plummet at the news. So soon… too soon.

"What's your centurion's name?" Karus asked.

"Centurion Agguus, sir," the optio said.

Karus knew Agguus. The man was reliable and not one prone to becoming overly excited. If he said Felix's line was about to be turned, well then, it was.

"Very well," Karus said. "Return to Agguus and tell him the Fourth will be pulling back promptly."

"Yes, sir." The legionary saluted and turned to go.

"And, Optio," Karus said.

"Sir?"

"Get that wound seen to," Karus said, "will you?"

"I will, sir."

Karus moved over to the wall. Felix spotted him and Karus waved him over.

"Time to give up the line and fall back to the next one." Karus hated the necessity of it, even as he said it. "The enemy is behind us on the left and will be flanking shortly. I'll alert headquarters and get them moving too… You focus on getting your cohort and those centuries you've placed on your flanks to where they need to go."

"Bah…just when we're starting to really kill them in good numbers, we have to fall back again." Felix frowned, looking disgusted. He turned and studied the fight for a long moment, clearly working through in his mind how he wanted to disengage from the enemy. A pullback and disengagement from a fight was always tricky, dangerous even. He turned his attention back to Karus. "I will get right on it, sir."

"Good," Karus said. "I will see you on the next line."

"Yes, sir." Felix saluted and moved off, shouting for his officers.

"Let's go," Karus said to Kol'Cara. "Time to fall back again."

Chapter Twenty-One

It was shaping up to be yet another brutally hot day. As he gazed up at the near flawless sky overhead, Karus thought the god of fire, Vulcan, would be well pleased with the heat in this land. He saw nothing other than the brilliant blue of the sky and the two suns. There were no dragons anywhere in sight. They had yet to return. He had no idea if they ever would.

He was standing just before the gate that led into the palace district. The main body of the last cohort to pull back from the city, the Seventh, was marching past and through the gate. Almost like a mother hen watching her chicks closely, Karus was there to see the last of his boys retire behind the safety of the palace walls.

The legion's surgeon, Ampelius, was working on his injured arm, fashioning a sling from a piece of white cloth. The arm and shoulder throbbed abominably from when the orc had tackled him the previous evening. To make matters worse, Karus was beat. He had not slept a wink. It had been a long, difficult, and frustrating night.

In truth, Karus was pissed. No, that was not correct. He was very angry, enraged even ... not at his men, for this was not their fault. His ire was at the situation he found himself in and how quickly things had deteriorated.

None of the legion's defenses had held up for as long as he'd hoped. They had held for a time, inflicted moderate casualties even, but in the end, the enemy had proven exceptionally adept at bypassing the legion's defensive lines. It had compelled the defenders to prematurely pull back time and again. That was one of the most frustrating things. At times, they seemed to know the city almost better than his men.

Karus was not one to make excuses and he recognized it for what it was, yet another example of the enemy having a say in how a battle unfolded. No matter how hard you prepared, planned… nothing ever went exactly the way you expected. Sometimes, it went very badly, which is what had happened.

All through the night, combat injures had mounted. In the end, Karus had made the difficult decision to simply give up the last defensive line, rather than attempt to hold and weaken his strength further. He could not afford that… not when defending the last line would only buy him maybe an hour or two. For his purposes and the plans he had put into motion, the palace walls would be sufficient to check the enemy for the time he needed for everything to play out. At least, he hoped this once, things would go according to plan.

Karus gave a grunt as Ampelius tied the sling securely into place, knotting the end. The surgeon gave it a tug to make sure it would not come loose.

"You could be a little gentler," Karus groused.

"I take it that hurt?" the surgeon asked, raising an eyebrow. Ampelius looked exhausted. His eyes were bloodshot and heavy with bags. Karus knew the man and his team of medics had been working through the night to treat the wounded as they came in. He wore a smock that was badly stained with dried blood, a testament to the wounded he had tended to.

"It's manageable," Karus said.

"Do you want the good news or the bad news?" Ampelius asked as he surveyed his handiwork.

"The good news," Karus said. "I've had enough bad news to last me a lifetime."

"I am fairly confident your arm's not broken," Ampelius said. "But you bruised your shoulder something good."

"What's the bad news?" Karus asked.

"I thought you didn't want bad news?" Ampelius said, then giving in, heaved a sigh. "It's gonna hurt for a few days. Best not to use it, eh? Take it easy, sir."

"You know what's going to happen here." Karus lowered his voice and pointed with his good hand to the stone wall behind them. "Soon enough the enemy will be trying to overcome these walls. Are you seriously telling me not to fight if it comes to it?"

"You are the camp prefect and in command of the legion," Ampelius said. "I do not have the authority to order you around. Nor would I want to. As such, I can only give you my advice. And that advice is to take it easy for a few days. If you don't... you may make your injury worse, to the point where it won't heal right."

Karus felt himself scowl at that.

"If you'd like, I can give you something for the pain," Ampelius said.

"Will it dull my thinking?" Karus suspected it would.

"Yes," the surgeon said simply.

"Then no," Karus said. "I will take the pain."

"I thought as much," Ampelius said as he picked up his bag. "If the discomfort worsens, call on me immediately. That might be a sign that there are internal injuries, ones not readily apparent."

"I will," Karus said.

Ampelius looked through the gate and scowled slightly. His eyes went to Amarra, who was speaking with Kol'Cara and Si'Cara just a few feet off, before returning his gaze to Karus. "It's a shame she can't heal anymore, like she did with the sickness. That would fix you right up."

"If she could, you'd be out of a job."

"Now that," Ampelius said, "would be a blessing."

"Would it?" Karus asked. "Would it really?"

"Contrary to popular belief, sir, I don't enjoy seeing good boys carved and cut up." The surgeon glanced back through the gate. "Well... you're all fixed up. I have other patients to see."

"Thank you," Karus said.

Ampelius gave him a nod and walked off through the gate.

Karus blew out a frustrated breath as he caught Amarra watching him. He shot her a wink. She gave him a small smile in return, her eyes flicking to his arm in the sling. When he had returned to the palace district, just before dawn, he had found her waiting by the gate with Si'Cara.

Thankfully, the elf had not allowed her out into the city during the confused and chaotic fighting of the night. Amarra had been immensely relieved to see him safe and, for the most part, sound. Despite being a sweaty, blood-soaked mess, she had given him a bear hug. The resulting discomfort had betrayed his injured shoulder and seen to the subsequent calling of Ampelius to examine the injury.

Even now, she watched him with suspicious concern that perhaps he had been more seriously injured than he had let on. Karus knew he looked dreadful. He probably smelled even worse. But by the gods, she was beautiful to his eyes. He felt refreshed by it, renewed even.

"Sir," Felix said, drawing his attention away from Amarra. He had been speaking with Optio Divius off to the side. The optio was wearing a tunic that had been blackened with ash. The same treatment had been applied to his arms, legs, and face. "Divius is ready to head back, sir."

"My men are in position and waiting, sir," Divius said.

So much was riding on what the man and his team would do that he could scarcely believe he was putting the legion's fate into the hands of just ten men. It seemed madness... but sometimes to win it took an unconventional approach—and a little madness.

"You have a fallback position?" Karus asked, for what the optio and his men were about to undertake was extremely dangerous. Divius's mission was also one of the reasons he had given up the last defensive line. If the optio was successful, in the span of a handful of hours, the actions of a few might just change everything.

"Yes, sir," Divius said. "We have a primary rally point and should be able to weather the storm there. If that is compromised, or the enemy catches on to us, each team has their own hidey hole."

Karus did not feel good about sending Divius and the picked men on this mission. There was a high probability that none of them would make it back to the legion. However, he well understood if anyone was capable of pulling off what he needed done, it was Divius and the men under his command. And so, Karus had given the order that might see the death of ten good men and one outstanding officer with much promise... even if he was a bit roguish.

"The legion is counting on you."

"I know, sir," Divius said. "We won't let you down."

"I expect you won't," Karus said. "I will see you when this is all over. Make sure that I do."

"Yes, sir." Divius hesitated slightly, and Karus saw the truth in other man's eyes, the recognition of what was likely to happen. It was clear he did not think he was coming back. Divius saluted crisply.

With his arm bound by the sling, Karus could not return the salute. Instead, he settled for a simple nod. Divius turned and jogged off toward one of the buildings that had a basement with access to the sewers. From there, he would make his way to where he needed to go.

"A heavy burden rests on that man's shoulders," Felix said.

"Yes," Karus agreed quietly.

The sound of fighting drew their attention as the Seventh's rearguard finally came into view, emerging from one of the main streets into the area that had been cleared before the palace district's walls. It was now a no man's land. Dozens of buildings had been knocked down and the debris completely removed. There had been several reasons to do this... one of which was to deny the enemy cover. Another was to open up a killing ground for the bolt throwers.

Varno's rearguard consisted of fifty men formed into two ranks. The rest of the cohort, in a column two abreast, were still making their way by Karus and Felix, marching wearily through the gate. Behind them, four seriously injured men were being carried on litters.

At the moment, the rearguard's security concerned him more than the cohort's casualties, for it was being tightly pressed by a veritable mob of the enemy.

With their shields locked, the legionaries took four steps backward, then stood firm for several heartbeats, until Varno blew on a wooden whistle. Then the formation would take three more steps back, steadily closing in on safety.

In the confines of the streets, with buildings to either side, Karus knew the centurion would have varied it up a bit, even occasionally pushing and shoving back against the enemy to keep them off balance. Without the protection of the buildings to his flanks, the enemy had begun to spread out to the sides of the formation. Varno picked up the pace slightly to compensate for that lack of protection.

There were several hundred orcs pressing against his line and even more behind on the street. All were light infantry, and for the most part, they were a disorganized mass of individuals. Varno's heavy infantry were more than holding their own. With every passing heartbeat, as the rearguard drew deeper into the no man's land, more of the enemy were emerging from other streets.

The disorganization of the enemy worked to the centurion's advantage in that there was no serious coordinated effort to break his line. The enemy fought as individuals, not as a cohesive team.

Varno snapped out a series of orders. The second rank spread out to either side, extending the first rank's line. He then bent the ends of his line back and around to keep the enemy from moving around his flanks.

As the Seventh's rearguard continued to fall back in good order, they left a trail of dead and injured orcs. Varno's mastery was on full display for all those on the wall to see. And the walls were crowded with men and officers of the legion, watching the drama as it played out. The centurion was handling his men extremely well. Steadily, yard by yard, he drew nearer to safety…five hundred yards, then four hundred fifty…four hundred.

"What about the bolt throwers, sir?" Felix asked. "The enemy's steadily working their way around his flanks. Our boys could use some covering fire to discourage that."

"Not yet," Karus said. "Varno will just have to deal with the enemy on his own for a bit more."

"What do you mean, not yet?" Felix said as two men fell out of the line. Both had been injured but were still on their feet. Varno snapped something at them that Karus could not hear over the sound of the fight, then pointed toward the gate. His meaning was clear and both men began hastily staggering their way painfully to safety.

"The bolt thrower crews have their orders," Karus said tersely.

Felix glanced up at the machines that had been mounted on the wall above the gate. Each had been set several yards apart and their crews of six stood by, watching the drama before them unfold. They were waiting for the order to go to work. As he turned back to the fight, a muscle in his jaw flexed. Both men watched silently after that.

Dropping his sword and shield, another man fell out of the line. He staggered a couple of steps before falling to his knees. A moment later, he toppled over onto his side and fell still. Varno bent down at the man's side, turned him over, and then shook his head.

The centurion straightened and blew his whistle once more. The formation backed up, right over the man who'd just fallen. A fourth man fell out of line, then ten heartbeats later, a fifth. The fighting raged on, and with each blow of the whistle, Seventh Cohort drew nearer the gate, until they were just one hundred fifty yards distant.

CRACK.

One of the bolt throwers released. The bolt, four feet long and as thick as a forearm, hissed by overhead. It hammered into the mass of orcs to the right side of the formation, ripping through four of the creatures before burying its iron head in the ground.

CRACK.

Another bolt thrower fired. An orc was literally torn in half by the missile, which hammered through his side and then drove into the ground between another's feet.

CRACK.

More orcs were hit. Karus glanced up at the gatehouse. Four bolt throwers had been mounted above it, just for this purpose, to provide cover and to keep the enemy honest. Though Karus had no intention of being honest. In the entirety of the city of Carthum, they had found nothing comparable to a Roman bolt thrower. It was quite possible the enemy had no concept of their range.

Another bolt fired. The first machine had reloaded. It shot a deadly bolt outward at the enemy, killing and maiming several. Learning to operate the machines effectively was a time-consuming and detailed process. It took months of training and experience to become merely proficient and meet the legion's exacting standards. To be superb with such a machine was something else. A crew needed to be able to not only reload rapidly, but also reliably hit what they aimed at. Some crews were so skilled they could hit a fly on a wall at one hundred paces.

And that's exactly what Karus's boys were doing, hitting what they shot at. They were killing the enemy with a professional efficiency that could only be admired. Several more bolts were fired, punishing the orcs further. At first a few disengaged. Then more, and finally all lost heart in pressing their attack, drawing back and away from Seventh's rearguard. The bolt throwers ceased their fire shortly after.

Felix gave a grim chuckle.

"It took me a moment," he said. "You don't want the enemy to know their range, do you?"

"No," Karus said. "I don't."

"Rearguard!" Varno hollered, his voice cracking from overuse and the strain of shouting orders. "Halt. About face." The formation spun around to face the gate. "At the double ... march."

In a half jog, with armor chinking, the rearguard crossed the distance to the gate, where Varno called them to a halt. The men looked ready to drop. He reformed them into a rough column and ordered them through.

"Nice job," Karus said to the centurion as the formation passed. Varno looked just as tired and spent as his men. He was also covered almost head to toe in green gore, with a spattering of red blood.

"Thank you, sir." And with that, Varno passed him by through the gate.

All who remained outside the walls were Felix, Amarra, Si'Cara, Kol'Cara, and the growing numbers of the enemy. The orcs had continued pouring from the streets into the no man's land before the palace walls. But they all seemed to understand the danger posed by the bolt throwers and did not come closer than two hundred yards.

Karus understood it was only a matter of time until their heavy infantry arrived. He wondered how long it would take them before they came up in strength to begin their assault against the walls. Would it be this afternoon? Tonight? He hoped the enemy commander decided to test his walls as soon as possible, for if he delayed, it might undo everything Karus had planned.

"How long do you intend to wait out here?" Felix asked, with a glance thrown to the gate. "It's bloody hot under these two blasted suns and I could use a drink of water or something stronger if I can find it."

"I thought to give it another moment," Karus said, "in the event some of our boys are still out in the city."

"Some undoubtedly are," Felix said, tone turning grim and hard. "But with those orcs out there, I don't see them winning through to us, not anymore."

"That only makes what I have ordered more difficult," Karus said.

"Gods help them," Felix said.

"Yes." Karus fell quiet for several heartbeats. "Their fate is in the hands of the gods now."

Felix did not reply.

Karus shifted his stance slightly and a lance of pain stabbed at him from his shoulder. He grimaced.

"Hurts, huh?" Felix asked.

"It does."

"What did Ampelius say?" Felix asked.

"That I am not to use it for a few days."

Felix grunted but said nothing. Karus glanced once more at the enemy. If anyone was out there in the city, they had no chance of getting to safety now. His heart felt heavy at that thought. He stifled a yawn. Gods, he was tired.

Felix looked over at Amarra and a sly grin traced its way onto the centurion's face. "If you ask, maybe she'll rub your shoulder for you…? Might make you feel better, sir."

"Funny," Karus said. He turned to the others and sobered. "Let's go. It's time to close the gate before that lot over there gets ideas… bolt throwers or no."

He turned and started through the gate. The walls above were fully manned. The enemy would not have as easy a time getting into the palace district as they had with the city, for it was a far smaller area and Karus had plenty of men to hold it.

He'd also had the district thoroughly checked for hidden tunnels. The only tunnel that led out into the city had been found weeks ago. It was the one in the dungeons that the druids had used to escape and had long since been collapsed.

Just inside the gate, a century of men was standing by for the purpose of closing it. Rank upon rank, six deep, Second Cohort stood just off to the side in battle formation. They were a guard, should the enemy attempt to rush the gate before it was closed and sealed. To them would fall the responsibility of pushing the enemy back so that the gate could be closed.

Beyond the Second, on the parade ground, Seventh Cohort had fallen out. Men sat on the ground with their heads in their hands. Others had lain down and immediately gone to sleep or dozed. A few had dipped into their haversacks and were ravenously eating whatever they found. Some were standing around staring at nothing, seemingly dazed, perhaps marveling or conversely feeling terrible guilt that they had survived when a beloved comrade had not.

Karus had seen it all before, experienced it himself even. Each man responded to the aftermath of a desperate fight in their own unique way. They would get through it, but never over it, for such things tended to stick with you.

Several medics were busy tending to the wounded, Ampelius too. Karus rubbed the back of his neck as he took it all in, feeling sour and angry. Deep down, he was really angry at himself. All that had happened lay solely upon his shoulders.

"Close the gate," Felix ordered after they had gone through and were clear.

Karus turned to watch as the century moved forward. Slowly at first, with great effort, they swung the heavily reinforced doors shut, one at a time. The hinges, needing an oiling, screamed as they worked. The metal locking bar was then hefted by ten straining men and dropped into place. It made a deep *thunk*ing sound that Karus found ominous.

"It all comes down to the next few hours, then," Felix said.

"That it does." Karus glanced around once more. "I am dog-tired and need some sleep." Karus paused and looked toward the gate. "It will take time for them to become organized. I'll be in my quarters. Wake me if anything happens."

"I will, sir," Felix said and saluted.

Karus turned toward the palace. Amarra joined him. Karus noticed the eyes of the nearest men upon her as they passed. They eyed her with hope, in an almost worshipful manner. At a discreet distance, Kol'Cara and Si'Cara followed. Together they headed across the parade grounds to the marble steps that led up to the palace. As they climbed the steps, he looked over at the beautiful woman by his side. He had a feeling she could sense his worry and fear of failing, letting her down…letting them all down, even his god. For after the night's events he had sure as shit failed in meeting his early goals for the defense of the city.

"Faith," she said to him. "Have faith."

Karus stopped at the top step and turned to face her fully. "At this point, that's all I have…though I've cheated a fair bit to weigh the ledger in our favor. I hope the High Father does not mind."

"I don't believe he will," Amarra said, for she well knew what he had planned.

Chapter Twenty-Two

The suns were in the process of setting as Karus made his way up the stairs to the wall. In a little more than an hour, it would be dark. Despite that, it was still bloody hot. Amarra, Si'Cara, and Kol'Cara followed. Of the two elves, only Si'Cara carried her bow.

"Make room," Karus ordered to a century of legionaries who were making their way down the stairs. The men stood aside as Karus and company continued up the steps. With every footfall, his shoulder stabbed him with pain. He tried the best he could to ignore it, but it still hurt just the same.

Reaching the top of the stairs, Karus stepped onto the wide stone walkway that ran the length of the entire wall behind the battlements. It was easily seven feet wide, with plenty of space for the defenders.

To his left, he spotted Dennig, Ugin, and Felix gazing out from above the gate itself, just a few feet away. Another Vass stood behind Ugin. He watched the humans manning the battlements with evident suspicion and a look of displeasure.

All along the wall, for as far as the eye could see, the legion and auxiliary cohorts were deployed, nearly to a man. The men had cleaned up, shaved, and maintained their kit too. He also had bathed and scrubbed up. It felt good to be clean. With their armor freshly polished, they looked sharp.

Karus felt a stirring of pride for them in his breast. They were the finest soldiers around and he loved them.

"Did you have a good nap, sir?" Felix asked, turning to Karus. There was a hint of a smirk on his face.

"It was better than no rest." Karus had managed four hours of sleep before he'd been awoken because the enemy had begun massing around the palace district. He had already spent time on the walls, studying the formations as they were coming up and deploying throughout the afternoon.

They had just put out a delegation, which was why he had been called to the gate by Felix. He still felt ragged, tired, and run-down ... also terribly sore. He stepped up to the wall and gazed outward. He sucked in a deep breath and slowly let it out.

The enemy army was finally fully assembled in all its glory and they had brought overwhelming force. Thousands upon thousands were formed up into neat, orderly, block-like formations that spread outward to either side and out of sight. The enemy had positioned their army completely around the district, effectively encircling it. They were essentially parading themselves before the legion.

Standard-bearers stood to the front of each formation, just behind the officers. The standards themselves were varied both in color and design, each depicting a different symbol. They meant nothing to Karus, but to the orcs it was likely a different story.

His eyes raked the units before him. Most of the formations positioned before the gate were heavy infantry. Their armor was plate, and uniform from unit to unit. It covered the chest, shoulders, and stomach, with a chain mail skirt protecting the groin. Each warrior wore a helmet and carried a shield and short spear. The light infantry formations

Karus had seen elsewhere were armored only with a chain mail shirt and helmet. They carried a sword belted to their side.

The enemy was silent, ominously so. Karus supposed the show was designed to impress. And impress it did. This only reinforced his belief the army on display was a well-trained and disciplined force.

"Now this"—Karus looked over at Dennig and gestured outward toward the enemy—"is a show... much better than the one they put on when they arrived."

"Quite," Dennig agreed. "I hope you plan to ruin it..."

"I do," Karus said.

First Cohort, which had the honor of guarding the section of the wall around the gate, gave a cheer. Karus looked back and saw that the Eagle-bearer had climbed the stairs. Under the fading light of the day, the gold Eagle glinted with reflected light. The men were cheering the Eagle as the bearer moved up to the wall and set the butt of the standard on the stone.

Karus was putting on his own show for the enemy. Granted, it wasn't as impressive, but it was a show nonetheless and a sign of the legion's defiance. He intended to send a message today, one that the enemy could not mistake.

Despite their hearty cheers and sharp appearances, he had a sense that his own men were concerned, worried even. There was a palpable tension, doubt, a brittleness of spirit... call it what you would, it was on the air and that worried him. The fight in the city had not gone as well as planned and clearly the enemy army was overwhelming in its magnitude. They had been through a lot since being transported from Britannia. This had been perhaps their greatest test so far.

They needed some help, reassurance that it would be all right. They needed confidence in their leadership… confidence in him. As Amarra had said, faith.

"Time to give you some strength," Karus said under his breath.

"What was that, sir?" Felix asked. "I did not quite hear that."

"Sound the horn," Karus ordered Felix.

"Yes, sir," Felix said and turned to a legionary who was standing there for this purpose. He gave the man a nod and he blew two long blasts from his horn. The sound of it echoed off the palace buildings. The men along the wall gave a cheer.

"Again," Felix said and the man blew his horn.

There was another massed cheer. Satisfied, Karus turned back to the enemy. Across the way, the delegation waited. A large orc in highly polished armor that reflected the fading light of the two suns stood just before the enemy's army. Karus supposed this was the enemy's general. Two dozen heavy infantry carrying large rectangular shields stood around him, as did another officer. There was someone else with him too and he was no orc.

Karus stiffened.

"Is that Logex?" Felix asked, aghast, seeing the man at the same time as Karus.

"Yes, I do believe it is," Karus replied slowly and it came out almost as a growl. It all made sense now. Before the refugees had turned on the legion, they had clearly found other tunnels leading out of the city… tunnels that had once likely been used for smuggling. Logex and those who had escaped with him had shown the enemy how to get into the city. Not only that, they had acted directly as guides. Ignoring the pain in his shoulder, Karus placed his hands upon the sun-warmed stone. His anger mounted like a thunderstorm about to break. There was a debt to be paid and Karus aimed to pay it in full.

An orc, who appeared to be a junior officer, separated himself from the others and walked slowly forward toward the gate. He was unarmed and came to a halt when he was fifty yards out. Si'Cara pulled her bow off her shoulder and nocked an arrow, though she did not aim it.

"Are you Karus?" the orc shouted in the common tongue. "I am told that you are he."

Amarra automatically translated for Felix.

"You are becoming famous, sir," Felix said.

"I am Karus, camp prefect of the Roman Ninth Imperial Legion," Karus said, ignoring Felix. He was much too angry at the appearance of Logex to be amused.

"I am Sub-Officer Nek." The orc gestured behind him. "My general would come forward and parley... without fear of violence. Will you guarantee that?"

"He may approach," Karus said, "without fear and say his piece. Upon my honor and that of the legion, we will do him no harm."

"That is most kind of you." The orc turned on his heel and slowly walked back the way he had come.

"Polite bugger," Felix said, "isn't he?"

"I wonder why they want to talk now?" Dennig asked, glancing over. "Why not before, when they arrived?"

Karus sucked in a deep breath of the hot, humid air and slowly let it out, calming himself through will alone. He forced down his rage at Logex and looked over at Dennig.

"They want an easy victory," Karus said, "an end without too much bloodshed. This parley is nothing more than an opportunity to give us a chance to surrender. That is the real reason they are putting on this show of overwhelming force. In their eyes, we're trapped. They are demonstrating, in no uncertain terms, there is no hope. Their general will offer us something, with the hope that we will accept and make his job of taking the city easier."

"How can you be so sure?" Amarra asked. "How do you know they will not attack immediately?"

"There are no ladders for scaling the walls in view," Karus said. "They do not intend to fight tonight, only to talk. An assault will take time to plan, prepare, and execute. Keep in mind, their supply has been strained nearly to the breaking point and much of their army was engaged in the assault last night. They may appear sharp, but like the legion, they are likely far from rested. No …" Karus glanced out at the enemy. "They will need a day or more, then such an assault becomes a possibility."

The delegation, Logex included, moved forward. Two of the heavy infantry guard walked before the general, their shields up for protection, and the rest followed close behind. Trust only went so far. They stopped fifty yards from the gate, almost exactly at the spot where the sub-officer had addressed Karus. Logex stood at the general's side.

"Thank you for agreeing to talk. I am General Iger," the enemy general called up to him. His voice was deep and confident.

"Say what you have to say," Karus said. His anger surged toward the man below. He found it a struggle just to contain it, for he wanted Logex dead. The enemy general had trotted him out on purpose. He clearly hoped to unsettle Karus. But, instead, he'd only angered him further. At the same time, Karus had never before spoken with an orc. It seemed almost outlandish, but then again, he now regularly conversed with dragons, dwarves, elves, and Vass, all alien beings. He was struck once more at how strange and fantastical his life had become.

"Your position is a strong one, defensible." Iger's tone was matter-of-fact. "I do not care to dispute that. There is no doubt in my mind. An assault will cost me many warriors to overcome your defenses. But in the end, we will prevail."

"And I don't doubt that we will prevail," Karus said. "Maybe our dragons will return."

"And maybe mine will come back before yours do," Iger snapped back.

"I think you touched on a nerve," Dennig said, loud enough to be heard by Iger.

"A filthy dwarf, elves, and a wretched Vass," Iger said.

Dennig stiffened. "Who are you calling filthy, orc?"

Ugin said nothing, just gazed down on the general.

"You keep interesting company," Iger said.

"So I am told," Karus replied.

"Do not force this issue," Iger said. "There is no need to fight."

"I disagree, and I will take my chances on the dragons."

"I do not wish to fight you." Iger held his hands out. "I do not know how I can make this plainer. All I want is the dwarven warband. You can march out of here with your arms, standards, and whatever supplies you can haul with you. Go west for all I care. You are not of this world. Its problems should not concern you. So why not just make it easy and give us the dwarves?"

"Really, it's not a bad offer," Ugin said to Karus. "You give them the dwarves and we go free."

"Do you think I can trust him?" Karus asked Ugin.

Dennig looked over at Karus. "You had best not be considering this. We formed a compact."

"No," Ugin said to Karus. "He is an orc and of the Horde. Your people follow the High Father, his god's enemy. He will not let you go, no matter what he tells you."

"I didn't think I could trust his word either." Karus glanced to Dennig. "I was just curious."

"You are killing me, my friend," Dennig said. "Really."

"This is not your world," Iger called, drawing Karus's attention back to the orc. "You are not our enemy. The dwarves are. Give them to us."

"Do you honestly expect me to do such a thing?" Karus asked.

"No," Iger said. "I do not. But I thought I would make the offer anyway."

"Sir," Felix said quietly. He jerked his head ever so slightly to get Karus to look eastward. A column of smoke was beginning to rise near the east gate. Those below could not see it, not yet. Karus's eyes tracked to the north. There was smoke there too. He struggled not to smile as he turned his attention back to Iger.

"You are correct, General Iger," Karus said and his tone hardened as he let some of his anger loose. "This is not our world and we are not of it. But…you most certainly made yourself our enemy. Now, it is my turn to make you an offer. Would you like to hear it?"

"You have a counterproposal?" Iger seemed intrigued.

"I do." Karus leaned forward slightly. "You will surrender the traitor, Logex, and then march away to the east. Go back to where you came from."

Logex made to speak, but Iger held up his hand for the man to keep quiet.

"Or what?" Iger demanded. "I am not the one trapped behind those walls. What will you do if I refuse?"

"I will destroy your army," Karus said, "killing many thousands of your warriors in the process. On this, you have my word."

Iger laughed. It was a harsh barking sound and reminded Karus of a mad dog. The orc shook a big hand in Karus's direction. "I do like you, Karus. I am told you are from your people's home world, the cradle of humanity. I find that astonishing … truly."

Karus wondered how the orc knew where the legion came from.

"You have brought together humans, dwarves, elves, Vass, and the taltalum," Iger said, sounding impressed. "Such an alliance between races I don't believe has ever been forged upon this world. You are so different than the humans of Tannis." General Iger paused and gave Logex a long look that clearly showed disgust. "They are weak, pathetic. You are strong. Your actions show you to be the threat my superiors think you to be." Iger paused and shifted his stance. "You have already proven yourself to be a worthy foe." Iger paused again. "I decline your offer. Do your worst, Karus … come tomorrow or the next, I will do mine."

"That was a nice bluff," Ugin said in a low tone that reeked with amusement. "Too bad it failed."

"Who's bluffing?" Karus said, looking over. "I will destroy his army, just as I have said."

"You are a real bastard, Karus," Logex hollered, apparently no longer able to contain himself. "You have earned what is coming, you and that whore of yours." Logex beat his chest with a fist. "And I will be there to see your downfall."

Karus eyed Logex for a long moment, then looked over to Si'Cara. She raised an eyebrow at him.

"It seems Logex did not lean his lesson the first time," Karus said. "Kindly educate him."

The elf's bow snapped up, and in less time than it takes for a heart to beat, her arrow was shooting away. It flew fast and true, taking Logex straight through the throat. He stumbled backward, eyes wide with shock and pain. His hands grasped the shaft that had gone clean through and tugged, as if to pull it free. Blood spurted out.

"Nice shot, little sister," Kol'Cara said.

There was a moment of stunned shock, then Iger's guards reacted, surrounding the general and bringing their shields up to protect him, while at the same time beginning to drag him backward toward their lines.

Left behind, Logex fell to his knees, then forward onto his stomach. His legs twitched spasmodically as his blood flowed out in a gush upon the ground.

"Dio has finally been avenged," Karus said.

"The bastard earned his fate," Felix said, "that's for sure."

"You violated the parley," Iger shouted in outrage and pointed an accusatory finger at Karus. His guards continued to drag him back. "You gave your word of honor."

"I only guaranteed your protection," Karus shouted back at the orc. "Not his, not a traitor, never."

Iger stopped and pushed his guards away so that he stood in full view of Karus again without protection. It was a risk to be sure, but Karus had to respect the orc's bravery, for there was no doubt Si'Cara could easily shoot and kill him.

"I would have killed him anyway." Iger gestured toward Logex, whose blood was staining the ground. "Once a betrayer, always a betrayer." He paused and looked back up at Karus. "I wish you had accepted my offer. We certainly don't need to be enemies."

"No, we don't." Karus's eyes flicked to the columns of smoke, which were becoming thicker, darker. "But nevertheless, we are enemies. And now, the parley is over. You may return to your lines ... oh, and when you see him ... give my regards to Vulcan, would you?"

"Who?" Iger asked, clearly confused.

Karus looked over at Amarra, meeting her gaze. He saw the warmth toward him in her eyes, the deep affection and love ... along with their shared faith.

"Sacrifice comes in many forms," Amarra said. "This city was once my beloved home. No longer. My home is with you and the legion."

Karus loved her for that. He switched to Latin. "Felix, signal the bolt throwers. Give the order to fire."

"Yes, sir." Felix turned to the legionary with the horn. "Sound the signal."

"What is going on?" Ugin asked.

"Watch," Dennig said, "and pray it works."

The legionary brought the horn to his lips and blew, one long blast. There was a slight hesitation, then one of the bolt throwers cracked. A bolt, trailing a thin stream of smoke, shot out from the wall to their left, over the orc army, and right through a building's window. The building was three stories in height and situated right next to the main street.

Two more bolt throwers cracked. Their bolts trailed smoke too as they flew outward and into the same building, through different windows. His best crews were manning the machines and their accuracy showed. Karus knew that on the other sides of the palace walls, and out of sight, the same thing was happening.

Below, Iger looked on, almost mystified. Then comprehension of what was happening began to dawn upon him. He understood Karus was attempting to burn the city, with his army deep inside it.

What he did not know was that the building the bolt throwers were shooting at was packed full of flammable oil, pitch, the strange black powder that burned and dried hay. He also didn't know that the oil depots by the city gates, which the legion had never had the opportunity to use, were on fire too. Divius and his men had seen to that when the first horn call had gone out, just before the parley. Within a short while, all main exits out of the city would be blocked by raging fires. That was the endgame to Karus's plan. He would destroy his enemy by fire.

Iger's speed at breaking into the city and moving up to parade the majority of his army in a show of strength was now working against him. He'd clearly not had time to search the nearest buildings, or if they had, the enemy had simply discounted what they'd found, considering it unimportant. The city was for the most part abandoned after all, and the defenders were newcomers.

As he sought to extricate his army, Iger would find out soon enough what waited. Karus almost smiled with satisfaction as Iger turned and began sprinting for his lines. He was shouting orders at his officers in his own tongue. It would take time to begin moving the army. Time that Iger no longer had.

The building had begun to smoke. Flames could be seen in the windows, first a little and then with growing intensity. The smoke quickly turned thick, ugly, and black, pouring out all of the windows.

"I think—" Felix never completed what he had intended to say. There was a tremendous explosion as the smoking building disappeared in a massive flash of flame. The shockwave and trembling of the ground that followed was so powerful that everyone along the wall was knocked from their feet, which likely saved many from injury, as the stone battlements offered protection from what followed. A heartbeat later, debris—masonry, plaster, wooden splinters, and more—hammered against the wall in a killing spray.

Ears ringing and shoulder hurting even more than before, Karus dragged himself to his feet. He looked around, fearing for Amarra, and saw Si'Cara helping her up. He breathed out a sigh of relief. She was fine.

The defensive wall itself had cracked. A gap more than a foot wide had appeared as if by magic, just inches from where he'd fallen. It ran from one side to the other. Karus stepped over it as he staggered to the battlements and looked out.

Five hundred yards away, a cloud in the shape of a mushroom was rapidly spreading skyward. The building itself was gone and those immediately around it had been flattened. Structures farther out were fully engulfed in flame and burning violently.

The army that had been arranged in neat block-like formations, particularly those positioned directly before the gate, had caught the brunt of the blast. Unlike the legion, they had not had a wall to shield them from the worst of it. The enemy's ranks had been thoroughly devastated. Thousands had been felled, with many having been ripped apart by the blast. Arms, legs, heads, torsos, and indescribable lumps of what looked like ground meat had been blown clear across the legion's killing field, all lying haphazardly about on the scorched ground before the city wall.

There was another booming explosion in the distance, from the other side of the palace district. It was followed shortly after by a strong gust of hot wind. Clearly one of the other buildings had gone up too.

Those of the enemy who were still alive began to pick themselves up or rolled on the ground, horribly injured, maimed, burned, all crying out in agony and torment. The formations in the distance that had not been directly impacted by the blast seemed confused, dazed even.

All sense of organization was gone. Karus could not see Iger anywhere. It was quite possible the enemy's general was dead, for he had been directly in the path of the blast.

Where before there had been an army, now there was only a mass of individuals seeking safety from the growing inferno, which was spreading rapidly from building to building. There would be no safety, for the city would burn. The heat from the conflagration could already be felt five hundred yards away on the wall.

"Blessed Gods," Felix breathed, taking in the sight and shaking his head in clear dismay. "That was unexpected."

"What?" Karus asked. His ears were still ringing. He rubbed at his left ear with the palm of his free hand. It was only then that he realized he'd lost his helmet. Where it had gone, he had no idea, but it had been ripped free from his head. The strap holding it in place had clearly snapped.

Felix shook his head and then leaned close as he gazed out at the growing inferno. "Can you hear me?"

Karus nodded.

"When I was a child in Rome, there was a fire that broke out. It burned several blocks, killed lots of people, and I mean lots. After it was over, they found people untouched by the flame. A doctor later said they died of asphyxiation. The fire sucked out all the air or some such thing like that."

"Now you tell me this?" Karus asked, looking over at his friend, wondering if he was being serious.

"I just remembered it," Felix said. "Besides, my family survived, and the fire burned all around us. The smoke was real bad and we almost choked to death, but it did not kill us. And it did not suck out the air like he said... not for us anyway."

"Was it as big a fire as the one we just started?" Karus asked, doubting it was.

Felix shook his head. "No. We're talking about burning an entire city here, Karus. There's no telling what will happen. The smoke might kill us all or the heat. Gods... it's already too hot. I am being singed just standing here. Have you ever done anything like this?"

"No," Karus said. "I don't think anyone has. Well, what's done is done. We now have to live with it."

"It's no doubt gonna get hotter."

The heat from the growing blaze across the way could be keenly felt, as if he'd stepped too close to a campfire. Karus shook his head slightly and worked his jaw. The ringing was beginning to subside a little, though he suspected he would be hearing it for days to come. He looked around the walls as men were picking themselves up or were just staring out at the destruction and growing fires in shock. Debris lay all over the wall and beyond it, far out into the parade ground. Pieces of wood and plaster were scatted seemingly everywhere.

It was time to reassert command.

"I think you're right," Karus said to Felix. "The heat's likely to increase as more of the city burns. Let's get most of the men off the walls and into shelter in the dungeons and underground spaces."

Out in no man's land, cinders were already on the air, carried by the wind. There had been no wind a short while before. Now there was a strong, hot breeze beginning to gust, almost as if a storm was brewing. Had the fire created it? "We need to make sure the fire brigades are watchful. We can't have the palace district burn around us, understand?"

"Yes, sir," Felix said. "I will see to it."

Felix left.

"I am thoroughly convinced," Ugin said, awe in his tone as he gazed outward at what Karus had wrought, "if there is ever a human that has some Vass in him, it is you. I pray that we never have to cross swords upon a field of battle."

Karus looked up at the big Vass. Ugin had meant that as a compliment. He gave a nod, accepting it for what it was. "I hope so too, for I would not want to fight you or your people."

There was another booming explosion off in the distance toward one of the gatehouses. Karus turned his gaze back out to no man's land. It was a mass of confusion, with orcs running this way and that, or milling about, thoroughly dazed. The enemy officers seemed to have lost complete control.

Crack.

The bolt throwers had begun to fire at the enemy, adding to the confusion. There would be no safety in the killing fields of no man's land. The bolt throwers would drive them away. He wanted the enemy forced out into the city proper and into the mounting inferno.

His gaze traveled to the growing columns of smoke toward the city's southern gate and his thoughts shifted to Divius. He hoped the optio and his men survived. Karus returned his attention to the enemy and his anger surged once again.

"Burn," he said.

Epilogue

With Dennig at his side, Karus stood a few yards outside the palace district's gate. They were both staring out at the destruction before them in awe. Thaldus stood a few feet behind his warchief, looking sour. He was likely mourning the loss of Martuke.

The gate had survived the blast when the building had gone up, but it was charred, blackened, and deeply pitted from multiple impacts. They had been unable to open it, as several of the hinges had melted. A team of men, using axes, had been forced to chop a hole through the wood to allow egress. That work had taken more than an hour.

The fires had raged for four long days before, for the most part, burning themselves out. As it devoured the city one building at a time, the blaze had turned into a true storm, a firestorm. It had generated its own fierce wind, which wailed and screamed about the palace district like a banshee.

When the wind wasn't howling, the cloying smoke was so bad, it burned at the lungs of those who had rotated aboveground in shifts to patrol and stand watch against the fire spreading to the palace district.

The heat generated from the flames had been brutal, hotter than the hottest day Karus could ever remember. Those who went outside could only do so for short periods, and even then, several men and dwarves had been overcome by the heat or smoke and needed medical attention.

Cinders carried on the wind had started several fires in the palace and administrative building. These had all been successfully extinguished. It was one of the reasons they had gathered all the buckets and containers throughout the city and filled them with water ahead of time. It also helped that the roofs of the buildings were tiled. And though the legion had wrecked the aqueducts and water sources, for fear of the enemy fighting the fire, they need not have bothered. Once started, in the way it had been, no amount of effort could have stopped the fire from consuming the city. That much had become clear.

As the storm raged, burning all in its path, the legion, dwarves, and camp followers had huddled in the lower levels and underground spaces of the palace district, including the dungeons. It had been tight, with little space for each person, but there had been no choice other than to make do.

The smoke from the fires had inevitably found its way to them, but it hadn't been too bad. Not once had breathing proved a real problem, though it irritated many people's lungs and there was much coughing and hacking. Karus wondered if that was due to the palace district being situated upon a large hill that overlooked the city. Or was it because he had pushed the city back five hundred yards from the palace walls, creating an effective firebreak? Regardless of the reason, they had weathered the storm and survived. He could not say the same for the enemy.

The city was gone, now nothing more than a charred and blackened ruin. All that remained were the stone walls, foundations, the occasional chimney, and a half dozen buildings that for some reason had been spared. And even those had been thoroughly gutted and were shells of their former selves.

Though the city still smoked and smoldered, Karus and Dennig had thought it safe enough to send parties out to reconnoiter. Their mission was to find out what had happened to the enemy, both in the city and beyond in their encampment.

After a few hours, the scouting parties had reported the enemy's fortified camp was still occupied. They had also found tens of thousands of dead orcs who had not been able to escape the city. After so many setbacks, Karus had succeeded in damaging the enemy's army far more than he had dared hope. The scouts had even made contact with Valens's cavalry, who were active beyond the city's walls.

Once they had heard back from the scouts, Karus and Dennig had made the snap decision to eyeball the enemy's encampment personally. Which was why they were standing before the blackened and charred gate. Kol'Cara and six of the Anagradoom were with them.

Felix had insisted Karus be accompanied by a century of men, as the scouting parties had found enemy survivors and taken prisoners. And so, Karus found himself waiting for the century to join them. Felix had gone to hurry them along.

The scouts had reported there were no organized enemy forces within the city. But still, Karus realized it paid to be careful. The remains of the enemy army were outside the city walls, in their encampment. More important, their numbers were supposedly significantly reduced. To what extent, Karus did not yet know.

Apparently, while the city had burned and much of the enemy's strength was caught inside, Valens had taken advantage of the opportunity and launched a dismounted attack on the enemy's camp. Striking at night, it had caught the enemy completely by surprise. Outnumbered, the dismounted cavalry had killed several hundred before being compelled to withdraw when the orcs had rallied and held firm. Apparently, from what the scouts had told him, it had been a close thing.

The enemy had simply refused to break, and Valens decided to cut his losses and disengage. The cavalry prefect's move had been a bold one, and though he had not succeeded, Karus applauded the effort.

Even more encouraging, the enemy appeared to be preparing to march, which was exceptionally good news. It meant they were leaving. They'd had enough. No matter how one looked at it, he had achieved a victory. The legion would live to fight another day.

Divius, Lanza, and two other legionaries from his team had reported in the day before. They had somehow survived the inferno that had torn through the city. Karus hoped the others had made it as well. But he knew that was unlikely. The entire venture had been terribly risky to begin with. Seven lives spent to save the legion and savage an enemy army. Though it pained him to lose those seven good men, it was a trade that Karus would take every time.

He turned as Ugin stepped through the hole that had been cut in the gate. His protectors filed out after him. They carried packs and appeared to be prepared for a journey. Karus understood what it meant. The Vass were leaving too.

Ugin stepped up next to Karus. His eyes were on the destruction. He said nothing. They stood there in silence for a time.

"We had to destroy the city to save it," Karus said, almost to himself, as his eyes raked the sprawling wasteland that spread outward before them. In the distance, only city walls were recognizable.

"What was that?" Ugin asked, looking over at him. "What did you mean you had to destroy the city to save it?"

"It was something I heard a long time ago," Karus said. "When I was a fresh-faced recruit, just out of basic training. My cohort was charged with helping an allied village ... to save it really. That was our mission. They were being regularly raided by their neighbors, who ironically were also allies of ours. The village was valuable to the legion, as we bought the food they grew, mostly barley and beans. We were sent to keep the peace. Our presence was supposed to deter the raiders, send them a message."

"It did not," Ugin said, "did it?"

"No," Karus said. "The raiders learned we were there and returned with the intention of finishing off the village, us included. Thankfully, the village had walls. They showed up with more than four thousand warriors."

Karus sucked in a breath and let it out slowly. That time, so long ago, was still vivid in his memory. It always would be, for it had been his first real fight. "We held that village for five long days, until someone back at the garrison decided we were overdue for a report. They sent two cohorts to check on us."

Falling silent, Karus recalled the smoke, the heat of the flames as the village burned around them, the seemingly unending waves of enemy as they sought to overcome the walls, his comrades dying. Most of all, he recalled his fear, the desperation of holding out hope that help would come, and the terrible exhaustion brought on by battle and lack of sleep.

"The defense of the village destroyed it," Ugin said, finally understanding. "Is that right?"

"Yes," Karus said. "Only fifty of us walked out of that bastard of a village. We went in there with more than three hundred men. A handful of villagers made it too. After it was over, those locals who survived moved on … they left … and never came back. But the village was saved, or so my centurion told me. We had done our job."

"Interesting." Ugin looked out over the ruined city. "And now Carthum is saved too."

"This time," Karus said, "it is we who were saved, at the cost of a city we don't want."

"I like that even better. What happened to the barbarians who attacked you in that village?"

"Their villages were razed in retribution." Karus took another deep breath that shuddered slightly and looked over at the Vass. "You don't mess with Rome. The legate wanted a message sent that could not be mistaken. All were put to death, including the women and children. Even though I wanted payback for the loss of my brothers, that was the worst duty I have ever had to perform. It haunts me to this day."

Ugin looked back over at Karus and gave a nod.

"Sir." Flaccus came up. He saluted.

Karus almost returned the salute, before he recalled that his arm was still in a sling. His shoulder was getting better, but still hurt something fierce when he unexpectedly shifted it. An auxiliary cavalry trooper stood with the centurion.

"This man just came in, sir." Flaccus's face was smeared with ash and he was sweating heavily, for it was brutally hot from both the suns and the aftereffects of the fire. Even though it had burned itself out, the stone around them still radiated with a portion of the fire's heat.

The centurion had been out in the city with the scouts, exploring and searching for pockets of the enemy. So far, they had captured around two hundred orcs who had somehow managed to survive.

"The enemy has begun withdrawing, sir," Flaccus reported. "They number a little over five thousand."

"What?" Karus was shocked. "Five thousand... that's all that remain?"

"Yes, sir," the auxiliary said. "They've begun marching back on the east road. I saw them go myself. I have a dispatch for you, sir, from Prefect Valens. The cavalry is shadowing them."

Karus took it and opened it with one hand. He scanned the contents and turned to Dennig.

"No sign or word from Torga yet," Karus told the dwarf.

"I would have thought he'd have been here by now," Dennig said, looking far from happy.

Where were the dwarves? What did it mean? Karus suddenly felt chilled. Had the burning of the city failed... they would have had to face the might of Iger's army as it attacked the palace walls. It would have taken time, but there would only have been one outcome: the legion's destruction. He handed the dispatch over to Flaccus to read.

"It seems," Flaccus said, after he had read it, "we've saved ourselves, with no help from anyone else."

"Yes," Karus said, then switched back to the common tongue and addressed Dennig. "I guess you're stuck with me for a while longer. Word has been sent to the wagon train and they are heading back to us. They should be here tomorrow afternoon. Once the supplies are loaded, we can march west together and put this city behind us. That is... unless you have changed your mind?"

"I see no reason to end or alter our compact." Dennig set the butt of the shaft of his magnificent axe on the ground before his feet. He rested a hand lightly on the polished steel of its head. "We will travel together, as we had originally planned. Eventually, I expect, we will run into my people and then we shall go our separate ways."

That last bit was not what Karus wanted. He held his tongue. There would be time enough to work on Dennig and see if the foundation they had started could be built upon. Now was not the time for that.

Thaldus, for his part, looked deeply unhappy. But he said nothing. Karus was beginning to suspect that was the dwarf's normal countenance.

"But our arrangement is done," Ugin said, drawing Karus's attention. "I will be taking my leave."

"So soon?" Karus asked. "It seems like we just found you."

Ugin chuckled politely at the weak attempt at humor.

"Where will you go?" Karus asked.

"Does it matter?"

"No," Karus said, "but I would part as friends."

"We are not friends. But… I appreciate your sentiment." Ugin paused, his eyes fixed upon Karus. "We are not enemies either. I would have it remain that way, especially after what I saw you… *Romans*… do to the orcs. You shattered an army of the Horde that outnumbered yours greatly. Such things are not known for happening on this world, at least not often. The Horde will look to settle the score. Next time you face them, they will send a more powerful force against you, backed up by priests with power."

Karus felt himself scowl. That was not a pleasant thought. What Ugin spoke of was a problem for another time, though. He would worry about that threat when it materialized.

The sound of wings overhead turned their gazes skyward. Cyln'Phax had returned, along with Kordem. Karus felt immense relief as he watched the two dragons land behind the palace.

Ugin looked at him, as if weighing something. He seemed almost hesitant. "A word of warning, if you will take it?"

Karus gave a nod, wondering what Ugin wanted to caution him about.

"That weapon you carry." Ugin pointed a thick finger toward Rarokan.

"What of it?"

"Your sword is from what my people call the Age of Nightmares. It is a relic from a time best forgotten ... a time we remember with great sorrow and pain."

Karus glanced down at the sword. "It talks to me."

"That does not surprise me." He tapped his own sword hilt. "Mine does as well. They tend to do that when a soul is imprisoned within. The soul and ability to take the spark of others is what gives your sword and mine its power. That power can manifest itself in many ways ... some good and some bad. It all depends upon the soul within."

When he had first learned of it, Karus did not much enjoy the thought that someone's soul was bound within his sword. It was fundamentally disturbing to him. He could not imagine what such an imprisonment would be like.

"Are you saying the soul within my sword is dark?" Karus asked. "Bad?"

"Not at all," Ugin said. "Yours is far more powerful a tool than mine, for a god had it forged."

"The High Father," Karus said.

"That is my understanding. There is a dread prophecy surrounding that sword." Ugin held up a hand to forestall the inevitable question that came to Karus's lips. "It is not my place to speak on it, nor would I … for if I did, you might leave it here in Carthum when you march or intentionally try to lose it or hide it. That would be bad for my people, as someone else would undoubtedly find the sword and use it. Relics like Rarokan have a way of drawing others to them, even when you don't want it to. Such things never remain lost or hidden forever. Trust me on this, you do not want the Horde in possession of that sword. Keep it close and guard it well."

Karus felt his scowl deepen.

"And you don't want it?" Karus asked. "You don't desire its power? To take it, that is? The Elantric Warden wanted it."

"Did she now?" Ugin asked, suddenly very interested.

"She tried to take it," Karus said. "She's dead."

"That is news." Ugin's eyes narrowed. "You continually surprise me, Roman."

"So why don't you crave its power?" Karus asked. "Like she did?"

"Likely because I have more sense," Ugin said. "I would be a fool to take it. Remember, there is a dread prophecy surrounding its bearer. Besides, even though he is not part of our alignment, I will not cross the High Father."

Ugin fell silent for a long moment, his eyes studying Karus, as a predator might look upon prey. "Be careful with it, for though it seems to help, granting you strength and other powers … it works toward a purpose of its own, as does mine."

"How do you know?"

"The wizard's soul that's inside your sword had ambitions without end. Just because he is imprisoned within does not mean he is any less a threat. His power expands beyond the blade and through you to the world around you. That is how he will influence events to his advantage. Be on your guard."

"I will keep that in mind," Karus said, though he did not see what he could do.

"Good." Ugin glanced toward the city, clearly eager to be off. His escort stood ready, waiting patiently, watching them.

"You mentioned powers the sword may grant," Karus said, curious to know more about Rarokan. He knew the sword could give him energy, make him faster, ease aches and pains, along with lighten darkness for him... but there was so much he did not know. "Can you tell me more? Anything that could help?"

The Vass considered him for a long moment, as if weighing whether or not to do so. "I am not fully sure what Rarokan can do. Given time, you yourself will surely find out." Ugin took a step closer, his eyes intense. "But... I might know of one power you may not be aware of that's fairly obvious... You and your legion arrived recently to this world, yes?"

"A little more than two months, now."

"And yet," Ugin said, "you speak the common tongue like you have been born to it. Does that not strike you as strange?"

Karus had not given it any real thought. He'd been forced to learn the language and then had been around Amarra, Dennig, and the elves, continually speaking it. Practice always made you better at something. But now that Ugin had mentioned it... He glanced down at the sword in its sheath. Since he had retrieved Rarokan, the common tongue had become much easier for him. Had it helped him master the language? He suspected the Vass was correct, and that worried him, for what else had it done without his knowledge?

Much... came the hissing reply in his mind. He froze, once again going cold.

"Karus," Ugin said, with a note of finality, "our arrangement has concluded. I have lived up to my side of the bargain and so too have you."

Karus said nothing. His thoughts were on the sword, fears swirling. What had it done?

"Do you agree?" Ugin pressed, tone hard, snapping him back.

"I do," Karus said, hastily. "Thank you."

"No," Ugin said, "it is I who should thank you."

Without another word, Ugin turned and started off, moving in the direction of the south gate, with his protectors settling into place around him.

"Ugin?" Karus called, a thought occurring to him.

The Vass stopped and looked back at him.

"Did you find it?" Karus asked. "The thing you were searching for?"

The Vass bared his teeth in a grin. "Perhaps, Karus, one day our paths will cross again. Until then..."

With that, Ugin turned away and, together with his protectors, continued off into the ruined city, leaving Karus with Dennig and the elves. Karus took a deep breath and almost regretted it, for a cloud of smoke swirled around them. Coughing lightly, he glanced over at Dennig. The dwarf met his gaze for a long moment and then turned it back outward toward the ruined city.

Behind them, Karus could hear the chink of armor and crunch of sandals as his escort emerged through the gate. He followed Dennig's gaze outward and wondered what the future held in store for them.

The End

Karus and Amarra's adventures will continue.

Important: If you have not yet given my other series—Tales of the Seventh or Chronicles of an Imperial Legionary officer—or The Way of the Legend a shot, I strongly recommend you do. All three series are linked and set in the same universe. There are hints, clues, and Easter eggs sprinkled throughout the series.

The Series:

There are three series to consider. I began telling Stiger and Eli's story in the middle years... starting with Stiger's Tigers, published in 2015. *Stiger's Tigers* is a great place to start reading. It was the first work I published and is a grand fantasy epic.

Stiger, Tales of the Seventh, covers Stiger's early years. It begins with Stiger's first military appointment as a wet-behind-the-ears lieutenant serving in Seventh Company during the very beginning of the war against the Rivan on the frontier. This series sees Stiger cut his teeth and develop into the hard charging leader that fans have grown to love. It also introduces Eli and covers many of their early adventures. These tales should in no way spoil your experience with *Stiger's Tigers*. In fact, I believe they will only enhance it.

The Way of the Legend is an adventure set in the same universe... and on the same planet as *The Karus Saga*. This series is a dwarven saga, based around an unlikely hero, Tovak, who struggles not only against his own kind, but the might of the Horde. It is set amidst a war of the gods and is full of action, intrigue, adventure, and mystery.

Give them a shot and hit me up on Facebook to let me know what you think!

You can reach out and connect with me on:

Facebook: Marc Edelheit Author

Facebook: MAE Fantasy & SciFi Lounge (This is a group I created where members can come together to share a love for Fantasy and SciFi)

Twitter: @MarcEdelheit

You may wish to sign up to my newsletter by visiting my website.

http://maenovels.com/

Or

You can follow me on **Amazon** through my Author Profile. Smash that follow button under my picture and you will be notified by Amazon when I have a new release.

Reviews keep me motivated and also help to drive sales. I make a point to read each and every one, so please continue to post them.

Again, I hope you enjoy *The First Compact* and would like to offer a sincere thank you for your purchase and support.
Best regards,
Marc Alan Edelheit, your author and tour guide to the worlds of Tanis and Istros

Enjoy this sample of *Reclaiming Honor, The Way of the Legend, Book One.*

One

Tovak Stonehammer breathed in the crisp air, clenching his fists in frustration and anger as he stared out at the grasslands of the plateau rolling by. Behind, yet another conversation about him was rolling by, just as easily as the landscape.

"Thank Fortuna we're almost there. I can't wait to get off this rickety old thing… I swear, the stench of the Pariah is getting worse every day. I'm afraid it's gonna stick to me."

The voice belonged to Kutog, an arrogant Dvergr from a wealthy family who had spent their entire journey making no secret of his family's wealth, influence, and his intense dislike for Tovak's presence.

Tovak was the Pariah.

"My father says it would be better to simply put them all to death." A round of agreement from the other recruits floated up behind Tovak. "Put the honorless scruggs out of their misery…"

Tovak didn't recognize the voice and wouldn't dignify the person by looking, which was what they likely expected. Knowing who it was only made it harder for him to go about his business. He'd heard such things many times before. It never made it any easier. He had long ago learned how to ignore those who insulted and reviled him while he was within earshot. It came with who he was, a Pariah. And though words hurt, he'd suffered much worse over the years.

"The warbands shouldn't take their kind," another voice said.

"If they weren't so desperate for warriors, they wouldn't," Kutog said. "Don't worry, he'll probably piss himself at the first sight of a goblin and run."

The group laughed.

Tovak burned with shame. He closed his eyes and breathed out a heavy breath. His objective was making it to the Blood Badgers, just like the other recruits he shared the journey with. For it would only be through building his own Legend that he could finally and forever cast off the stigma of Pariah. Until then, he would endure. He had no choice.

Tovak was far from what had been his home—a place to which he would not return, at least if he could help it. He certainly never desired to see it again. The memories were just too painful. The great reinforced iron wheels of the *yuggernok*—one of the massive cargo wagons of Garand'Durbaad—ground its way across the Grimbar Plateau, carrying him one turn of the wheel at a time closer to his dreams of Legend. The yuggernok and three others of its kind traversed the rolling grass prairie in a small convoy on their way to resupply the Blood Badgers Warband.

Tovak ignored the voices behind him and whispered a prayer to Thulla as he watched the plateau pass by. He unclenched his fists and tied a prayer knot of gray cloth into a small braid hidden behind his thick auburn beard, marking the prayer's passing.

And the Way shall be opened to the faithful, so they may be tested and reclaim that which was taken from them. The passage, lifted from *Thulla's Blessed Word,* echoed in his thoughts. He knew Dvergr scripture as well as the priest who had taught him. Like no other, that passage had sustained him through the rough times for as long as he could remember. The prayer knot was one of twelve required by scripture, and he maintained them all without fail, as one of the faithful.

He had his faith, he had his dream, and he was going to be at the forefront of the next Great March—the exodus of his people.

It was enough, enough to sustain him.

The incessant rumbling of the yuggernok, its massive wooden frame creaking and groaning with every turn of the great iron wheels, had taken some getting used to. The wagon was pulled along by a team of six *oofants*—distant cousins of elephants. They were larger, shaggy beasts of burden capable of travelling tremendous distances. Fully grown, they normally stood fifteen feet at their humps, though some occasionally reached twenty feet tall. They had long, curved tusks that reached out to lengths of eight feet and made formidable weapons against predators and raiders alike. Each of their thudding feet added its own tempo to the low, subtle thunder of the yuggernok's passage. During the long nights, Tovak had at first struggled to sleep through the racket, but in time, the sound had come to lull him to sleep as the miles passed.

Setting out from Garand'Durbaad, the small caravan of yuggernoks had traveled for two weeks, and in that time, Tovak had grown increasingly restless. His body, accustomed to the rigors of physical labor and the Academy's military training, yearned to be active once again. The only time he was able to stretch his legs was when the oofants needed rest or water.

Early on, out of boredom, Tovak had even offered to help the teamsters tend to the animals and the rig. Duroth, the lead teamster, had rejected him, saying only that they didn't want a dumb, young Pariah's bad luck. So, he had passed the days and nights by riding in the back of the covered wagon, watching the mountains in the distance slide by.

A ruddy pair of suns squatted just above the nearby ridgeline separating Grimbar Plateau from the heavily forested, orc infested lowlands to the northwest. As the two suns set, they took with them the warmth of the day. It would turn cold again soon as daylight shifted to shadow and shadow to night, but Tovak was accustomed to cold nights spent shivering under his blanket.

He was no stranger to the cold. Under the mountain, the stone floors and cold barns where he'd worked and slept had been chilly. Hardship was something to which he had become accustomed. He shrugged his shoulders into his threadbare woolen blanket for warmth, doing his best to mind its frayed and torn edges. Unable to afford the cost of a replacement, he'd had it for years. In truth, it was almost like an old friend.

As the deepening shadows from the mountains stretched across the rolling countryside, he silently watched the tall grasses of the prairie. Almost hypnotically, they bent and swayed with the wind.

"Stand to," a harsh voice shouted, jarring Tovak out of his thoughts. He recognized Duroth's bellow and wondered if the old drunkard had been at the jug yet again. "I said, bloody stand to."

Tovak had learned to follow Duroth's orders or face the consequences, which could and often did include a cuff or, if enraged, a beating. Duroth was shorter than the average Dvergr, ill-tempered, and possessed with a genuine enthusiasm for swearing... particularly by taking Thulla's name in vain. He had long, gray hair and a braided beard tied with simple black bands.

At the start of the journey, Duroth had made it clear to everyone that he'd been a training instructor with the Blood Badgers once and still held the auxiliary rank of sergeant. This meant he outranked the recruits and was the ultimate authority on the oversized wagon.

Tovak and the other recruits stepped out from their berths into the central passageway that stretched from stem to stern along the interior of the yuggernok. Like Tovak, they had all recently achieved the Age of Iron and were now fit to join a warband and grow their Legend. Unlike Tovak, however, they already had secured appointments to various companies in the Blood Badgers.

It would have been easier if he'd had a clan or sponsor to arrange for his appointment. But as it was, a Pariah could only hope he would be able to join a company once he was standing before its commanding officer. As always, Tovak was on his own. No one cared a fig for a Pariah. Well, to be honest, very few did.

There were twenty recruits on board Duroth's yuggernok. They, Tovak along with them, placed their backs to the curtains of their berths and faced forward, stiffening to attention.

Tovak stood before the three-by-six-foot area of floorboards Duroth had laughingly referred to as Tovak's "berth." Without a clan, sponsor, or patron, he had been forced to pay for his own passage. Tovak had spent a week trying to arrange for a berth aboard one of the caravans, but it was always the same. One teamster after another simply turned his nose up at a Pariah.

Tovak had been losing hope when a strange impulse finally pushed him in the direction of an older yuggernok that looked to be on its last legs, barely travel-worthy. Its owner, Duroth, was its match in appearance, and he'd had a strong reek of spirits upon him. The teamster's initial reaction had been identical to the others: "Fortuna don't look kindly on Pariahs." However, when his eyes had found Tovak's purse in hand, his tune had changed. "Maybe we can work something out..."

In exchange for ten copper *suuls*, a substantial chunk of Tovak's hard-earned savings, Duroth granted enough space at the back of the yuggernok to lay out his blanket each night. It was twice the cost of a standard berth, and Duroth made no secret of having taken on a Pariah, which made Tovak's journey a lonely one.

At least he'd gotten aboard.

The corridor, such as it was, held the sleeping bunks for the other passengers and the crew. The yuggernok could sleep up to thirty Dvergr in narrow bunks shielded only by curtains and a weatherproofed canvas roof.

When unoccupied, the bunks were disassembled for additional storage space. Stacked above each bunk were crates, sacks, casks, and amphorae, all supplies destined for the Blood Badger encampment. The supplies had been strapped and tied down so they didn't shift or move during transport, and the teamsters regularly checked to make certain everything was still safely secured.

Tovak knew from speaking with them that Duroth's yuggernok was the only one in the caravan carrying passengers. The other two hauled only supplies.

"Thulla curse you young scruggs," Duroth hollered from the front as he stomped slowly down the corridor. "We're almost to the encampment. Soon enough, I'll be done with the lot of you. And I say the sooner you bugger off the better. No more nursemaiding for me, Fortuna be praised. You'll be someone else's headache after today. Bloody Thulla, I can't wait to get rid of the lot of ya."

Duroth stopped before Tovak, and his rheumy eyes narrowed.

"I said eyes forward!" he said, his breath thick with spirits. "You best get used to acting like warriors if you expect to join the Blood Badgers."

Tovak kept his face calm, impassive. Standing a head taller than Duroth, what he really wanted to do was grab the short drunkard by the collar and throw him over the edge of the platform. But that was not in the cards. The other teamsters would likely not look kindly upon such actions.

"I don't know what I was thinking," Duroth growled in a low tone so that only Tovak could hear. "I never should have let one of your kind aboard my rig," he seethed, poking his finger into Tovak's chest. "Thulla's bones, they'll probably blame me if something happens to the Blood Badgers... All you Pariahs are bad luck, boy."

Tovak shifted his gaze forward, staring over Duroth at the supplies stacked and strapped down on the other side of the corridor. He bit back the suggestion that Duroth had been too drunk at the time to see anything but the purse and more coin for another bottle of spirits.

Duroth hesitated a moment more, his jaw flexing as he considered Tovak. He let out a heavy breath that was part sigh. The stench of spirits was almost enough to make Tovak gag. Then, the old Dvergr turned and stomped back the way he'd come.

Like so many other times, Tovak wanted to say something... do something. Frustrated rage bubbled up inside him, but he kept his mouth shut. Duroth was in a position to kick him off the yuggernok and perhaps even keep him from joining a company.

All Thulla's sons and daughters have free will, and it is His domain to mete out reward and consequence as He sees fit. Tovak had always liked that passage and found a measure of comfort recalling it. He took a deep breath and pressed his lips together in silence, when something occurred to him. Duroth's drinking might have been the only thing that had allowed him to gain a berth. The great god worked in mysterious ways. Tovak sent up a silent prayer of thanks.

"The main encampment is in sight," Duroth continued, loud enough for all to hear. "Gather up your belongings and be ready to get your sorry asses off my rig the moment we come to a stop. We won't be serving no dinner for you either." He came to a halt halfway down the corridor, leaned around a recruit, and swept the curtain aside. He made a show of peering within the berth. "And clean up before you go. Don't leave nothin' behind. Your mommas didn't come along for the ride, so anything I find after your feet hit dirt is mine."

"Who does that drunken bastard think he is?" the recruit beside Tovak hissed.

Duroth swung around in a flash. The old teamster's eyes settled on Kutog, though it had not been him. Duroth stomped back down the corridor and stepped right up into Kutog's face, his nose only inches away from the recruit's chin. He slowly ran his eyes up and down Kutog's larger frame and then glared up into the recruit's eyes.

"Anything you want to say to me, rich boy?" Duroth demanded. "Or perhaps I should have a few words with your new commanding officer to let him know what a Thulla-cursed, disrespectful little cuss you are? One word from me and you'll be without an appointment, in the same boat with the Pariah there." Duroth jabbed a thumb in Tovak's direction. "What would Daddy think, eh? How would you like that?"

There was a long moment of silence.

"No, sir," Kutog said. "Sorry, sir. I have nothing to say."

"That's what I thought." Duroth let out a disgusted grunt and turned on his heel. Without another word, he marched back up the corridor to the steps that led to the teamster's bench. He stopped at the first step, turned back with a disdainful sneer, and then climbed up, disappearing.

Tovak let out a breath he hadn't realized he'd been holding. It seemed that the others did the same, and then they went back into their berths. Many of the recruits traveled with armor, weapons, and even multiple packs containing their possessions. Compared to the others, Tovak had very little. All he owned fit into his small, battered, and patched pack.

Turning around, Tovak grabbed his blanket from where he'd discarded it, folded it carefully, and laid it aside. The other side of his berth opened up to the prairie, with only a couple of stacked crates between him and the rear deck of the yuggernok.

"At least I didn't have to walk," he said under his breath, for he had at one point, prior to securing passage with Duroth, thought he might need to. He picked his pack up from the deck and set it upon a nearby crate that had served as a table for him during the trip. The sigils stamped upon the side in black lettering indicated it was destined for someone named Struugar Ironfist, of the Baelix Guard. Tovak had spent much of his journey daydreaming about who Struugar might be and what the crate might contain. He'd had little else to do.

He untied his pack and peered inside to make sure he wouldn't be leaving anything behind for Duroth to confiscate. He found a small toiletry kit, a bone-handled comb, a book wrapped in cloth, a small wooden box, a knife, and his spare tunic. He also had another pair of socks, which had been patched numerous times by his own hand. He ran his fingers along the cloth-wrapped book, feeling the smooth fabric. It was the same type of cloth used for prayer knots, and as his fingers brushed the surface, he offered up thanks to Thulla for it coming into his possession.

Within the cloth was his copy of *Thulla's Blessed Word*, kept hidden from condescending eyes. In truth, the book was old and battered, its stitching coming loose in places, but it was one of his few treasured possessions.

A pang of sadness tinged with shame washed over him at the necessity of hiding the book from prying eyes. His people had mostly abandoned Thulla. They blamed the god for the problems they faced. Part of Tovak understood the why of it, but it still bothered him to his core that he had to hide his faith.

"'And the Way shall be opened to the faithful, so they may be tested and reclaim that which was taken from them'," he whispered. Tovak closed his eyes for a long moment. He breathed in and then out.

If only he could show his people that suffering was one of the paths to Thulla, not a reason to turn away from the great god. Was that not one of the primary lessons taught through the tale of the hero Uliand Stormhand in *Thulla's Blessed Word*?

As the first holy warrior of Thulla, his trials had been unparalleled and had only made Uliand stronger, or so the scripture taught. The loss of his family, torture, years spent fettered in chains, all of it had prepared him for divine service. The god tested his flock, and faith brought salvation. Indeed, Tovak's own faith had been his compass, his foundation, and his anchor during the worst of times.

Folded inside the book was his Warrant of Passage, proof of his graduation from the Pioneer Academy. He unwrapped the cloth and pulled the yellowed parchment out. With it, Pariah or not, he had the right to travel to a warband of his choosing and apply for a posting. The document represented years of work. It was the first step in his dream of proving that he was just as worthy as the next Dvergr and not the disgrace everyone thought him to be.

The Warrant even bore the coveted Crossed Hammers, a mark of excellence granted to top students. Not only did Tovak know his numbers and letters, but he'd also completed basic military training and gone on to complete pioneer school, a grueling twelve-week program. The Academy taught scouting skills to those deemed to have promise or the potential to become a pioneer. He hoped this achievement would allow him to sign up with one of the coveted pioneer companies. It was with the pioneers that he saw himself rebuilding Legend and breaking free of the Pariah's stigma.

He pulled a small, plain wooden box out of his pack and slid open the cover. Inside was a spirit deck, containing forty-eight placards, hand-painted by Tovak's priest, Father Danik. After *Thulla's Blessed Word*, it was his most cherished possession, and certainly his most valuable. Most Dvergr believed that spirit decks were simple folly, but among the faithful, they were believed to be a direct connection to Thulla, allowing one to divine a measure of the god's will.

The deck had been gifted to him by the cleric. Since the passing of his parents, Danik had been the one person who had offered Tovak any real measure of kindness. It was through Danik that Tovak had discovered and embraced his god. For that, he would be eternally grateful.

Stepping up to the crate he used as a table, Tovak closed his eyes and thought on Thulla.

"Of the way ahead, what must be foremost in my heart?" he asked, shuffling the deck.

He then laid out four cards, face down, before him. One by one, he flipped them over. The first card was the Traveler, depicting a lone Dvergr in white cloth, leaning upon a walking stick with a long, open road before him. The second revealed Thulla, the Taker, the deity standing with a scowl upon His face and a closed fist held against His chest. The third exposed the Road Hidden, which showed the Traveler standing before a high hedgerow, and beyond it an open, straight, cobbled path between high mountains rising on either side. And finally, he turned over Thulla, the Giver, where the god stood smiling, His hands outstretched and a bounty of fruit in one hand and a clay jug in the other.

Tovak pondered the message before him. He was obviously the Traveler. The card had come up frequently for the past few months, but the second card concerned him. What might Thulla be taking from him as his journey progressed? He had so little. What more could Thulla ask? The lesson, perhaps, lay in the next card. A new path would be made available to him, and down it would lie Thulla's bounty, but the way would not be clear. Tovak slowly nodded his head in understanding.

As always, he would keep going. Faith was the one thing that nobody could take. He would keep his faith, and with it seek out Legend with every trial. Each test that lay before him would only serve to make him stronger.

He returned the cards to the deck and slipped them carefully back into their box.

The smell of woodsmoke now filled the air. There were shouts outside, followed by a trumpeting of oofants. He glanced over the back of the yuggernok to see a formation of Dvergr warriors in full plate armor emerge into view. They were marching in the opposite direction of the wagon, passing within a handful of yards.

With an officer and a standard-bearer at the front, they looked disciplined, and dangerous. Tovak couldn't help but smile. Soon he would be one of them—a Blood Badger. The warriors carried packs and yokes. A sergeant walking alongside the formation waved. Tovak waved back but, to his embarrassment, realized the warrior had been waving to one of the teamsters driving the massive wagon. He felt his cheeks heat as the sergeant looked directly at him, and then they were past.

Tovak removed his Warrant of Passage and set it on the crate. He then put everything carefully back into his pack, including his dagger, which had been lying on the floor-boards. He tied the straps tight and gave a tug to make sure the knot would not come loose.

Gazing upon the Warrant, a warm feeling washed through him. Even as a Pariah, his skill had seen him admitted to the Academy. He could scarcely still believe he had graduated and earned a Warrant, and with it, his goal now lay tantalizingly within reach. He folded it carefully along its creases and tucked it into his tunic pocket.

His field blanket came next. It took only a few moments to roll it up. He used short lengths of rope to tie the ends off and then secured it to his pack with a strap. Standing quickly, he slipped the strap over his head, settling the rolled blanket under his arm. He slipped on his pack next.

A rough bump almost knocked him over. The great wagon rattled and creaked loudly, as if in protest. Tovak looked outside again and felt a thrill of excitement. They were passing into the encampment. A deep trench and turf wall with a wooden barricade formed the outermost defensive line. Sentries slowly walked the wall, gazing out onto the prairie. To Tovak's eyes, they looked impressive in their armor and invincible. He imagined himself as one of them, guarding the encampment and helping to keep everyone secure.

The yuggernok passed through the encampment's open gate, where a detail of armored, shield-bearing infantry stood on either side, ever watchful. Full of anticipation, Tovak moved out onto the rear deck to try to get a better look at the camp, but much of it was blocked by the massive wagon and stacks of supplies. As they continued forward, the smell of smoke grew thick in his nostrils, and he quickly realized why. Dozens of campfires came into view. He picked up the stench of waste, mixed with the appetizing aroma of cooking. Tovak's stomach rumbled with hunger. As Duroth had said, there would be no evening meal for him tonight. He would have to fend for himself.

There were hundreds of tents, both large and small. He spotted an officer's pavilion, a blacksmith, a leatherworker, even a large cooking tent with a dozen long tables set off to the side with cooks and their assistants hard at work, preparing an evening meal.

Dvergr warriors were everywhere now, gathered around fires, marching in formation, and some going to or fro on whatever business they were about. Dozens sat around the nearest campfires, some in armor, others in their service tunics. Tovak saw women and children too.

He had never seen so many Dvergr gathered in one place, and he was only now coming to understand the scale of what the word "warband" really meant. The stories he'd heard as a child did not do them justice. The steady beat of hammers from a forge filled the air. Dogs barked and chased after one another, fighting over scraps.

The yuggernok passed through another defensive turf wall identical to the first. Within that were more tents, as well as an artillery park off to the left. In the fading light,

Tovak's eyes fell on a line of bolt throwers. Beyond them were several rows of catapults, massive machines with great iron wheels. Two of the machines were at least twenty feet tall, with massive beams and wooden arms for throwing stones.

In the fading light, he spotted a team of engineers working on one of the dread machines. They looked to be replacing a support beam. The yuggernok turned away and the artillery park was lost from view. Then the great wagon came to an abrupt, jerking halt. Tovak almost lost his balance. The heavy locking bolt was thrown in place with a hollow *thud* that shuddered through the floorboards.

They had arrived.

The center of the encampment was a veritable city of tents, formed around a wooden watch and signal tower. The structure rose thirty feet into the air. Tovak could just make out sentries on the tower's platform. He knew from his studies they would be equipped with a large war horn.

Tovak reveled at the sights and sounds that surrounded him. The clatter of wooden swords against shields drew his eye to what appeared to be hundreds of warriors training, sparring against one another in an enclosed area surrounded by carts. Officers and sergeants moved amongst them.

Formed into tight ranks, a company of warriors stomped by, moving in the direction the yuggernok had just come. Excitement, anticipation, and a wave of nervousness rippled through Tovak. This was where he was meant to be. He could feel it in his bones. Soon, his days of being an outcast, one barely tolerated by society, would be over. He would be a pioneer.

A growing clamor of voices rose behind him. Tovak stepped away from the railing and moved to the end of the corridor. It was full of the recruits, slinging gear over their shoulders as they got themselves ready to disembark.

"I can't wait to get to my company," a recruit said with no little amount of excitement. "My brother's been with them for two years now. It will be good to see him. Hard to believe tonight I will be part of Sixth Company."

"The Sixth are second-rate," Kutog jeered. "Everyone knows First Company is the best, and that's where I'm headed."

"Bah," the first recruit said. "What do you know?"

"My company has no equal, you dumb scrugg. Everyone knows that." Kutog struck his chest with a fist. "They only take the best, and that's me. My father told me they reject nine out of ten applicants. The Sixth takes whatever they can get, because that's all they can get."

"The best my ass," a voice replied. "You can wipe mine if you want."

Kutog spun around, but clearly could not see who had said it. His cheeks flushed with anger. Tovak almost grinned at the smug bastard's consternation.

"Make way," a voice called. "I said, make way."

It was Kyn, the youngest of the teamsters but still considerably older than Tovak. He moved down the corridor with an old, battered ladder that had seen better days. He held it over his head. His long, wild hair and heavily braided beard were the color of copper with only hints of gray. He wore a hardened leather breastplate and long hide pants tucked into knee-high boots. Two white painted slashes on his shoulder armor indicated he held the rank of an auxiliary corporal. His bare arms revealed an array of red tattoos depicting mystical patterns from shoulder to wrist. Like a captive beast, the outline of a dragon coiled around his right arm. He held the ladder easily, and as he approached, the recruits moved aside to allow him to pass.

"Get the latch, will you?" he asked Tovak as he reached the end. "Open the gate too."

"Yes, sir," Tovak replied and moved to the gate on the far side of the deck. Kyn had been the only one of the teamsters who hadn't gone out of his way to treat him badly or outright ignore his presence... although they hadn't exchanged more than a handful of words during the trip.

"Don't call me sir," he said. "I work for a living. The name's Kyn or Corporal, your choice."

"Thank you, s—" Tovak cut himself off. The habits of the Academy had become ingrained. Anyone who was serving had been a *sir.* "I mean Kyn," he corrected and then opened the gate for the teamster, swinging it wide and out into open space.

Kyn lowered the ladder over the side and then sank two rods at the top into holes bored into the deck. The bottom of the ladder almost touched the ground. Kyn gave the ladder a jerk to make sure it was secure, then stood.

Kutog stepped around Kyn and then roughly shoved Tovak aside with his shield. "Out of the way, Pariah," he growled before dropping his pack to the ground below. It landed with a heavy thud. Kutog mounted the ladder and, holding his shield to the side, climbed down one-handed.

Tovak's temper flared again. He closed his eyes and took a deep breath, forcing himself to calm down. When he opened them, he saw Kyn shake his head at Tovak.

"Boffers," the teamster grumbled under his breath. "There's always them bastards that think they are right better than the rest of us."

"It's all right," Tovak said, although he wanted to call Kutog out and beat him senseless. He dared not, though. There was too much at stake.

"You're a lot more forgiving than I would be." Kyn gave Tovak a scowl. "I'd have given him a thrashing for that. If he were on our crew, I tell you, I'd have whipped him or gotten whipped in turn. But at least I'd have stood up for myself. People like him only respect strength."

Tovak could have told Kyn that it never went well for him when he stood up to the likes of Kutog. Bastards like that always seemed to return with friends, and Tovak had none of his own. He could have said a lot of things, but none of it would matter. He knew that. "I've come a long way to get here, and he's just not worth the effort," was all he could manage. It sounded rather lame.

"If you say so," Kyn replied, sounding far from convinced, then glanced back at the other recruits, who were still getting themselves ready. "How long have you had your Age of Iron ring? You seem older than the rest."

"Four months," Tovak replied, glancing at Kyn's hand. He had noticed the ring before. "Yours is truly striking."

Kyn looked surprised by the compliment, holding up his hand to show off the incredibly detailed silver band, made in the form of a dragon with an obsidian orb set in its mouth. "My father crafted it for me."

"It's beautiful work," Tovak said, in honest admiration. "Your father has real skill." His hand involuntarily went to his own Age of Iron ring, a simple band of rough iron he kept hidden beneath his tunic on a copper chain.

Kyn paused and glanced behind him as more recruits began working their way to the ladder. "Say, I never did catch your name."

"Tovak," he said simply.

"Well then," Kyn said, clapping him on the back, "welcome to the Blood Badgers, Tovak." He glanced out at the encampment that stretched about in all directions. "And don't you worry none about that bastard." He indicated Kutog, who was heading off toward the center of the encampment with a determined stride. "He'll be getting the education of a lifetime over the next few weeks. He's full of himself now, but in a few hours, he won't be. First Company's a line formation. They're always under the eye of Karach. Lots of spit and polish and guard duty, if you know what I mean. He'll be the new guy in his company. If he shows too much cheek, they will cut him down and teach him a little humility or beat it into him if needed."

Tovak liked the thought of the latter. Kutog needed a good beating.

"Karach's warband is the best mix of small clans and clan-less warriors in the whole thanedom, misfits really, all of us." Kyn pulled Tovak aside so that the recruits could begin making their way down the ladder. They began to file by. Several cast Tovak unfriendly looks before they disappeared down the ladder. Kyn seemed not to notice and instead gestured outward. There was a proud note to his voice. "I've been with the Badgers for ten years now. Let me tell you something, Tovak. All them other warbands look down on us because we're a mixed bunch. This warband knows what's what."

Tovak wondered where Kyn was going.

"Who gets all the tough jobs? Who gets all the shit assignments? So, Tovak, I ask you, who is it the Thane sends for when it matters most?" Kyn paused expectantly.

"The Blood Badgers?" Tovak offered.

"That's right, the Blood Badgers," Kyn said, with a pleased grin. "Because we always get the job done. Karach

Skullsplitter is the best warchief to ever lead a warband. He's hard, but fair. We're all misfits here. Karach has taken us all in and now we're family."

"I see," Tovak said, gazing about the encampment.

"Do you?" Kyn asked. "You will not be the first Pariah the Blood Badgers have accepted. Nor likely the last."

Tovak blinked at that.

"My advice is to do your best," Kyn said. "Find a good company and build your own Legend. In time, things will change."

"Kyn," Duroth shouted from behind on the steps that led up to the driver's bench. "Quit your loafing and get that boffer's feet on the ground. We'll be unloading all night if ya keep jawing with the Pariah."

"You better get on down," Kyn said, turning to Tovak. "Old Duroth might be loud, but he's right, and despite the bark, he's really not so bad once you get to know him." Kyn glanced around at the stowed cargo. "We've got a lot of work to do before we can turn in for the night."

The rest of the recruits had already debarked. Tovak stepped up to the ladder, turned, and then leaned forward as he put his foot on the first rung. His Age of Iron ring slipped out of his tunic and dangled free. He quickly tucked the cheap token back inside, but not before Kyn spotted it.

Kyn turned knowing eyes to Tovak.

"Don't you worry none," Kyn said. "You're gonna fit in just fine around here. Do you know where you're headed?" he asked, stepping up to the edge of the deck.

Tovak began to descend the ladder, then paused and looked back up. "I'm off to join the pioneers, but I don't really know where to go."

"Not everyone can make it in the pioneers," Kyn warned. "Most get turned away."

Tovak resumed climbing down the ladder. He jumped the last foot and his boots slapped down on the ground.

"I have a Warrant of Passage from the Pioneer Academy," Tovak said, patting his pocket where the document rested. "I even received a mark of excellence."

"Well done," the teamster said, sounding impressed, though his eyes took on a sad tinge. He blew out a breath and then pointed toward the center of camp. "In that case, you'll want to find Dagon Trailbreaker. He's the captain of the Second Pioneers. Everyone around here knows who he is. I've never met him, but I hear he's a real bastard"—Kyn gave a shrug of his shoulders—"but with a mark of excellence, he might just take you in, Pariah or no. Head toward the center of camp and look for a tall green and black banner with a *durvoll* on it, you know, the big dog-looking thing with six legs."

Tovak nodded. "Thank you."

"Safe journeys, young Tovak... May your Legend never fade."

"May you always find the Way." Tovak bowed his head briefly.

Gazing down on Tovak, Kyn hesitated a moment, looked about to say more... then turned and was lost from view.

Tovak bit his lip. Had he just read pity in the other's eyes? Tovak shook his head. Perhaps he'd just imagined it.

As he stepped away from the ladder, he found himself moving with a lighter step than he'd had in a very long time. Garand'Durbaad lay far behind him, as did his past and the pain that came with it. The mere possibility of what lay ahead filled him with a sudden excitement.

"They don't know my family," he said quietly, a smile creeping onto his face. It was why he had chosen the Blood Badgers. The warband was a mix of all the clans. "I am finally my own Dvergr." He traced a finger over his Age of Iron ring, feeling it beneath his tunic. It might be of the lowest quality, but it marked the beginning of his adulthood, where he could truly shape his own future.

It was enough.

If you would like to read more, and I hope you do … follow the link to Amazon: Reclaiming Honor

Made in the USA
Columbia, SC
18 June 2024

37235908R00259